DUBAI

Robin Moore
DUBAI

1976

DOUBLEDAY & COMPANY, INC.

GARDEN CITY, NEW YORK

All of the characters in this book are fictitious, and any resemblance to actual persons, living or dead, is purely coincidental.

ISBN: 0-385-04927-7
Library of Congress Catalog Card Number 74-33654
Copyright © 1976 by Robin Moore
All Rights Reserved
Printed in the United States of America
First Edition

To Mary Olga

Who was there all the way; from restless Lebanon to the deserts of the Arab emirates, from emerging Oman to the teeming Creek of Dubai and the smugglers' coves of Ajman and Umm Al Quain, who dug up ancient coins in a buried village in Ras Al-Khaima, helped research intrigue-ridden Tehran and observed the war in the Golan Heights.

A more beautiful, devoted, and adaptable bride is unimaginable.

Part I
FITZ

CHAPTER 1

Fitz left the intelligence staff meeting at the U. S. Embassy in Tehran at 10:30 A.M. He turned onto Rozvelt Avenue, the large street dedicated to the U.S. president who organized the famous Tehran summit meeting near the end of World War II, and began the one-hour walk to the giant Bazaar, forerunner by a century to the supermarkets of America. He enjoyed walking Tehran's streets, and of all his foreign assignments this was the most challenging and exhilarating of his twenty-year military career, combat duty in Korea and Vietnam excepted.

Tehran might seem to the casual visitor a city devoted exclusively to street selling and buying. Everything was for sale. But to Fitz it was the world's foremost city of intrigue, strategically located between the Middle East and Asia. And Tehran was the great international transfer point between Israel and the Arab world. This was the city in which to pause, switch or alter passports, and then proceed.

Reaching Shahreza Avenue, he turned right and walked the three blocks to the square, and turned left on Ferdowsi. If he had a home of his own, Fitz reflected, as he walked down Ferdowsi Boulevard, he would go into one of the carpet dealers and haggle for a beautiful rug. He had been to Tabriz and watched the care with which the carpets were woven. The proliferation of exotic household goods on sale along the route to the Bazaar never failed to remind him that he was, in truth, one of the world's homeless and rootless citizens. But he had learned not only to live with this situation but to enjoy it, feel comfortable with it. In his particular line of work this was an advantage.

Personally he had nothing to lose, so he was better equipped psychologically than most military intelligence officers abroad to treat the national objectives of the United States above all other considerations. He had few personal opinions about the current power struggles in the midst of which he lived. Whatever policy the American ambassador under whom he served espoused became Fitz's policy, perhaps with one exception. He couldn't help but feel, after ten years' service in such Arab countries as Jordan, Syria, Iraq, Egypt, and the Gulf states (he was always careful to think and say Arabian Gulf, not Persian Gulf, in Arab countries), that there was a very legitimate Arab point of view on the Middle East conflict between Arab and Jew. It was his observation that American diplomacy was weighted in favor of Israel and that the Arab outlook was either distorted in the American press and in American thinking, or it was ignored. He had seen all sides of the question in intimate, close-up detail. He had learned to speak Arabic well and Hebrew passably and he understood the grievances and aggressions on both sides equally. And he still thought the Arab world, which to date had made little effective protest within the American power structure, was getting the splintered end of the stick. However, good and anonymous intelligence officer that he was, he kept this one personal opinion to himself.

It bemused Fitz to be so frequently considered Jewish because of his last name, Lodd. Just because Israel's international airport at Tel Aviv was Lod and frequently mentioned in the press, many colleagues who didn't know his background thought that with a Jewish name he must be a Jew. Emmy Lodd's only deviation from strict midwestern Congregationalist Christian doctrine, which included more than a suggestion of anti-Semitism, had been the bearing of an illegitimate son. Him.

As he came closer to the Bazaar he crossed the relatively quiet tree-lined Ferdowsi Boulevard and, taking a cross street to the left and a jog to the right onto Naserkhosro Avenue, he was soon in the noisy, dirty, traffic-clogged streets that surrounded the Bazaar, advertised as the world's largest marketplace under one roof.

Fitz entered the Bazaar through the gate across from Naserkhosro, passing the large jewelry store which specialized in the pale-blue semi-precious turquoise for which Iran was noted. Then he plunged on through the milling crowds deep into the Bazaar, looking down the lanes of shops stretching more than a hundred yards in any direction.

A shopkeeper standing outside his door plucked at Fitz as he walked by. "Gold coins!" he proclaimed. Fitz paused and the shopkeeper intensified his importunings. "I have the finest gold coins from all over the world. Americans buy much from me." The Persian winked broadly. "The best hedge against inflation."

"Where did you hear about inflation?" Fitz asked with a friendly smile.

"See this one," the Persian persisted, thrusting a large gold coin into Fitz's hand. The intelligence officer stared down at it. It was the Ethopian Menelik II, a very rare coin minted in 1889, the obverse side depicting Emperor Menelik II, the reverse side featuring the Lion of Judah. This was the credential of Hassian's intelligence service.

Fitz produced from his pocket the duplicate of the coin and displayed it. "Where?" he asked.

The shopkeeper took his own coin back and nodded down the lane. "Downstairs, the Bazaar Bozorg on the other side."

Fitz pushed his way through the shoppers and sightseers into the jewelry shop. He walked through the entrance and, seeing a flight of stairs at the rear, he went to them and descended to the basement of the shop.

A man with a gray, badly trimmed beard looked up through a pair of bifocals. He was dressed in conventional Western garb, as were most shopkeepers in the Bazaar. The gold-rimmed glasses gleamed in the light from a brass lamp suspended above the desk behind which he sat, gesturing at an empty chair beside the desk. Fitz placed his Menelik II gold coin on the desk and took a seat. He reached for a pad and pencil in his suitcoat pocket.

"Proceed, friend of Hassian," Fitz urged.

"You have something for Hassian?" the bearded one asked suggestively.

Fitz patted his coat pocket. "I will evaluate the worth of the information and fill this envelope accordingly." He took from an inside coat pocket a brown envelope and placed it on the table. "I listen most attentively."

The friend of Hassian commenced his recital. "Beginning next week the Shahenshah"—he bowed his head reverently as he referred to Mohammed Pahlavi, light of the Aryans, occupant of Iran's Peacock Throne—"has authorized almost a fifty percent increase in the monthly arms shipments to the Kurdish tribesmen in Iraq."

Fitz nodded. "We became aware of this when the Shah asked the Embassy to process his request for additional American armaments. Still—" Fitz removed a thousand-rial note, about fifteen dollars, and placed it in the envelope. He continued to listen attentively.

"The pressure increases on the Shah to raise oil prices even in excess of the 1963 agreement of Tehran."

"Come, friend of Hassian," Fitz began impatiently. "You can do better than that."

The older man flashed a wily smile and then began pouring out items of intelligence concerning the Middle East. Sometimes Fitz reached into his pocket for additional money, other times he sat stonily.

"There is a very important piece of news I just learned." The information monger's lips smacked over the words. "The oil exploration in Trucial Oman on the Arabian side of the Gulf is going very well. We heard from the oil workers on holiday in Beirut that oil is under the water just nine miles off the island of Abu Musa, claimed by the Emirate of Kajmira." Fitz started to interrupt wearily but his informant held up a hand. "The important news is that the Shah has decided to forcibly occupy the islands of Greater and Lesser Tumbs, claimed by the Emirate of Ras al Khaimah, and establish military bases."

"You mean send in his navy, troops? Take those islands away from the Trucial States which are under British protection?"

"The British will be pulling out soon enough. In just a few years from now, by 1971, the Trucial States rulers will be on their own. Then the Shah will certainly occupy the Tumbs and Abu Musa immediately."

Fitz nodded appreciatively. This was the kind of long-term intelligence that would be useful to the State Department in planning a reply to such a move. Fitz added another thousand rials to the sheaf of bills in the envelope.

"So little?"

"That's what it's worth," Fitz replied.

"Then perhaps I will not sell you my final news. It's worth far more than anything I have told you this morning."

"Hassian knows I pay well for good intelligence. Let me hear your final news."

"It is worth five, ten thousand rials, maybe more. This we just learned from our agents negotiating the new gas pipeline from Iran to Israel. They themselves only came across it by accident."

At the mention of Israel, Fitz stiffened. There was, he knew, something about to happen. It was May and tensions had been building steadily between Israel and its Arab neighbors of Egypt, Jordan, and Syria. He reached into his wallet once more and pulled out ten one-thousand rial notes. "How many of these go into the envelope depends upon your news, friend of Hassian."

The glasses gleamed in the overhead light as the bearded man looked down at the bills in Fitz's hand. "And what if you choose not to believe what I tell you, only to find out in ten days' time I was correct?"

"I have always been more than fair. I always will be. Why do you ask that question?"

"Some have not believed it and refused to pay. Those most in danger laugh off this news, but I know it to be true."

"Then tell me."

"Very well." The eyes, magnified through heavy lenses, fixed themselves on Fitz. "Israel will launch a war on Egypt, Jordan, Iraq, and Syria within ten days' time. Israel has decided not to wait for the attack they believe will come."

"In ten days?" Fitz exhaled sharply.

"Maybe less. In three days it will be the first of June. Anytime after that date the Israeli attacks will start."

"And you have already sold this news? Surely the Arabs are prepared."

The old, bearded man laughed bitterly. "I told you, they can't believe it. They only believe what they want to hear. If there is to be a war it will be started by them, at the time and place of their choosing." He shook his head. "Al-lah. It is always the most important and crucial information that is hardest to sell because nobody wants to believe it."

"I believe it," Fitz said decisively. He pushed the ten thousand rials across the desk along with the envelope. "I wonder how the legions I helped train in Jordan will stand up to an attack by the Israelis with all their sophisticated weaponry?" Fitz sighed. "Arabs should never make war, it requires too much organization and efficiency."

Pushing back his chair, Fitz stood up. "Contact me in the usual way if you hear any more details."

The bearded man stood up. "It was a pleasure to do business with you. You are the first customer who believed that Israel will start the war."

Fitz smiled wryly. "The question is, will my embassy, my government, believe me?" He turned, mounted the stairs, and left the jewelry shop and out in the Bazaar regained his bearings and took the shortest route out of the labyrinthine shop-lined lanes to the street, a walk of almost ten minutes through the teeming marketplace.

Finally reaching the outside, Fitz pushed his way through the incredibly populated streets, walking through the snarled traffic almost half a mile before the traffic abated enough so that the taxis could move. Then he stepped out into the street, hailed a cab, and when it paused gave the address of the French Club. The driver nodded and Fitz stepped into the back seat beside two ladies returning from a shopping expedition, their packages inundating the cab. Gingerly he pushed enough bags off the seat so that he could sit down and the cab started off. The Tehran system of carrying several different passengers at a time to their various destinations was a mixed blessing.

The French Club was one of the exclusive and thoroughly delightful clubs in the city and the weather in May was similar to that in the eastern part of the United States, delightful spring days that made eating on the green lawn of the club a great pleasure. Fitz's three years in Paris as an officer in NATO had established his credentials to belong to the club, that and the fact that he spoke French.

As he sipped the typically American gin and tonic, which he liked despite the look of distaste it received from the French members who had never cultivated a taste for what they considered a harsh drink, Fitz thought how much he enjoyed this tour of duty in Tehran. Iran, Persia as he thought of it, appealed to him thoroughly. And now finally, at the age of forty-two, he was on the full colonel's list for the second time. He had been passed over once merely because he hadn't had the lobby at the Pentagon to push for James Fitzroy Lodd's silver bird. Having achieved his commission via Ohio State ROTC, he was not a member of the West Point Protective Association. This time around, however, he had been assured he would make full bull on the promotion list. If he didn't it would be retirement for him.

In the years he had spent in Iran, Fitz had given frequent thought to retiring here and getting into some form of business. Not that he knew much beyond intelligence gathering and handling every type of weapon manufactured in the world, but these skills could be valuable to some profit-making organization in the Middle East.

He thought about the impending Israeli attack on its neighbor countries. Good strategy, and so bold and unexpected that even when one of the best private spy systems in this part of the world revealed the information, the intelligence services of the nations most surely to suffer deeply refused to believe it. It was reminiscent of Hitler's refusal to believe that the Allied D-Day attack on fortress Europe would come at Normandy despite inexcusable security leaks which clearly signaled the time and place of the greatest invasion in the world.

There was little possibility that his own superiors would believe the information, for that matter. Nevertheless, he would pass it along through the U. S. Country Team in Iran and it would be the responsibility of either CIA or the Military Attaché to forward the information by coded cable to Washington.

Fitz's counterpart in French intelligence, seeing he was alone, suggested they lunch together. Another advantage of this club was that the intelligence officers of most major world powers with representation in Tehran had penetrated it. It was a fine informal forum for the members of the international intelligence community to lie to each other, exchange information when appropriate, and probe one another's awareness of current sensitive situations.

Try as he would, in as delicate a way as possible, over drinks, a delicious French meal with imported wine, and finally a *digestif*, Fitz could not discover whether his French rival had purchased the same information concerning the Israeli attack that he had acquired this morning from Hassian's service, much less whether he believed such an occurrence could really come about.

On the matter of oil they were both able to be more frank with each other. Yes, the Frenchman had heard just this morning that the Shah would eventually annex the Tumbs Islands and perhaps Abu Musa as soon as the British withdrew their military protection of the Trucial States. And of course everyone suspected that the Shah had already drawn up his plan to raise Iranian oil prices in excess of previous agreements on gradual escalations.

Fitz returned to the Embassy at 2 P.M. There was the usual crowd of Iranians seeking visas to visit the United States waiting in the chancery. Only in Iran, Lebanon, and Israel did the population go about its business all day without the three- to four-hour midday rest period observed throughout the Middle East. In his office Fitz picked up the telephone on his desk and called Major General Fielding, senior U.S. military member of the Ambassador's country team. Asking for an appointment, Fitz was told to come over to the General's office immediately.

Fielding was only five years older than Fitz, yet the rank gulf between a lieutenant colonel and a West Point two-star general was formidable.

Since both officers were wearing civilian clothes, Fitz did not salute but took the proffered chair beside the General's desk.

"What's on your mind, Lodd?" the General asked affably. "What gem of intelligence that can't wait until the staff meeting tomorrow have you uncovered?"

"I was making the usual rounds, sir, after the meeting this morning and turned up something I think should be cabled to Washington. It may fit in with intelligence gained from other sources."

"What is it?" The General leaned forward. He had learned to respect Fitz's ability to ferret out important information, and he was aware of Fitz's experience in the Middle East.

"Hassian's intelligence service has always been most reliable. Today it came up with the information that the Israelis are going to attack Egypt, Jordan, Iraq, and Syria simultaneously within ten days' time at the most, maybe less."

General Fielding stared at Fitz intently. "The Israelis attack? I can't believe it. They don't want war. We have a peace mission actively working to avoid war in the Middle East."

"The Israelis obviously feel that if they don't attack first, by surprise, they'll be overwhelmed by the Arabs."

"I'll cable this information on to Washington, of course." A
gleam came into General Fielding's eye. "Actually that one-eyed
bastard would love to pull off an attack like that. It's what I'd do
in his case."

"Pity that the Israelis and the Arabs can't get together and
work things out," Fitz offered. "You can't blame the Israelis for
wanting to keep their country together, but the Arabs have their
side of the question too. A million and a half Arabs displaced, living in detention camps because they have no homeland any more,
gives a black face to every believer in Allah and his prophet
Mohammed alive in the world today."

"Damn it, Lodd, I don't see why the big, successful, rich Arab
nations want to waste time and money fighting with the Jews
about a bunch of ragtag refugees that can't do anything to help
them, a type of Arab the others don't like anyway. They are perfectly willing to go up against the latest weaponry we've given Israel and die for these Palestinian bastards."

Fitz shrugged and gave his superior a helpless smile. "You
haven't lived with the Arabs or you'd understand. The infidels,
the Jews, have put one over on Allah. This is an affront to every
Arab in this part of the world. I admit it sounds like some medieval concept of a holy war but it means everything to religious
Arabs. And as for being killed in battle?" Fitz gave General Fielding a quizzical look. "Have you ever read the Koran?"

"Their Bible? No."

"You should. You'd understand them better. In *The Women*
the Prophet said, 'Whoso fighteth in the way of Allah, be he
slain, or victorious, on him We shall bestow a vast reward.' "

The General nodded. "Makes dying in battle a real personal
thing. We die for our country, they die for Allah."

"That's right, sir. And in *Repentance* the true believers read,
'Go forth and strive with your wealth and your lives in the way of
Allah.' And the rulers of all the rich Arab countries are true
believers and this is what they are doing."

"So," General Fielding sighed, "we're in for another Mideast
war."

"In ten days," Fitz added. "Or less."

"In Washington they won't believe that Israel will start the war

unless old Eshkol in Jerusalem personally calls President Johnson."

Fitz chuckled. "I think you're right, sir. The Arabs don't believe
it either."

"Oh, Fitz, by the way, I have an official request which came
through the Information Officer at the Embassy for a newspaperman to interview you."

"Why me?" Fitz asked, alarmed. He had always made it a point
to avoid the press, although that had been difficult in Vietnam,
where he had come to mistrust and heartily dislike most newsmen.

"The reporter in question apparently knows you. Met you in
Vietnam and heard that you are very knowledgeable on the Middle East."

"A reporter knows me?" Fitz asked incredulously.

"His name"—the General consulted the memo—"is Sam Gold.
Mean anything to you?"

Fitz grimaced. "Yeah. So he finally left Saigon? He was a writer
for one of the most influential American papers, I can't remember
which one—in New York or Chicago, I think."

"New York *Star*," the General prompted.

"What I do remember is that he was never known to leave
Saigon and go out in the field. He got all his information from in-
terviewing officers and other newsmen in from the field. And he
wasn't above twisting words around to make a better story. I don't
want to see him. I was lucky he didn't get me in trouble in Vietnam, I had enough as it was."

"According to this memo from the I.O., the Ambassador would
like you to see him. In fact, you probably have more insight into
the situation here in the Middle East than any other American
employed at the Embassy. Will you talk to him, Fitz?" It was
more a command than a question. "You don't have to tell him
anything, just let us give that New York newspaper the courtesy
of talking to one of its reporters. O.K.?"

A pause, then reluctantly, "O.K."

"He'll be over at four o'clock. I'll have him sent to your office."

"I'll be waiting for him."

Just why Fitz dreaded the interview he couldn't have said.
Perhaps it was merely his distrust of the press in general and Sam

Gold in particular. Fitz had been assigned to U. S. Army Special Forces in Vietnam as Chief Intelligence Officer when he first met Sam Gold. For the second time in his career he found himself wearing the green beret of the elite unit. He was well qualified to rejoin the unit, having been a paratrooper and an instructor at the guerrilla warfare school at Fort Bragg. This assignment had followed his tour of duty as an adviser to King Hussein in creating a special commando group in the Jordanian Army. The King had been so pleased with Fitz's work that he had offered him a five-year contract as a general in the army at fifty thousand dollars a year plus all his expenses. But Fitz was an American Army officer and had no wish to terminate his career.

Back in the fall of 1965, Lieutenant Colonel Lodd was known to have more information on U.S. cross-border operations into Cambodia, Laos, and even North Vietnam than any other single officer in the command. Occasionally when some outrageous, and sometimes true, rumor of Green Beret-initiated cross-border operations reached the press and the newsmen demanded clarification, it was Fitz's unenviable job to have to mislead the persistent reporters seeking sensational stories. No matter what he said or how he answered the questions of the press, he was alternately reviled and quoted by Sam Gold, whose sensational stories for his sensation-hungry newspaper invariably caused at least a flap a week at High Headquarters.

Sam Gold, short, rotund, and deceptively pleasant-mannered, entered Fitz's office precisely at four o'clock. He had a paper cup of coffee in his hand. This is how Fitz remembered him from Saigon, always a cup of coffee.

"Good afternoon, Colonel Lodd. It's a real pleasure to see you again."

"Hello, Mr. Gold," Fitz replied guardedly. "You asked specifically to talk to me?"

"Why not? For old times' sake, you know. All we went through together in Saigon, I figured as soon as I saw your name on the Embassy list here that the two of us could get into things quicker than if I started out cold with someone else. Besides, wherever you are you always know what's going on. What is hot over here? Are we still sending arms up to help the Kurdish guerrillas overthrow the government of Iraq?"

"Have I stopped beating my wife? Eh, Gold?"

The reporter laughed. "I'm just trying to understand the scene over here, Colonel. After five years in Vietnam I knew Southeast Asia better than any reporter—or soldier," he added. "Now I have to start all over again and learn what goes in the Middle East. You were up with the Kurds on an assignment once, before Vietnam, weren't you?"

"I spent some time in Iraq. And yes, I did join a U.S. mission to the mountains to give medical care to the tribesmen, the first they ever had, and train them in hygiene."

"We're still trying to help the Kurds, aren't we?"

"Not by providing them with arms," Fitz countered.

"Then how come they do their fighting with U.S.-made guns?" Sam replied. "We give them to the Shah and he passes them on to the Kurds, right?"

"What the Shah does with the arms we sell him is beyond my knowledge."

"But we're still pouring the stuff into Iran, right?" Sam Gold smiled ingratiatingly. "I don't mean to be poking into sensitive subjects, Colonel. Just tell me to shut up if I hit too close. You always did in Saigon."

Feeling on the defensive, Fitz tried to backtrack. "Of course the rumor you just repeated has been abroad for years. And of course we all know the Kurds are using preponderantly U.S. weapons, but there isn't a week goes by that some weapons salesman from the United States doesn't pass through Iran. Some of them call at the Embassy, others make their sales surreptitiously. But let me repeat, the position, so far as I know, is that we do not provide arms for any power or group without making the sale public. We have no secret arms deals that I know of in the Middle East. Did I answer your question?"

"Not exactly, Colonel. But then you never did in Saigon either. Let's get onto something else. How about oil?" Gold asked.

"What about oil? That's a big subject."

"When is the Shah going to raise oil prices and what is the Embassy position?"

"Why don't you ask the Embassy I.O. that question? It's certainly nothing I know about. I'm in military intelligence as you know."

"It could become a military matter."

"I doubt it. Again, that's policy." Fitz began to wonder if somehow Sam Gold had managed to get onto Hassian's private intelligence service. But Hassian had always maintained he dealt only with intelligence officers. It certainly wasn't to his advantage to have all his hard-learned information published where anyone could read it for free.

"Help me on something else, Colonel." Again the ingenuous appeal for assistance. He smiled sadly. "I don't really know anything about this part of the world. I'm not here to write a story, I'm just looking for background information. I don't expect I'll even be filing stories for a couple of more weeks. I wouldn't know where to look for one yet."

"Knowing you, Mr. Gold, it won't be long before once again I'll be getting calls from the Ambassador asking me how the hell Sam Gold got onto that story." Fitz felt somewhat relieved that this interview wasn't going to be the basis for a news article.

"We all have our functions, Colonel. Now let me ask you, in the Arab-Israel conflict Tehran is pretty neutral, wouldn't you say?"

"Yes, I would say. The Iranians are not Arabs nor are they Jews. Iran trades with both sides and tries to maintain friendly relations all over the Middle East."

"My information is that the war is going to start up again pretty quick. That's why I'm over here of course. Is there any background information you could pass on to me regarding this?"

"You are as aware of the tensions as I am. It wouldn't surprise me to see fighting breaking out."

"The fuckin' Arabs are a bloodthirsty lot, aren't they? Some night they'll probably swarm all over Israel and kill every Jew in sight. And for no reason except they hate Jews. Yet the U.S. keeps giving the Arabs planes and weapons."

"Mr. Gold, as a responsible journalist you have to realize that there are two sides to this question." Fitz tried to keep his tones level. "For some reason the American press by and large takes the same approach to the problem that you just shot from the hip. If the Jewish-oriented population and communications media of America would be less hysterical about the problem and take the trouble to learn and understand the Arab side of the question, and by the same token the Arabs could see the Jewish side, perhaps the United States could form some sort of an evenhanded policy that could lead to the achievement of a lasting peace in the Middle East."

Sam Gold smiled broadly, took out his notebook and scribbled in it and then put it away. Fitz didn't like the complacent look on the reporter's face. Sam dropped his cigarette into his coffee cup, placed it on Fitz's desk, and stood up.

"Thank you, Colonel. You've been most helpful."

"I haven't given you much background, Mr. Gold." Fitz was worried now.

"You've given me something better. A point of view." He smiled and put out his hand. Fitz was forced to stand, terminating the short meeting, and shaking the reporter's moist, limp hand.

"If there's any more background material you want, let me know," Fitz said lamely.

"Thank you, Colonel." The sly smile still on his face, Sam Gold left Fitz's office.

Fitz felt a knot of deep concern form in his stomach. He wasn't sure what had happened in the interview but he was positive that he would regret having agreed to see Sam Gold.

CHAPTER 2

Two days later, on the thirtieth of May, Fitz was dismayed at the Embassy intelligence report that King Hussein had flown to Cairo and with great fanfare and dramatics signed a military pact with his former enemy, President Nasser. The following day an Egyptian general was sent to take command of Jordan's forces.

"So much for the effectiveness of the Jordan legions," Fitz remarked to General Fielding. "They'll never fight efficiently under a foreign Arab commander. And I think Hussein knows it. He never really wanted to destroy Israel—throw every Jew into the sea the way that idiot Nasser is shouting."

On his trip to the Bazaar on June 1, Fitz learned that all over the Arab world the mullahs in the mosques were preaching a "Jihad" or holy war. The intelligence Fitz purchased predicted that Israel would attack airfields in Egypt, Jordan, Syria, and Iraq within three days.

It was on June 4, one day before the expected air strikes were actually carried out, a time of intense emotion and fear in America for the very existence of Israel, that Sam Gold's story broke.

The reporter, in an exquisitely timed background story, first summed up the situation. Egyptian infantry divisions, armored formations, and air force units had moved in strength across the Suez Canal into the Sinai Desert, massed within striking distance of the Israel frontier during May. Before the end of the month this military buildup amounted to some 90,000 men, 900 tanks, 350 planes, and great concentrations of artillery.

On May 17 the Egyptian Government had demanded the withdrawal of UNEF (the UN Emergency Force), and Secretary General U Thant had complied.

On May 22 Egypt had announced the closing of the Straits of

Tiran, the entrance to the hundred-mile-long Gulf of Aqaba
leading to Israel's southern port of Eilat.

On May 26 President Nasser declared that the war "will be
total and the objective to destroy Israel. We feel confident that
we can win and are ready now for a war with Israel. . . ."

Then the story which had been headlined *Anti-Semitism in
U. S. Embassy in Iran on Eve of Israel's Fight for Life* went into
an account of reporter Sam Gold's interview with Lieutenant Colonel James Fitzroy Lodd, military intelligence attaché to the U. S.
Embassy in Tehran.

"There will never be peace in the Middle East until the hysterical Jewish population and Jewish-oriented communications media
of the United States take the trouble to learn the Arab side of the
problem over here, according to Lieutenant Colonel James Fitzroy
Lodd in an interview with this reporter on the 27th of May, the
day after President Nasser made his statement about destroying
Israel."

Sam Gold conceded that Lodd had also added, "And by the
same token the Arabs should also see the Jewish side of the question."

But the damage had been done. Even though the six-day war
which erupted the next day crowded most other news off the front
pages, newspapers throughout the country carried excerpts from
Sam Gold's story. Congressmen with large Jewish constituencies
denounced anti-Semitism in the U. S. Foreign Service. Five days
later the war was over. A Congressional investigating committee
was formed to inspect the U. S. Embassy in Tehran and other U.S.
embassies, all to the intense embarrassment of the Ambassador.

Fitz was stunned by the reaction in Washington over Sam
Gold's account of the interview. Although General Fielding sym-
pathized with Fitz and believed that the reporter had shamefully
distorted the sense of Fitz's statements, the pressure on him from
Washington for a full accounting of the incident was becoming
increasingly heavy. A simple denial was not sufficient. A Jewish
congressman from New York demanded Fitz's immediate dis-
missal without bothering to ascertain whether or not the reporter
might have misquoted him.

To his chagrin Fitz received the first friendly communication
from his stepfather in years, the much older man who had mar-

ried his mother despite her then three-year-old illegitimate son. "You know those hebes for what they are, son. God bless," the cable had been worded, and of course read by several members of the Embassy staff.

For all the wrong reasons his stepfather was congratulating his mother on her son's unwanted attention in the press. Fitz had never been close to his stepfather, a wealthy widower who had sent him off to a succession of boarding schools in order to have his pretty young wife all to himself. Fitz just hadn't ever known a family life. When he was old enough to understand his origins and read history, his mother told him that his real father's name had been Jim King. He was a charming insurance salesman but when Emmy informed him she was pregnant he left town, never to be seen again. Fitz realized that Fitzroy meant a bastard son of the king. His mother had retained some sense of humor in bestowing that middle name on the son and Fitz had refused ever to use his father's first name, preferring Fitz, which reminded him that he was a bastard.

When General Fielding called Fitz into his office two weeks after the story had appeared, he looked up at his intelligence subordinate sadly. "They have asked me to try and get you to retire, Fitz. At Department of the Army they've already taken you off the promotion list to full colonel."

"Don't I get a chance to explain to D.O.A., to tell my side of the story?"

"You could sue Sam Gold and the newspaper but that won't help your career. What did you ever do to that character?"

"Nothing except withhold information I felt shouldn't be released for security reasons when I was in Vietnam."

"Well, the irresponsible little bastard did you in this time. You've got over twenty years, so you're clear on your pension. Why don't you retire and then sue the paper?"

"Sue? Where would I get the money to hire lawyers to sue a powerful American newspaper? If I'm through in the Army I've lost everything that meant anything to me anyway."

"Well, nobody can make you retire but you know what kind of assignments you'll get until you are automatically retired after being passed over for promotion a second time. It's too bad you haven't got somebody powerful in Washington to fight this thing for you."

Fitz thought about Lieutenant General Oscar Bealle, unfortunately retired these last five years and living in Arizona. Perhaps this was his only real friend in the world, the man responsible for Fitz making the Army a career. From the time Fitz had been able to understand completely his own background he had been an unusually self-sufficient youth. He had an inward perception of himself as a person nobody was going to do much for. He knew he would have to take care of himself.

At the various boarding schools he attended he was always a good student and athlete and he was also gregarious. As he grew older he became more and more obsessed with the notion that nobody was ever going to do anything for him unless they in some way benefited too. This outlook was strengthened by the increasingly cool reception he found at his mother's home as his stepfather grew older and more irritable at the presence of his wife's bastard son.

He entered college the last year of World War II. He had mixed feelings about going into the Army but was prepared to do so if drafted. However, he saw no way that he could benefit from military duty and discovered that by taking a reserve officer's schedule at Ohio State University he could stay in college until he graduated, at which time he would be an officer and a gentleman.

As always, he did well in studies, joined a good fraternity of young men with families ready to put them into lucrative business posts, and found to his immense surprise that his greatest interest was the military studies to which he had first submitted and then devoted his major attention. Political science, geography, and history combined with military science fascinated him, and Colonel Oscar Bealle, in charge of the Reserve Officers' Training Corps, urged Fitz to make a career in the military. The Colonel, a West Pointer wounded in the early days of the war, was well connected in the Army and promised to follow Fitz's career and become his mentor.

Although his common sense bade him take up one of the many promising offers in business that were made him in his senior year, some strange inner compulsion pushed Fitz toward the military. It was as though he could remember a past brilliant military career, a promise to himself that he would continue it, perhaps in some future life if such things existed. Fitz made Colonel Bealle a happy man when he agreed to make the military his career. The Colonel in turn promised him one thing: he would make it his business to see that Fitz was not wasted by the United States Army.

Fitz looked General Fielding in the eye. "The only man who could have helped me once is retired and not even living around Washington."

"I'm sorry, Fitz," Fielding replied simply.

"We used to have a motto in the Berets. 'Never Give Up.' I don't know why I should give up so easily."

"That meant never give up in battle," the General snapped. "This is politics, something no soldier ever fought successfully. It will be easier on everyone if you put in for retirement. Those congressmen with the big Jewish constituencies will use your case for the next six months to get solid with their voters."

"Couldn't I call a press conference and straighten the whole thing out?"

"They'll trip you up and make it worse. It would be easier on all of us, from the Ambassador on down, if you just retired."

"Maybe so," Fitz replied somberly. "By the way, what ever happened as a result of the cable about the Israelis attacking just when my intelligence said they would?"

"Nothing, I guess. As far as I know, Washington was caught completely off guard, just the way the newspapers said, when the attacks came."

"I'm going back to my office and think about the whole thing, sir."

"Let me know what you decide to do. Perhaps before the end of the day?"

Without answering, Fitz left the General's office and walked down the hall to his own modest office. Morosely, he stared down into the Embassy lawn. Flowers were blooming and the grass was green and close-cut. The bitterness that assailed him at the futility of his plight rose in his breast. He considered trying to contact General Bealle, but then there was little the retired officer could do other than to offer sympathy. When Bealle had been in power Fitz found that indeed he was not wasting his time in the Army.

When the Korean War came along Fitz was happily commanding a company of the Wolfhound Regiment in Japan. Although
the U. S. Army in Japan had become notoriously soft, Fitz kept his
company well motivated and combat-ready. He was convinced
that the United States would become embroiled in Asiatic
conflicts and his continued studies and ability to analyze the
world news made him pick Korea as the likeliest trouble spot.

When North Korea overran the border with the South, Fitz
and his company were among the first troops to be sent into combat. Although companies around them were decimated, Fitz and
his Wolfhounds managed to preserve the unit and Fitz was
quickly promoted to major and made a battalion commander.

And then, as the tide turned seriously against the Americans
and the casualties were rising astronomically, Fitz received orders
transferring him back to Japan and assigning him to a special intelligence job.

Leaving his men was a wrench. He knew that the battalion was
in for severe casualties but preferred to stick with his troops rather
than take a safe headquarters job.

In Japan he found that Colonel Bealle was now a two-star general and the Intelligence Officer at MacArthur's headquarters in
Tokyo. Fitz was assigned to a newly organized unit of the Army,
the U. S. Army Special Forces, working under Colonel Aaron
Bank, a former OSS officer in World War II.

Fitz worked long and tirelessly with this new concept in a military unit made up of soldiers who were paratroopers, rangers, and
combat men from World War II and the present war in Korea.

Ten years later Fitz's unit was to earn the sobriquet Green
Berets. With an impressive record in Korea, Fitz and the Special
Forces returned to the United States. By the mid-fifties Fitz was a
lieutenant colonel of thirty, and recognized as a soldier-diplomat
as well as a fine combat man.

Then the United States began to get seriously involved in the
problems of the Middle East. At the time it was the government's
policy to support and keep close ties with the Arab world at the
same time that it maintained friendly relations with Israel. That
was when Fitz was the chief U.S. military adviser to King Hussein
of Jordan.

Today Fitz couldn't help but think that he had made a mistake in turning down King Hussein's offer to make him a general. On the fifty-thousand-dollar salary with all expenses, his own plane, quarters, servants, and traveling allowance to visit America, he could have built up a nice fortune by now.

He wondered what Marie and his son Bill were thinking of the news story about him. Bill at thirteen still didn't think anything other than what his mother told him.

That had been quite a moment in his career, his marriage.

Marie had worked in General Bealle's office in Washington at the end of the Korean War. Bealle and his wife frequently had urged Fitz to become a family man. Fitz thought he loved Marie and he wanted a son, his own son whom he would train and bring up, and try to make up for his own illegitimacy. So he and Marie were married in a military ceremony at Fort Myer.

Fitz, thinking of the trouble he was in over the news story, remembered the final counseling General Bealle had given him just prior to his retirement. Fitz and Marie had dinner with the General and his wife, and after dinner Bealle had taken his protégé into the study, which was filled with cardboard boxes full of the mementos of the General's career.

"There's one more thing I can do for you, Fitz. Two, really. I can give you some advice and I'm owed one favor that will make it possible for you to take my advice if you want it."

Fitz had listened attentively as Bealle had pointed out to him that nobody was going to profit careerwise from service in Vietnam. "It's a losing war, the politicians are playing hell with it, and a lot of good officers are going to have their careers ruined when they're used for scapegoats by higher officers and politicians. Keep away from Vietnam if you're really interested in making it all the way—two, three, hell maybe even four stars. You've had two successful tours in Vietnam, that's enough. Now, I can get you assigned back to the Middle East. I can't tell you what the job will be exactly, but something in training or intelligence. Three years over there and you'll be something of an expert. When the Vietnam thing is over, even before it's over, the Army and the government will be looking for men with Middle East experience to promote up to star rank."

"I'd like to go back to the Middle East, Oscar. I was very happy on my last assignment there."

"And you should be able to take Marie and little Bill with you on this tour."

Fitz had reached across and shaken his old mentor's hand. "I don't know how to tell you how much I appreciate your advice and help, Oscar."

"I'm afraid it's the last thing I'll be able to do for you, Fitz, but it should be all you'll need. Just try and stay out of controversy and you'll make it all the way."

Fitz received the assignment that was to change his life. The Shah of Iran had been deposed once, but the CIA had quickly countered the Communist insurrectionists and restored the Shah to the Peacock Throne. Fitz was assigned as a special military adviser to the Shah, working under the supervision of the U. S. Embassy.

Fitz went to Iran alone, leaving his wife and son safely at their comfortable quarters in Virginia until he could determine whether it was appropriate to bring them to Persia.

With the war raging in Vietnam and public attention removed from the Middle East, Fitz helped the Shah organize an Iranian equivalent of the Green Berets and for two years visited the countries around the Persian Gulf on special missions for the U. S. Embassy, frequently initiated by Shah Pahlavi, who in turn acted favorably on policy suggestions of the U. S. Government.

Those had been the good days of Fitz's assignment even though Marie refused to come or bring Bill over for a visit. She had no desire to live in the Middle East, and Fitz was so busy visiting the Arab countries around the Persian Gulf on special missions that he felt it was just as well that Marie live where her friends were around Washington.

With the assignment of General Fielding to the Embassy, Fitz's freedom to handle Gulf matters his own way was much curtailed. Fitz was reduced to being an intelligence officer. He was looking forward to getting his promotion to full colonel and reassignment, hopefully, within the Middle East so he could continue working with the Arab leaders he had come to know and like.

As Fitz pondered his alternatives—and there seemed none to voluntary retirement—it particularly distressed him to be thought of as an enemy of the Jews. In order to maintain perspective during his tour of duty in Iran, he visited Israel at least three times a

year, making friends anew and cultivating past relationships. He
numbered doctors, intellectuals, craftsmen, politicians, and particularly the Israeli fighting men among his friends. He freely admitted to his Israeli friends that he had been part of an American
mission under the Eisenhower administration to gain the friendship and support of Arab nations, Jordan in particular.

Fitz was proud of the Israeli spirit and would have been happy
to be assigned to advise Israeli Army units. But the Israelis needed
neither advice nor outside recruits. "Just give us the weapons,
we'll do the rest," they proclaimed, and they lived up to their
word. For the first time since the Romans conquered the Hebrews
in Old Testament days, they had their country, ruled by themselves, and they would die to keep it.

It was with a divided soul that Fitz observed the scene in this
part of the world he had come to love and understand. He understood the importance of close friendly relations with the Arabs.
Obviously Arab oil was the largest factor, but Arab ingenuity combined with their recent and constantly increasing wealth made
them a major force in the world of economics and diplomacy.

In two years Fitz had watched the basically pro-American Arab
states begin to slip from the U.S. sphere of influence and all the
reports, memos, studies, and warnings he sent up to the Ambassador and presumably to Defense and the State Department in
Washington might just as well have been filed in some sand dune
in the Arabian Desert.

The one woman in the Intelligence Department of the Embassy walked into Fitz's office and laid a folder on his desk. "Here
are some cables that came in for you this morning, Fitz," she said.
Then, looking down at him with deep, lachrymose brown eyes,
she said, "It's all so damned unfair. So cruel. The Shah has the
right idea. He would close down the paper and put that reporter
in jail."

Fitz smiled wryly. Laylah Smith was a beautiful girl at twenty-
six and her flash of righteous indignation brought fire to her face
and eyes. Long black hair rippled down below her neck. She was
the offspring of an American diplomat and Iranian aristocrat and
was particularly valuable to the Embassy as an American girl who
spoke Farsee, the language of Iran.

Fitz stood up, looking uneasily past the open door out into the hall. He put his arm around her shoulder for a moment. "Things are going to work out fine, Laylah. You'll see."

She brightened. "You're not upset?"

"I was, I guess I still am. But God, Allah, take your pick, works in mysterious ways his wonders to perform."

"You have some more generous invitations," Laylah replied brightly, gesturing at the folder she had brought in.

"Yes," Fitz sighed, "and for all the wrong reasons." He opened the folder and looked through the cables. From Arab leaders he had befriended and helped he had received a stream of laudatory cables. He looked through today's communications and after a few moments picked one out.

"Now here's an interesting one. From Dubai."

"Yes, I read it," Laylah said. "But you don't have to leave Tehran. You could retire here. You have friends who would make you very rich in a short time."

"I don't know what I'm going to do." He frowned. Then he glanced out at the hall and kissed Laylah's lips briefly. "I'll tell you about it over caviar and iced vodka tonight."

She smiled and then turned and left the office.

Fitz sat down once again to read the telegrams. The first one was a gut twister, from Tel Aviv. "We know here you got, in the vernacular, a bum rap. What happened? Can we help? (signed) Shlomo."

Fitz pressed a button on his desk and before the messenger from the cable room arrived Fitz had composed an answer to his friend, deputy to the Israeli Minister of Information. Then he began to read the other telegrams. When he came to the one from Dubai he studied it carefully. His old friends on the Creek hadn't forgotten him.

> We would welcome you to become part of our busi-
> ness community. There are many opportunities here.
> We would be honored to have you as our adviser. We
> await your visit. Customs and Immigration have been
> notified to extend full courtesy.
>
> (signed) H.H. the Ruler, Rashid

Fitz thought about Dubai and the true merchant prince who ran his small shaikhdom in the Trucial States so effectively. Although Dubai had no oil royalties unlike his wealthy neighboring shaikhdom, Abu Dhabi, Shaikh Rashid bin Sa'id al Maktoum had turned his small state into the most thriving entrepôt on the Arabian Gulf. It had become rich without oil although oil exploration was always being carried out in the desert behind Dubai Town and under the ocean offshore. Once called the Pirate Coast, the area now was referred to as the smuggling coast. Not that anything was smuggled into Dubai—there was no duty and no contraband with the exception of hashish and opium—but large fortunes were being made in what was politely known as re-export. Shipping such forbidden or high-duty goods as gold, cigarettes, and liquor into India, Pakistan, and Iran.

An invitation to become an adviser to Rashid could not be lightly dismissed. And whereas Fitz had received many invitations to visit and even to take up residence in Arab states, Dubai seemed to promise the most rewarding financial benefits—if that was now his interest in life.

At four o'clock Fitz was not surprised to be called into General Fielding's office. He sat stiffly across the desk from his superior and waited for him to open the conversation.

"Have you made up your mind what you want to do?" the General asked, embarrassment making his tone gruff.

"I want to try and hold on to my military career but I guess that's a lost cause now."

Fielding remained silent, waiting for Fitz to say something more. After a few moments of uncomfortable stillness Fielding said, "Some congressman from New York is planning to be here in a few days. It would be nice if we could cable State and Defense and say the problem is cleared up, so this junketing representative looking into anti-Semitism in U.S. embassies could be headed off."

Fitz shrugged. "O.K. I guess it's the only way. You have the papers prepared. I'll retire and look around for a new life."

Fielding, a broad smile on his face, stood up, came around the desk, and put an arm on Fitz's shoulder. "Good decision, Lodd.

And you know that whatever you get into we at the Embassy will help you in any way we can."

A bitter smile flicked across Fitz's lips as he recalled Oscar Bealle's warning: Keep away from Vietnam; don't get into anything controversial and you can go all the way.

"I'll have everything ready," Fielding continued. "Back pay, allowances, pension forms. We'll take care of everything in the morning."

They certainly were anxious to get the pariah out from their midst, Fitz thought.

Part II
GOLD

A searing blast of heat greeted Fitz as he walked out of the Iran Air jet at Dubai's new international airport.

To his delight he found Ibrahim Matroos, resplendent in white *kandura*, his *kuffiyah* held in place by the *aghal*, a double-strand black camel rope, waiting for him at the bottom of the plane's steps. Ibrahim was one of Rashid's important courtiers.

"Old friend, you honor us with your presence," Ibrahim said in English.

"*Aleikum as Salaam*," Fitz returned in Arabic. They shook hands warmly.

"You have chosen the evil time of the beginning of the heat to come, I am sorry," Ibrahim apologized. From June to September the temperature averages 120 degrees, sometimes dropping to 100 at night. The humidity reaches nearly 100 percent. Most activity was at a standstill and the European community left the Arabian Gulf area during the summer.

"You are cleared at Customs and Immigration," Ibrahim said. "As soon as your bags come we will proceed to the beach guest house. His Highness is most concerned with your comfort."

"When are you going to get air conditioning?" Fitz asked, glancing up at the overhead fans beating futilely at the solidity of the heat.

"In another year, Inshallah. Allah willing," he translated.

"I hope he so wills."

Sitting in the back seat of one of the Ruler's big British automobiles, his suitcases in the trunk, Fitz slowly began asking Ibrahim about the state of affairs in Dubai. The heat, even in the fast-moving automobile with all windows open, was so oppressive that Fitz found his thinking slowed, his words coming slowly.

They were soon in sight of the Creek. The Maktoum Bridge

built some years before arched over the blue water of the naviga-
ble stream which made Dubai the most important shipping center
on the Trucial Coast. To their right, toward the Gulf, rose the
two- and three-story buildings of Deira, the new Carlton Hotel on
the Deira side of the Creek looking like a modern skyscraper
against the rest of the town.

Fitz thought back to the stories he had been told of how
Shaikh Rashid had united Dubai and Deira in 1939 when his father, Sa'id, was still alive and ruling. Rashid's cousins, the Al
Mana family, controlled Deira. There was considerable rivalry between the families, particularly over who should collect custom
duties from the many dhows that put into the Dubai Creek. The
pearling industry provided especially lucrative payments to the
proprietor of the Creek.

Finally Rashid solved the problem. He was thirty years old and
still had not taken a bride, a most unusual circumstance for an
Arab. In one stroke he took Shaikha Latifa of Abu Dhabi, who
was living with her Al Mana cousins, as his bride, and his wedding
party of warriors, permitted to cross the Creek and land on the
fortified Deira side for the ceremony, immediately attacked the Al
Mana men, driving them out of Deira once and for all.

The marriage, despite its disquieting prelude for the bride, was
a model of success even to this day, in the Arab world. Rashid had
never taken another wife although by law he was allowed four at
any given time, and Shaikha Latifa's palace, the harem, was always full of a multinational mob of urchins she adopted, cared
for, and educated.

"The Ruler will see you in the morning," Ibrahim said as they
crossed the Maktoum Bridge from the Deira side to Dubai. "He
regrets that he had a long-standing appointment this evening with
the Ruler of Sharjah. The new highway is one of the matters they
will discuss."

"That's fine with me, Ibrahim."

"You will have some of your countrymen to talk with at the
guest house. Several other visitors are in Dubai for discussions
with the Shaikh. Since the discovery of oil offshore last year,
Dubai has been busier than ever."

Ten minutes after crossing the Maktoum Bridge the car completed the last leg of the trip, driving over the desert sands to the

beachfront guest house built a few years before by the Ruler. "Personally," Ibrahim said, "I would not want to be down on the ocean but the Westerners seem to like it here."

"I guess I can cool off a little with a swim," Fitz observed.

"As you like, but don't wander up the beach away from town too far. Twice the slavers have stolen people right off the beach at Jumiera and sold them to the caravans going to Saudi and Oman."

"Westerners?" Fitz asked in surprise.

"Even Westerners, though they don't get the money for them that a young black brings unless, of course, they captured a female."

"Were the Westerners ever rescued?" Fitz asked.

"The Trucial Oman Scouts did bring back the last Westerner taken, in poor condition but nevertheless alive. That was more than five years ago."

The automobile stopped in front of the guest house and Fitz stepped out onto the sand. The driver went around and opened up the trunk, taking Fitz's two suitcases out and carrying them to the door, upon which he pounded after placing the bags on the doorstep.

A dark-skinned Pakistani servant in smock and slacks and wearing a turban opened the door, bowed, and picked up the suitcases. Fitz followed him into the spacious interior of a long sitting room facing out over the ocean. Somehow, although it was certainly hot, the room seemed cooler than the temperature outside.

Three Western men were sitting around the room in shirts open to the waist, wearing loose-fitting slacks, and holding drinks.

Ibrahim greeted the other guests and introduced Colonel Lodd. Then he left Fitz with the others, promising to return at seven in the morning to join him for coffee before taking him to visit with the Ruler.

"We're all going over tomorrow, Ibrahim," a tall, silver-haired, ruddy-faced Englishman named John Stakes said. "We could take Colonel Lodd with us."

"The Ruler has asked that I personally conduct Colonel Lodd to his presence," Ibrahim replied, leveling a steady gaze at the Englishman. Then, nodding to the others, Ibrahim left the beach house.

Tim McLaren, a hearty, dark-haired American in his early forties, walked over to Fitz and shook his hand. "Pleasure to meet
you. This is a big surprise to have you walk in here. You must be
the best-known American in the Arab press today. Glad to see you
here."

The other American was a slightly built though somehow in-
tense-looking man, appearing to be in his late thirties or early forties. He had been introduced as Fender Browne and, in an unmistakably U.S. midwestern twang, he welcomed Fitz to the guest
house and confessed he was in the oil business. "Tim McLaren
here is more legitimate, I gotta admit," Fender Browne drawled.
"He's a banker. Gonna set us guys up with a real U.S. of A. bank
here. Air-conditioned bank," Fender added.

"Air-conditioned?" Fitz asked. "You bringing in your own generator?"

"Of course. An air-conditioned quonset hut on top of our vault.
All I need is the Ruler's final O.K. tomorrow and we'll be taking
deposits, making loans, and selling gold in one week."

"That doesn't sound too secure," Fitz observed.

"You know this part of the world, Colonel." McLaren took a
sip from his highball. "There's very little stealing. A felon's hand
is cut off in most of these states. Rashid, of course, abandoned
this practice but thievery is rare."

Then, suddenly remembering, the banker said, "I'm sorry, Colonel, I didn't offer you a drink. Naturally the Ruler doesn't stock a
supply but I had the foresight to bring a few bottles of scotch
with me. How about it?"

"I wouldn't mind at all," Fitz replied.

"Help yourself. The bottle's on the table over there. And the
royal refrigerator does make ice."

As Fitz made his drink the expansive banker was saying, "Yes,
sir. These Trucial States and Oman across the hills are about the
last places left where you can still get in on the ground floor.
That's what First Commercial Bank of New York is doing. We'll
be here to help the rest of the pioneers make it."

"I'll be around to see you, Tim," Fender Browne chimed in,
walking over to where Fitz was standing and refreshing his drink.
"With the drilling beginning offshore, Dubai Oil Drilling Operations, we call the company DODO, is going to need more and
more of my equipment."

Browne turned to Fitz. "I was with Aramco for fifteen years. Worked up to tool pusher and then ran the supply and maintenance shop over in Saudi. Then I decided to try and make it on my own. I heard they were exploring here in the Trucial States and I knew where all the equipment was stored, some of it forgotten and rusting away, along the Gulf."

Fender Browne took a long belt of the banker's scotch. "I started supplying the exploration parties and seismic crews in Abu Dhabi, here, and in Sharjah with stuff they couldn't get and pretty soon I had me a warehouse in Abu Dhabi and now I'm after a few hundred acres on the Creek to set up the only independent oil field supply company on the Gulf south of Kuwait."

"And you are going to need capital, Fender," Tim McLaren boomed.

"I sure as hell am. You get that air-conditioned quonset hut set up and those vaults full of gold real fast because if Rashid lets me have that land on the Creek my oil field supply company will never see competition on this gulf. And here's where the oil is at."

McLaren gestured at Fitz. "What are your plans, Colonel? You planning to stay with us here and serve the Ruler and yourself?"

"In the first place it's ex-Lieutenant Colonel," Fitz said with a sad smile. "Just call me Fitz; everyone else does."

"Well, Fitz, you've come to Dubai a famous man in the Arab world," John Stakes interjected. "Seems a pity the American Army saw fit to cashier you just for speaking the truth about the Jews. They bloody well are a hysterical lot."

"But that's not what I said, nor what I think," Fitz began.

McLaren lifted a hand. "Fitz, my boy, don't say another word. I'm sure you were misunderstood, misquoted, and mistreated. But you're here now, on the ground floor, in the first wave, so to speak. There's going to be plenty of opportunities for the second, third, and fourth wave of entrepreneurs who come to Dubai, but we'll be sitting firmly in control. So if you take the advice of an old Mideast hand, you'll never explain what you really meant. Let the shaikhs think what they want to think and you just stay close and pick up the loot that comes your way."

"Amen to that, Fitz," John Stakes chimed in. "I'll be glad to put you in the way of several attractive propositions, old boy."

"Thanks," Fitz said.

"I agree too, Fitz." Fender Browne held his glass up. "There's a place on the Creek for you."

It was a relief when the morning came and it was no longer necessary to try to sleep in the hot night.

Ibrahim was in front of the guest house to pick Fitz up. He was wearing, as he had been advised, an open short-sleeved sports shirt and slacks and sandals. Fender Browne, John Stakes, and Tim McLaren had a car and driver sent to them and followed along after Ibrahim.

"At this time of the year we try to finish all business before nine-thirty or ten in the morning," Ibrahim explained. "Indeed, some of the less faithful believe that even Allah himself deserts the Arabian Gulf these days and leaves it to the forces from hell. It is a time of year to exist through in whatever way possible."

A ten-minute drive across the sand from the coast and they reached Rashid's new palace, a blue and gold one-story edifice. They drove up to the main portals with lesser doors on either side and stepped out of the automobile.

"You've been here before," Ibrahim said.

"Yes, but the last time I visited Shaikh Rashid this palace hadn't been finished. He lived closer to the Creek then."

Ibrahim led the way up the steps, into the palace, and down a long corridor which despite the fierce heat outside seemed to be only warm. Honor guards carrying bayonet-tipped rifles lined the corridor, coming to some semblance of attention as Ibrahim and Fitz passed and then sagging into a semi-leaning, semi-upright position against the wall.

They stopped before two tall, barrel-vaulted doors and a pair of guards swung them open. Fitz followed Ibrahim inside. The room was large and rectangular with a high ceiling. On the benches around the room Arabs and a sprinkling of Westerners awaited their turn to discuss their business with the Shaikh. The coffee slave constantly made the rounds of the room filling the cups of those waiting from a copper pot with a pelican beak. At the far end of his reception room, behind an ornate, ivory-inlaid table, sat Shaikh Rashid. The Ruler looked up and a benevolent smile spread across the kindly weathered features of the black-bearded craggy face that looked out from the white *kuffiyah*. He stood up and motioned Fitz to approach.

Ibrahim led Fitz past the rank of standing Arabs and Westerners. Shaikh Rashid waved the Arab sitting beside him away and gestured to the now empty chair beside him. Fitz and the Ruler shook hands and then both sat down.

"*Qarrat 'ainii*," Rashid said, using the congratulatory greeting to a close relation or particular friend who has come back from a journey.

"*Wejh nabiik*," Fitz replied, meaning "the face of your prophet."

A cup of coffee was put before Fitz. He sipped it, finishing the cup, and then, shaking it to denote he wanted no more, he handed it back to the slave.

"So, dear friend, have you been made comfortable?" Rashid asked.

"As comfortable as the heat will allow," Fitz answered with a smile.

After a few more exchanges of pleasantries Rashid's expressive face became serious. "I was sorry to read of your troubles and your loss of position in the American Army," he began in slow, distinct Arabic to help Fitz understand.

"Our fate is not our own to manage," Fitz replied, spreading his hands.

"But Allah helps him who helps himself. When I heard of this statement you made that your American Jews should try to understand our position and not be so irrationally emotional I was proud that an American employed by his government would say such a thing. We well realize that the Jews are most powerful in matters of money and public opinion in your country. Furthermore, I know you, I think. We have talked on many occasions about many things. I know you to be a man who harbors his words and thoughts most carefully. It is my belief that you did not say what the American press quotes."

The Ruler smiled knowingly at Fitz and reached a hand across the table to touch his. "We have seen our words and motives given a black face almost every day in the American press. It would serve your American newspapers well to warp whatever it was you really said into the form in which it appeared. But what is important"—he paused as though weighing his words—"Well-informed, intelligent Arabs everywhere have heard that you apparently defied your government and people on our behalf. That is all you need now, since you speak our language, to become one of the richest and most powerful Americans in our world. It is my wish that you would make Dubai your home and headquarters. You will be under the protection of the Ruler. Everyone who does business in Dubai or hopes to do so will know that you have our ear.

"We are not a rich state"—Rashid paused—"yet." He nodded to himself as though possessed of some secret knowledge. "But Allah willing and with the hard work of our people and foreigners who come here to make money for themselves and the state, we will very soon be the most important and modern state on the Arabian Gulf, in all of the Arab world."

Rashid's eyes gleamed and Fitz found himself absolutely convinced that this Ruler would do exactly as he foresaw for his small state.

"We will be an oil-producing country in another two years but Dubai must not depend on oil. Our reserves are small compared to those of our neighbor, Abu Dhabi. We must constantly be looking for opportunities to lead the Arab world in commerce and industry. But in the meantime"—he gave Fitz a wink—"we must go to the source of every moneymaking scheme available to us and pump its wealth into our treasury. You and I will be partners. Within a few years I foresee the government of the United States coming to you for advice in making policy in the Middle East and asking your help to correct the mistakes it is making today."

Rashid once again smiled benevolently on Fitz. "Do you find these words meaningful to you?"

"Yes, Your Highness, I like what I hear."

"Good. You will join us? Stay in the guest residence as long as you like. I will see that you are granted land wherever you desire on which to build a home. Your office will be in our building on the Creek. A car and driver will be made available to you until you are ready to purchase your own."

In English, Fitz found himself saying aloud, "Not bad for a bastard from Ohio."

Rashid looked up. "Something I should know?"

Fitz shook his head, smiling. "No, just an American expression of gratitude. It would lose in translation."

Rashid nodded, satisfied. "Ibrahim will see that you have everything you need. Tomorrow night I am having a few of our most prominent Western visitors for dinner. Ibrahim will bring you to us. Go with Allah."

Fitz bowed his head momentarily. They both stood up and shook hands, Fitz taking his leave. Ibrahim came forward and escorted him from the room. Fitz nodded to his three guest-residence mates as he left and they smiled back at him. It was evident to everyone in the room that Shaikh Rashid had placed his mantle of protection around Fitz's shoulders and another anointed Westerner belonged to Dubai.

Outside the palace Fitz climbed into the car beside Ibrahim and they drove away. "Where do we go now?" Fitz asked.

"The Ruler wants you to meet Majid Jabir first," Ibrahim replied in Arabic. "We'll go now to his office in the customs house."

"He's a customs collector?" Fitz asked.

"He's a little of everything. He came here a few years ago from Qatar, where he worked under the British adviser on customs and immigration. Majid has one extremely valuable accomplishment, as you will soon see. Fortunately for Majid his parents possessed sufficient wealth to send him to the English school in Qatar from the time he was a young boy. He speaks almost perfect, idiomatic English. None of us in Dubai possess Majid's ability to converse with and completely understand the Westerners."

"Then Majid Jabir is not a native Dubai Arab?"

"No. For some reason he displeased his British superior, who thought that sending Majid to Dubai would be a form of exile or punishment. As Allah would have it, this was the best thing that ever happened to Majid. When he became customs collector he went out to each dhow, carrying his black umbrella over his head for protection from the sun, and personally took the payments from each dhow captain. Then, unlike his predecessor, instead of turning the money over to the British superintendent of the port of Dubai, he took it directly to the Ruler. I can tell you that Shaikh Rashid was much pleased at this direct action. Rashid himself used to go from dhow to dhow collecting customs and he appreciated seeing for himself the day's receipts. Majid became close to the Ruler from that time on. Now he is more important than any man on the Creek and he has his hands in most of the business enterprises."

"In our language then, Majid is the Ruler's bag man," Fitz said with a chuckle. At the perplexed look on Ibrahim's face Fitz explained in Arabic. "Bag man is the person who collects the money and holds it for the person in high position who can make things happen but doesn't want to become directly involved in the receipt of money."

Ibrahim grinned and nodded his head. "That is very accurate. Majid is the bag man. But there are others."

"What will Majid expect of me?"

Ibrahim shrugged. "Almost anything. Since he is well aware of your background as a fighting man and intelligence gatherer, there are many uses to which he can put you, all of which will be highly profitable to you as well as the state."

The car had almost reached the Creek when it paused before the ancient square mud-brick fort that had once protected the Dubai side. "The Ruler hopes someday to turn the fort into a museum," Ibrahim commented. Passing the fort, the car drove up to the two-story office building used by the Ruler's advisers.

Ibrahim and Fitz stepped out of the car and walked into the office building past a khaki-uniformed guard, wearing a red and white checked *kuffiyah*, and then up a staircase to the second floor. Fitz followed his guide down a hall and into an office with wide windows commanding the Creek. Looking out over the panorama, standing up behind a desk, was a young-looking Arab, clean-shaven, wearing the traditional white *kandura*, or *dish dasha* as the robe was sometimes called, and *kuffiyah*.

Ibrahim introduced Fitz to Majid Jabir, who carried on the conversation in precise English. "I have looked forward to the pleasure of meeting you, Colonel Lodd," Majid began. "It is my understanding that the fact you are here means you have decided to throw your lot in with us, so to speak."

"His Highness was very generous in his proposal," Fitz replied noncommittally. "I of course see nothing but boundless opportunity here on the Arabian Gulf."

"You have been active in the Middle East many years," Majid

stated. "You should be well qualified to make your fortune with us. Have you any ideas of where to start?"

"The money is in oil, I suppose," Fitz began.

"Yes, but it is also in many other directions. I don't have to explain Dubai to you, an intelligence officer. I can only confirm that we are as wide open as you have always suspected. Duty on goods coming in is negligible. Re-export is our biggest business today, and as long as the price stays at thirty-five dollars an ounce, gold is our biggest re-export item. We have just one problem—pirates. Our high-speed dhows occasionally run into pirates in the form of naval vessels of other countries who stop our ships and take the cargo. Just this year our most important gold shipper has lost two cargoes valued at over five million dollars each."

"A staggering loss," Fitz commented.

"True. Of course successful shipments provide a staggering gain. As much as two hundred percent profit on the cost of a gold shipment. It occurred to me that while you are settling in with us you might be able to advise one of our chief gold exporters, a particular friend of the Ruler, on methods of safeguarding valuable cargo."

"I don't know what I could do, Mr. Jabir," Fitz replied, at a loss to understand what the customs man was suggesting.

"Why don't you have a talk with the Shaikh's friend," Majid suggested pointedly. "If you can help him you will be doing a service to Dubai, and, you will find, to yourself."

Ibrahim, seeing that the meeting was temporarily terminated, stood up. Majid gave a helpless shrug. "Colonel Lodd, please forgive me for being short this morning. I am looking forward to seeing much of you, talking at length with you, and learning more about American aims in the Middle East from you. But"—he gestured out the window sadly—"I am still the customs collector and I see two dhows waiting my visit. I will be at the Ruler's dinner tomorrow night. Oh, and may I remind you, whatever it is you and Sepah—he is the chief organizer of our merchant re-exporters—decide to do, neither His Highness nor any of us who attend the Ruler must have any knowledge of it. You understand?"

"I'm afraid I do, Mr. Jabir." Fitz smiled ruefully. "Until tomorrow evening, then."

CHAPTER 4

It was a short drive along the Creek to Sepah's home. "Sepah's father, Yousef, was one of the largest pearl merchants on the Gulf," Ibrahim explained. "Then after your great war the Japanese flooded the market with their cultured pearls and that was the end of the Arabian Gulf natural-pearl trade. Yousef finally went back to his native Persia to live out his days, but Sepah and the Ruler had become almost like brothers. Rashid convinced Sepah he should stay in Dubai and help build up the Creek as a great international trading port."

"I guess they still have a way to go," Fitz remarked.

"Of course, but if you had known us just ten years ago you would be amazed at our progress."

"I have seen the changes in just the past three years since I first visited here," Fitz agreed.

The car pulled up in front of a house whose luxurious mien was exaggerated by its setting among the mud houses and stores along the Creek. It was a long, low white house, the roof of which could just be seen over the walls surrounding it.

"Whatever Sepah does, he must do it well," Fitz observed as they drove through the gate.

"This was his father's home and though it was built forty years ago it is still one of the finest houses on the Creek. It's been said that the Ruler greatly coveted this house, much finer than the home in which the royal family lived. So it is a measure of his regard for Sepah that Rashid asked him to stay in Dubai when his father left. Had Sepah also gone, Rashid could have taken the house, since it is on the Ruler's land, loaned to Yousef for his lifetime and his son's lifetime provided they lived in Dubai."

Just as Fitz and Ibrahim reached the door of the house it was opened by a servant, who admitted them into the large living room looking out over the Creek. It was cool inside and Fitz breathed deeply, grateful for the respite from the heat, which by this time in the morning had reached above 110. "Sepah and Rashid are among the very few people with air conditioning. Sepah brought diesel generators and air-conditioning units down from Kuwait. Another great service he performed for the Ruler."

At that moment Sepah entered the room. His dress was remarkably Western, Fitz thought. A billowing blue shirt tucked into loose-fitting tan slacks, a pair of sandals on his feet. Sepah seemed unusually trim for a man his age, about fifty, Fitz estimated. His brown face had the weathered look of a man who spent much of his time outdoors. He looked to be a hard man who had physically worked to achieve the obvious success which vibrated from his person and surroundings. Here was a man with whom Fitz instinctively felt empathy.

Sepah extended a strong hand to Fitz and without waiting for Ibrahim to make introductions he said in English, "Welcome to my house, Colonel Lodd. This is an honor." He gestured toward an overstuffed sofa, and Fitz walked across the magnificent Persian carpet which covered the long floor and took a seat.

Sepah noticed Fitz's admiring gaze. "Of course, you have just come from Persia, or must I call my father's country Iran? You have seen many fine carpets."

"Even in Tabriz I saw nothing to compare to this one, Mr. Sepah."

Sepah laughed, white teeth gleaming in his deeply tanned face. "There is no Mr. to my name. Just Sepah."

"Call me Fitz." Fitz smiled ruefully. "I'm not a colonel any more. I retired from the U. S. Army, as you probably heard."

Sepah nodded. "Yes, to our good fortune, and as you will see, your own." Sepah indicated the sofa and the three men sat down. "I'm sure you are wondering why the Ruler sent you to me," Sepah continued. He smiled at Ibrahim. "And not directly at that, but through Majid Jabir." He gave Fitz an owlish look.

"I know that in due course you will tell me," Fitz replied, settling back in the comfortable sofa.

"Since you were in intelligence in Iran, you must be conversant with the results of the Shah's import embargoes."

"Those results being smuggling?" Fitz returned.

Sepah's white-toothed smile broadened. "In Dubai we use the term re-export, but no matter. You have the right idea. Fortunately, with my father's help, I was able to purchase some fine boats from the pearl fleet when that trade was destroyed. As a matter of fact, I purchased the two fastest boats on the Creek—at that time," he added.

"The pearl trade!" Fitz sighed at the romance he thought was inherent in diving for pearls. "Those must have been great days."

Sepah cocked an eye at his visitor, a humorous look coming to his face. "Do you know anything about pearling?" he asked.

"Just what I've read. Being a great underwater enthusiast, I would love to have gone pearling."

"It is too bad you never met a pearling ship coming back to the Creek after spending the hottest four months of the year under a fierce sun on a dead-calm sea. What a pitiful sight to see the thin, dried-up divers return from a successful diving season. Of course, to see the unsuccessful boat arrive is a tragedy. The divers' daily ration consists of a little water, a handful of dates, and a small bowl of rice. They can stay down longer if they are undernourished."

Sepah shook his head at the vision. "I know; I began as a diver in order to learn my father's business. When I came to his house after my first season I was covered with sores, walking with my legs spread apart to ease the pain when my dried-out, ulcerated skin and the erupting infections in the crotch rubbed together. Because all the fresh water must be saved for drinking, the divers were never able to wash the salt from their skin."

"That's an aspect of pearling I never heard about," Fitz admitted.

"Shaikh Rashid tried to stop the abuses of the *nakhoudas*, or captains as you would call them. He forced them to take casks of lime juice to relieve the scurvy on their ships even though they complained of the expense. You might well ask why year after year these wretched men went out despite their sufferings and the underwater dangers of sharks, stingrays, and red jellyfish whose lash is agony for hours and feels like a burn with a hot iron."

"Why did they?" Fitz asked.

"Debt. They always had to borrow from the *nakhouda* and then to pay him back they dove for just one more season. Rashid did as much as he could to improve the divers' lives, but it was Dubai's biggest industry and he could only do so much."

"How many seasons did you dive?" Fitz asked.

"My first was my last," Sepah replied. "Then I worked up from crew member of a dhow to *nakhouda* and captained the ships that carried my father's pearls and other goods to the seaports of the Gulf and beyond."

"And then you got into re-exporting?" Fitz prompted.

"I built a modest trade in commerce up and down the Gulf, much of which involved taking cargoes of embargoed items into India, Pakistan, and Iran. Since the Shahenshah has been trying to encourage his country's native tobacco growers, he has placed an embargo on importing American cigarettes."

"I know about the cigarette business," Fitz said. "If one does not have the advantage of an embassy post exchange and wants decent cigarettes, he buys them on the black market."

Sepah nodded. "My boats have been taking good American cigarettes into Iran since the embargo was first announced." He paused, glancing out the window at the shipping passing up and down the Creek. "There are many other items of course which are profitable but the richest and most dangerous re-export item is gold. And it is in this item that I am experiencing ruinous reverses. And when I suffer, most of the merchants along the Creek suffer with me. When the merchants suffer, the Ruler suffers. Quite honestly we believe that with your help I should be able to run four heavy gold shipments to Bombay in the next year. To date I have lost two high-speed dhows and ten million dollars of gold. This, as you can imagine, is most distressing to me and the syndicate which purchased the gold."

"I don't know what I can do to help," Fitz interjected. "If you get caught inside the territorial waters of India with contraband in your hold, nobody can help you."

"That is true of course. However, the Indian Coast Guard has taken to cruising a hundred miles and more off their shores looking for boats like mine. And while we can outrun most Indian ships, they have a small fleet of fast, light ships, hardly more than sixty or seventy feet long, which can catch up to us on the high seas.

"The first time this happened my *nakhouda* obeyed orders to halt. He was on the high seas and completely within his rights. Nevertheless, the Indian ship trained its machine guns on him and on pain of death ordered the entire cargo of gold transferred. Once this had been accomplished the Indian vessel hulled my boat with its guns and sailed off, leaving it sinking. The *nakhouda* and some of the crew survived by clinging to wreckage and were fortunately saved by another Dubai dhow a few days later."

Fitz thought about the story a few moments. "So you contributed heavily to the Indian Government's cash reserves."

"No." Sepah shook his head. "I will explain. I spent more than a year in India building up my organization there. That's where the real danger and work in this operation occurs. My receivers in Bombay send men out in boats beyond the three miles legally patrolled by the Coast Guard. They take the gold from my ship and land it back on the beach at night. My receiver delivers the gold to a safe hiding place where it is locked up securely. Then he goes to one of my several trustees and gives him the key to where the gold is secured. Then it is the job of the trustee to make contact with one of our trusted agents, who consummates the sale of the gold to the buyers in India and collects the money, which he gives to the trustee. It is this trustee who sends the payment for the gold back to me in Dubai."

"A very complicated process," Fitz commented.

"True. And all of my men in India are intelligence gatherers of a quality enjoyed by few intelligence agencies. They report that when an Indian Coast Guard ship captures a gold cargo it is split among the crew of the ship and high-ranking shore officers, making all of them wealthy for life. The Indian Government never learns about the capture." Sepah laughed. "If such a prize came to the attention of high government officials they would take it for themselves. In no case does the confiscation of gold on the high seas benefit the people of India."

As an intelligence officer Fitz was professionally interested in Sepah's organization. "It must have been a difficult and dangerous business setting up your network in India."

"Of course. And frequently while I was receiving small gold shipments in India to test and perfect my machine, my people were either apprehended and made to talk or they turned informer for money. Each time this happened I changed identity.

The Ruler gave me ten different passports when I went to India and I used every one of them. The reason I have few competitors is that it is so difficult to set up the organization in India."

After a long silence Fitz finally said, "I still don't see where I can fit in."

Sepah stood up. "That I am going to show you now. I'm sorry to have to take you out of this cool room, but the rewards will more than compensate you for spending the hot summer with us here."

Sepah led the way out of his house and into the inferno of mid-morning heat. Instructing Ibrahim to follow, Sepah stepped up agilely into his Land Rover and started out. It was a short drive to the boatbuilding yard beside the Maktoum Bridge. Sepah pulled up in his vehicle and Ibrahim's driver drew to a halt beside him. Sepah jumped out of the Land Rover and strode across the litter-strewn sand toward a boat that looked to be half built.

Six men, each with a dirty skullcap on his head, had shed their graying *dish dashas*, and wearing only T-shirts and the *ouzaar*—the sarong-like calf length of cloth that goes under the *dish dasha*—were pounding nails into the hull of the boat. An Arab wearing a *kuffiyah* over his head came up to Sepah and shook his hand.

Sepah turned to Fitz. "This is Abdul Hussein Abdullah. His grandfather began building boats here and Abdul followed his father into the business. He builds the finest dhows on the Arabian Gulf. This boat you see he is building for me. He promises me that it will be the strongest and fastest boat sailing the Gulf. Of course, he hasn't seen the Indian Coast Guard patrol launches," Sepah added glumly.

Sepah followed Abdul as they walked around the boat, which Fitz estimated to be about one hundred feet long. "It will be ready to sail in two months," Sepah said proudly. They climbed the ladder behind Abdul to the highest strip of hull siding and then went down another ladder into the ship's hold.

"Look around carefully, Fitz," Sepah said. "See how Abdul has reinforced the beams of the hull? Your mission with us starts here. I want this dhow armed in such a way that it can destroy any Indian patrol launch that tries to pull up to it on the high seas."

Fitz shot a startled glance at Sepah, but the gold smuggler merely stared back, nodding. Realizing that Sepah was serious,

Fitz turned from him and began examining the inside of the hull in earnest.

"What kind of power are you planning?" he finally asked.

"Three Rolls-Royce diesels. That's why the hull beams are triply reinforced. This boat will go through the water at forty miles an hour when necessary. Of course, we'll cruise at a much lower speed. We must have room for cargo as well as diesel fuel."

Fitz continued evaluating the inside of the hull. "Is it still possible to change some of the planking in the hull?" he asked Abdul in Arabic. Fitz knocked with his fist along one of the planks halfway up the hull. Abdul nodded his head.

"What is your thought?" Sepah asked. "Gun ports?"

Fitz shook his head. "They would be too obvious. Is it possible for me to get a blueprint of this boat?"

Sepah laughed. "The blueprints are all in Abdul's head. But I've watched enough of these boats built so that I can draw you a plan."

"Can I have a look at a finished craft, one that this dhow will closely resemble?"

"Certainly," Sepah replied. "Have you seen enough of the interior?"

Fitz nodded. The hull seemed to contain the day's heat in a sodden, torrid pool. They climbed out of the hull and Sepah led the way back to the car. "Follow me across the bridge to the Deira side and I'll show you a finished dhow."

As they drove across the bridge Fitz looked down over Abdul's boatyard. There were two other dhows a-building but most of the workmen seemed concentrated on Sepah's boat. Over on the Deira side they drove along the quay a short distance and then Sepah stopped. Leaving their cars, Fitz, Ibrahim, and Sepah walked up to a dhow pulled up against the concrete wall of the Creek.

"There's a fine boat," Sepah said. "Abdullah turned it out last year."

They stared at the half-moon-shaped craft with the high protruding prow and the mast raked forward. If one didn't know, it would be easy to mistake the rear end of the boat for the front end. At the back of the dhow, on the high poop deck, stood a wheelhouse large enough to afford living quarters for the ship's captain.

Fitz studied the boat for some moments and then his eyes rested on the wheelhouse. "Can we go aboard?" he asked. Sepah nodded and they walked up to the edge of the quay and stepped across onto the dhow. The deck was heavy planking with a cargo hatch amidships. Fitz strode down the deck and walked up the steps to the poop deck and through the open door of the wheelhouse. Inside he faced the front of the ship looking at the instrument panel, the levers which worked the engines, and the steel circle with eight spokes running from hub to beyond the outer edge of the wheel by which the craft was steered. At the back of the wheelhouse was a bench which ran its width.

"At what point during the building is this cabin put on the deck?" Fitz asked.

"When the boat is finished completely and ready to go to sea a crane picks up the finished deckhouse and drops it into place," Sepah replied.

"Fine. I think I've seen what I need." Even though he was hardly exerting himself, sweat trickled down his face, neck, and back.

Sepah led the way from the wheelhouse onto the deck and then back to the quay. "We will return to my house," he said. Ibrahim and Fitz followed Sepah's Land Rover back across the bridge to his residence.

The air-conditioned living room was a plunge into a pool of cool air and the relief was immense. Although he had spent many years in hot countries, seldom had he experienced the heat of Arabian Gulf states in the summer.

As they seated themselves a servant wheeled in a cart containing various bottles of soft drinks as well as liquor. "I think we're entitled to some refreshment," Sepah said jovially. "Although I'm half Arab, I'm all Persian when it comes to the enjoyment of liquor." He surveyed the display a moment and then abruptly turned the conversation back to business. "Well, what do you think, Fitz?" Sepah asked.

"What sort of armament do the Indian boats carry?" Fitz asked.

"One fifty-caliber machine gun mounted on the bow, twin thirty-calibers aft," Sepah replied.

"Nothing more?" Fitz asked.

"This is what my people in India tell me; they see the patrol launches in Bombay every day. And that's plenty to shoot our unarmed dhows apart."

Fitz sipped his gin and tonic contemplatively. "What we're talking about is making your dhow into a high-speed Q-boat. That's what the Germans did in World War I. An innocent-looking freighter suddenly dropped its superstructure and blasted at the attackers with heavy cannons."

"Right," Sepah agreed. "That's what I want."

"Well, what I would suggest is a pair of M-24 20-mm. cannons in the hold that will fire through a slit the width of one longitudinal strake which can be swung inboard. The guns would be equipped with a silencer and the bullets charged with smokeless nitroguanidine grains. Thus as a patrol launch approaches you blow it out of the water without the crew knowing what's happening to them. They see no weapons, no flash, and hear no reports. All of a sudden their boat goes to pieces as though its own engine had blown up. Then you drop the sides of the wheelhouse and with twin thirties pick off the deck gunners and destroy the radio room before the operator can send out a message."

Sepah's eyes brightened as he pictured the destruction of his nemesis. "Masterful," he breathed. "Go ahead with the plan."

Fitz shook his head, smiling at Sepah's enthusiasm. "I told you what to do, not how to do it," he cautioned. "For instance, where do you acquire this armament?"

"That's your job, Fitz." Sepah grinned back.

"You ask a great deal, Sepah. I am a retired United States Army officer on pension from my government. To attempt to purchase such armament to be used against a friendly government is just about a hanging offense, to say nothing of losing my pension."

Sepah studied his guest a few moments. Then: "Fitz, I guess we haven't made the position clear to you this morning. You aren't just going to tell me what to do, you are going to do it. And then you will accompany me on our first voyage in the Q-boat to India and teach my men how to blow up an Indian patrol launch.

You see, when we make this trip to Bombay we will have a minimum of eighty thousand ten-tola bars aboard." Casually he reached over to the table beside his sofa and picked up a small gleaming gold bar which nestled comfortably in the palm of his hand. "Have you ever seen a ten-tola bar? It weighs three and three quarters ounces." Sepah pushed it toward Fitz, who took it in his hand. "Our cargo will cost us ten million dollars here in Dubai at the standard price of gold. In India that will represent a sale of three times the figure, thirty million dollars. So you must see, there is considerable profit in these little boat trips."

Sepah leaned forward. "You, Fitz, have a great opportunity to share in these huge profits. Here's our proposition, and I speak for myself and the others involved in financing this shipment. For your part in this venture we will give you two percent of the profits of our first trip and one percent of the next three trips. Wait! First figure what two percent of a twenty-million-dollar profit comes to. Then, for doing nothing, no matter where you are, you will receive one percent of ten million dollars more or less for the next three trips—assuming no accidents of course. But with your arms and training we should not have any accidents during this trading season. By my count you will make well over half a million dollars, tax free, here in Dubai."

Slowly Fitz finished his drink and put it down. "It will be an expensive proposition to purchase these arms," he said tentatively.

"Don't worry about the expense. Can you get the guns and have them installed on the ship in two months? We can only get four trips in between one storm season and the next. Four trips a year. We must be ready to leave by September."

Fitz thought about the proposition. "The United States has been bringing into Iran twenty-millimeter cannons with silencers and nitroguanidine bullets," he began. "The Shah sends them along to the Kurds up in the mountains of Iraq. This armament is ideally suited for the insurgency the Kurds are carrying on against the Iraqi Army."

"You can get them," Sepah said positively.

"I guess there is some way. And then I'll have to arrange to get the weapons to Bandar Abbas. From there I'm sure your people can take over."

"Certainly," Sepah replied. "How soon?"

"I'll have to go back to Tehran and make the contacts with some of my friends from the Shah's intelligence section. How do I pay for these arms?"

"Pick any bank. The money will be there."

Fitz turned to Ibrahim. "By the way, if I'm going to stay in Dubai, where will I live? I can't become a permanent resident of the Ruler's guest house."

Ibrahim looked at Sepah, who put a hand on Fitz's shoulder. "I am just finishing a house on land the Ruler gave me down on the beach at Jumiera. I will give the builder orders to hurry and it should be finished in two weeks. You can live there until you build your own home. I feel certain the Ruler will make a beautiful piece of beach land available to you. Oh, and my new house is air-conditioned. So this summer will not be a bad one for you when you are at home."

"And the Ruler has arranged for you to borrow a car from the royal garage," Ibrahim added. "There are two Mercedes-Benz sports cars not being used."

"How about a Land Rover?" Fitz asked.

"Certainly, if that's what you want," Ibrahim replied.

"It's much more practical," Fitz said. "There's just one more thing." A hesitant smile curled the edges of his lips.

"Whatever you want," Sepah urged.

"I know the policy of issuing a visa to a single woman in these countries. You don't do it. But there is a young lady working in the American Embassy in Tehran whose company I enjoy. If possible I would like to bring her here for a visit."

A worried look came across Ibrahim's face, but Sepah laughed his assurances that the matter would be taken care of whenever the lady was ready to come. "Now Ibrahim here, he's a conventional old Bedouin. He'd have a Westerner such as yourself starve for female companionship since no Arab woman may meet any man outside the family except for the man she will marry, and even then for the first time on the wedding night. But the Ruler and I understand that even the Westerner needs his woman while he is among us."

"Thank you, Sepah."

"And now, I think it is time we had some lunch. We can make more detailed plans afterwards."

CHAPTER 5

After cocktails and dinner at the Ruler's guest house John Stakes took Fitz aside. Both Fender Browne and Tim McLaren were in jovial moods. The Ruler had granted them what they wanted. Now it was only a question of doing what they knew best—Fender setting up an oil field supply center and Tim establishing a bank.

"Fitz," the white-haired Englishman began, "I think I have an interesting proposition for you. We could be of great help to each other, you know."

Fitz smiled wryly. "Shoot, John. This seems to be my day for propositions."

"This has to do with Arab investments in the United States. My associate in this venture, a young American, will be over here in about two or three weeks. His name is Thornwell, Harcourt Thornwell from Boston."

"Fine city," Fitz encouraged.

"Indeed. Young Thornwell's family are basically bankers but their investments included both a newspaper and a television station in the city. When Courty, as his friends call him, came out of Harvard he went directly into the family communications interests and he sat on top of both the newspaper and the television station. For eight years he was a figure in communications to be reckoned with all over America and he persuaded his family to let him expand. They owned three other television stations and four newspapers around America at the height of Courty's reign."

"Bully for Courty." Fitz stood up. "I think I'll have a nightcap, maybe it will help me sleep."

"I'll join you. I am in the process of making a most cogent point, you know."

"Oh, quite."

After they had each made themselves a drink and resumed their seats John Stakes continued.

"What I'm getting at is that Courty knows every newspaper publisher and television station owner in America. He is only thirty-two years old but he's probably the best-known individual now *out* of the business. You see, his Boston banking family sold out the communications empire Courty had built up, for a very large profit. The bankers decided they were in the business of money management, not communications. I met Courty, a very depressed young man, last year at his home in Jamaica. He's not married and a very beautiful blond girl from France was trying to console him on the loss of his business."

"How did you happen to meet him?" Fitz asked.

John cleared his throat and took another sip of his drink. "Well, since you will undoubtedly check me out, I will admit I have a reputation—undeserved of course—as something of an opportunist. It is my business to know of interesting propositions and bring them to the attention of those who can afford to go into them. I was early on in oil concessions throughout the Middle East. That's how I have come to know so many of the rulers here."

"And you heard that Courty was a rich young man and therefore a potential investor in one of your nefarious deals."

"My schemes are basically sound, old boy. In any case, I did make an effort to meet Courty at the Tryall Golf Course, where he plays. He had me up for dinner."

"And what con were you trying to work on Courty?" Fitz was finding himself interested in the story.

"As a matter of fact, it worked the other way. Courty came up with the scheme himself and I found myself drawn into it."

"This is the dodge you think I should be part of?"

"Precisely."

"I'm all ears, John."

"Courty is by no means short of cash, but what he wants to do requires enormous amounts of money. He wants to start a communications network that will be the most powerful in America."

"Why doesn't he just buy the New York *Times*?"

"He wants to add it to his interests but he feels it will have to suffer through two or three more strikes before he can acquire it," Stakes replied.

"I think I understand what you're leading up to. Go on."

"During the week I spent with Courty," Stakes continued, "he and I discussed his plan. It's all he's been thinking of since his family sold out the stations and newspapers. But where would he find the necessary money? It is literally a billion-dollar project. Then I began telling him about the money the rulers of the oil countries have and will be making. And that was when the great idea struck us. The Arabs have absolutely no constituency in the United States. The communications industry which molds public opinion is Jewish-controlled. If the Arabs want to get their story across in America they should buy control of U.S. communications. Harcourt Thornwell will manage the acquisitions and create a cohesive newspaper and television network and the Arab oil shaikhs will supply the money and make America into a pro-Arab country."

"There is only one thing all the Arabs I ever knew wanted more than to be loved, and that is to be richer," Fitz pointed out.

"Such a network could make huge profits," Stakes said. "Courty felt it could be more profitable than any other enterprise the Arabs could invest in. Look at how rich your President has become just owning the television station in one city in America."

"Of course, no one dares give him any competition in Austin, Texas," Fitz observed. "But it is a stupendous concept."

"That's what we are going to tell the Arab leaders," Stakes went on. "Here is a way to make America understand them and they'll earn money at the same time."

"Where do I fit in?" Fitz asked. He grinned. "You know that question is beginning to haunt me today."

"Where you fit in is that the Arab leaders won't forget you, an American Army officer who was cashiered for comments about the Jews. After all, it's what they think you said that counts," Stakes said. "If you were to visit the strategic Arab rulers and leaders with Courty and myself, they would be even more inclined to go along with us. Naturally, to use a vulgar Americanism, you'd be in for a piece of the action."

"Naturally." Fitz was silent a few minutes. "It is a hell of an idea. It might even work, although to get Arabs working together, cooperating with each other on such a big undertaking, would be difficult. They can't even win a war with a ten-to-one ratio over their enemy."

"I have been out here many years. What you say is true. But take Rashid as an example. When he heard what had happened to you for speaking out in favor of the Arabs he gave you a piece of his shaikhdom."

"You want me to travel around the Middle East with you selling Arab oil money on coming into this project?"

"Not only oil money, although that's the biggest source. We'll get money from Arab banks and even Rashid, who, I can tell you, was enthusiastic about the idea. He wants to put in money from his various business enterprises."

"I have certain commitments as of today." Fitz hesitated. "Still if we planned things carefully I could probably travel around with you on this deal."

"Fine. I'll need a couple of weeks to plan our travels and insure that we are received everywhere in the highest possible circles. As I said, Courty will be over in about two or three weeks himself. Incidentally he is financing all our expenses."

"That's good to know." Fitz stood up. "It's been a big day. I'm going to have a word with Tim McLaren about Middle East banking procedures and then try to get some sleep."

CHAPTER 6

Once the Iran Air jet was off the ground bound for Tehran via Bandar Abbas and Shiraz, Fitz settled back into the coolness of his first-class seat. For a few days, perhaps a week, he would be away from the heat of the Arabian summer. For some reason it never seemed to get as hot in Persia as on the Arabian side of the Gulf. He stared down at the bright blue water lapping the yellow sand of the coast and then the jet was out over the Gulf heading north toward the Straits of Hormuz. It was a flight of little more than half an hour before the plane began to descend into Bandar Abbas.

The port, a smuggling center since the idea of customs duties was first introduced millennia before, is a picturesque coastal village from the air, with a hundred miles of inlets, beaches, and islands around it. Even the Shah's modern air force is unable to control the illicit traffic that comes in, the most profitable being L & M cigarettes from Dubai.

At Bandar Abbas all the passengers deplaned, went through immigration and customs inspection, and then reboarded the plane. Fitz's thoughts about Laylah Smith became more intense as the plane came closer to Tehran. That uncomfortable feeling of guilt and doubt lanced him when the notion of making love to her came to him, which it so frequently did. She was a beautiful young woman with a brilliant life ahead of her. Since her mother was from one of the finest old families of Tehran and her father a senior foreign service officer from an equally impressive Philadelphia family, she had the best of two worlds. She was more in demand at the in-group gatherings in Tehran and up on the Caspian coast than even the American Ambassador. She had been courted by the Shah's cousin and managed to tactfully convince him she did not want to get married just yet.

What did she see in him? At forty-two he was sixteen years older than she. A colorless, passed-over lieutenant colonel, now retired. Yet she had made the year he had known her far happier than his previous years in Tehran. She included him in many of her parties and frequently the two of them dined alone and even went up to the Caspian seacoast for weekends together—of course in separate rooms. She knew he was married "after a fashion" as he described it. Both he and Marie wanted the divorce, he insisted. It was just that they didn't get around to doing it.

The prospect of knocking on the door of her apartment in two hours made him tingle with pleasure. Maybe now that he was no longer working at the Embassy he would find it in himself to take a more swashbuckling approach to their relationship. But that old gnawing realization that he was some sort of an inferior being wouldn't let go.

At Tehran's Mehrabad International Airport he quickly made his way to the taxi stand and gave the driver Laylah's address in the Shemiran section of town. Here, where the Shah's guest palace stands, was one of the most beautiful parts of Tehran. It was inevitable that when Laylah came to work for the Embassy her mother's family would have engaged an apartment for her near their home.

Briefly he wondered if the two cables he had sent her—a formal one to the Embassy, a more personal message to her apartment— had reached her. Of course they must have. It would be embarrassing to arrive unexpectedly. She might be having cocktails with some other man. He hadn't even given her a way of heading him off.

The cab drove through the familiar streets to Laylah's small apartment building. Except for the deep open gutters that ran down both sides of the street in this section of the city at the base of the mountains, the area could have been one of the expensive residential sections of any city in the United States, Fitz had often thought.

The cab stopped and Fitz stepped out, swinging his small suitcase out of the car. He still had his own apartment in Tehran. He had thought of going home to change first but he lived in a far less fashionable part of town almost ten miles through traffic clogged streets from Laylah. His pulsebeat suddenly became irregular as he rang the bell to her apartment. Then he waited for the answering buzz that would permit him to open the front door. It came. Fitz pulled the door open, walked inside, and heard Laylah open the door to her second-floor apartment.

"Fitz?"

He bounded up the steps to her. She tilted her head to him and he held and kissed her. How he loved this girl, he thought to himself as everything in the world but the embrace and kiss disappeared.

"Come on in." She pulled him inside. "Everything's ready. The vodka is ice-cold."

Fitz put his suitcase on the floor next to the door and walked into the large, beautifully appointed apartment. The two worlds of Laylah Smith were clearly reflected. The carpet, the vases, the carvings, and costly objects reflected the Persian influence of her mother's side of the family. Then there were pictures, her desk, an overstuffed chaise longue on which reposed an overstuffed pink elephant which was pure college-girl America. The place never failed to make Fitz vividly aware that he was just a scruffy old lieutenant colonel who in a lifetime had never been in more than two or three established family homes. But he loved Laylah's apartment. And he realized that he must come to terms with the fact that he was fortunate to have attained such intimacy with her as he now enjoyed and anything deeper was out of the question.

"Sit down, Fitz." She gestured toward the chintz-covered sofa. "I want to hear everything you've done." She went from the sitting room to the small kitchen and he heard the refrigerator open and shut. Then she reappeared carrying a silver tray with a frost-covered bottle of vodka and the round blue tin box of caviar on a sparkling silver dish. The chopped egg yolk and chopped onion were in two smaller silver dishes and she placed the tray on the coffee table in front of the sofa and then sat down beside Fitz. "I can hardly wait to hear all about Dubai."

"Well, I've always found it fascinating," he began. "But in the past few days I've learned more about the inside workings of that strategic little shaikhdom than I ever did in intelligence memos and my various trips there."

"I've heard it's terribly hot this time of year."

"Fierce. But of course from October until March or April the climate is comfortable."

"Do you think you'll find anything worthwhile to do?"

"Profitable, let's say."

"Will you live there?" she asked. He thought he detected a wistful tone in her voice but it was probably wishful thinking on his part.

"I think Tehran will always be my base. I certainly don't intend to give up my apartment here. But I've found a very nice air-conditioned house on the beach in Dubai to live in. If things go well I'll probably get a permanent place to live while I'm there."

"It all sounds so exciting, Fitz."

"You must come and visit me. My house has three bedrooms and baths," he added.

"When?" She smiled challengingly.

"It's damned hot right now."

"But your house is air-conditioned and you're on the beach. As long as you can get cool once in a while the heat wouldn't be so bad."

"I'll work on a visa for you with the Ruler. They don't allow single women into Dubai, or any of the other Arab states on the Gulf."

"How very arrogant of them."

"Arab customs are different from yours in Iran."

"Of course we're not Arabs," the Persian side of Laylah said disdainfully. She reached for the vodka bottle and poured them both a pony-glassful. Then she spooned the gray-black caviar onto a piece of melba toast, topped it with the egg and onion, and handed it to him.

"I'll bet you didn't get anything like this in Dubai." Fitz took it, sipped the vodka, bit off half the toast and caviar, and washed it down with more vodka.

"I'll bet I didn't," he replied.

Laylah talked about the Embassy as they ate caviar and sipped iced vodka. "General Fielding is all happy now," she reported. "With you gone nobody knows anything about military intelligence, so the old fart"—she mockingly clamped a hand over her mouth—"is now the resident expert. I think I know more than he does just from what you've told me and what I can pick up at parties. Of course, Fielding doesn't understand a word of Farsee, so we can say anything we want in front of him."

"I suppose the Ambassador is relieved to have me out of the Embassy, out of the Army, for that matter."

"You know how ambassadors are about anything that rocks the boat." She paused. "What are you going to do, Fitz?"

"I don't know that I should burden you with the knowledge."

"Is it something not quite legal?" Her eyes sparkled in excitement. "Maybe I can help you."

Fitz shook his head. "That I wouldn't let happen. I have to buy some merchandise here that they can't get in Dubai."

"What sort of things?"

"I'll tell you all about it when it's over."

"Just a hint?"

"Is our friend Colonel Nizzim around? Would you call him? I want to see him as soon as possible."

"That's a hint. You have something to do with Kurds in Iraq?" she probed, laughing.

"Yes and no."

"It all sounds very mysterious."

"I'll tell you everything—after it's done. Of course, you'll have to meet me in Bandar Abbas in about four or five days. Ever been down there?"

"I've always wanted to go. It's supposed to be a big smuggling port, isn't it? Fitz! You're not getting into some smuggling scheme?"

"Not really. Would it shock you if I was?"

"Not at all. Everybody I know buys smuggled American cigarettes. There must be a lot of money in it."

"What I'm doing here doesn't involve smuggling anything into Iran. But I have no desire to test the legality of what I have in mind. I do know that Nizzim enjoys a high life style and he likes women. That takes money. I have money for him and he has control of what I want."

"Even General Fielding knows that Nizzim supplies the Kurdish tribesmen with arms the Shah buys from the United States. Why do you need arms? You aren't going to do something dangerous?"

"You are too smart for me, Laylah." Fitz took another sip of vodka and a bite of caviar.

"Oh, Fitz!" There was excitement and new admiration in the way she looked at him. Now that he felt like an adventurer, all of a sudden Laylah didn't seem quite as unobtainable to him. He felt as confident in himself as he might have had he made bird colonel. He had always told himself that when he was a full colonel he would feel more like a man that could at least hope to truly interest Laylah in a lasting relationship. He hardly dared even think the word "marriage." Still he had most of the details of a divorce from Marie worked out.

Now, for the first time since the debacle resulting from the interview with Sam Gold, Fitz felt there might be hope for him. He looked at Laylah, smiled, leaned toward her, and kissed her. She kissed him back, a real woman's kiss promising more.

He would make himself very wealthy and powerful, using Dubai as a base. So much so that he might even be made an ambassador to an Arab country someday. Laylah would be an ideal ambassador's wife, he dreamed as the kiss became prolonged.

"I'd better call Nizzim before he gets out," Fitz heard Laylah say as she finally pulled away from him. He watched her trim body move under the light summer dress as she went across the room to the telephone.

She consulted her book of numbers and then dialed. "This is the number he pressed upon me one night at a party." Laylah laughed. "It is his private line that he alone answers. I think he told me that only the Shah, a few generals, and now I have the number."

"He'll be most disappointed at the nature of your call—"

"Hello." Laylah's throaty voice on the phone would have undone any man, Fitz thought. "This is Laylah Smith. Do you remember me?"

From across the room Fitz heard the explosive string of endearments emerge from the phone, which Laylah held away from her ear as she grinned at Fitz. Finally she said, "Yes, yes, of course we will. Very soon. I understand about tonight. I didn't expect you to be free. I just wanted to say hello to you and also to tell you that an old friend of yours just came back to Tehran. Colonel Lodd,

Fitz Lodd." This news obviously carried small moment to the
Iranian colonel. Then Laylah handed Fitz the telephone.

"Hello, Colonel Nizzim. Fitz Lodd here."

Confronted by Fitz, Nizzim hadn't much choice but to be cour-
teous. The two men had worked closely on various intelligence
matters, in particular the manner in which the Kurdish tribesmen
were resupplied with weapons and ammunition.

They talked ambiguously a few moments and then Fitz asked
Nizzim to have lunch at the French Club with him the following
day. Nizzim accepted and Fitz put Laylah back on the line to
keep Nizzim's hopes up about his chances of a quiet dinner with
her someplace and dancing afterwards.

"Always ready to be useful in a good cause," said Laylah. "How
about telling me a little more about it, now that I'm involved?"

"How about us going up to the Darband Hotel for dinner? And
afterwards we'll pick a place where we can dance in the neigh-
borhood."

"I'm not letting you get away without telling me everything.
You know I'm good at keeping secrets. Did anyone in the Embassy ever find out we were dating?"

"I'll make you a promise, Laylah. Meet me in Bandar Abbas.
I'll make reservations for both of us at the Naz Hotel. The Iran
part of my mission will be accomplished by then and I'll tell you
everything. O.K.?"

"But suppose you get in trouble and need help. How can I help
if I don't know what you're doing?"

"A point we'll consider after dinner over a nightcap."

"Fair enough," Laylah agreed.

CHAPTER 7

Fitz had carefully timed his arrival at the U. S. Embassy. Earlier he had made the trip from the First Commercial Bank of New York branch in Tehran to the Embassy, clocking the precise number of minutes the drive through the traffic required. At exactly 11:30 A.M. he walked into General Fielding's outer office without an appointment. The General's secretary looked up at him as though he had returned from the dead. Her jaw dropped. "Colonel Lodd!" she gasped. "We've been trying to find you everywhere! Where have you been?"

"Just around the Gulf. What's it all about?" Of course he knew exactly what it was all about but he had decided to play the complete-innocence role.

"I'll tell the General you're here."

Moments later Fitz was ushered into Fielding's office. "Good God, Lodd! Where have you been?"

"I thought I was retired, not AWOL," Fitz replied.

"Your papers, man! Your diplomatic passport, your Embassy credentials, most of all your diplomatic immunity clearances from the Iranian Government, signed by the Shah himself! Where are they? The Ambassador is wild! He doesn't know whether to tell the Shah that we forgot to collect the papers from you and look like fools here or hope we could find you and get these papers back."

"The papers are secure. When I left the Embassy with my retirement papers, you were all in such a hurry to get me out before some congressman arrived you forgot to ask me for the special diplomatic clearances. Since I was leaving early the next morning for Dubai, I dropped the documents off in my safe-deposit vault at the First Commercial Bank of New York."

"Do you have them with you now, Lodd?" Fielding asked hopefully.

"No, sir. But they're safe. I'll get them over to you."

"Right away, Lodd. They're still live. We didn't want to embarrass the Ambassador by telling the Shah we had let those documents get loose."

"I trust you knew I would take care of them and turn them in," Fitz replied stiffly.

"Oh, of course. I told the Ambassador it was just a matter of a few days. We tried to locate you at your residence, everywhere. If they fell into the wrong hands a lot of damage could happen. Infiltrators, smugglers, anyone with those papers could move throughout the country, past checkpoints, at will."

"I realize that of course. Tell the Ambassador not to bother notifying the Shah."

General Fielding picked up the phone. "Get me the Ambassador," he barked. He held on to the phone, his eyes fixed on Fitz in front of him. "Where were you?"

"Dubai."

"I thought so. We couldn't reach you there. We should have some U.S. representation somewhere in those states." Fielding's eyes rolled in his head.

"Mr. Ambassador, General Fielding here. Colonel Lodd is with me now, sir." The General skewered Fitz with his glare. "No, sir, not with him. He has the documents in a secure place. He'll bring them around later on." Then Fielding nodded and smiled. "Yes, sir, I'm very much relieved too, sir. We were all in such a hurry to process Lodd's papers for him, of course. Yes, sir." Fielding hung up and settled back in his reclining swivel chair, looking as though a great weight had been lifted from his mind.

"So. How are things going for you, Fitz?"

"Still getting acclimatized to civilian life, sir." Fitz had accomplished half of what he had come here to do. His papers were still live. Now he needed to get some information and then go after the guns.

"I just got back from Dubai last night and over there I came across a new element of Communist subversion I thought might interest you."

Fielding became seriously attentive. This was the sort of thing he should know about and be able to make a report on to the Ambassador. And Fielding knew that Fitz was an outstanding intelligence gatherer and evaluator.

"What form is this subversion taking?" he asked.

"It appears that at the southern end of Muscat and Oman, in the state known as Dhofar, the Chinese Communists are trying to stir up resentment, the usual thing. Needless to say, if they could promote a successful rebellion and put Communist-oriented leadership into Oman, they would control the Straits of Hormuz and therefore the entire Persian Gulf. We may end up supporting an Iranian military effort in aid of the Sultan of Oman."

"You think so, Fitz?"

"I think it's likely. I spent some time with Colonel Buttres of the Trucial Oman Scouts the other night after dinner at the Ruler of Dubai's palace. He's very concerned about the situation. For your information, it wouldn't surprise me if we began seeing the weapons we've been passing along to the Kurds being diverted down to Oman."

"I'll be damned. Why haven't we heard about this before here?"

Fitz shrugged. "What are we sending up to the Kurds now? Still the M-24?"

"That seems to be the most effective weapon up in those mountains," Fielding agreed.

"Any shipments gone over to Colonel Nizzim recently?" Fitz asked casually.

"Just three days ago, as a matter of fact." Fielding stopped himself abruptly. "Damn it, Fitz, I forget. I can't talk to you about such things any more."

"A little exchange of information between us can only be of benefit to you, sir."

"I appreciate whatever you can pass along to me, Fitz. You were always an outstanding intelligence officer. But things have changed. You're retired now."

Fitz had everything he needed for the present, and since there was no need to further irritate himself by sitting in General Fielding's presence, he replied, "Yes, sir. I forget too."

"Very sensitive, the whole Kurd situation." Suddenly Fielding snapped forward in his chair. He looked down at his wristwatch.

"Look here, Fitz, if you're going to get over to the bank before it closes you'd better start moving. You haven't much time. I'll send an aide with you in an Embassy car. He can drop you off anywhere after you give him the papers." He picked up his phone and pressed a button. "Send in Captain Portes. Urgent!"

Fielding and Fitz stood up. "Thanks for dropping by, Lodd. Just give the papers to Portes. He'll bring them back and give you a receipt." Portes entered Fielding's office, was given his orders, and then Fitz followed him outside into the courtyard where General Fielding's staff car was waiting. The Embassy gate swung open and the staff car pulled out, forcing its way into the congealed Tehran traffic.

"What time does the bank close?" Portes asked nervously.

"Twelve noon."

"That doesn't give us much time." He swallowed and looked out the window at the tangled mass of cars about them.

"No," Fitz agreed.

The staff car finally arrived at the First Commercial Bank of New York at ten minutes after twelve. "They might still let us in," Portes suggested.

"Might," Fitz agreed. Earlier he had called on the manager of the bank, given him the personal note from Tim McLaren asking for complete cooperation and the letter of credit for up to ten thousand dollars. Fitz had transferred two thousand dollars to his personal account and taken eight thousand in cash. Then he had asked the manager of the bank not to open for anyone after the twelve-noon closing that day, even if the American Ambassador himself called.

Fitz ambled out on the sidewalk following Captain Portes, who had leapt from the staff car where it had stalled in traffic a block from the bank's entrance. He reached the massive steel slab which had been rolled into place on the dot of noon as Captain Portes stood pounding on it.

"Hey, no sweat, Portes." Fitz put a hand on the frustrated captain's shoulder. "I'll get here in the morning and bring the papers over to you. O.K.?"

"The General and the Ambassador want them now." The captain's voice squeaked in agitation. "You should have seen the sweat around here when they discovered you didn't give them the clearances before you left."

"An unfortunate oversight, but nothing serious. After all, I am here and one more day isn't going to make any difference."

"Maybe if the Ambassador called the bank personally," Portes thought aloud.

"Maybe," Fitz agreed. "Tell you what, I have an appointment for lunch. I'm looking for a job, you know. Leave me at the restaurant and then if the Ambassador can get the manager of the bank to let us in you can come back and get me."

"Why don't you come back to the Embassy?" Portes pursued.

"I said, Portes, I need a job, God damn it! I'll take a cab and see you when I see you."

"I'll take you where you want to go, Colonel."

The staff car dropped Fitz off at a restaurant a block from the French Club. He stepped out, thanked the captain, and walked into the restaurant. He waited until the staff car had disappeared in the traffic and then left the restaurant and walked the block to the French Club.

Colonel Nizzim was waiting for him in the pub-like bar. They shook hands and went into the main dining room. The French maître d' recognized Fitz and ushered him and Nizzim to one of the corner tables. They sat down and Fitz ordered a bottle of white wine to sip while they awaited the menu.

Nizzim was, as Fitz expected, more interested in talking about Laylah Smith than reminiscing about some of their joint intelligence ventures. Nizzim kept giving Fitz accusing looks as he extolled the virtues of this half-American, half-Iranian beauty. There was no need for them, at least not yet, Fitz thought. It had been a circumspect evening and he had returned to his own apartment by one in the morning after kissing Laylah good night.

Finally Nizzim asked, "How do you like civilian life over here?"

"It's very expensive," Fitz replied. "I still do a few things for my government, incidentally," he added.

Nizzim nodded and bemoaned the expenses of maintaining his position and then, as though sensing something to his benefit about to be brought up, he asked, "And what is the nature of these things you are doing?"

Fitz looked about conspiratorially and then said in low tones,

"I wouldn't want it known generally, but we are supporting a movement something like the Kurdish insurgency. You realize, of course, that this whole business of me being forced to retire was a cover?"

Nizzim nodded wisely. "I always knew it was something like that." Then he laughed. "That story about the Jews in America influencing the Army was too crazy to believe."

"In my new job you can be of help to me and I have a big budget now to get things done. Real money to spend that I don't ever have to account for."

Nizzim leaned forward. "You are the best man your country could have chosen. They know who to trust with unaccountable funds." He drained his glass of wine and Fitz refilled it. Speculatively the Iranian officer looked at Fitz. "How can I help you?"

"I'd like to turn over two or three thousand dollars to you, whatever it will take, to buy back some weapons we want to supply covertly to anti-Communist Dhofar tribesmen in the south of Oman."

"Why can't you just send them in?" Nizzim asked. "Not that I wouldn't be delighted to assist you," he added hurriedly.

"There must be no way that these arms can be traced back to shipments sanctioned by my government. We need some weapons right now. You received a shipment of arms including M-24 20-mm. cannons three days ago."

"How did you know that?" Nizzim asked sharply. Then he answered his own question. "Of course, for a moment I forgot. You are still with the Embassy, just on a different basis."

"That's right, Nizzim. Now, how do I pick up two M-24s complete with sixty-round drums, twin mounts, silencers, and smokeless nitroguanidine ammunition? I also need a fifty-caliber machine gun and two thirty-caliber machine guns and mounts and ammo. I'll pick them up anywhere you say in Iran."

"What will you pay for this equipment?" Nizzim asked.

"Whatever it takes," Fitz replied, knowing that Nizzim gave the weapons to the Kurds free of charge. "Three thousand dollars?" he suggested.

A crafty smile spread across Nizzim's face. "Four thousand dollars should do it, but only to help you in your mission, Fitz, my friend."

"Can I pick them up, say tonight, here in Tehran?"

Nizzim looked shocked. "Oh, no. I must be very careful how I handle this. All the weapons assigned me go directly across the border to the Kurds."

"Tell me how we arrange this?"

"How do we handle the money?" Nizzim asked.

"Two thousand dollars when you give me the time and place to make the reception, two thousand when the weapons and ammo are placed in my truck." Fitz picked up his own wineglass and finished it. "And the reception must be no later than tomorrow night."

Nizzim grinned. "Very good, my friend. Tomorrow you will drive to Tabriz to buy a beautiful carpet for your home. I will meet you there in front of the Blue Mosque on Khiaban Pahlavi at six o'clock tomorrow night and lead you to one of our Kurd resupply stations on the Iraqi border."

"Tabriz is four hundred miles from here and I still have to buy a truck." Fitz emphasized the word "buy."

The grin on Nizzim's face became wider. "I can sell you an American light weapons carrier, in good condition, for"—a speculative pair of eyes turned on Fitz—"two thousand dollars? You did say the funds are unaccountable."

"I did, Nizzim. Two thousand will be fine. That's a total of six big ones as we say in the U.S."

Nizzim laughed. "Yes. Six big ones, my friend."

"You'll provide me with current plates and markings on the weapons carrier?"

"Of course. But I can't guarantee you personal immunity through the checkpoints."

"I have the papers for that. Just let me pick up the vehicle today."

"I will give you the address to meet me at six o'clock this evening. You will have a pleasant evening in town and tomorrow you drive to Tabriz."

"Very good, Colonel." Fitz was pleased at the way the day had gone so far. "With our business out of the way shall we order the best lunch the French Club has to offer?"

During the luncheon, which lasted two hours, Fitz so captivated Nizzim with tales of U.S. intelligence activities, all in strictest confidence of course, on the Arabian side of the Arabian Gulf that the Iranian officer agreed, as they were leaving the table, to deliver the weapons carrier to Fitz that evening at six o'clock in the parking lot behind the Darband Hotel.

"You have asked for delivery at the furthest point in the city of Tehran from the road to Tabriz," Nizzim pointed out. Fitz nodded sagely and then winked, provoking sharp laughter from Nizzim. "You Americans, you go to more effort to deceive each other than the enemy."

It was almost three when Fitz saw Nizzim into his waiting staff car, two thousand dollars richer than when he had started luncheon, with another four thousand to come. The Iranian intelligence colonel was in an understandably jovial mood.

Now he had until six o'clock to meet Laylah at her apartment, and then as exhausting a three days and nights ahead of him as he could recall having to face in many years. He decided to take a cab back to his apartment when the door porter of the French Club called him back in to take a telephone call.

"Fitz." He recognized Laylah's voice over the phone he had picked up in the porter's booth. "I'm outside the Embassy. I hoped I'd find you there. I've been in the Ambassador's office. He is upset about some papers you have not returned."

"Where are you calling from?" Fitz asked.

"I'm secure. I'm using the telephone in the Iranian Crafts Center across the street from the Embassy."

"Come on over here for a drink. Right now," he added insistently. "And don't worry about the papers. I'll be getting them out of my safe-deposit box when the bank opens at eight in the morning. I hope the Ambassador and the Embassy appreciate the lengths to which you have personally gone to recover these documents, as though I wouldn't personally deliver them."

"Oh, Fitz—" she began.

"Now!" And he hung up.

It hurt him to be so abrupt but there was no help for it. He went back into the club, instructed the doorman that there would be a young woman coming over shortly, and then had a gin and tonic at the bar. He had just finished it when a distressed-looking Laylah came in the front door of the club. He went to her,

smiling lovingly, put an arm around her, kissed her, and led her
out the sliding doors behind the dining room to the lawn beyond.

Once he had seated her he waved to a waiter, ordered them
each a drink, and then reached across the table and took her
hands in his. "I'm sorry I sounded so abrupt on the telephone but
I happen to know the Embassy has had that line tapped for two
years. It's the phone everyone uses when they have to make a fast
call they don't want going through the switchboard."

Laylah sighed with relief. "Oh, Fitz. I thought you were angry
with me."

A thrill shot through him that Laylah would care that much
how he felt about her. "I had to cut you off. At least now they'll
think that you were acting in the best interests of the Embassy.
Now what else were you going to tell me?"

"The Ambassador has ordered that you be kept under surveillance until he has those clearance papers back."

The drinks arrived and Fitz took a tentative sip as he pondered
the situation. "They'll know that you and I are together here at
the French Club from the tap on the phone."

"How stupid of me."

"Not stupidity, just inexperience. Didn't your father tell you
what it's like at a big U.S. embassy? Everyone spys on everyone
else."

"That all seems too dramatic to be American," Laylah said.

"Tehran is the center of intrigue in the Middle East, Laylah.
You know that. Now listen to me. You want to help me? I am
doing nothing that is contrary to U.S. interests. But in order to
carry out a commercial venture in which I'm involved I need
those papers for three more days."

"I want to help, Fitz. You got incredibly unfair treatment from
the Embassy and the government."

"I'm not crying about that. It's the way things go sometimes.
But I kept those papers back just on the chance I might need
them once more. Right now they are at my apartment. Probably a
couple of Embassy spooks have it staked out. I'll have to go back
anyway and then lose the tail."

"You can stay tonight at my place," Laylah offered.

"They'll have you covered too now, although I was going to ask
you if that would be all right."

"I don't care what they think," Laylah declared.

"The problem is, Laylah, that I want the Embassy to think I played the game fair with them, sent the papers back as promised, yet still I want to keep the clearances until Friday, four days from now. You see, I'm going to need the goodwill of the Embassy in the months and years ahead. So far they can only blame themselves for not picking up my diplomatic immunity credentials."

"Well, now that we know what the problem is, we can solve it." Fitz loved the positive tone with which Laylah made the statement.

Half an hour later Fitz and Laylah left the table on the lawn of the French Club and he walked her to the front door. "I'm just sorry we won't be together tonight, Fitz," she said. He felt the goosebumps on his arms and the back of his neck when she said it.

"So am I. I had it all planned. But we'll make up for it in Bandar Abbas this weekend. See you Thursday night. Just check into the hotel. I'll call you when I get in. It will probably be late."

"I'll be waiting."

He watched her turn and walk out of the club. He didn't bother to see her to the street. He knew someone would be waiting to follow her. The U. S. Embassy in Tehran was that kind of a place. It had to be if it were to remain effective. It was the way he would have handled the situation.

Fifteen minutes later Fitz took a cab to his apartment in the unfashionable but convenient area of town near the Bazaar. Whether or not he was followed made little difference. There was sure to be a stakeout on his place. The cab left him off in front of his small building, pinched between two larger, taller commercial structures. Without looking around he walked up the three flights of stairs and let himself into the cluttered apartment he had lived in for the last two years. He quickly satisfied himself that nobody had broken in and searched the place. Then he went over to a small safe he had dug into the brick wall. Opening it, he removed the diplomatic clearance papers and put them into the inside pocket of the sports jacket he wore. Then he packed his toilet articles, a clean pair of slacks and sports jacket, two shirts, underwear, and a bathing suit into the neat attaché case and he was ready to go. In the money belt which added perceptibly to the beginnings of the paunch about his midsection was tucked five thousand dollars' worth of U.S. and Iranian currency. Another thousand dollars was neatly stacked in the two wallets he carried, one in his trousers pocket, the other in his jacket pocket with the clearance papers. Now one more detail needed attention and he was ready to go.

Fitz sat down at his desk and from a drawer pulled a brown manila envelope with the official seal of the U. S. Embassy stamped on it and a few pieces of copy paper. He addressed the envelope to Miss Laylah Smith, c/o The United States Embassy, from Lieutenant Colonel (ret.) James F. Lodd, and placed the blank sheets of paper inside. Then he licked the gummed flap, sealed it, and placed his handiwork on top of the clothes inside the attaché case, snapping it shut. He looked at his watch. Almost five o'clock now.

He let himself out of the apartment, double-locking it behind him, and descended the stairs. On the street he looked straight ahead as he strode toward the Bazaar, a ten-minute walk. He could almost feel the surveillance team behind him although he was careful not to look around. Soon he came to the Bazaar and made a sudden turn into one of the long arcades lined with shops. Late afternoon was a popular hour in the Bazaar and Fitz quickly lost himself in the throngs. Brushing past importuning shop-keepers standing just outside their stalls, he kept turning into the crowded alleys, walking with knees bent to keep his head slightly below the average height of the shoppers. For ten minutes he worked his way deeper and deeper into the middle of the Bazaar and then out toward the street on the opposite side from which he had entered.

A cab with three people in it stopped as he waved it down. "Anywhere. I want a ride," Fitz said in Farsee. The driver grinned and let him into the back seat with two old women. He slammed the door shut and slid down in his seat as the cab started out into the traffic. Fitz glanced at his watch. He rode with the driver for fifteen minutes and then got out with one of the passengers and paid the fare. He was reasonably sure he had lost his tail but he walked a few blocks to make sure. Nobody seemed to be following him now. After five blocks of walking he hailed another cab, this one with only two people in the back seat, and asked for the Darband Hotel. The driver nodded and Fitz hopped into the front seat. Fifteen minutes later, at exactly six o'clock, the driver let Fitz out at the Darband Hotel. He paid the driver and walked through the front door. There were few people on the road up to the mountain resorts and night clubs at this hour and nobody was following him. He walked through the lobby, past the bar, and out the back door of the hotel to the parking lot. At the far side of the lot, under a tree, stood the sturdy little weapons carrier he was looking for.

It was a compact sort of truck, halfway between the two-and-a-half-ton truck and a small pickup. Over the bed of the truck was a frame enclosed with canvas. This was one of the most utilitarian pieces of equipment the U. S. Army motor pools offered, perfect for Fitz's needs.

He walked over to the vehicle and inspected the tires. Every one of them in good condition, including the spare. Fitz lifted the flap at the rear of the truck. Another spare wheel was bolted to the side. Nizzim was being cooperative, Fitz thought. Mentally he resolved to add another five hundred to Nizzim's bribe. Undoubtedly he would need the Iranian's help again in the future.

He felt a hand on his back and whirled about, startled. "Hah. You are satisfied, my friend?" Nizzim chortled.

Fitz took two deep breaths before answering. "Very." He looked at the license plates. Official military. "Yes, you have done everything as promised."

"Good. I shall see you in Tabriz tomorrow at six. It is over seven hundred kilometers, so you must get an early start. You aren't driving one of your Cadillacs, you know."

Fitz grinned back. "I don't know of a Cadillac that will carry two M-24s, a thousand rounds of ammo, plus a fifty-caliber machine gun and a couple of thirties." Fitz reached into his wallet. "Here, another five hundred dollars on account."

Nizzim's eyes raised and he smiled with pleasure. "But thank you. It is a pleasure doing business with the U. S. Government."

"We'll do more together. How about a drink?"

Nizzim looked at his watch. "I regret that I haven't the time. I am due at a reception at seven." He smiled. "I am led to understand that Miss Smith of your embassy will be there."

"Give her my regards, Nizzim." Fitz felt a pang of jealousy

sting his gut. Nizzim would have another chance to see Laylah while he waited, in hiding, until the next morning.

"Until tomorrow." Nizzim turned and was gone. Fitz walked around the weapons carrier to the driver's seat, took the ignition keys from the lock, dropped them in his pocket, and headed back for the hotel. Nothing to do until tomorrow.

Might as well have some vodka and check in under an assumed name.

CHAPTER 8

At eight-thirty the following morning, thirty minutes after the banks opened in Tehran, Fitz parked the weapons carrier on Iranshahr Street and walked the few blocks to the U. S. Embassy. Carrying his attaché case, he walked through the gate and into the chancery of the Embassy. The receptionist recognized him as he handed her the envelope. "You will send this in to Miss Smith as soon as possible this morning?" he asked.

"Yes, Colonel Lodd," the Iranian girl at the desk replied.

"Would you stamp the date and time of delivery on it, please?" Fitz requested.

The receptionist placed a corner of the envelope into the time stamper. It snapped down, leaving a record of the delivery.

"Thank you." Lodd smiled and left the Embassy. In another twenty minutes he was leaving the city on the road to Tabriz.

The highway running north and west was comparable to any superhighway in the United States. The weapons carrier rolled along at an average of sixty miles an hour, only occasionally slowed by slower-moving vehicles. Fitz calculated he could easily be in Tabriz by five in the afternoon. He had eaten a good breakfast at the hotel and had some sandwiches made up. A single gas stop should be sufficient.

Although Fitz had been to Tabriz before he had never made the drive. Under other circumstances it would have been enjoyable. The countryside was interesting and there were occasional spectacular views as he began climbing into the mountains north and west of Tehran.

Nizzim had given him a good vehicle, and a little over eight hours of solid driving after he had left the Embassy, Fitz was parked on Khiaban Pahlavi, the main street of Tabriz. This was one of a number of carpet-weaving centers of the Middle East, and Fitz, rubbing his back, which ached from the long drive, looked at the samples of the local handicraft industry laid out on the sidewalks for sale to the dealers who came through. The other industry seemed to be silversmithing. Every other store sold silver ornaments. Fitz tried to concentrate on the carpeting, but he was already exhausted from the long drive, and he had thirteen hundred miles or more ahead of him after loading the weapons carrier at the border station, yet another hundred and twenty miles southwest of Tabriz around Lake Urmia.

At six o'clock he was parked in front of the decrepit-looking Blue Mosque when he heard his name called. There was Nizzim just getting out of a staff car. The Iranian colonel walked over to Fitz. "Buy some carpets," he suggested. "You'll never have better bargains than here. After dark we'll start out for the border station."

Fitz stood with his thumbs digging into the small of his back, one on either side of his aching spine.

"Nizzim, isn't there some off-duty soldier you know that would like to make some extra money as a driver?"

"I can find you a man. I would have suggested it myself but I thought you wanted this all to be a big secret."

"If you can find a man who will stick with me from here all the way south to Bandar Abbas, I'll pay him well and send him back to Tehran or Tabriz by plane."

"I'll bring you a man from our headquarters, but I'll have to take a look at your papers. I wouldn't want to be responsible for one of our men getting into trouble."

"Of course not," Fitz agreed. He reached into his pocket and brought out the leather folder containing his diplomatic passport and the special clearance, signed personally by the Shah, instructing military and civilian police personnel to extend every courtesy to the bearer. Nizzim looked at the papers a moment and then took out a notebook and wrote out the numbers on the special clearance. "You'll forgive me if I check to make sure this is still current? Not that I mistrust you, but it's a formality with which police and military are ordered to comply."

"Of course. I understand," Fitz replied affably.

"This is a very nice paper to have," he commented, handing the document back. "Even the picture of you is good. If all checks out, as I know it will, I'll have your driver here in half an hour."

While Nizzim was driving to the local military headquarters, Fitz looked at the carpets for sale. They would be useful to cover the crates of weapons and ammunition and also make fine gifts. Both Sepah and Majid Jabir collected fine Persian rugs and Fitz would need carpets for his own house someday. He let himself dream about the fortune he had been promised for helping make the gold shipment successful.

In the time it took him to haggle over the price of four fine tapestry carpets and load them into the back of the weapons carrier, Nizzim had returned from district military headquarters accompanied by an Iranian soldier wearing the stripes of a sergeant.

"Sergeant Aram here will take care of your driving," Nizzim announced. "He doesn't speak English but your Farsee is good enough to converse with him."

Fitz welcomed the sergeant in his native language and they agreed upon a price, the equivalent of one hundred dollars plus transportation back to Tabriz from Bandar Abbas. "You had better go to the Tabriz Inn and get some supper," Nizzim suggested. "Then the sergeant will drive you to our border station just beyond the town of Naqaden. Since he knows where it is, I'll go along ahead and have the weapons ready to be loaded when Sergeant Aram brings you around. Naqaden is about a hundred and twenty miles from here." Nizzim chuckled. "Now at last you'll see how the weapons you send us actually get to the Kurds."

After eating and having a well-deserved drink of vodka, Fitz slumped gratefully into the front seat of the weapons carrier beside Sergeant Aram, who started the vehicle and began the long drive over mountain roads to the Iranian border with Iraq. The first fifty miles over the wide highway which ran beside Lake Urmia were easy, but then they started over the mountains. Fitz wondered if he could have made the trip alone over the tortuous trails at night. Yes, somehow he would have made it but what an exhausted wreck he would have been when he finally arrived in Bandar Abbas. The sergeant seemed elated at the prospect of earning the hundred dollars, a month's pay, in just a few days of driving.

Fitz dozed in short spells between sudden jolts into wakefulness as the truck hit ruts and potholes that threatened to bend its axles. There were no lights on the roads of course but the sergeant seemed to know his way. When Fitz looked at the luminous dial of his watch and noticed they had been on the road four hours, he asked the sergeant how much longer they had to go. Aram shrugged. "Maybe another thirty kilometers," he replied in Farsee.

It was after midnight when they finally pulled up in front of the well-lit military compound beyond the town of Naqaden. A line of trucks of all sizes and makes waited to drive through the gate in the barbed-wire fence surrounding the buildings. The drivers and what appeared to be body guards all wore turbans and vests with bullet-filled pockets in them. This was a Kurdish supply convoy loading up, Fitz realized.

The process that began with policy decisions in Washington stemming from CIA information on the Communist orientation of the Iraqi Government in Baghdad, came to fruition here at a mountainous border post in the region known as Kurdistan. The territory of the Kurd tribesmen ran through three countries: Turkey, Iraq, and Iran, and the Kurds considered themselves a separate political identity, an identity which the Iraqi Government steadfastly refused to recognize. By supplying the Kurds with modern armaments, Iran kept the Iraqi Government permanently bleeding troops and supplies in the fight against the fiercely independent mountain people. This effort did much to keep the expansionist-minded, Communist-leaning Iraqi Government from aggressive acts against neighboring countries.

Sergeant Aram drove the weapons carrier into the compound past a Kurd truck and up to the loading dock. Colonel Nizzim was waiting for them. He beckoned Fitz to jump up onto the loading dock and then pointed out the crates that were waiting for them.

"Do you want to inspect the M-24s?" he asked. "They're still packed in Cosmoline."

"I'll take a look," Fitz replied. With a steel wedge bar he pried the top off one of the crated cannons and, despite the preservative grease, he went over each part of the weapon until he was satisfied it was complete. He nailed the top of the crate down and then inspected the second crate. The second 20-mm. cannon was complete and Fitz signaled to Sergeant Aram to have the two crates loaded into the weapons carrier. The sergeant had already pulled the carpets from the back of the truck.

"How about the sixty-round magazine drums and machine guns?" Fitz asked.

Nizzim looked slightly distressed. "I'm sorry, Fitz, we don't have a single fifty-caliber in supply. The drums are in that box. Four of them," he quickly added.

"Good Christ! No fifty-calibers? I thought you said in Tehran you had some."

"I thought so. Will the new thirty-calibers do?"

"I guess they'll have to." Fitz was already envisioning an encounter with the Indian patrol launch armed with a fifty-caliber machine gun on its foredeck. Well, the cannons would just have to do the distance work. They had a longer range than the fifty-calibers.

"I'll throw in a couple of Armalite submachine guns and forty-five-caliber grease guns," Nizzim offered.

Fitz shrugged. "O.K., bring 'em out. And what about the recoil-absorbing mounts for the M-24s?"

"They're up here with the drums, ready to be loaded." Nizzim pointed at two more crates. "Help yourself."

Fitz opened the crates, inspected the mounts and ammunition drums, grunted in satisfaction, and gestured for them to be loaded. He also looked over the thirty-caliber machine guns and sent them onto the weapons carrier. "Ammo?" he asked.

"A thousand rounds of 20-mm. nitroguanidine smokeless rounds, just as you requested." Nizzim kicked an ammunition crate. "Another thousand rounds of thirty-caliber," he said, pointing at a smaller crate, and both were wrestled to the edge of the loading dock and then into the heavily loaded rear of the weapons carrier.

Nizzim turned from Fitz and took a box the size of an orange crate from a table and handed it to him. "Silencers for the M-24s."

Fitz put them on the floor and opened the case and examined the large collars that would fit over the end of the cannon barrels, stifling the sounds of the shells firing. "Very good, Nizzim." He laughed mirthlessly as he repacked the case. "I'll bet our Kurdish friends take a heavy toll of government troops with this gun."

"It's the most popular weapon we give out," Nizzim agreed.

"I'll take the Armalites you offered and the grease guns," Fitz reminded the Iranian officer.

"I'll send them right out. Would you like to come into the office with me?" Fitz followed Nizzim to the rear of the loading area and into a small office. When the door was closed Fitz unbuckled his belt and pulled up the money belt.

"Four thousand dollars, right?" Fitz asked as he counted out the money and placed it on the desk.

"That's right, my friend," Nizzim replied, his eyes gleaming as he picked up the sheaf of U.S. currency and began counting the money. He slipped the bills into his pocket after checking the cash. "Everything is right. I hope your mission goes well from here."

"With the help of Sergeant Aram, I think it will," Fitz answered. "So, I will take the light weapons too and we'll be on our way. We have only three days to drive the thirteen hundred miles to Bandar Abbas."

Back on the loading dock Nizzim gave Fitz the four light machine guns and a supply of ammunition for them, already boxed. He also handed Fitz a .45-caliber automatic pistol which fired the same ammunition as the two grease guns. "This might come in handy someday," he suggested.

"Good luck, Fitz," Nizzim called out as the sergeant and Fitz loaded the last box into the back of the truck and then threw the four carpets over the crates.

"Thanks, I'll need it." He climbed into the cab beside Sergeant Aram, who stepped on the starter and gunned the engine a moment before driving out of the compound. A Kurd truck pulled up to the loading dock as the weapons carrier drove off.

For the first thirty miles of the long, exhausting haul to Bandar Abbas, more than thirteen hundred miles to the south, they retraced the track that had led them through the heavy bushland to the outpost. Over and over Fitz wondered how he could have found his way through this impossible, roadless terrain alone. At Mahabad they drove by the headquarters of the Iranian Army Third Corps and headed southeast over a poorly paved road to Buksan and picked up the main highway south. The hundred and fifty tortuous miles from the border outpost had taken almost six

hours and the sun was well above the horizon as they turned onto
the highway south. Twenty miles further on they came to Saqqiz,
a fairly sizable town where they stopped for a breakfast of omelets
with chopped herbs and then Fitz took the wheel and Sergeant
Aram, exhausted after eight hours of hard driving, fell asleep in
the front seat beside him.

Now that he was on a main road heading south toward Bandar
Abbas, where he would be meeting Laylah, Fitz was in the best of
spirits. It was easy driving and the miles fell behind him at a good
rate. Two hundred miles after he had started driving he reached
the town of Bisitun, made up of single-story mud-brick houses,
and turned off on a poor road for Khurramabad, ninety miles due
south. He could have stayed on the highway and driven twice that
distance to get to Khurramabad but he took the unpaved shortcut. Sergeant Aram was fast asleep beside him and Fitz didn't
want to wake him up. He might just as well have done so, he soon
realized. The shortcut was a rough, hilly, rutted road and he held
his breath as he drove across the fragile-looking wooden bridges
spanning the rivers the road crossed. Aram was soon jounced
awake and he stayed awake until they finally reached Khurramabad early in the afternoon. Once again they stopped at an
inn, to eat the typical luncheon of chelo kebabs, rice and lamb
chunks broiled over charcoal. Fitz filled up the tank with gas and
had the engine checked and they were off.

It was two hundred miles south over the Iranian equivalent of a
superhighway to the city of Ahwaz, where Fitz had planned that
they would spend the night at the Royal Hotel in town and then
on Wednesday morning proceed nonstop the nine hundred or so
miles to Bandar Abbas. Sergeant Aram drove and they arrived at
Ahwaz late in the afternoon.

The only parking lot was a dusty area beside the hotel on
Pahlavi Avenue. Fitz decided that he would get one hotel room
and let Sergeant Aram sleep until one in the morning while he sat
in the weapons carrier to guard the cargo. Then at one Aram
would relieve Fitz and at six in the morning they would start out
again. They had dinner together in the Royal's dining room and
when it was dark Fitz settled into the front seat of the vehicle, the
forty-five pistol at his side.

From time to time he stepped out of the truck and walked

around to the rear, pulling at the canvas covering to make sure it was secure, and then went back to sit in front. To keep from falling asleep he planned in detail how he would mount the 20-mm. cannons in the belly of Sepah's high-speed dhow. He would have to construct a steel frame through which the barrels of the cannons would protrude, caging them and preventing them from raising or lowering sufficiently to blast out the side of the boat.

At eleven o'clock a watchman walked through the parking lot and noticed Fitz sitting in the front seat of the car but said nothing to him. However, a few minutes later two local police officers entered the lot and walked over to him, shining a light into the cab.

"Why are you sitting out here?" one of the officers asked.

In his best Farsee, Fitz replied, "I have valuable carpets I purchased in Tabriz. I am watching them. I am an American attached to the United States Embassy in Tehran and I am trying to see more of this beautiful country."

The other officer demanded to see Fitz's identification, which he produced. When they saw his safe-conduct pass signed by the Shah himself, both officers became friendly, even patronizing.

"We will watch your truck," one of them offered. "One of us will not let it out of his sight for the rest of the night."

"Thank you, but I am happy out here. I have a companion who is driving with me, a sergeant in your army. He will relieve me at one o'clock. So if you come by later and find a Sergeant Aram here, he is working for me."

Both officers touched the bills of their caps and left Fitz alone. He was convinced that the officers would indeed have watched over the truck and its contents but he knew he would be unable to sleep, worrying about the cannons and machine guns. He was better off here.

At one o'clock Fitz left the truck long enough to walk into the lobby of the hotel. Rousing a sleeping desk clerk, he asked him to go up to Room 6 and knock on the door until Sergeant Aram answered. Then he hurried back to the truck and stood at its rear until, fifteen minutes later, Sergeant Aram, rubbing his eyes, appeared. Fitz told him about the police officers and reminded him to send someone up to knock at the door before six and then Fitz went upstairs and lay down on a bed for the first time in forty-eight hours and went to sleep.

The following morning after breakfast they took to the road again, driving for the most part through low-lying farming land until late in the morning the road led into hilly, rocky country, and just before noon they reached a point ten miles from the town of Kazerun, where the main road turned inland to the historical city of Shiraz.

They turned off to the right and were now headed directly toward the Persian Gulf and the seaport of Bushire. By midafternoon they had passed the road into Bushire and were continuing south, finally reaching the Gulf fishing village of Bashi.

The deep-blue water of the Persian Gulf was a welcome sight. They now faced a drive of over six hundred miles along rough, usually unpaved roads to Bandar Abbas. It was late afternoon with at the most four hours of daylight left in the sky.

From now on they could expect rough going and probably frequent halts. This was the smuggling coast and the Iranian Army patrolled it as carefully as possible, maintaining frequent checkpoints along the road. It was for this last stretch of the journey that Fitz had been so anxious to have the Shah's clearance.

They began the long final leg of the trip with Aram driving. No sooner had they left the town of Bashi than they encountered the first roadblock. Two soldiers with rifles leveled stopped them.

The sight of Aram's uniform relaxed the guards and then Fitz passed them the clearance paper, which they studied a few moments before handing it back and saluting.

"I'm afraid this is going to be the longest five hundred miles of the trip," Fitz said. Aram nodded silently. They went through two more roadblocks before darkness fell. However, even at night the Persian Gulf, always close to their right, reflected the moonlight so that they could see the coastal terrain through which they were proceeding. Because the road was narrow, rough, and twisting they couldn't drive more than twenty-five to thirty miles an hour but they pushed on south with determination.

Frequently they could see sailing dhows out on the Gulf, their sails lit by the pale moonlight in the sky. This was not a good night for smuggling but nevertheless every twenty miles, sometimes less, they came to a checkpoint and were required to identify themselves.

Sergeant Aram snorted disgustedly each time they were stopped. "The smugglers pack up their cigarettes on camels and drive them straight overland where there are no roads for army vehicles," he grumbled disdainfully. "These green troops wouldn't know a smuggler if they walked into him."

Steadily they proceeded on south, Aram working the wheel, clutch, gear shift, and brakes doggedly. Fitz made up his mind to double the money promised the sergeant and thanked his fates for the thousandth time that he hadn't tried to make this drive alone as he had originally planned.

As the sun rose above the hills to their left and shimmered off the Gulf, they were driving through Bandar Muqam. On his outdated map Fitz calculated that they were about two hundred and fifty miles from Bandar Abbas. He relieved Sergeant Aram at the wheel and began the last lap of the journey. Between the condition of the road, the many checkpoints which his Embassy papers got them through, and the difficulty they had finding a place where they could eat something, it was early afternoon before the island of Qishm loomed out of the waters of the Gulf to their right, signifying that they were ninety miles from Bandar Abbas. The road improved slightly as they approached the large southern port city, Iran's important seaport on the Persian Gulf.

It was about five in the afternoon when Fitz and Aram triumphantly completed their thirteen-hundred-mile journey from northern Iran to its port on the Straits of Hormuz in the south. Fitz had relinquished the wheel to Aram when they sighted Qishm Island so that he would be at least slightly more rested when they reached the port. Laylah would probably be arriving about the same time. They had actually made the trip a few hours ahead of schedule.

"Drive straight to the Naz Hotel on Reza Shah Avenue," Fitz instructed. "There should be messages there." Aram parked at the front entrance to the hotel and a porter came out to meet the dusty truck.

"Stay with the truck while I check inside," Fitz said as he stepped out onto the pavement. The porter held the door open for him and he walked up to the desk.

There were two messages for him. "Miss Smith, of the Embassy, would arrive at seven in the evening." The second message said that a representative of the Sepah shipping company would meet him in the lobby of the hotel. No sooner had he read the message than he noticed a brown-skinned young man wearing dark glasses and a white suit, yellow tie, and white shoes rise from a chair in the corner and approach him.

"Colonel Lodd?" the man asked.

Fitz nodded and the man held out to him a letter. Fitz opened it and read the prearranged code identifications from Sepah. This was clearly the authentic communication. He turned to the man who had handed him the letter. "Have you been waiting long?"

"No. As a matter of fact, you arrived earlier than I expected."

"I had some help with the driving."

Fitz led the man outside to where Sergeant Aram was waiting in the driver's seat of the vehicle. He motioned Aram to step out and then Fitz reached inside and pulled out the attaché case containing his clothes. The sergeant had only a canvas bag. An Iranian in a green fatigue suit materialized beside the man who had met Fitz in the lobby and took his place behind the wheel of the weapons carrier.

"By the way, Sepah owns this truck," Fitz reminded the man as they pulled the doors shut. The driver started the engine and drove off.

"So," said Fitz, "mission to Iran accomplished." He turned to Sergeant Aram. "Shall we have a drink now?"

Aram grinned and nodded, following Fitz into the bar, where he found a table off in a dark corner. They sat down, ordered drinks, and then Fitz took two hundred dollars' worth of rials from the wallet in his jacket pocket and handed them to Aram. "A bonus for a job well done, Sergeant," he said.

The smile on Aram's face broadened as he saw he was getting double what he had expected. "*Al Humdulillah*," he exclaimed in gratitude. "This will make it possible for my wife and me to do things to our small house we have only dreamed of."

Fitz was touched at the true ring of gratitude in the sergeant's voice. "After we have had our drinks I will buy you a ticket back to Tabriz. If you would like to stay here for a few days, you will be my guest in the hotel."

"Just one night to get some sleep, Colonel. Then I will go home. My wife will be missing me and I want to tell her of our good fortune."

Fitz registered for the room he had reserved, made sure that Laylah's room was being held for her, and was able to get the last room in the hotel for Sergeant Aram. Friday being the Sabbath in Iran as in all Islamic countries, Thursday night at a resort hotel was a difficult time to get rooms. With Sergeant Aram settled Fitz took a long, leisurely bath and put on clean clothes for the first time since he had left Tehran for Tabriz.

CHAPTER 9

At seven o'clock Fitz was sitting in the lobby watching for Laylah to arrive. She walked into the hotel at seven-fifteen and even as she was asking for messages Fitz came up behind her.

"Fitz," she cried, whirling around. "I thought you'd probably get here in the middle of the night."

"I was fortunate to get some help driving. How's everything at the Embassy?"

She made a doleful mouth at him. "Everything's fine for you, but I'm sure the Ambassador and General Fielding think I'm a wisp-witted dame." She turned back to the desk. "Let me register and I'll tell you about it." Fitz watched her write her name and U. S. Embassy affiliation on the card. The clerk called a bellboy to take her suitcase up to her room.

"Let me freshen up a bit and I'll be right down. No more than fifteen minutes, I promise. Order me the usual and I'll join you in the bar."

Excitement and anticipation coursed through him as Fitz picked out a table at the window overlooking the harbor. For some reason ever since he had turned over the weapons carrier to Sepah's representative he felt like a whole new individual. Not many men could have procured two 20-mm. cannons, transported them the length of Persia, and delivered them to a smuggler to ferry across the Gulf to Dubai. Soon he would be installing them and then taking them into combat on the high seas, making half a million dollars for himself in the process. No reason ever again to feel himself colorless, a bit too insignificant to interest a beautiful, glamorous young woman.

That's what he told himself, but when Laylah appeared in the doorway of the bar, attracting the attention of all the patrons, the old feelings of self-doubt assailed him once more. He stood up and walked toward her. Seeing him, Laylah entered the room and, all eyes of the international crowd upon her, she went to Fitz and took his hand. He led her to the table and seated her. The vodka he'd ordered, in an ice bucket, had just arrived and the caviar was on the table.

"You are the most beautiful girl in the world, Laylah," Fitz sighed. "I've been thinking about this moment all week."

"So have I, Fitz. You do have those papers with you?"

"Of course."

"Good. What a week of deception I've been through. The envelope you left arrived on my desk on Monday morning. All day I prayed the Ambassador wouldn't check with the receptionist and I even left at noon Monday before he could call me in. I took the envelope home with me and then on Tuesday the Ambassador himself called me. He had finally discovered that you had left an envelope with the receptionist first thing on Monday morning, so you were always in the clear with the Embassy."

Laylah sipped her vodka a moment. "Well, on Tuesday I said yes, you had left an envelope for me and I had assumed it was some pictures you had promised me and so I took it home but had been too busy to open it. He made me promise to bring it in on Wednesday. So you were still all right. On Wednesday all I could do was telephone in and plead a woman's prerogative to be sick. I felt like such a fool. And then the Ambassador himself called me at home and asked me to open the envelope and tell him what was in it. I was prepared of course. I told the Ambassador that there was a diplomatic passport and special clearance papers with your picture on them signed by the Shah. The Ambassador asked me the passport number and the serial number on the clearance papers. And of course you had given me that information at lunch at the French Club. So all is well at the Embassy.

"I begged off sick again today, tomorrow is the Sabbath, and on Saturday morning I deliver the papers in an envelope stamped received last Monday. So they will think you are a good boy and I'm a dumb dame but all's well. You can go back to the Embassy for another favor any time."

"You're not only beautiful, you saved this mission for me. Several times when I was stopped they checked clearance cancellations from Tehran. I couldn't have done it without you, Laylah."

She smiled happily, proud to have been of help. "And now, with your momentous mission behind you, I think you owe me the thrill of telling me what it was all about."

"Sure, but keep it secret, Laylah. Only stage one has been accomplished. The worst is ahead."

"I promise there's no way anyone would ever get out of me anything you say."

After another caviar and vodka Fitz said, "O.K. I acquired a load of arms and ammunition, two 20-mm. cannons, and two thirty-caliber machine guns from the border station where Colonel Nizzim hands them over to the Kurds to use against the Iraqis. With the help of a great Persian sergeant I brought them all the way down here and turned them over to a smuggler to take back to Dubai. In Dubai they will be used to arm a high-speed gold-smuggling boat so that if an Indian Coast Guard patrol launch tries to stop it on the high seas, the smuggler can blow the Indian boat out of the water. What do you think of that?"

"I don't know, Fitz," she replied, truly perplexed. "Somehow it all sounds sort of internationally illegal, like it could cause trouble."

"The first Indian boat that comes after that dhow is in big trouble, I promise you that."

"Isn't that the legal job of the Indian Coast Guard?"

"On the high seas? Absolutely not. Within three miles of the Indian coast, perhaps even twelve, I would say yes. But it is on the high seas that the Dubai boats are hit and the Indian crews keep the gold for themselves. It's piracy, that's what it is. I don't mind helping the Dubai businessmen save their cargoes."

"I hope you are getting a fair share for what you are doing," Laylah said after thinking about the situation.

"I am. Visit me in Dubai and you'll see."

"As I asked before, Fitz, when?"

"Whenever you like. Give me a couple of weeks to get settled and then fly on over."

"I will."

At midnight Fitz and Laylah stood out on the terrace of the hotel alone, looking over the port city and the brightly lighted ships at dock and anchored out in the stream. Laylah was leaning against Fitz's chest.

"It's lovely here. I've been wanting to visit Bandar Abbas for a long time," Laylah said. She turned slightly to him. He bent his head and kissed her. Laylah returned the kiss. "You must be very tired, Fitz. It's been an exhausting four days for you."

"I wouldn't waste time being tired," he said softly. "By the way, I ordered a bottle of champagne to be delivered to your room before the bar closes. I thought perhaps we could drink it on your balcony. We won't have dinner again together until you come to Dubai."

"It's a lovely idea, Fitz. Let's have another dance and then we'll go up."

The Iranian musicians trying to sound like an American dance band did a creditable job and for another half an hour Fitz held Laylah close to him as they danced. The music was strictly out of the nineteen forties and fifties, nice waltz and fox-trot music, none of the strident rock sound which took all the romance out of dancing. It was just about closing time when they entered the elevator to go up to Laylah's room. He didn't really know what might happen between Laylah and himself but the evening had been a memorable one already. Laylah handed him the key to her door and he opened it, followed her in, closed and locked the door behind them, and put the key on her dresser.

The bottle of champagne in the ice bucket could be seen out on the terrace, a table with two chairs beside it and champagne glasses and napkins on the table.

"This is one place we'll have to visit again," Fitz said huskily. "I suspect I'll be here from time to time on business."

"My dashing gun runner and gold smuggler," Laylah teased.

"I'll make a million dollars in two years and buy an ambassadorship somewhere out here," Fitz chuckled. "Will you be my ambassadress?"

Laylah came easily into his arms. "Of course I will, Fitz. I have a lot of connections with the Republicans if they get in next year. Fifty thousand dollars ought to get you an Arab country. I understand Iran will be going for several hundred thousand. It's supposed to be almost as desirable as Paris or London."

"Give me a year and I'll be able to buy the post here."

Laylah turned her face up to him and they kissed for a long while. Then she pulled gently away from him. "We wouldn't want the champagne to get warm."

"I'll open it." Fitz and Laylah went out on the terrace, where he popped the cork and poured them each a glass of champagne.

Laylah held up her glass. "To your future on the Persian Gulf— the Arabian Gulf where you'll be," she amended.

"To our future, Laylah," he replied. They sipped their champagne a few moments, looking out over Bandar Abbas. Then they put their glasses down and once again they were in each other's arms. "How long have we known each other, Fitz?" Laylah asked dreamily.

"One year and half a month, since you first came to the Embassy last summer," Fitz replied. "You had dinner with me for the first time three weeks after I met you."

"Say!" There was surprise in Laylah's tone. "You have a good memory."

"I remember everything about us," he replied. He took another long sip of champagne to give him a little extra shot of self-assurance. "You know," he heard himself saying, "here tonight, in the strange and romantic setting of Bandar Abbas, wouldn't it be great to give each other something very special to remember? As you just pointed out, we've known each other a year now. Isn't it time, to use a diplomatic expression, that we escalated our relationship?"

"Why, Fitz!" Laylah exclaimed in mock shock, "I've never heard you talk like this."

"Neither have I," Fitz replied truthfully. "Maybe I'm changing. For the more interesting, I hope, if not for the more virtuous." He reached for the bottle of champagne and filled both their glasses again. As they drank and kissed, Fitz realized that if it wasn't now the chances were that it would be never. He held his glass up. "To Bandar Abbas, may it be the site of our first time making love."

Laylah held up her glass, gently clinked the rim of his with hers, and they both drank deeply, put their glasses down, and came into each other's arms. After the long kiss Laylah separated from Fitz.

"Why don't you pour the last of the bottle into our glasses and bring them inside." As Fitz followed her suggestion Laylah disappeared into the bathroom and Fitz put the glasses down on the bedside table.

Now, he wondered, would he be a satisfactory bed partner for Laylah? He had read that modern college-educated girls like Laylah in this decade of advanced sexual enlightenment encouraged new and unusual types of erotic play and he was very un-up on such matters. Maybe for this, the first time, the plain old missionary position would be sufficient. Fitz had, during his years in the Middle East, found occasion to bed some exotic Persian and Bedouin girls. He never knew how effective his role had really been in such encounters since these girls were always polite.

He felt he was really out of his class with Laylah, but here they were together. No time to let his eternal self-doubts plague him. He finished half of his glass of champagne and felt stimulation and sensation dispel trepidation and uncertainty. For good measure he helped himself to half of Laylah's glass of champagne. She didn't need it, so cool and self-assured, confident in her knowledge that she was a total woman.

Fitz was in a frenzy of anticipatory delight when he heard the bathroom door open. Laylah's heavy long black hair hung loosely to her shoulders about the sheer summer nightgown she wore. Fitz, who had been sitting on the edge of the bed, stood up and, putting his arms on her shoulders, held her away, drinking in the exquisite sight.

"You are the most"—he paused, searching his limited vocabulary of love—"the most ravishing woman in the world, Laylah."

She laughed. "I'll bet you've said that before."

"Never," he declared. His arms trembled slightly and he pulled her close to him. She raised her face and he kissed her, feeling the firm breasts, which had been so clearly revealed under the filmy negligee, pressed against his bare chest.

"Fitz, your belt buckle is hurting me," she whispered. He let go of her long enough to undo the buckle and unbutton his slacks. Laylah stayed close to him as his pants dropped to the floor and now in just his shorts he stepped out of them. He felt he was being clumsy but Laylah seemed to be patient with him. He sensed her motion toward the bed and the two of them moved onto it together. He removed his shorts and was naked against the

loose nightgown around her. Somehow, very smoothly, Laylah
wriggled out of the gown altogether and their bodies were pressing
together.

"I love you, Laylah. I have as long as I've known you," he murmured against her lips.

"Why didn't you mention it before, Fitz?" she murmured back.
"Think of all the time we've wasted."

"No more," he vowed.

"No more," Laylah agreed.

And indeed no more time was wasted that night. When the
morning sun reflecting off the Gulf filled the room with bright
daylight, waking Laylah and Fitz, they turned to each other and
until they made ready to go downstairs for lunch, none of the
morning was wasted either. For all Fitz's feared inexperience in
what he thought of as modern sex, Laylah had not found him
lacking and by noon she exuberantly pleaded to a surfeit of
lovemaking that would require a week's recovery period.

"Just the time it will take to get my house in Dubai ready for
your arrival," Fitz laughed.

That afternoon Fitz saw Laylah off on the last flight to Tehran.
He had wanted her to spend another night in Bandar Abbas but
they both realized the necessity for her presence in the Embassy
at 8 A.M. Saturday morning, the first day of the Islamic week.
There was of course the matter of turning Fitz's credentials over
to the Ambassador before his impatience reached the explosive
point.

Fitz was obliged to spend one more night in Bandar Abbas
since his flight to Dubai left at eleven in the morning and he certainly had no intention of going until he had shared every moment with Laylah left them before her return to the capital.

CHAPTER 10

Abdul Hussein Abdullah had towed the dhow he was constructing for Sepah away from his boatyard and the prying eyes that could look in on it from the Maktoum Bridge spanning the Creek between Deira and Dubai. The dhow was now berthed in a special drydock at the mouth of the Creek on the Dubai side close to the new construction work being waged against the Gulf to create Port Maktoum, the new deep-water docking facility which would provide berthing space for the largest ships and oil tankers that plied the Arabian Gulf waters.

It was two in the morning and the temperature had dropped to a bearable ninety-five degrees as Fitz with the help of Abdul's blacksmith worked under lights in the hold of the new dhow. It had taken great ingenuity to install the mountings for the twin 20-mm. cannons in such a way that the recoil wouldn't tear the bottom of the boat apart. Fitz and Abdul had devised a method of recoil absorption that would conduct the stress of the bucking twin M-24s evenly around the frame of the dhow. Even so, Fitz had pointed out, sustained firing of the cannons could easily warp the sturdy frame of the ship. The job of the cannons would have to be accomplished in a matter of seconds in two or three short bursts of fire.

Fitz was justifiably proud of the feat he had accomplished in mounting the cannons. A tubular-steel frame encasing the barrels of the guns had been built inside the boat's hull. Even in the heat of battle an inexperienced gunner would be unable to swing the cannons into a position where they could shoot out the hull of the dhow from the inside. It had taken longer to install these guardrails inside the hull than it had to put in the gun mounts. The firing slit in the side of the hull, when swung open inward, was barely a foot in width and twenty feet in length between two reinforced ribs on both sides of the boat. There was also a gun port in the stern of the dhow, giving the twin M-24s a monumental stinger capacity should the boat be attacked from the rear. Certainly the first time an attempt was made to stop this dhow on the high seas the offensive ship would be destroyed. It would not be until there was a survivor of such an interception able to tell the authorities what had happened that effective countermeasures could be taken. The twin thirties and the submachine guns should take care of that problem for a while, Fitz thought grimly as he worked in the heat to get the ship ready for its first gold-"reexporting" trip.

By three in the morning, with the heat and humidity taking their toll, Fitz pronounced his twin 20-mm. cannons combat ready. As always, Sepah was on hand during the time Fitz was working on the gun mounts as though memorizing all the technical details of the American's efforts.

Fitz straightened out, rubbing his back, which ached badly.

"Will you have a drink with me before going home?" Sepah asked Fitz.

Fitz, of course, wanted to get back to the delightful small house Sepah had loaned him on the beach but it was important to maintain the very cordial relations they enjoyed, so he accepted the invitation. In the Land Rover which had been loaned him by the Ruler, Fitz followed Sepah's vehicle to the Persian's home and gratefully consumed the cool air inside as gin and tonics were made for them by an ever-alert servant.

"So the guns are ready?" Sepah gave Fitz a grin of immense satisfaction.

Fitz nodded. "All but the thirty-caliber machine guns. A night's work when the breakaway deckhouse I designed is put in place," Fitz replied. "But you said it would be the end of September when you make the first voyage. That's a month away."

Sepah nodded. "There is a dire demand for gold in India and Pakistan today," he explained. "Many weddings are being postponed until the proper amount of gold to adorn the bride can be obtained by her parents. The rich Indians are desperate to convert their silver bars, and the American and British currency and traveler's checks they have acquired, into gold. Instead of the eighty thousand ten-tola bars we had expected to send, we'll probably take over a hundred thousand. Perhaps as much as fifteen million dollars in gold will be sailing on the strength of your guns and of course your own skill as a gunner."

Fitz's lips compressed. The immensity of his responsibility filled him with uncertainty. "I suppose that makes my two points more valuable?"

"Indeed it does, Fitz. And there's not an investor in my syndicate that begrudges you that share."

"I just hope they are keeping the guns a sacred secret," Fitz intoned.

"With the money they are investing? You don't have to worry about the secret of the guns getting out."

"Nothing seems too secret around here. Eyes are everywhere."

"My biggest concern is that you brought enough ammunition," Sepah went on, ignoring Fitz's comment. "This dhow has a lot of sailing to do in the years to come."

"I had an overload in the weapons carrier as it was," Fitz replied. "Five hundred rounds to each gun should last you through five or six firefights. It should only take a few well-placed twenty-millimeter explosive shells to break up a patrol launch. I'll teach your men burst control. And if later you need more ammunition I know where to get it for you."

Sepah patted Fitz's shoulder. "I know, Fitz. I have full faith in you. My future is at stake on this next run. That's why I'm going on it myself and if at times I seem a bit overanxious try to understand."

"Just as long as the Indian Coast Guard has no idea an armed smuggling dhow is in existence we'll be all right. But too damn many Arabs have seen me working on that dhow."

Sepah shrugged. "I did have a call from Colonel Buttres of the Trucial Oman Scouts. He was wondering about a shipment I brought in from somewhere in the Gulf some weeks ago."

Fitz looked up. "The guns?"

"I wasn't going to alarm you, Fitz. Buttres may have many spies about the waterfront and he may have some idea that I brought in some hardware, but he also knows that I do nothing without the Ruler's knowledge and cooperation, so he won't be meddling further."

Fitz sighed, leaned back, studied his drink, and sipped at it.

Then he said, "Now that the twenties are installed I'm going to bring my young lady from the American Embassy in Iran over here for a visit."

"Now would be a good time," Sepah agreed. "Have you done anything about a visa for her? It may be a problem."

"You think so?"

"Oh, we'll get around it. But you know how these Arab countries are about women. Unless you are bringing in a wife, and even then it's difficult, they don't like young Western women walking around stirring up the lust of young unmarried Arabs. The whole sex question is a delicate one here. From childhood Arabs are taught that it is sinful to even think of sexual relations and the worst thing a youngster can do to disgrace the family is to so much as talk to a member of the opposite sex in some concealed or intimate place. They cannot conceive of a man and woman given the opportunity to be alone together resisting the temptation to have sex."

Fitz nodded. "I am well aware of this attitude. But I hope the Ruler doesn't insist on Westerners embracing all Arab customs."

"Of course not. I'll see him tomorrow and tell him you need a visa. Just write down all the details for me." Sepah went over to a desk and took out a pad of paper and a pen, which he handed Fitz.

Fitz printed Laylah's name, address, and Embassy affiliation and handed the pad back to Sepah. "Incidentally," he said, "Tim McLaren's bank was most helpful in Iran. I hope you can give him some business as you build up the gold load."

"Of course. Ask him to come see me. We'll buy gold from his bank and process the Indian payment for the gold through him. Does he deal in silver?"

"I'll ask him tomorrow."

"On this coming trip I expect that we will be paid heavily in silver. At current prices silver is worth one dollar and twenty cents an ounce. Gold we buy for about thirty-five dollars an ounce and sell it in India for about one hundred and five dollars an ounce, a two hundred percent profit. Thus we take back one hundred and twenty-nine pounds of silver for each pound of gold we trade. There is no law in India about buying and selling silver. They seem to have unlimited quantities of it and we can sell as much silver as we can warehouse here."

"I'm sure McLaren has every angle in the financial community going for him."

"By the way, Fitz, Majid was very pleased with the carpet you brought him from Tabriz, and of course I was happy with mine. It happens that Majid buys and sells fine carpeting as a sideline throughout the Arabian Gulf and he recognized the quality of your carpet. As of course my wife and I did," Sepah added. "Does this girl from the American Embassy speak Farsee?" he asked.

"Her mother's family are Persian, her father's American," Fitz replied. "She is bilingual, and extremely valuable to the Embassy."

"You must bring her around for an evening with us," Sepah invited. "My wife, of course, is Persian and she seldom has a chance to talk to a woman in her native language."

"Get Laylah's visa and you're on."

"By the way," Sepah asked, "have you thought about what you'll do when you finish the job for my syndicate?"

"I seem to get endless propositions," Fitz said. "I'm thinking over a number of things."

"If you keep investing in our re-exporting ventures you'll do very well."

"I believe it. And Majid has some oil ideas. There seem to be limitless opportunities here."

"In a month at most we'll set out. Two weeks later your active participation will no longer be required and you can do whatever seems interesting."

"Sepah," Fitz asked, "how long does it take the syndicate to distribute profits? And incidentally, how do I know how much gold we are transporting?"

Sepah laughed, motioned the servant to make two more drinks, and when they arrived he answered. "Well, Fitz, in the first place you'll see all the gold aboard the ship with your own eyes, but more important, in this business of re-exporting a man's word is everything. We can have no contracts, no letters, no agreements in writing. Everything is based on a man's word. The penalty for not keeping your word is severe. As a matter of fact, we are having a little trouble with a trustee in India right now. It will be settled by a man we are taking on our trip. He will slip into India and kill this trustee. Such examples from time to time keep everyone honest."

Fitz was sorry he had mentioned the subject. Sepah continued. "As to time of profit disbursement, you can ask your friend McLaren how long it takes to process the payments we receive here for the gold. When everything has been converted into hard currency in Dubai, the money is divided up. Perhaps it takes as long as a month."

Fitz nodded. He finished the drink in silence. "Sepah, if you will excuse me I need to get a little sleep."

Sepah stood up and shook hands with Fitz. "Of course. Things are going well, I am highly pleased. We will do much together. And, Fitz, it is seldom that an outsider is asked to become part of an established syndicate such as ours."

"That I realize, Sepah," Fitz said as his host opened the door. "And I will do my best to see that you remain established."

They exchanged understanding smiles and then Fitz walked out into the cloying heat to his Land Rover.

CHAPTER 11

His exertions over the four or five hot and humid hours that night, combined with the two drinks and the refreshing air conditioning in his home, dropped Fitz into a deep sleep from which he begrudgingly awoke when his Pakistani servant, Peter, knocked at his door.

"Sahib Sake here," Peter announced. That was as close as he could come to the name Stakes.

"Tell him I will be with him soon. Give him coffee."

"Give him coffee one time already."

"Give him coffee two time while I get awake and dressed," Fitz commanded.

He did not rush taking a shower and dressing. Twenty minutes after he had been awakened, Fitz, wearing slippers, slacks, and a loose-fitting short-sleeved shirt, walked into the living room, where the tall, white-haired, ruddy-complexioned Englishman was waiting. Fitz couldn't help being curious about Stakes, the man talked very little about his background. He had the cultured accent and hint of a stammer which, combined with chiseled features and an almost hawklike nose, gave him all the trappings of the English aristocracy. Yet he was obviously an opportunist living off his wits. Possibly a younger son of an old family who had disgraced himself somewhere in the past.

"Good morning, John," Fitz greeted him.

"Sorry to get you out of bed, old boy." Stakes walked to him and shook his hand.

"I was up late last night," Fitz confessed.

"For the last week or so of nights, I'd say. It didn't take you long to get yourself involved here."

"Nothing very exciting, really." He wondered how much Stakes and the others knew about what he was doing and decided that a half-true explanation might be in order.

"One can't work out in the sun on the Gulf this time of year, you know. Boatbuilding has always been a great hobby of mine, and the local boatbuilder, Abdullah, is giving me a course of instruction in the construction of high-speed dhows."

Stakes smiled knowingly. "Quite. You got to the heart of things here right away, what?"

"Tell me what's on your mind, John." Fitz sipped the cup of tea Peter brought him and ate some buttered toast.

"First, Harcourt Thornwell will be arriving in a few days. After he's picked up the feel of the Gulf we'll be ready to start out on the first step of raising pledges of a billion or so dollars among the Arab leaders to put Courty's plan into action." Fitz nodded but did not reply.

"One thing I was wondering, old boy. Your fellow countryman has never been out here before and it will take him some time to acclimatize. I was wondering if perhaps you could put him up here with you?"

Fitz shook his head. "Any other time I'd like to accommodate you, John. But I have a visitor. A young woman from the American Embassy in Iran coming over to spend a week here. She'll need the guest room. Sorry."

"Oh, I quite understand, Fitz. Just thought that if you happened to have a free room . . ."

"Then I would have been delighted. In any case, he'll probably find the Ruler's guest house more interesting. If he listens to the talk there he'll learn a lot more about the Gulf than he would here."

"Yes. Pity Shaikh Rashid doesn't see fit to air-condition the place."

"There's always the Carlton Hotel over in Deira."

"If you can get a room. I wish some American would build a small, swinging hotel and bar. Import some girls to sing and be around. There's just nothing to do here. Courty is a young man and used to what he calls night action. I don't know how we'll entertain him."

Fitz stared at John Stakes a few seconds as an idea flashed through his head. "You're right, John. A really good bar, with entertainment. A place to meet and talk deals under pleasant conditions is badly needed here." He let the idea percolate a few moments. "What's your schedule when Thornwell gets here?"

"I'm waiting for replies to my letters now."

"And you want me to make this junket with you?" Fitz asked.

"Of course. We have to convince the leaders whose money we are after that we are sincerely working on behalf of the Arab cause."

"Are we?"

Stakes was taken aback. "What do you mean? Everyone knows you were cashiered from the U. S. Army for speaking up on behalf of the Arabs."

"I know what I am. I don't know what you and Thornwell are. Is he really interested in spending the rest of his promising life working for better understanding of the Arab world by Americans?"

"That would be a by-product of the communications empire he wants to establish. I just received a letter from him in which he indicated it might be possible to buy *Life* magazine from Time, Inc."

"I'll look forward to talking to him. If I like what I see and hear, of course I'll go along with you if that's what you want."

"Courty has already made up an elaborate presentation with the help of some of the Arab delegates at the United Nations. The Arabs were impressed to hear that you are part of the plan."

"I'll reserve final judgment until Thornwell gets here. We'll have to do some detailed planning, as I do have a two-week commitment coming up in about a month."

"I'm sure we can work around it, Fitz. Courty should be here in three or four days."

There was a ring at the door and Peter went to open it. Fender Browne was led into the living room. Fender and John Stakes greeted each other and then the Englishman made a discreet withdrawal, his business, for the time being, concluded with Fitz.

"Sorry to come over unannounced like this, Fitz," Fender began.

"No problem. When in Arabia do as the Arabs do. If you need to see a man go see him."

Peter appeared with fresh cups and an Arab-style, pelican-beak copper coffeepot. Fitz and Fender Browne discussed the new warehouse area, which was across the Creek on the Deira side and above the bridge from Abdullah's boatyard.

When they had both finished their coffee and Peter had removed himself from the room, Fender Browne began talking in earnest.

"It was the Ruler who suggested that I come to you with this thought, Fitz," he opened. "Rashid felt that working together we could pull off a very lucrative oil deal. He seems to have a lot of confidence in you."

"I appreciate his support," Fitz acknowledged. "Obviously I wouldn't even be here without it." Nevertheless, Fitz was acutely aware that the Ruler had not summoned him to the palace since his return from Iran and all communications had been expressed through third parties.

However, Fitz was wise enough in the ways of the Arab-world hierarchy to understand what was going on. It was necessary for him to prove his reputation as a firmly pro-Arab American and then to prove himself as a man who can be trusted and counted on in delicate transactions before the final acceptance into the community of the Creek was bestowed upon him.

And there was another thing which Fitz uneasily realized all too well. He was venturing into a most dangerous international area in arming and acting as combat gunner for a gold-smuggling syndicate. If he, an American, should be captured in the act of firing on the Indian Coast Guard on the high seas, an international incident would be provoked and disavowed by the Ruler and all his advisers. Majid Jabir had made this clear to him. And if he were captured, Fitz would be absolutely on his own. Up to now the Dubai gold re-exporters had dropped their gold overboard when menaced by Indian Coast Guard patrol launches and thus no charges could be preferred against them. With the advent of Fitz joining the syndicate a new tactic was being attempted. Only when it had been successfully employed and Fitz excused from further personal participation in the area of smuggling could the Ruler afford to officially receive him again.

"What's happened is that some of the drillers who helped form DODO discovered likely offshore oil reserves at what they call the Fatah Field. This will be worth one hell of a lot of money to

Dubai. Naturally the oil personnel are very close to Rashid and they happened to mention that one of their seismic crews had come to the conclusion that there is a potentially big oil field in the territorial waters of Kajmira about nine to ten miles from the island of Abu Musa, which belongs to Sharjah. Since Sharjah can only claim a three-mile territorial waters limit around Abu Musa, here is a great big beautiful offshore oil field, under lease to no oil company yet, and the Ruler of Kajmira with only fifteen miles of Gulf shoreline doesn't even know he has an oil field out there."

"Why doesn't the Dubai company claim the field?" Fitz asked.

"It's tied up with Dubai, which is all it can handle."

"Where do we come in?"

"You go to the Ruler of Kajmira. He knows all about you and would like to meet you. Tell him you have big oil contracts, get the exclusive rights for two or three years of oil exploration, and then make a deal with one of the major oil companies. And when you make the deal they agree to use my oil field supply facilities in Dubai exclusively."

"How about grabbing off rights to Sharjah's waters?" Fitz asked.

"Seismic exploration reveals no oil-bearing structures under Sharjah waters even though Abu Musa belongs to Sharjah. Remember, this new field is nine miles from the island, well beyond its territorial waters."

"It all sounds very exotic and interesting," Fitz finally allowed. "I just don't see why the Ruler of Kajmira would give me preference over somebody else."

"Go up there and get to know him," Fender Browne urged. "Rashid will help you. Naturally he's in for twenty percent of any deal we make."

"My plate is getting quite full here in just a few weeks," Fitz commented wonderingly. "Do I need a letter from the Ruler here to see the guy up in Kajmira, what's his name?"

"Shaikh Hamed bin Sultan al Sulim. He's an old man and has ruled since 1929. Just go up there and tell him Majid Jabir, which means Shaikh Rashid of Dubai, sent you. The less letters and stuff in writing, the better."

Fitz nodded. Nothing that could indicate a relationship between him and Dubai officialdom could be committed to writing yet; not until the gold voyage was successfully completed. "I hear the beaches are good up there," Fitz said. "I'll just drop in on Shaikh Hamed and see what happens."

"That's the route." Fender Browne sounded pleased. "Make the most of it while you're a hero. And keep me up to date."

"I sure will. And now I've got to get over to the Creek and send a cable to Tehran."

"Are you going back there?" Fender asked, worried perhaps about anything that might hold up Fitz making contact with Shaikh Hamed.

"No, but a friend over there is flying here pretty quick."

The telltale grin on Fitz's face made Fender ask, "A woman? By God, I don't blame you. There sure is nothing here."

"You'll meet her, Fender."

"I'd like to. My wife should be coming in from London any day. My house is just about finished."

"We'll have ourselves a beach party," Fitz suggested.

After Fender Browne had left, Fitz pulled on a pair of shoes and, stuffing his wallet in his pocket, he told Peter he'd be back in an hour or less and ventured out into the heat of the day, thoughts of Laylah vividly in his mind.

When Fitz returned to the air-conditioned sanctuary of his house on the beach, he saw a Land Rover with the official white and red colors and markings of the Trucial Oman Scouts parked in front of his house. There was also an official-looking black sedan of British manufacture in front of the Land Rover. As Fitz drove into his driveway a note of concern dispelled the flowing spirits that had filled him since he had sent the cable to Laylah. He leapt from his vehicle and strode up to his front door. Peter pulled it open as he gained the doorstep.

Colonel Buttres, TOS, here. Also the *mua'atamad*." The British Political Agent was always called the *mua'atamad*.

"Thank you, Peter," Fitz said walking in, striding down the hall and into the main sitting room looking out over the beach and the Gulf. "Gentlemen," he greeted his guests. "To what do I owe this honor?"

"Good morning, Fitz," the Colonel greeted him.

"Same to you, Kenneth." Fitz shook the Colonel's hand. "And

Brian." He took the hand of Brian Falmey, the British Political Agent. "Come sit down."

The three sat facing each other beside the large picture window giving onto the white sand and blue Gulf waters.

"I've been meaning to drop around, Fitz, since we last talked at Majid Jabir's place a couple of weeks ago," the Political Agent said.

"And I'm glad you let no more time go by," Fitz countered cheerfully. "Is there some way a neophyte to this side of the Gulf can be of assistance to you old hands?"

"Possibly, Lodd," Falmey replied. "We felt it was time to appraise you of some of our problems in hopes you might understand them and if not help us with solutions, at least not make our task more difficult."

Fitz raised an eyebrow. "Make your task difficult?"

"The chief concern of Her Majesty's Government here in the Trucial States is to keep peace between the various rulers. It is not an easy job, I might add." Brian Falmey, O.B.E., was a typical Brit Foreign Office type, Fitz thought. Pompous, his arrogance thinly disguised beneath a slightly condescending manner. "But we have been here over a hundred and fifty years now and we aren't prepared to shirk our duties."

Before Fitz could utter a rejoinder Colonel Buttres took up the conversational reins, talking in a military vein, one officer to another. "You see, Fitz, the Trucial Oman Scouts are particularly sensitive about armaments we have not cleared coming into the area. And we are approaching an especially difficult time in British relationships out here. It won't come as a surprise to any of us, including the rulers, when London announces that England is no longer prepared to police the Middle East, in particular this Arabian peninsula. Already the Chinese Communists are organizing insurgency operations, as I mentioned to you the first time we met, at the Ruler's dinner, when you had only been in Dubai a couple of days."

"I remember well," Fitz murmured.

"The Communists are openly building up so-called Liberation Fronts in Oman and Yemen and going underground right here in the Trucial States. They are just waiting to attack in Oman, especially when it is announced that Britain will no longer be protecting the existing states. If they can win in Oman the Communists will dominate the Straits of Hormuz and all the shipping into and out of the Gulf."

"I have been in a number of discussions on just this situation since I arrived here," Fitz said blandly, "but what does all this have to do with me?"

The Political Agent, Brian Falmey, answered Fitz. "Simply that everything points to the fact that you and certain Dubai businessmen seem to be involved in bringing military hardware right up the Creek and unloading it. We know that the Communists are paying top money for arms to use down in the Dhofar province of Oman. We'd hate to see our enemies suddenly supplied with sophisticated insurgency weaponry, the sort the Vietcong are using against you today in Vietnam."

"Perhaps you should study our problems in Vietnam. You just might learn some things that would help you here," Fitz retorted. "Whether a few weapons get through to some fledgling Communist front operation in the south of Oman isn't what's going to make the difference between a successful or unsuccessful insurgency. What's going to make the difference is whether or not you get rid of that medieval monster Sultan Sa'id bin Taimur. He's the one that exercises life-and-death rule over his subjects. He's the last of the rulers to have his subjects whipped to death in public for the smallest infractions of his religious laws. He's the answer to Communist prayers. If we hadn't waited so long to get rid of Ngo Dinh Diem, perhaps we wouldn't have such a disastrous war going in Vietnam right this minute." Fitz had always believed that a sharp attack was the best defense, and certainly the old Brit Political Agent was left speechless for a few moments.

"Now look here, Lodd, we didn't come to talk politics," he finally protested. "We're here to suggest that bringing arms into Dubai without discussing it with myself and Colonel Buttres can only be viewed in the most unfavorable terms."

"Are you suggesting that I brought weapons into Dubai?" Fitz kept his voice low but righteous indignation bristled forth.

"Not that you directly imported weapons into Dubai, of course not," Falmey answered. "But we strongly suspect that in some way you are connected with some weapons that arrived on the Creek a few weeks ago."

"Do you think that I, an American citizen, a retired United States Army officer, would in any way help the Communists?"

"Oh, absolutely not, old boy. Certainly not—intentionally," Colonel Buttres hastily interjected.

"But any arms that arrive here might get into Communist hands," Falmey said. "What are you doing every night working on your Persian friend's new dhow?" he shot out after a pause.

"I don't see that indulging in my hobby, boatbuilding, is so suspicious," Fitz replied evenly.

"Oh, come off it, Lodd." Falmey flashed an impatient glare at the American. "You know what we're talking about. Our only concern is that supplying arms to whoever pays you for using your experience and connections in this respect might become habit-forming. We know the Ruler likes you because you openly expressed what most of us think about the Jews but our advice to you is don't spoil a good thing for yourself. You could become very rich very fast here. But don't forget that politically and militarily we guide the various rulers here and they follow our advice implicitly."

"And what sort of advice are you offering Shaikh Rashid concerning me?" Fitz challenged.

"None at all, just yet." Falmey reached into the side pocket of the lightweight safari jacket he wore and pulled out a pipe, to which he applied the jet of a butane cigarette lighter, and puffed a few moments. "Our suggestion is that we let whatever may have happened during your first few weeks here go ignored. But we trust that any further trips you might make to Iran do not result in more weapons turning up on the Creek." He puffed in silence for a few moments. "You see, even the Ruler does not really comprehend the insurgency problems, which are apparent to you who have studied counterinsurgency and fought Communist guerrillas. And by the way, your thoughts on old Sultan Sa'id have been expressed at the highest levels in Foreign Office meetings."

Brian Falmey stood up. "We have taken up enough of your time, Lodd. But I do believe we all understand each other."

Fitz and Colonel Buttres stood also. "Fitz, I would like to have you come out to TOS headquarters in Sharjah. It would probably remind you of some of your own operations. I'll drop you a note and perhaps you'll join myself and the other officers for dinner in the mess. You wouldn't mind if we picked your wits a bit about your experiences in Vietnam? We British haven't had a really good insurgency to fight since Malaya."

"Be delighted, Ken. I'll probably have a young lady visiting here for a week or ten days."

"Bring her along. The men would really enjoy that. I'll expect you both."

Fitz walked to the door with the two Brits and opened it.

"Oh, by the way, Lodd." Falmey's afterthought was studiedly casual. "Don't get into trouble in that homemade Q-boat. We have nothing against a bit of gold smuggling, but we wouldn't like to hear of a shooting incident between a Dubai dhow and an Indian patrol launch. There is the odd British adviser aboard Indian naval craft from time to time, you know."

Fitz, caught off guard, was unable to control the startled expression that came to his face. Falmey chuckled mirthlessly. "Oh, you needn't worry, we're not going to tip off the wogs. Our job is to protect Rashid's interests."

"Yes," Fitz concurred. "He is spending millions of pounds with British engineering firms."

CHAPTER 12

The flight from Tehran arrived in Dubai at thirty minutes after noon. Fitz stood up in the large hall above the runway watching the Iran Air jet taxi up to the spiral concrete ramp and cut its screaming engines. A motley procession of turbaned Indians, Arabs in robes and *kuffiyahs* on their heads, some followed by black-shrouded women walking obediently a few steps to the rear and left of their husbands, and a few Iranians and Westerners trickled out of the plane and up the ramp. And then Fitz's heart caught as he saw Laylah, a queen among the rabble, descend the steps from the jet, cross the concrete, and start up the ramp circling to the terminal. Her long black hair gleaming and rippling, she smiled into the sun as she stared up at the visitors behind the glass walls of the upper floor of the building. Fitz waved vigorously. She saw him, waved back, and then was ascending the spiral walkway.

Fitz walked over to the white-robed and headdressed immigration officer as a reminder that his female visitor was a special guest of the Ruler. It took a long time for the straggling passengers to pass through Immigration and finally Laylah reached the officer. He looked at her in wonderment. Never had he seen such a strikingly beautiful young woman, her lightweight, near diaphanous dress revealing the full breasts and trim figure underneath. It was precisely such provoking sights of femininity that the Arab culture most strongly guarded against.

Since the immigration officer was expecting the young American woman, he quickly passed her through after eying her a few moments. Finally her suitcase was placed in front of her and the alerted customs officer merely waved her through the door.

Although he wanted to take her in his arms and kiss her, such a display would have been gauche in the extreme here. He took Laylah's bag.

"I'll greet you properly when we get home," he promised.

She followed him from the terminal. He placed her bag in the rear of the Land Rover and helped her up the high step into the passenger's seat and then walked around and jumped up into the driver's seat on the right-hand side of the British-made vehicle.

"Welcome to Dubai, Venice of the Gulf, Port of Pearls." He leaned over and kissed her. Laylah kissed him back, the point of her tongue vibrating between his partially open lips.

"My God, it's hot and humid," she said after the kiss.

Fitz started up the engine. "We'll be air-conditioned soon." As they drove along, Fitz listlessly pointed out the sights but Laylah hardly looked about her, the effort was so great in the midday inferno. Crossing the Maktoum Bridge, Fitz turned toward the Gulf and the beach area known as Jumiera. Shaikh Rashid's palace was off to their left and Laylah turned her head slightly to look as Fitz announced it. Ten minutes later they were parking in front of the house and Fitz leaned on the horn, summoning Peter.

He hustled the suitcase into the front door, Fitz ushering Laylah in behind the Pakistani servant and closing the door after them. "Oh, Fitz, what a relief," Laylah breathed. "How did anyone stand it here before air conditioning?"

She wandered over to the large picture window and looked out over the beach and the waters of the Gulf. "How beautiful. You must be very happy."

"I am now that you're here."

Peter reappeared from the hallway to the rooms. "Memsahib want a drink?"

"A gin and tonic?" Fitz asked.

"Why not?" She looked back over the beach. "I'll bet it would be fun to run out there and jump in the water."

"Right now?" Fitz asked.

Laylah shook her head slowly. "Afterwards."

"No point in wasting time," Fitz agreed. Peter returned from the kitchen with the two drinks. Fitz took them. To Peter he said, "Wait for lunch." Then he led Laylah back down the hall to his bedroom, which also looked over the blue waters, put the drinks

on the bedside table, and she sank onto the double bed beside
him.

"I've been really waiting for this," he said, pulling her to him.

"Me too." They kissed for a few minutes and then sat up word-
lessly and shed their clothes. Fitz's new sense of self-confidence
gave him a feeling of freedom and power. Laylah wanted him as
much as he wanted her. And he was, or soon would be, a successful and powerful man, fully worthy of holding and loving a young
woman like Laylah. In Bandar Abbas, Laylah had, he realized,
supplied much of the impetus in their actual sexual play; this time
he would initiate the flow of passionate intercourse.

They kissed deeply, lying beside each other as he murmured
love phrases into the hollows between her neck and shoulders and
kissed her breasts and then gave loving attention to each of the
nipples until they jutted out. Instinctively he knew she wanted
him to continue his kisses down her body. He buried his face in
her belly, his tongue darting into her navel as she held his head
tightly to her.

As he retreated down her body his feet reached the end of the
bed, on which they were lying crossways, his face burying itself
into the silky black hair. His tongue found its way through the
thick, compellingly scented dark pubescence and made the intimate contact. After some moments Fitz looked upwards along her
flat stomach and, seeing her beautiful face framed between her
breasts, her head on a pillow, he was surprised to see tears welling
in her eyes and, as he continued the sensual kissing, the tears
streamed down her face. Clearly they were tears of ecstatic pleasure, for her fingers, entangled in his hair, held his head to her.

Suddenly she moaned and then cried out to him, her fingers in
his hair pulling his head up her body. He wriggled his way
completely back onto the bed, his body next to hers. Laylah's
fingers disengaged themselves from his hair, reaching for and guiding him into the softness he had lately been kissing. Joyfully he
knew that he had succeeded in giving her even more delight than
he had their first time, a month ago. He felt her capture and pul-
sate around him, her buttocks moving hard against him.

"Oh God, Fitz!" she cried, her tear-filled eyes wide. "Now! I
want it all! Now . . ." Her cries trailed off as he felt all the
strength of his being gush into her and the tension drain from

both of them, his limp body atop hers. Vaguely he realized that despite the night of rather puritan if vigorous lovemaking they had shared in Bandar Abbas, they had in their first moments of this encounter, only the beginning of a whole week together, reached a plateau higher than anything they had known before.

For some time the only sound in the room was the gradually slowing breathing of the two as they lay together, savoring their experience.

Finally Laylah breathed in a low tone, "Fitz?"

"Mmmm?"

"Have you been practicing or something?"

"Here?" His voice rose. "You've got to be kidding."

Sleepily she said, "Wow! And six whole days to go."

They lay together a few more minutes and when Fitz felt able he reached over to the bedside table, found his gin and tonic, the ice mostly melted by now, and took a long drink.

"Me too." Laylah's voice was almost inaudible.

Unsteadily Fitz handed her the glass. She took a sip and handed it back to him. He put it on the table and fell back beside her. After a few more minutes Laylah stirred again.

"Why don't we go for a swim. Then we can come back to bed refreshed."

Fitz couldn't believe what was happening. He had made this glamorous, unattainable girl want him, give herself to him as he had wanted to give himself to her. Truly he would never again be drab old Fitz Lodd.

He watched as Laylah sat up on the edge of the bed and stretched, her breasts, their nipples pointing upward, silhouetted in the glare of sunlight beyond the translucent curtains. Lightly she jumped to her feet and walked across the bedroom and opened the door. The door to her room was directly across the hall from his door.

Fitz did not move quite as briskly as Laylah but he managed to get up, pull open a dresser drawer, and take out a bathing suit. In the almost three weeks since Sepah had invited him to move in here he had only once, the second day, had a swim.

Holding hands, Fitz and Laylah walked out the sliding glass door facing the walled-in section of beach outside the house. At the far end of the enclosure Fitz opened the gate and they were out on the wide beach, stretching hundreds of miles along the Arabian Gulf in either direction.

Laylah started running toward the water, Fitz right behind her. The waters of the Gulf were in the mid-eighties, but with the air temperature about a hundred and twenty degrees, the water felt cool by contrast and they splashed around for fifteen minutes before coming out into the heat. Back inside the enclosure they sipped on gin and tonics until the sun had evaporated the water from their bodies and the heat became once more oppressive.

After lunch, at about three-thirty, they went back to the master bedroom and after more lovemaking fell asleep. Dusk was gathering when they woke up.

"I forgot to tell you, we're having dinner at the home of my associate in the project that started on my last trip to Iran. He's Persian and so is his wife. She hardly ever has a chance to talk Farsee with anyone here."

Laylah brightened. "I'll be happy to chat with her. How old is she?"

"I suppose in her thirties, she's younger than Sepah."

"I'd better start to get ready. I haven't unpacked."

While Laylah took a long, leisurely bath and washed her hair, Fitz sat in the living room, relishing the delight of having Laylah with him in his house and starting out on a new, exciting, and prosperous career.

Then Laylah, her hair turbaned in a thick towel, came in, holding a round gadget by its handle, a long spout coming out the other end.

"Fitz, my hair dryer doesn't work when I plug it in."

"That's because we don't have electricity yet. It takes all the power from the generator to keep the air conditioning going."

"What am I going to do?" she wailed. "My hair takes hours to dry by itself."

This was a situation Fitz had failed to foresee and he thought about it for a while. "I guess the only thing we can do is turn off the air conditioning and switch the power over to the house circuit."

Bemused by this additional delight of having a woman in his house, Fitz went out to the kitchen and thence to the generator house beyond, next to Peter's quarters. "Peter!" he called. There was no answer. He banged on the door to Peter's room but still no answer. Then, wondering if Peter had perhaps become sick or somehow hurt himself, Fitz pushed open the door.

Peter was not hurt and not sick by the normal definition of the term. Rather Peter was sprawled on his bed, his hand on the floor of the room near to a quarter-filled bottle of scotch. "Oh my God!" Fitz thought. "I'm going to have to keep the liquor locked up." All the little niceties of having a real home were becoming apparent to him. He left his servant's room and walked around to the generator shed. The working of the homemade electrical supply had been explained to him by one of Sepah's engineers and it took little time to switch the generator power over to household current. By the time he returned to the living room the temperature in the house was already rising.

"Dry your hair as fast as possible, my sweet," Fitz called to her. He heard the hair dryer whir into action and he stood in the living room, feeling the outside heat seep in.

It took less than ten minutes for the temperature to climb into the nineties. He walked back to the guest bathroom.

"At some point you'll have to reach a compromise between how much heat you can take and how dry your hair really has to be," Fitz said, laughing. He walked out and pulled the sliding glass doors open to catch what breeze might come across the Gulf and opened the front door to create some slight air movement. What a hard land this must have been to live in during the summer, he thought. And of course it still is for most of the people. During the day he could see the people in the streets suffering in silent misery. He understood why it was the Arabs seemed to age much faster than Westerners. It was easy to understand why most of the British residents of the Trucial States leave the Gulf during the insufferable summer months.

Finally Laylah appeared in the living room, perspiration on her face. "I hope your friends' home is air-conditioned."

"Sepah has one of the few air-conditioned houses in Dubai. And before I forget to tell you, he owns this place. He's just letting me use it until I can get a place of my own."

"I'll help you look, Fitz." She walked over and kissed him. He stood up and started to hold her. "Hey, love," she protested, "get the cool going first."

Fitz nodded and went back to the generator shed and switched the juice back to air conditioning.

It was fast getting dark now and Fitz went around lighting oil lamps and candles. There were just two electric lights hooked into the generator when it was on air conditioning, an outside light to guide Fitz home and one bulb in the hall which partially illuminated the living room. In minutes the house was cool again.

"How long do you have to go on like this?" Laylah asked.

"Shaikh Rashid, the Ruler, hopes to have central generators and electricity for all of Dubai in a couple of more years. When the oil royalties come in he'll really be able to modernize his country."

"I think I could learn to like it here." Laylah smiled suggestively. "Of course there would have to be a lot of incentive."

"I would be happy the rest of my life trying to provide that incentive," Fitz said earnestly.

Fitz and Laylah stepped out into the hundred-degree evening and ambled to the Land Rover. He helped her into the vehicle and then walked around and swung himself up into the driver's seat, started the engine, and backed out of the driveway.

Beautiful, if somewhat wilted, Laylah walked up to the front door of Sepah's home on the Creek, which opened for them before they could ring the bell. They were bowed in by a Pakistani servant who, Fitz realized, closely resembled Peter. Probably his brother, since Peter had been assigned to Fitz's house by Sepah's staff.

Laylah preceded him into the cool home, and as the servant closed the door Fitz muttered to him, "Peter is drunk."

"Yes, sahib. Must lock up all liquor," the servant agreed.

Sepah took Laylah's hand and bent low, kissing it as Fitz introduced her. Then he introduced Laylah to his wife, Sira, and as Laylah greeted her hostess in her native Farsee, Sira smiled happily. For a while all conversation was held in Farsee. Fitz was weak in the language but he could make out what was being said and hesitatingly attempted a contribution to the conversation.

As Fitz had hoped, Sepah's servant brought out the Iranian caviar and iced vodka and placed the tray before them. It was a delightful scene, Fitz thought. Sira was wearing a basically Western-type white slip of a dress with a brightly colored silk shawl thrown over one shoulder. Laylah was similarly attired and the two women looked quite exotic. Both Fitz and Sepah wore Western slacks and short-sleeved open shirts. In the time he had known Sepah he had never seen him affect the Arab *dish dasha* and *kuffiyah*.

As the two women talked about what was happening in Tehran, Sepah and Fitz took a few moments to talk business.

"It may be that we will make our run a little earlier than I thought."

"Whenever you say," Fitz replied agreeably. "As soon as the thirty-calibers are mounted my job will be finished."

"Not quite," Sepah reminded him.

"I'll be ready to head out to sea when you are."

"It's mainly getting the syndicate to enlarge the value of the shipment now. We're going to leave the Creek with the biggest load of gold that ever went out of here on a single boat."

Sira protested the business conversation and the two men began talking with the ladies about everything from Persian rugs to the new hotels going up in Tehran. Sira, it seemed, could only abide half a year in Dubai. She did not like sitting at home when her husband went out so many nights to the Arab gatherings from which women were barred. She did not wear the black veil and mask of the Arab women and this made her an outcast among the women of the Arab society in which her husband moved.

After they had finished the caviar and a servant had cleared off the coffee table, Sira led the way to the dining room. A real Persian shish kebab was served with a vintage Chablis imported from France. Laylah declared that even in Tehran she had not enjoyed a dinner so much. Sira, Sepah announced proudly, had cooked dinner herself.

When dinner was over, Sira took Laylah back to her private parlor as Fitz and Sepah repaired to the living room. "Majid Jabir may drop around," Sepah mentioned. "He wants to hear how we are progressing. He is most important to the syndicate. As you may have surmised, the Ruler is looking forward to receiving us *after* this very controversial and delicate voyage has been completed successfully."

"I sensed something of the sort," Fitz allowed.

"If it wasn't that both of us were actually going to be aboard the ship, if you had merely rigged the armaments for it, things would be different. But naturally, if after a fight in which we destroy Indian boats and kill Indian personnel we should be caught, the Ruler and his advisers have to be in a position to disclaim any responsibility."

"Of course," Fitz agreed. "I don't see why a man as successful as you is taking the chance of personally commanding the voyage."

"Perhaps I didn't make myself clear, Fitz. There have been three accidents in a row at the hands of the Indian Coast Guard on the high seas. If this trip is not successful, I am wiped out. Everything I have in the world, everything I have saved is at risk. So why not send the finest *nakhouda* on the Gulf, myself, to captain this expedition."

"You answered my question."

A servant materialized, walked to the door, and opened it. Majid Jabir entered, wearing the flowing robes and headdress. Sepah stood up and welcomed him, showing him to a seat. Except that his left hand was not constantly caressing a string of worry beads, he appeared the epitome of the upper-class city Arab. It was known that Majid was often sent on special assignments to Beirut and London on Shaikh Rashid's business and that he had a complete London-tailored Western wardrobe, which indeed he preferred for these occasions.

The three talked for some minutes, Majid accepting a cigar though nothing alcoholic to drink. This was something he had not yet learned to handle.

Majid smiled at Fitz, perhaps a little apologetically. "I hear you had a visit from Colonel Buttres and the *mua'atamad*."

"You didn't tell me." Sepah looked surprised as Fitz answered in the positive.

"I was going to. The TOS seems to have a pretty good intelligence system. Those two Brits worked me over a bit, the Mutt and Jeff system, you know? Ken Buttres was the good guy on my side, Falmey the hostile, indignant one."

"It is annoying, to understate the matter," Majid said, "to have the British still telling us how to run our own countries here on the Gulf. They hold us in a form of bondage, really. They do have the gunboats, the military, and the RAF to enforce their damned truces and agreements. We'll all be better off when they get out."

"If they get out," Sepah added.

"Oh, they will. When I was last in London I discovered that the Prime Minister and his Labour Government have absolutely made up their minds that England can no longer police the world and in particular the Arabian Gulf. It won't be long before they announce they're pulling out of here, giving us independence from their ruling our rulers."

"I always thought you liked the British and were dependent upon them for protection and guidance." Fitz deliberately primed the Arab's sense of outrage.

"We like the British businessmen, not that they aren't part and parcel of the British Government, a Brit is a Brit, but at least the businessmen play the game, find out what's what, and act accordingly. Not so their diplomats and Political Agents for the most part. They treat us like children, manipulate us as though we couldn't handle our own affairs."

"Well, I can tell you old Brian Falmey treated me like a lower-form boy at an English public school last time I saw him a few days ago."

A wide grin spread across Majid's face from one edge of his *kuffiyah* to the other. "He came to me too, wanted to know what I knew about you. He actually said, Fitz, that it was his opinion that you were involved in the Iran link of an arms-importing syndicate." Majid looked at Sepah. "The *mua'atamad* even implicated you."

"What did you say?" Sepah asked.

"Only that anything you were involved in had the effect of improving the economy of Dubai, which is prospering without oil and able to spend millions of pounds with British engineering interests."

"He didn't talk to you about a Communist insurgency?" Fitz asked.

"Oh, he came up with some nonsense about guns coming into the Trucial States might be on their way to Communists, whatever that means."

"I have to admit Falmey and Colonel Buttres may have a reason for concern on that front," Fitz remarked.

Majid looked from Fitz to Sepah. "Now there's the true Westerner. Always worried that there's a Communist ready to jump out from behind the nearest tree."

"And there usually is," Fitz concluded. "In any case, the Brits believe in Dubai re-exporting. Falmey said he wouldn't tell on us to the wogs, meaning that the secret of the hull buster in the guts of Sepah's dhow will be kept."

"Oh, they are with us on that," Sepah agreed. "We buy enormous quantities of gold from London."

Majid, obviously, was unwilling to be drawn too deeply into a conversation that might directly lead into the arming of a Dubai boat. He was, after all, the top Arab in Customs, there being only a friendly British adviser above him in this capacity. "Fitz," he said, changing the subject, "forgive me for not thanking you immediately when I walked into here for your princely gift. It is one of the most valued carpets in my collection."

"I'm happy that I was able to pick a carpet that would appeal to your cultured taste," Fitz replied.

Sepah stood up. He walked to the dining room and called out for his wife to join them. In moments Sira and Laylah entered the room.

Majid's eyes ranged appraisingly over Laylah and he went to her, took her hand, and kissed it as he was introduced. Then, after greeting Sira, he turned to Fitz. "So this was the reason for your visit to Tehran recently. Now I understand." He turned to Laylah. "I hope you find Dubai pleasant, Miss Smith, despite the heat at this time of year. If you will stay with us for another month, or return, you will find that except for the summer we have a very salubrious climate here in this part of the Gulf."

"I am looking forward to getting to know your country," Laylah replied.

Majid made a deprecating gesture. "Oh, this isn't my country, Miss Smith, although I am trying to make it so. Allah, in his infinite wisdom, saw fit to allow a rather abrasive tension to develop between the British director of customs in my native Qatar and myself as his chief Arab deputy. Fortunately, the most distant and dreary exile he could conceive of for me where there was a vacancy in the customs department was Dubai. I was given the opportunity to come here or"—he spread his hands—"cease working under the direction and guidance of Her Britannic Majesty's Customs." Majid smiled broadly. "Someday I will reward that Brit suitably with a high-paying job on contract to us here even though he was only Allah's messenger. He didn't really intend to send me to the center of the greatest opportunity on the Gulf."

"The Lord works in mysterious ways his wonders to perform," Laylah intoned, giving Fitz a smile.

For another hour the talk concerned Dubai and the people who lived in the Creek community and the many more who would be coming, particularly when oil production began. Then Fitz and Laylah excused themselves, leaving Sepah and Majid to discuss whatever business they had alone.

The air had cooled to the mid-nineties and when they arrived back at Fitz's home and parked the Land Rover, Laylah suggested a midnight swim.

"I'm not sure we should," Fitz said. "I've heard that the slavers still come out here to Jumiera and take people off the beach to sell as slaves in Oman and Saudi."

"Oh, Fitz. In this day and age? That's ridiculous."

Ten minutes later they were once again out under the stars, a crescent moon providing a soft shimmering light. Naked, they walked to the edge of the Gulf where the waters gently lapped at the sand. Fitz couldn't help but be uneasy and he looked up and down the beach as they splashed into the water. Certainly there was nobody to be seen and soon he relaxed and played with Laylah in the warm Gulf seas. When they had enough swimming Fitz followed Laylah onto the sand and they ran back to the enclosure, where their towels were waiting. It thrilled Fitz to the core of his being to towel the salt water from Laylah's body. Gently he dried each firm breast, kissing the nipples as she laughed merrily. Then he dried her long legs from ankles up to the black tuft at their confluence and reluctantly turned her around to rub her back. When she was dry Laylah took her towel and thoroughly dried off Fitz before they went back into the cold house.

He led her through the living room and the hallway to his room, where he embraced her and pulled her onto the bed.

"Help," she cried, "I've been captured by a white slaver."

"Yes," he roared in mock ferocity, "and I am going to hold your beautiful white body in bondage—forever!"

"Forever?"

"Yes." Then they were holding and caressing each other as though forever would end tomorrow.

CHAPTER 13

At one in the afternoon two days later, with Peter dressed neatly in white slacks, a white shirt, and a red band around his waist and two helpers he had borrowed from Sepah's house in the kitchen, Fitz and Laylah gave Fitz's first luncheon party since his arrival in Dubai. John Stakes brought the newly arrived Harcourt Thornwell.

Thornwell was tall, in his early thirties, and wore a seersucker suit, regimental stripe tie, and white shoes. He carried himself with the aristocratic self-assuredness of one born and brought up in old-family affluence. He was the epitome of upper-class America, the America Fitz never could hope to be part of and to which he felt inferior. Thornwell and Laylah were part of the same world, Fitz recognized, and he wished the handsome young Bostonian had not arrived in Dubai while Laylah was here.

"Please," Thornwell said to Fitz and Laylah, "don't call me Mr. Thornwell, that's my father. I'm Courty, always have been, I guess I always will."

"Welcome to Dubai, Courty," Laylah said graciously. "I've only been here a few days myself."

"Courty," Stakes said, "let me introduce you to Majid Jabir. Then we can come back and talk to Laylah and Fitz." Courty allowed himself to be pulled away.

"He seems to have come down with an instant crush on you," Fitz remarked to Laylah. "Can't say as I blame him."

"He's a very nice-looking young man," Laylah remarked. "I'm sure we'll get into a game of who-do-you-know in Boston and Philadelphia. I'll bet he went to Harvard."

"Is that so great?"

"Not really. It's just that he has that clubman look."

"His family are supposed to be old, rich, and established."

"Yes. I know of the Thornwells. I wonder what he's doing here."

"I'll tell you all about it, unless he tells you first, in which case I'd appreciate your passing it all along to me."

Colonel Buttres and Brian Falmey arrived together and walked over to Fitz and Laylah. Fitz introduced the two British gallants to Laylah, with whom they were charmed. "Brian and Ken think I have some mysterious reason for wanting to go to Iran," Fitz said to her, laughing. Then turning to the Brits: "Gentlemen, does a man need, would he indeed have time to attend to, any other incentive than this in Tehran?"

The colonel and the *mua'atamad* were vehement in agreeing with Fitz.

"Colonel"—a mischievous look came into Laylah's eyes—"is it true that there is still slavery in this part of the world? I mean, do slave sellers invade the beaches here and carry off people to take to slave markets someplace?"

"I would be very careful, if I were you, Miss Smith," Buttres said with a twinkle in his eye. "Any man given the chance would pinch you off Jumiera beach and take you out to his desert stronghold."

"How exciting," Laylah replied.

"I should think she'd easily be worth three hundred camels," Brian Falmey attempted jocularly.

Fender Browne arrived with a handsome Scandinavian-looking woman in her late thirties or early forties and introduced his wife, Inga, to Fitz and Laylah and the others who hadn't yet met Mrs. Browne. Sepah arrived with Sira, who moved to Laylah's side as her husband and Tim McLaren melted off into a corner to talk business.

As the party went on, Laylah made one announcement. "There are extra bathing suits in the bathhouse outside if anybody wants to swim. I'm going in."

None of the Arab guests chose to swim, but Laylah and Courty Thornwell and Colonel Buttres decided to take a plunge in the Gulf and were joined by Fender Browne and his wife, who had brought their swimsuits.

As Fitz stood alone at the side of the wide picture window looking out at the bathers splashing in the warm blue Gulf waters,

Majid Jabir seemed to materialize beside him, the robes and headdress imparting a spectral appearance to the Arab's presence.

"Fitz." There was an urgency to Majid's tone which focused Fitz's attention on the adviser to the Ruler. "I learned a piece of intelligence this morning which I believe you could put to good advantage."

"Your information is always the most important," Fitz replied. "What have you got?"

"Thornwell and Stakes want you to accompany them to see Shaikh Zayed of Abu Dhabi and help them convince him to put money into this communications syndicate in America, yes?"

Fitz nodded.

"And you need to see Shaikh Hamed of Kajmira regarding the oil concession," Majid continued. Again Fitz nodded.

"It has come to my attention that over the Sabbath, next Thursday and Friday, Shaikh Hamed is traveling to Al Ain to visit with Shaikh Zayed. Hamed needs to fix his creek and wants to borrow the money from Zayed to steel-plate the crumbling sides the way we did here in Dubai. Zayed is the only one of the Trucial States rulers presently taking oil revenues."

Fitz nodded in interest. "I've always heard that if you want an interview with Zayed he is most receptive out on that oasis."

"Quite true. Zayed is a Bedou at heart. He lived out on the Buraimi Oasis most of his life while his brother Shakbut was Ruler, and then when the family decided to depose Shakbut and make Zayed Ruler he still retained his interest and love for Al Ain. He is building a dual highway directly across the desert from Al Ain to the Gulf and having trees planted the entire hundred and twenty kilometers. Hamed could dredge his creek, shore it up, and build a new town of Kajmira for a fraction of what that job will cost."

"He could also buy several large daily newspapers in the major cities of the U.S. for that money, with a couple of television stations thrown in," Fitz commented.

"Thornwell's scheme could work," Majid said thoughtfully. "But of course he doesn't know Arabs."

"I tried to explain to him that attempting to get two rulers working together harmoniously on a joint endeavor was unrealistic. But maybe, in this case, it just might work."

Letting the subject of Thornwell drop, Majid went on. "Now
Hamed really needs money. Rashid has shown the states that even
without oil, if their creeks are in good order and they can adjust to
Western ways to a certain extent, they can develop a successful
economy. Hamed is an old man but he wants the best for Kajmira
and for his sons. I think you could get that oil concession to
explore and develop for three years by paying under a million dollars in three installments a year apart. This would also help him in
his negotiations with Zayed for a loan."

"You think I should go to Al Ain then?"

"I happen to know old Hamed is looking forward to meeting
the notorious American colonel. And the same is true of Zayed."

Fitz frowned slightly. "I just hate to leave Laylah alone for the
two days it will take to get there and back."

"Take her with you," Majid urged. "Zayed has a nice guest
house, surrounded by date palms. I'll send a driver up tomorrow
to make all the arrangements for you and request appointments
with Zayed."

"How do we find Hamed?"

"I'll talk to him on the telephone tomorrow," Majid promised.
"This is a good opportunity for you and all of us."

"That would be a good solution, Majid." Fitz looked out at the
swimmers, noticing that young Thornwell was never more than a
foot or two away from Laylah as they splashed in the diminutive
surf. "We'll go out in two or three days. By the way, I understand
that Rashid is interested in both of these deals. Wouldn't it help
for him to send a letter?"

"I believe Fender Browne told you it was best to leave Shaikh
Rashid out of the oil affair for the time being."

"Maybe you would like to send a note?" Fitz teased, knowing
perfectly well that as long as there was the slightest chance of his
being compromised in the coming gold expedition nobody official
wanted to be tied too closely to him, or Sepah for that matter.

"Completely unnecessary," Majid almost snapped. "I'll have
the driver stop by the palace and tell the Ruler's secretary to expect you in Al Ain."

"I'll plan to be there, Majid." He walked out into the enclosure
and through the gate to the back edge of the beach. Laylah,
splashing about with Thornwell, saw him, waved, and started

GOLD   129

swimming toward the beach, calling to the others to come to
lunch. Fitz hastened back into the air-conditioned villa. Tim
McLaren came up to him.

"I want to thank you, Fitz, for getting Sepah thinking in terms
of my bank. I think we'll be doing some business in the next couple of weeks."

"How are your deposits coming along?" Fitz asked.

"I expect you will have some substantial sums soon that will
need care."

"I hope so, Tim. I suppose you're getting in on some of the
gold sales to Sepah?"

"That I am. It won't be long before I'm able to convince them
back in New York to build a real bank here. We're already outgrow-
ing the quonset hut."

Peter and his crew outdid themselves preparing luncheon.
Laylah was clearly the hit of the party and Fitz couldn't help
think what a great life it would be here if she were his wife. Then
he frowned to himself. Of course, there was the problem of Marie,
but she had promised him a divorce if he would come back to the
States and work it out.

By four in the afternoon most of the guests had left to go home
and only John Stakes and Harcourt Thornwell were still at Fitz's
house. By now Courty was thoroughly smitten with Laylah. Fitz
found it difficult to stifle the vague hostility which possessed him.
Thornwell was really the type one would visualize Laylah marrying. Like herself, he was from a substantial family, he was personally wealthy, the right age for her, and a handsome young man.
By now they had established a number of mutual acquaintances
and even decided they had met briefly at someone's family Christ-
mas party in Chestnut Hill outside Philadelphia.

· John Stakes was eagerly trying to get the discussion centered on
business, and finally Courty brought out the large leatherette presentation case he had carried with him. He opened it up, making
an easel which he set on the dining-room table so Fitz and Laylah
could study it.

"Very nice," Fitz couldn't help observing.

"This is the one we use if we can't show the movie presentation
I made. I had some Arabs at the UN help me," Courty explained.
"As you can see, the presentation is divided down the center of

each page. Arabic and English opposite each other." Thornwell
flipped the first page over and Fitz was startled to see a picture of
himself peering out of a newspaper column pasted to the page
with the Arabic translation of the column to its right.

"I never saw that clipping," Fitz remarked.

"When John told me you would become part of this plan I dug
up most of the press coverage on your statement about Jews.
Hope it doesn't distress you too much to see what they said about
you, particularly in the New York *Star*, but this should be golden
to the Arabs we show it to."

Briefly Fitz skimmed the commentary. "Anti-Semitism in the
U. S. Army," read the headline. If this was a sample of the tempest
Sam Gold had stirred up, Fitz didn't wonder that the Ambassador
was so anxious to have him retire quickly.

Courty Thornwell flipped a few more pages. "How unfair,
biased, and hypocritical!" Laylah exclaimed.

"Wait until you see some of the other coverage on Arab affairs
I have put into this presentation," Courty said. "And then I'll
show you the television shows I taped and had put on 16-mm.
film so that the Arabs we visit can see for themselves the way they
are treated in the media."

As Fitz and Laylah watched, Courty flipped the pages of his
presentation. Story after slanted story on the Arab world came up.
"Now come on, Courty," Fitz finally interjected, "the U.S. press
isn't really as anti-Arab as this selection of clippings would suggest. Somewhere, some writer must have had something fair to say
about Arab leaders and Arab aspirations."

Thornwell shrugged. "Maybe, but I didn't come across any."

"I was in the United States for three years at college before I
came to Tehran a year ago with the Embassy," Laylah said. "I
didn't get the impression that the newspapers were as anti-Arab as
this presentation makes it look."

"Let's just say that the print media is biased in favor of the
Jews," Courty replied. "Perhaps my presentation comes on a little
strong in this respect but that's why I'm over here after all, to get
a few billion Arab petrodollars committed to buying a big share of
the U.S. communications industry. You know how the Arabs
think—in outrageous hyperbole. Everything is exaggerated. If I
came on showing that the American newspapers are fifty-one to

forty-nine in favor of the Jews, John Stakes and I aren't going to get that big Arab money behind my plan to put together the most powerful communications organization in the world. It's as simple as that."

He went on flipping the pages, stopping at some of the more scurrilous stories of Arab atrocities against Jewish soldiers in the Six Day War. When he had gone through the presentation Courty flipped the pages back. "Well, what do you think?"

"If I was an Arab leader I'd be pretty upset," Fitz allowed. "What newspapers do you think can be bought by this pro-Arab communications company?"

"The way the unions are acting in New York it won't be hard to pick up a paper if we move fast," Thornwell answered. "And I happen to know that Time, Inc., is in big trouble with *Life* magazine. It's just a question of having the money ready and grabbing at the right time. So it may take ten years to put the whole thing together. The main thing is that it can be done if the money, big money, is available. Someday the unions are going to seriously threaten to put the New York *Times* out of business. We should be ready to grab it. The Sulzbergers and the Ochs family aren't going to put up with losing money on a large scale indefinitely in order to keep their paper, but it would be well worthwhile for the Arabs to lose a few million a year and keep giving the unions everything they ask for until that left-wing Jewish rag, the New York *Star*, folds trying to keep up."

"I think you are an anti-Semite, Courty," Laylah declared.

"Not at all, not even slightly. I'm just pro getting a powerful communications organization into existence. This is the only way for me to do it I can see."

"How do you intend to get TV stations?" Fitz asked. "They're all gold mines, I hear."

"True, but at the moment the American Broadcasting Company is in financial trouble. A hundred million dollars would take it and with it control of one third of the network television news America sees on its sets. This is what I've got to make the Arabs understand." He turned to Fitz. "I should say what *we* have to make the Arabs understand. We are giving them an opportunity to buy American opinion. How do we sell them, Fitz?"

Fitz slowly shook his head. "I don't know, Courty. I am not

sure that the Arab mind can grasp the concept. They have no frame of reference to help them understand what you are trying to explain to them. The rulers over here are an insular lot, even the best of them like Rashid. King Faisal of Saudi Arabia is your man to get this action going, but I doubt if even he could understand the value of investing a billion dollars, which of course he has, monthly, in U.S. communications."

"I disagree, Fitz," John Stakes broke in. "I know these people, probably longer than you have. I think we can convince them. Are you willing to try at least?"

"The profits will be enormous," Thornwell said. "My family corporation made a four hundred percent profit on their paltry few millions I shoved into newspapers and television stations when that board of Bostonians decided there was going to be a depression and sold out. You'll be in for a nice piece of the action, Fitz."

"It will be interesting to see where we get," Fitz replied noncommittally. "The reason the Arabs can never win a war is that you can't make them work together, even within the same family. The Arab world is devoted to fratricide, patricide, and regicide. That's how rulers change. Even Faisal, the mightiest Ruler in the Arab world, is bound to be deposed or assassinated by restless members of his family."

"But you will give it a go, Fitz?" Stakes asked anxiously. "It is mostly on the strength of our conversation a couple of weeks ago that Courty came over here." Courty nodded his head.

"As a matter of fact, we're going to give it a try in just a few days." Fitz explained to Stakes and Thornwell about the coming trip Shaikh Hamed was taking to Al Ain.

"We'll be able to see two rulers in the same town," Fitz said. "That is an opportunity you don't get very often."

Both John Stakes and Courty Thornwell were delighted with the news. The Ruler of Abu Dhabi was number one on the list of rulers they wanted to expose to the presentation.

"I'll tell Majid Jabir to have his messenger contact Sir Harry Olmstead, who runs Shaikh Zayed's stud farm. Sir Harry was the Political Resident when Zayed became Ruler in Abu Dhabi in place of his brother Shakbut. He is probably Zayed's best friend among Westerners. A fine old gentleman. He can be very helpful to us."

"Good, we'll need all the help we can get."

"I understand that Zayed has built a guest house on the farm. That's probably where we'll stay."

"It all sounds exciting," Laylah said. "I'd love to meet a real Arab Ruler."

"If anyone can arrange it, it's Sir Harry," Stakes said confidently.

With the sun dropping toward the desert floor behind them, Thornwell querulously asked John Stakes, "What do you do for action in this country when the day is over?"

"Not much, my boy," Stakes replied. "It's a good place to come if, like me, you enjoy reading a great deal."

"There's just so much time you can spend with your nose in a book," Thornwell answered. "Aren't there any bars or night clubs or something of the sort? There must be enough people here to keep a good joint making money for its owners."

"I've been thinking the same thing," Fitz agreed. "As a matter of fact, I've been toying with the idea of opening up a small hotel and restaurant with entertainment."

"Whoever does it first should end up with a lot of business," Thornwell commented. "They'd have plenty from me."

Fitz, who had shared Laylah with his guests all day, Thornwell in particular, was in no mood to invite the young man to stay around any longer. Laylah would be returning to Tehran soon enough. In a subtle effort to get Thornwell and Stakes on their way, Fitz said, "Maybe tomorrow night, after dark, you could bring your projector and the films over so we can see the television presentation. I'll have to turn off the air conditioning long enough to run the movies but we should have a look."

"I'll be glad to, Fitz," Thornwell confirmed.

"We're having a meeting with the Ruler in the morning," Stakes added. "Will you join us?"

"I'd like to, John, but for various reasons I think it would be better if I didn't. Rashid knows we're working together and he'll give you a most attentive hearing. I will of course see Zayed in Abu Dhabi with you. I'll go to the other countries with you as long as the trip doesn't conflict with certain commitments here."

"Good enough then, Fitz." Stakes glanced at Thornwell, who was having difficulty taking his eyes off Laylah. "Tell you what, after our meeting with the Ruler we'll come by and tell you what happened."

"Fine. We'll be here."

"We can have a swim and some lunch," Laylah added, and Thornwell brightened considerably.

Just about noon the following day, after Courty Thornwell, Stakes, Fitz, and Laylah had finished a long swim in the Gulf, an emissary of Sepah's arrived with a letter. Fitz opened and read it and then looked at Laylah in disappointment. The message read that the deckhouse was to be swung into place tonight on the new dhow and Fitz should be present to install the hardware. There was no way he could tell Sepah that he didn't want to leave Laylah.

"What's the matter, Fitz?" Laylah asked.

"Sepah has work for me tonight, unfortunately. As soon as the temperature goes down a bit after dark I'll have to meet him."

"Can I come with you?" Laylah asked.

"I'm afraid not. This is a job I have to do at the boatyard."

"We'll look after Laylah for you," John Stakes volunteered, obviously pleased at the opportunity.

"Sure, no problem," Courty chimed in. "And we'll be here to have a nightcap with you when you get home."

This wasn't Fitz's idea of how Laylah could best spend her evening, getting to know young Thornwell better, but there was nothing else to do. It was better than leaving her alone.

"I guess that's the best way to handle it," Fitz reluctantly agreed. "We'll have some supper here and then I'll have to leave you." He dismissed Sepah's messenger. "Well, I'm glad all went well with Rashid today."

"Yes, he's quite enthusiastic," Stakes said. "Of course, he can't put in the big money just yet but he can be very influential with the other rulers."

About ten that evening Fitz arrived at Abdullah's boatyard. The lights were turned on the dhow and a crane was in place, ready to lift the deckhouse up to its position on the high rear deck of the boat. There had been considerable redesign on the deck-house and the traditional high thwarts that ran around the poop deck were missing, the only clue as to the real purpose of the deckhouse. Also, although the dhow was built to look like a sailing ship, the mast was hinged to fall straight forward along the deck, carrying all the rigging with it, so that the high poop commanded an unobstructed 360-degree sweep of the sea around it.

Without the railings, while an inattentive sailor might be swept into the ocean, the twin thirty-caliber machine guns, which it was Fitz's task to install this night, could be depressed at a sufficiently low angle to shoot down into the water less than twenty feet from the ship's hull.

Sepah was standing by the hull when Fitz arrived and led him up the ladder from the sandy ground to the main deck and thence up the steps to the poop.

The pedestal which Fitz and the shipbuilder's blacksmith had fashioned was already bolted into place. It was now necessary to place the gun mounts on the pedestal and the twin thirty-calibers into the gun mounts. Then the spurious wheelhouse would be lowered over the mounted machine guns. Although there was a wheel mounted in front of the machine-gun pedestal, the actual wheel and navigation room was situated directly under the poop deck. The spoked wheel above could be used going into and out of port and even on the high seas, but it was instantly removable when the guns were readied for combat.

It was a six-hour job to install the guns and then lower the wheelhouse over them and bolt it into place. A great deal of ingenuity on the part of Fitz and Abdul Hussein Abdullah, the boatbuilder, had gone into the construction of the wheelhouse. In seconds the port, starboard, aft, and forward sides of the wheelhouse could be pushed outwards, falling flat to the poop deck, and the four hinged studs that supported the structure swung aft, carrying the roof with it, flat on the poop deck to the rear of the wheelhouse. Then the twin thirties with their armored plates attached to the mounts to protect the otherwise exposed gunner were ready to spit steel-jacketed bullets at any would-be aggressor.

"Magnificent!" Sepah exclaimed when the installation was complete and Fitz gave the first demonstration of knocking down the wheelhouse and bringing the guns to bear on an imaginary Indian patrol launch attacking them on the high seas.

Fitz breathed a sigh of relief. "I have completed my work except for training some likely gunners but that will have to be at sea." He was sweat-soaked and covered with the grease in which the weapons had been packed until now.

"You have, Fitz," Sepah agreed. "Now it is up to us. We must have our sea trials in the coming two weeks. My mechanics inform me that we should put thirty hours at low speed on the three diesels before running them at top speed. And we are still enlarging our syndicate to take the greatest gold shipment yet to India."

"Laylah leaves on Sunday and I have tentatively scheduled a trip to Kuwait, Saudi, and Abu Dhabi for that next week or ten days. So if I am on deck in two weeks will that be all right?"

Sepah nodded. "There's no need of you going on the sea trials. You can give your student gunners their instruction out in the Arabian Sea. But no more than two weeks. We have to get this trip in before the shamal season hits the Gulf. We can't take a chance on running into one of those storms with the cargo we're carrying."

"I'll stay in constant communication with you, Sepah."

"Please do. And, Fitz, we all appreciate what you are doing. You can be sure that almost every established trader on the Creek has an interest in this venture. All the way to the top. That's why I am personally going to be the *nakhouda* on this voyage." Sepah clapped Fitz on the shoulder. "I would ask you to come and drink and dream with me for an hour but I know what is waiting for you."

In his total absorption with the intricate task of completing the installation of the dhow's armament, Fitz had forgotten temporarily that not only was Laylah waiting but Courty Thornwell was keeping her company.

"You're right," Fitz agreed. "I guess I'll get along home now." He stepped into his Land Rover and drove quickly out of Abdullah's boatyard and then through Dubai Town and beyond it out onto the sandy road that led toward Jumiera. As he drove he wished there were some way he could come into the house unobserved by Laylah until he could get cleaned up. He didn't need a mirror to tell him how grease- and sweat-begrimed he was. He reached his house and pulled the Land Rover into the driveway. The car that John Stakes used was also there.

"Good old Courty," Fitz thought resentfully. "Right in there pitching."

"Fitz!" Laylah cried happily when he opened the door, letting himself in. Courty was nursing a highball, sitting on a chair in the corner, and there was no sign of anything more than the most casual conversation having taken place. "We've been worried about you. You said you'd only be gone a couple of hours. Oh, you look so hot and tired. Go in and take a shower while I make you a drink. How about a gin and tonic?"

"I'd love it." He nodded to Courty, then to Laylah. "I promise I won't be as long cleaning up."

Laylah came to him in the bathroom while he was in the shower and put the drink down. "Did you get whatever it was done?"

"Sure did," Fitz called from behind the shower curtain. He felt better now and was a little ashamed of himself for deliberately underestimating the time he would be working. He had wanted Laylah and Courty to be expecting him back at any moment all evening.

Once washed, shaved, and dressed in clean clothes he returned to the living room. It was five in the morning. He felt pleasantly weary with a sense of accomplishment. "It won't be long until the sun rises from behind the mountains and brings us a new day," he said. "Tomorrow at just this time we'll leave for Al Ain."

Laylah smiled at Thornwell. "It was sweet of you to talk to me all night, Courty. Now I understand much better what it is you're trying to do."

"Good. Maybe you can give me a hand in Iran then." He stood up. "So long, Fitz. See you later."

After Thornwell had left, Laylah walked to the bedroom with Fitz, her arm around him, and together they lay down on the bed.

"Laylah, I love you," he murmured. And then he was sound asleep.

CHAPTER 14

The desert tires on Fitz's Land Rover floated it over the sand. With one hand resting intimately on Laylah's knee, he drove through the sand along the coast of the Arabian Gulf. Courty Thornwell and John Stakes sat in the back seat.

Fitz faced a difficult task driving all the way up the Gulf coast to the point in Abu Dhabi where he would turn in from the coast and head directly over the desert to Shaikh Zayed's Al Ain retreat in the Buraimi Oasis. He grinned to himself at the disgruntlement of Thornwell being jounced around in the back seat.

It was early in the morning and the sun was just turning the sky pink as they left the beach of Jumiera behind them. "In just another few years we're going to see Americans living in air-conditioned houses two and three deep along the whole beach," Fitz predicted. He sighed. "What a pity."

"That's progress," John Stakes boomed from the back seat. Courty Thornwell stared morosely out over the sand and said nothing. It meant little difference to him if they put up a solid row of ten-story-high condominiums along this beach. Only one thing bothered him, Laylah and Fitz together up front while he sat on the hard rear seat. He tried to concentrate on what he would say to Shaikh Zayed when he finally had the opportunity to make his presentation.

The Land Rover bumped along on the hard-packed sand as Fitz followed the ruts of the countless vehicles that had traveled this route before them. "I understand Rashid is getting ready to put a four-lane highway along here," Fitz observed.

"That's right," Stakes agreed. "There's a construction company I have an interest in that I put together with Shaikh Rashid to build the road for him. The big problem, of course, is labor.

They'll just have to let more illegal Pakistanis into the country to work on these roads."

"Is it difficult for illegal immigrants to come into the country?" Laylah asked.

"I should suspect that Jack Harcross, Chief of Police, spends half his time turning away illegal immigrants," Stakes replied. "And the Trucial Oman Scouts seem to think these illegal immigrants are all agents of Communist China trying to start an insurrection." Stakes looked out over the Gulf up and down the coastline. "Of course, with all this coastline to patrol I suppose they can put all the illegal immigrants into here they can carry across," he observed.

Courty broke his long silence. "I don't think I'd like to walk through this sand to Dubai."

"I've seen them lying in the sand burned to black leather," Stakes replied.

"Poor souls," Laylah said. "All they want is a chance to work, make money, and send it back to Pakistan and India to their families. Why do the police make it so hard on them?"

"I suppose one reason is that it is most offensive to an old-line police officer like Jack Harcross to see the law broken whether or not the law makes sense." Again Stakes looked out over the water contemplatively. "There is, of course, the fact that a number of Dubai shipowners make a very handsome profit smuggling these Pakistanis, Baluchis, and Indians into the Trucial States. And when large-scale building gets under way here it should be even better."

Fitz was able to maintain a speed of about thirty-five miles an hour through the sand and two hours after they had left Jumiera they arrived at the border of Abu Dhabi. Arab soldiers, menacing looks on their faces, flagged the vehicle down. Fitz came to a stop, opened his door, and stepped out onto the hot sand. He held out his passport and Laylah's, which the officer looked at as though he could read English. Stakes and Thornwell both stepped out of the Land Rover and stretched themselves walking around a bit. The officer examined all four passports and then motioned Fitz to proceed. In Arabic, Fitz asked how far it was to the place he would turn inland to get to Al Ain. The officer, pleased at hearing his native tongue spoken so well by a Westerner, gave Fitz long, detailed, and most inexplicit directions, nodding and smiling as he spoke and gestured in all directions.

The turnoff was well marked, distinguished by a sprawling tent city. Bulldozers were at work on both sides of what appeared to be construction of a major highway and laborers were planting palm trees. "I wish I'd been able to set up the construction contract between Shaikh Zayed and the road-building company," Stakes said ruefully. "This is going to be one of the biggest jobs ever done in the Arab world as far as road building is concerned. The figure I heard was five hundred million pounds Zayed is prepared to spend to build the highway from the coast out to Al Ain and plant trees along both sides of it. For two years now he's been establishing nurseries along the route and irrigation projects so that the trees will grow the entire eighty miles of the road."

"Christ, what a project," Thornwell exclaimed. "If he can do that he can certainly spare the price of a couple of television stations with maybe a newspaper or two thrown in."

"No doubt about it," Stakes said. "It is not, can he afford it, but will he spend the money with you? That's what we have to persuade him to do."

"I have some really persuasive material," Thornwell said confidently.

"You sure persuaded me, Courty, a year ago," Stakes interjected. "Now comes the real test."

Three hours from the time they had left the Gulf behind them they were rolling through the sparsely planted area of the edges of the Buraimi Oasis. The oasis, forty miles long and ten miles wide, was about ten miles from the mountains which formed the natural boundary between the Sultanate of Oman and the Emirate of Abu Dhabi. As they progressed further into the oasis large groves of green date palms surrounded them. Then they came into the town of Al Ain. Glass and concrete buildings were going up among the mud houses and stores.

"Well, here's a good example of what oil can do. They're planning to put up a brand-new seven-story Hilton Hotel with a penthouse for the various members of the royal family to keep their harems in when they visit."

"Abu Dhabi has had oil six or eight years, hasn't it?" Fitz asked.

"That's right. But it also had Shakbut as Ruler until just a couple of years ago. Then they decided that he must be removed as Ruler of Abu Dhabi and his brother Zayed put on the throne in his place."

"*They* being the Brits?" Fitz asked wryly.

Stakes chuckled, "*They* being Sir Harry Olmstead, whom you'll soon meet. Old Shakbut, or Sharkbait as we sometimes called him, kept the treasury under his bed, you know."

"Under his bed?" Laylah asked in surprise.

"That's right, literally under his bed. He never trusted banks. When he went to pull out his chest of money to pay up the construction company for building his palace, it turned out that these insects they call fish—a flying carpenter ant, I believe—had literally eaten all the currency that Shakbut had been hoarding. There was a sort of fine paper dust at the bottom of the chest."

"How much money did these *fish* eat?" Courty asked.

"Nobody knows for sure but it was a great day for the Bank of England. There was a minimum of three and maybe four million pounds that would never have to be redeemed. So old Sharkbait had just given the British Government a present of four million pounds."

"You really know your way around these Arab countries, don't you?" Fitz said admiringly. "How come you're not a multimillionaire yourself?"

John Stakes sighed deeply. "I have the contacts, but it seems that when it's my turn to share in the largesse of contractors and oil companies out here, I'm in no position to force my occasionally fragile rights. I take what I can get and I'm happy to have it. If I had the absolute backing of Shaikh Rashid or Zayed or the Shah of Iran or any of the great rulers here, I could be like our friend Majid Jabir and ask for millions in baksheesh. The way Majid operates, he asks for five or ten million dollars for his services once a deal has been consummated and when the representatives object he shrugs and says we'll cut it in half. That's why they call Majid 'Shaikh Cut-It-in-Half.' He asks for two million and gets one. And the rulers back him up."

Stakes turned his attention to the road. "Now just keep going straight ahead. It's about eight miles to Zayed's stud farm. I can see why Zayed loves this place. Since he was a little boy the

Buraimi Oasis has really been his home. That's why he was so frustrated that Shakbut would do nothing for Al Ain. Since the day Zayed replaced his older brother the fortunes of Al Ain have blossomed considerably, as you can see."

Fitz drove the Land Rover along the deep tracks in the sand, following them through the date-palm orchards for several miles. Finally John Stakes patted his shoulder from the rear seat and said, "Take your next right."

Fitz made a right turn through a gate and started to drive down a long road, at the end of which he could see what looked to be stables.

"All right, you'll see a house on the right. Turn in there, that's Sir Harry's house." Fitz spotted the house, turned his car into a circular drive and came to a stop in front of a long, rambling one-story wooden house. It did not resemble any of the Arab houses he had ever seen but looked like a British version of an American ranch house. It was surrounded with palm trees and as Fitz turned off the ignition and put on the brakes an old but vigorous-looking man opened the door of the house and strode out into the driveway. He wore a battered brown felt hat and a sports shirt and slacks tucked into the tops of ankle boots. As the old man approached the Land Rover, John Stakes opened the door on his side and jumped out.

"Sir Harry, good to see you again."

Sir Harry Olmstead stared at Stakes and after a moment's pause said, "Hello, John. Welcome to Al Ain again."

Fitz stepped out of the Land Rover and walked around to the passenger side. Opening the door, he helped Laylah step down to the sand. Thornwell got out of the back of the Land Rover and joined the others as John Stakes made the introductions. "Come in out of the heat," Sir Harry urged. Fitz and Laylah followed Sir Harry into the cool main room of his house, Thornwell and John Stakes directly behind them. Sir Harry took his hat off and hung it on a peg beside the door. "Now, let me get your names straight so I won't forget them. John, of course, I know. And who is this lovely young lady?"

Laylah introduced herself and Fitz followed suit. John Stakes introduced Harcourt Thornwell. Sir Harry led them from the long, rather formal-looking living room into a comfortable sitting

room behind it which looked out over a garden. With windows
on two sides wide open and a breeze blowing through, it was
pleasantly cool. Sir Harry gestured at the chairs and clapped his
hands. Immediately an Indian servant appeared.

He collected drink orders and went back to the kitchen to fill
them.

"Would anyone like to have a swim after you're relaxed?" Sir
Harry asked. "I have a small but very pleasing swimming pool
which Shaikh Zayed built for me.

"After lunch I'll take you over to the guest house where you'll
be staying." They talked a few minutes about Al Ain and the farm
until the drinks arrived. As the conversation continued, they
covered such subjects as the agricultural development in Al Ain
and the irrigation systems being put in as well as the construction
programs under way. Thornwell had a hard time containing himself and not asking outright when they were going to see Shaikh
Zayed. It was obviously on everybody's mind, but patience is considered a prime virtue in Arab countries. When the drinks had
been finished, Sir Harry was ready for a swim. Laylah and Fitz decided to join him and went back to the Land Rover to get bathing
suits from their joint overnight case. John Stakes and Harcourt
Thornwell declined the invitation to swim. Sir Harry showed
Laylah and Fitz to the guest room and first Laylah and then Fitz
went inside to change.

He gave her a wry smile as she walked out of the guest room
and he went in to put on his own bathing suit. "Too bad we can't
swim our way," he chuckled in a low voice.

Sir Harry and his two guests swam back and forth across the
pool several times and then Sir Harry pulled himself out. Fitz and
Laylah did two more laps of the pool and then climbed out themselves. Still in their bathing suits, the three of them sat on the veranda in the shade, and the warm air quickly evaporated the water
from their bodies.

The servant brought them each a second drink and Thornwell
and Stakes joined them out on the veranda. "Do any of you like
to ride horseback?" Sir Harry asked. "We have some magnificent
Arabian stallions here."

"I used to enjoy horseback riding very much, Sir Harry," Laylah
said.

"Then perhaps tomorrow you will ride with me," Sir Harry suggested. "I ride for one hour every morning between six and seven before breakfast. It gets a really good appetite up."

"I should think so," Laylah said. "I didn't bring any riding clothes or boots with me unfortunately or I'd take you up on the invitation."

"I think I can find whatever you'll need. Unfortunately Fitz will not be able to join us since I have made a very early morning appointment for him with Shaikh Hamed." This was the first occasion Sir Harry had made mention of the purpose of the visit. All of them leaned forward expectantly, waiting to hear what else Sir Harry might have to say about meetings they had traveled so many desert miles to attend.

Sir Harry smiled at the obvious eagerness of his guests to learn about the plans that had been made for them to meet with Shaikh Zayed. He took another sip of his gin and tonic and put it down on a table beside him. "Shaikh Zayed will be here at six-thirty this evening to meet with you. I suggested that hour so that the sun will be behind the mountains and the cinema you wish to project for the Ruler's consumption will be easy to see. We don't have shades or draperies here."

"That's fine, Sir Harry," Stakes enthused. "I am sure that Shaikh Zayed will be extremely interested to see Thornwell's presentation."

Sir Harry turned to Fitz. "Majid Jabir sent a man from his office in Dubai all the way out here to see me and request that I make the arrangements for you, Colonel Lodd, to meet with Shaikh Hamed while he is here. Personally I don't know what luck you'll have with him, but obviously he needs money and Shaikh Zayed is under the impression that if he lends Hamed what he wants, he will have a very difficult time paying it back. So if you were to succeed where others have failed and find oil in Kajmira, it would be a great thing for the Trucial States and Hamed."

Sir Harry smiled as though at a fond memory. "That Majid Jabir is quite a lad. At least I think of him as a boy still although he must be thirty-five now."

"Majid was very strong about me seeing Shaikh Hamed," Fitz said.

"Yes, you'll find him very receptive. Quite aside from the fact that you're associated with Majid Jabir, Hamed, like all the Arabs, is delighted with the way you told your countrymen about this whole Jewish problem."

Sir Harry's servant appeared and the old Britisher stood up. "I believe lunch is ready." He walked over to the table. "I'll take this opportunity to set Miss Smith on my right and, Colonel Lodd, please sit on my left. We'll give Mr. Thornwell a chance to sit beside the lovely Miss Smith. And, John, you sit next to Colonel Lodd." They all took their places and the servant set a large platter of fish in front of Sir Harry, who looked at it approvingly. "The airplane is a wonderful thing. We have fresh fish flown in every morning from the Gulf. It took a while for the desert Arabs to get used to eating fish, but now it's taken on. There is no doubt but what the addition of fish to the diet here has been very salubrious to the health of the Arabs out here." The fish was served and a bottle of cold white wine brought in, which Sir Harry poured.

Sir Harry's guests were duly impressed with the luncheon service. All the more so since it was so unexpected to find a man like Sir Harry Olmstead out in the middle of the desert still preserving many of the British amenities and customs even though he had been intricately involved for so long in the Arab world.

At three o'clock, when they had finished lunch, Sir Harry suggested a tour of the stud farm. "It's a little cooler now with the sun not directly overhead and I think you'll enjoy seeing some of Zayed's finest horses."

Sir Harry sat up in the front seat of the Land Rover with Laylah and Fitz as he drove them the short distance from Sir Harry's home to the stables. Politely and with as much enthusiasm as they could engender, Harcourt Thornwell, John Stakes, and Fitz complimented Sir Harry on the magnificent horseflesh they were observing. They were of course anxiously awaiting the meeting with Shaikh Zayed and kept going over and over again in their minds the things they would say when the presentation actually occurred. Finally Sir Harry suggested that they all go back to the guest house, get settled, perhaps take a nap, and come back to his house at six. Sometime after that Shaikh Zayed would arrive. Sir Harry showed them to the guest house, where a servant took their baggage to their rooms. Since there were only three rooms available, Harcourt Thornwell and John Stakes shared one room, Laylah had another, and Fitz had the third room to himself. Fitz then drove Sir Harry back to his own residence and returned to the guest house.

He went into Laylah's room and kissed her. "A damn shame one of our precious nights is being taken from us," he said.

Laylah gave him a sympathetic smile. "It's good for you. You need one night's rest at your age, you know."

"At my age I need every bit of you I can get. Damn, but I hope this presentation amounts to something." Sitting beside Laylah on her bed in the cell-like room, he began to stroke her hair and kissed her again. "You know something," he whispered, "I think we have just about time to—"

Laylah put a hand over his mouth. "Shush. These walls are like paper."

Fitz sighed. "I suppose you're right. We wouldn't want to make Thornwell absolutely miserable, would we?"

"As a matter of fact, I could use a thirty- or forty-five-minute nap," Laylah said. "And I think it wouldn't do you any harm either. You had to do the driving."

"You're right. I want to be at my best with Shaikh Zayed."

CHAPTER 15

At precisely six o'clock Fitz, Laylah, Thornwell, and Stakes arrived at Sir Harry's house. The old Brit let them in and they
checked the motion-picture projector they had set up earlier in the
large front room. At six-thirty the ruler of Abu Dhabi had not arrived. "He's usually very punctual," Sir Harry apologized, adding,
"for an Arab." Just as he finished the statement the roar of powerful automobile engines could be heard as Shaikh Zayed's motor-
cade turned into the grounds of the farm. Three Mercedes-Benzes
careened into the circular driveway in front of Sir Harry's house,
the lead car coming to an abrupt halt in front of the door. The
other two cars parked behind the first one. The door to the Mercedes opened and an armed *jundi*, as Arab soldiers are called,
stepped out onto the sandy ground. He was followed by Shaikh
Zayed and one of the Ruler's advisers. Both of the men wore the
full robes complete with *kuffiyah* headdress and walked toward
Sir Harry's home.

Fitz couldn't help admiring the regal appearance and bearing of
the Ruler of Abu Dhabi. He was tall, and the robes notwithstanding, it was obvious he was a lithe whip of a man, a true desert
monarch. Although Fitz knew his age to be over fifty, the
beard was jet black and his face youthful, open, and lean. Here
was a Ruler any man, Westerner or Arab, could only respect and
wish, in some way, to serve.

Another *jundi* had simultaneously leapt out of the front seat to
be standing behind Shaikh Zayed. From the second and third car
more Arab associates of the Ruler stepped gracefully to the ground
and in a swirl of *dish dashas* and *kuffiyahs* the Arabs joined
their Ruler. Sir Harry stepped from his doorway to greet Shaikh
Zayed and take his hand. He led the Ruler and his advisers into
the large front room, which had been prepared for them to see

Thornwell's presentation. The sofa had been turned facing the screen and Sir Harry gestured toward it. Shaikh Zayed nodded and sat down alone in regal splendor on the sofa, his retinue taking chairs beside him, the soldiers standing at the door.

Once the group of Arabs were seated about their Ruler Sir Harry brought the Westerners one by one to meet him. Shaikh Zayed seemed to be particularly charmed with Laylah. He looked with extreme interest upon Fitz when he found out who he was. Fitz talked to the Ruler of Abu Dhabi in Arabic and a pleased look of satisfaction came across Zayed's handsome, alert visage. Fitz knew Zayed was basically a Bedouin at heart, a prince of the desert rather than a city-dwelling Arab. Thus the greetings were more direct and less flowery than would have been the case, for instance, with Shaikh Rashid. For twenty years, prior to becoming Ruler, Shaikh Zayed had governed Al Ain and the province of the Buraimi Oasis. So Fitz spent several minutes expressing his delight and pleasure with the new development coming into Al Ain and particularly the signs of agricultural sophistication that were evident everywhere. This pleased Zayed greatly. Zayed gestured for a chair to be brought up so that Fitz could sit down and converse with him.

"All the Arab rulers were pleased and proud of the way you told your countrymen about the Jews," Zayed began. "In America, of course, they have no idea what really happens here. As sacred as the city of Jerusalem is to Christians and Jews alike, it is equally sacred to the Arabs."

"I of course realize that, Your Highness," Fitz replied. "It is my fondest wish and the most desired outcome by all thinking Americans that some arrangement mutually agreeable to the Arab world and the Jews can be discovered." Fitz realized he was taking something of a risk even going so far as to say that the outcome should have some satisfaction for the Israelis. However, he could not ignore the sense of guilt he felt, knowing in his heart that the reason the Arabs were all attentive to him, listening to him, appreciative of him, was based on one huge misunderstanding. Each time an Arab leader brought up the fact that he had been cashiered out of the United States Army for championing the Arab cause against the Israelis, it distressed him.

Zayed considered Fitz's last statement a moment. Then he nodded. "Yes, an evenhanded solution must be discovered. But in the past the Americans have been more evenhanded toward the Israelis than they have toward the Arabs. We resent this. I think you made a very profound statement which we all know had an enormous impact throughout your country when you spoke of the hysteria of the Jews. That is the problem."

Fitz did not agree with Zayed but there was nothing to gain and much to lose by trying to set the record straight at this point. Instead he plunged right into the problem at hand. "My friend from the United States here, Harcourt Thornwell, is in your country specifically to discuss the lack of evenhandedness in America's dealings with Israel and the Arab countries. He feels he may have a solution for you, Your Highness. I agree with him. I think that what he has to say can be perhaps the most important suggestion an American could make to an Arab leader today."

Zayed glanced over at Thornwell and nodded to him. Thornwell, standing just a few feet from the Ruler, said in English, "Your Majesty, it is a pleasure and honor to be able to discuss with you my thoughts on solving Arab problems with public opinion in the United States."

Fitz translated the statement into Arabic, making a slight change. "My countryman, Mr. Thornwell, is honored to be able to show you how he feels the Arab world can change the thinking of the American Government and make it more responsive to Arab needs."

"We are ready, Colonel Lodd. Please proceed."

Fitz turned to Thornwell and nodded at the motion-picture projector. Immediately Courty went over to the machine, pressed the switches, and the presentation was under way. The attention of all the Arabs was instantly captured by the opening of the presentation. A wide shot of the city of Jerusalem taken from the air filled the screen. The narration was in Arabic.

"This is Jerusalem, the Holy City of the world's three major religions—Christianity, Judaism, and Islam." The camera zoomed in to a tight shot of the Dome of the Rock. Shaikh Zayed and the other Arabs caught their breath and gasped at the excellence of this photographic marvel.

"This is the Dome of the Rock, one of the world's most beautiful mosques, sacred to the entire Arab world, which commemorates this place from which, according to Moslem legend, the prophet Mohammed ascended into heaven astride his favorite white steed, Buraq." In silence the camera held on the spectacular mosque. The room was suddenly electrified with the excitement of the Arabs watching.

To himself Fitz said, right on Courty, right on. You really know how to put over a piece of propaganda. Abruptly the scene changed to a montage of the fighting in the Six Day War. Each sequence was captioned with an NBC, CBS, or ABC television network news logo. Each sequence was carried with the American announcer's voice explaining what was happening. Then the American announcer's voice was decreased in volume and an Arab voice came over, giving the translation of what the American announcer had been describing.

Although the various correspondents' reports that had been played on the network news may have been somewhat pro-Israeli, Fitz felt that Thornwell had perhaps gone a little too far in making the translation sound anti-Arab and pro-Israeli. Actually Fitz felt the correspondents had tried to be reasonably objective in their reporting. Then came the atrocity scenes and descriptions of what Arabs had done to captured Israeli troops, how they'd been tortured, beaten to death, and summarily executed while the Israelis had taken the captured Arabs and put them in hospitals, tried to minister to their wounds. This produced from the audience the expected shouts of "No! Untrue!" and other protests. Abruptly the scene returned to the Dome of the Rock. And the murmurs of disapproval from Zayed and his retinue died out. Over the picture the Arab voice said, "To whom does Jerusalem justly belong?"

Cries from Zayed and his retainers came forth. "Islam. Allah's will is that Jerusalem should be Islam."

Indignant shouts were uttered by the Arabs watching the presentation. The voice went on: "Why does America feel that Jerusalem and Palestine is the rightful heritage of the Jews? The government of the United States, being an elected body of men, reflects the views of the greatest number of people in America. Each man who serves in the Congress of the United States, which with the President of the United States rules the nation's affairs and foreign policy, is elected by people from his part of the

United States. The President is elected by all the people in the
United States. If they want to be elected they must mirror the
view of the majority. How is the view, the thinking, the desires of
the people of America formed? For the most part the opinion of
Americans is formed by the free press of America, its great newspapers. The network television news and, with eighty million
Americans on the road in their automobiles every day, the radio
stations they listen to, form their opinions. Let us have a look at
what the newspapers of America are telling Americans about the
Middle East."

With that a montage of the major newspapers and *Time* and
Newsweek as well as other influential publications were shown on
the screen and the Arab announcer translated specific portions of
them. The selected translations from the editorials were particularly pro-Israeli and anti-Arab, causing great consternation among
the attentive Arabs.

The announcer enumerated the circulation of the various newspapers that were shown and translated circulation into the power
of the newspapers to make opinion which was important and
could cause, in fact does cause, shifts of policy among the elected
members of the United States Government, always thinking in
terms of the next national election.

The New York *Times* and the Washington *Post* were displayed, followed by *Newsweek*, and then the on-screen logo of the
NBC, CBS, and ABC networks were shown one right after the
other. "Here are some of the most powerful influence panderers in
the world today—all are Jewish-owned, all reflect the Jewish point
of view."

Other newspapers, periodicals, and radio and television station
identifications shown or laid into the sound track and translated
by the announcer added up to a tremendous impact, and at the
end of this montage the announcer said simply, "This is why
America is pro-Israel. The Arab nations have traditionally been
pro-America. We have sent our sons to American universities and
they have come back with high regard for their American friends.
Yet the Americans do not reciprocate this point of view. There
are of course many answers to this. We can punish America if we
want to with further oil embargoes, but that doesn't solve our fundamental problem, which is simply: How can we make the Ameri-

cans see our problems and our point of view? How do we make America pro-Arab? How do we make the Americans realize that an important segment of Islam, the Palestinians, have been driven from their homes and lands, all their possessions taken from them, and forced for the last twenty-five years to live in concentration camps like these."

On screen came a series of pictures of the Palestinian refugee centers in Lebanon, Syria, Jordan, and the Sinai Peninsula.

Now the presentation was rolling into its finale. On the screen appeared a shot of King Faisal of Saudi Arabia. This had a solid impact on the audience. King Faisal is not merely the richest of the Arab oil rulers, he is also a spiritual leader of the world's 600 million Moslems because his kingdom encompasses Islam's two holy cities, Mecca and Medina. This thought was instantly transferred to the minds of those Arabs watching the screen intently.

As the camera moved in for a closer shot of King Faisal, the voice in the background said, "The King, who is sixty-four, wants to pray within his lifetime in the third most holy city of Islam, Jerusalem—at the Dome of the Rock. And he wants to walk there, and walk without setting foot on Israeli-held territory. What are the chances of him doing this?"

A number of murmurs were heard from the audience as the scene of Faisal faded into the wide-shot picture of the city of Jerusalem and then narrowed down to the mosque at the Dome of the Rock.

"Force of arms itself will never achieve King Faisal's goal and the goal of all Arabs—Palestine for Palestinians. Islam needs the backing of the United States to achieve this noble objective. To secure the backing of the United States requires a program to re-educate the majority of the American people who are not Jews. Yet the Jewish minority controls what the American people read in their newspapers, see on their television news broadcasts, hear on their radios as they drive to and from work each day. It is not necessary that this condition in America survive.

"The Moslem world working closely with Americans sympathetic to its objectives and highly trained in the field of communications in the United States can recast the opinion of Americans and thus the opinion of their leaders. The means of doing this is to use our vast oil wealth to buy important American communications entities. We can at this time through American businessmen buy one of the three major television networks. It is conceivable that we could buy control of the New York *Times*, particularly if they suffer another of their periodic strikes which weaken the financial structure of a newspaper. It is possible that we could buy either *Newsweek* or *Time* magazine or *Life* magazine, which is going through severe financial problems at this time. It is possible to buy independent radio and television stations all over the United States. It is merely a question of money, and money is what we have in such abundance that it staggers the imagination of even the richest, most powerful, and most influential American businessmen, bankers, and investment counselors.

"In America everything is for sale, but other Americans do not have the money it takes to purchase the type of communications network we have shown you in this presentation. We Arabs can and should own, through our American friends, the most powerful communications network ever formed in the history of the world. After we have conquered the American communications media, we will go to Western Europe and in fact everywhere that a free press exists in the world today. The voice of Islam can and will influence the world. Listen carefully to what your American friends who have brought you this presentation have to tell you now."

Arabic music playing over the Dome of the Rock continued for ten seconds and then the film ended. Thornwell and John Stakes, who had rehearsed this during the afternoon, were standing by the light switches and the room was illuminated. The Arabs were sitting in a state of semi-shock after the lights went on. Fitz brought Harcourt Thornwell over to Shaikh Zayed, who bade them both be seated.

"That was a most compelling presentation," Zayed said. "How much would it cost to accomplish this entire plan?"

Fitz translated the question for Thornwell, who thought for a moment, smiled, and said, "Tell him if he has to ask how much it costs he can't afford it."

"Your Highness," Fitz translated, "Mr. Thornwell says that there is no way to give you a specific price on this project. The point he makes is that you can very easily afford it if you want it.

When I say you, Your Highness, I mean you and the other rulers of Islam."

The Shaikh gave Thornwell a crafty, knowing smile. He nodded his head in understanding. Then Zayed turned back to Fitz. "Have you spoken to Faisal about this plan yet?"

"We go to see King Faisal next, Your Highness. If we went to him with a commitment from you it would of course greatly strengthen our position. We are also planning to see Shaikh Isa in Bahrain, Shaikh Khalifa in Qatar, and Shaikh Sabah of Kuwait."

"I have heard that Rashid is very favorably impressed with your plan," Zayed pronounced. It was well known that Zayed had respect for Rashid. He was well aware of how Rashid had built up Dubai without any oil revenues. Even though Dubai and Abu Dhabi were natural enemies, being neighbors, and there was a time when Zayed and Rashid had derived their entertainment from harassing each other, they now worked together. With the discovery of oil in Dubai, Rashid's nation would be immensely wealthier than it already was, and Rashid was an important factor in Arab-world decisions.

"I believe that you have shown us a highly important objective for Islam. I assume Mr. Thornwell here will direct this program in the United States."

Fitz translated for Thornwell, who nodded affirmatively.

"This program you suggest would cause great controversy in the United States if it were known what Mr. Thornwell is planning. Is that the reason Mr. Thornwell did not have his picture or name mentioned in the presentation we just witnessed?" Zayed astutely studied Thornwell's face as Fitz translated the question. As a matter of fact, this was a point Fitz had wondered about the first time he saw the presentation.

Thornwell had his answer ready.

"Tell the Ruler that I am not the only American involved. There are many other highly competent and skilled communications men who will work with me and will be showing this presentation to influential Arab leaders all over the world wherever they may be. We expect to show it to all of the Arab delegation leaders at the United Nations. For the sake of my colleagues who will also be giving this presentation, it was necessary that I not spotlight one individual, myself, to the detriment of the others.

The reason for this is that when others show the presentation to Arab leaders they will feel that they are not talking to the number-one man if I'm the only individual shown." Thornwell paused briefly, then asked, "Do you buy that, Fitz?"

"I don't know. But it doesn't matter whether I buy it. I feel certain that Zayed will. The Arabs have a very fine respect for face, which is what you're talking about."

Fitz translated Thornwell's reply to Zayed, who nodded and appeared to accept the answer. Thornwell leaned forward anxiously and said to Fitz, "Ask him when we can get some sort of a commitment out of him. When can we know that he will be a major contributor to forming this communications empire? I'd like to get his commitment for a fifteen- or twenty-million-dollar preliminary contribution right away so we can get on with our planning. Explain to him that *Life* magazine is in even more serious trouble than we knew when we made the presentation. Tell him that the American Broadcasting Company is in trouble. Tell him that the American Broadcasting Company was trying to sell its stock to ITT and the U. S. Government stepped in and stopped this because of what they considered the monopoly situation it would create. Tell him—"

"I'll tell him what I think I should," Fitz replied shortly. He turned to Shaikh Zayed. "Your Highness, at this moment there are many bargains in the United States that may not be around much longer. Mr. Thornwell is anxious to put his plan into action and would like to know when you could give him an answer or negotiate further with him on this whole matter."

Shaikh Zayed looked around the room at his other people, nodded very slightly, and a retainer stood up. Shaikh Zayed himself remained seated. "Tell Mr. Thornwell that we will give this serious consideration."

"Could I tell him when we could continue these talks, Your Highness?"

Zayed stood up and smiled. *"Bukra Inshallah."*

"What did he say?" Thornwell asked.

Fitz translated the familiar phrase. "He said, 'Tomorrow, Allah willing.'"

"Tomorrow! Great. That's what I call action."

Fitz smiled consolingly. "Don't get your hopes up. *Bukra*

Inshallah actually means in effect: 'When I'm ready, that's when I'll talk to you further.'"

Zayed perceived that his American friend who understood Arabic perfectly had given Thornwell the true definition of *Bukra Inshallah* and smiled enigmatically. And to Fitz he said, "Tomorrow you'll be seeing Shaikh Hamed. He is looking forward to your meeting. I understand Majid Jabir is associated with you in this venture. That is good. Kajmira needs to make an oil strike and if you can succeed where others have failed you will be doing Shaikh Hamed, and of course yourself, a great service. Your reputation as a friend of the Arab world goes before you when you see Shaikh Hamed tomorrow. I feel certain you will have a good audience."

Fitz bowed his head to the Ruler, working hard not to show his elation at what Zayed had just told him. "Thank you, Your Highness. I appreciate your interest."

Zayed extended his hand to Laylah, who took it and smiled at him. As Fitz knew, it was always somewhat of a treat for Arabs to have attractive Western women come to see them. No Arab woman would dare approach a man other than her husband without being fully veiled and under long-planned circumstances. Shaikh Zayed said to Laylah as he held her hand, "I hope I will have the pleasure of seeing you again. I understand you must leave tomorrow to go back to Dubai. But perhaps the next time we will spend more time together." He turned to Thornwell after Fitz had translated his words and shook Thornwell's hand. "Truly we will give this serious and immediate consideration."

Fitz translated the phrase and Thornwell brightened up somewhat. Sir Harry Olmstead escorted the Arabs out to their cars, saw them off, and then returned to the main room, where Thornwell was packing up his equipment. "You made a very strong impression, very strong indeed, Thornwell," Sir Harry said seriously. Then, turning to John Stakes, he said, "You were very silent and unobtrusive during this entire meeting, John."

Stakes smiled. "Yes, I felt that, between Fitz, Laylah, and young Thornwell here, any comments I might have made would have been superfluous."

"You're quite right, John. Well now, I think there's some supper ready for us and perhaps after that presentation a drink would be in order."

"You are the most generous of hosts, the most gracious," Laylah said sincerely. "Someday I hope you will come to Tehran so that I can return some of your hospitality, Sir Harry."

"It's been a pleasure, my dear." Sir Harry took her arm gently and led her toward the veranda.

CHAPTER 16

At six o'clock the following morning Fitz rapped gently on the door to Laylah's room next to his in the guest house. A few moments later she opened the door and let him in. They embraced quietly and he kissed her tenderly and passionately. "What a lousy night," Fitz muttered.

"I missed you too, Fitz," Laylah whispered into his ear. "But we will be home soon."

"You can be sure of that. As soon as I finish with Shaikh Hamed, we'll take off for Dubai." He pressed her to him again. "Are you really going to go horseback riding with Sir Harry?"

"Of course. I promised I would. I wonder how he happened to have boots and those jodhpurs that just about fit me perfectly."

"I think that old Sir Harry does find interesting companions from time to time, even at his age. Now get yourself ready so we can go over and have a bite of breakfast."

At six-thirty they joined Sir Harry on his veranda.

"Sir Harry, if you can give me directions how to get to Zayed's guest house, I'll be on my way to see Shaikh Hamed."

"It's not far from here. I'll draw you a little map."

By seven-thirty Fitz was knocking on the door at Shaikh Zayed's guest house for visiting Arab leaders. An armed guard opened the door and Fitz identified himself.

Even at seven-thirty in the morning Shaikh Hamed was conducting a busy majlis. In the room in the guest house allotted to visiting princes, there was a special room which the visiting prince could use for meetings. Hamed sat in an armchair with a table beside him and around the walls of this room were seated fifteen or more retainers and others having business with Shaikh Hamed, even on his visit here to Al Ain. The coffee pourer was busy filling the small cups of Hamed's visitors. Fitz recognized two of the men who had been at Sir Harry's the evening before to see the presentation. They nodded to Fitz as he walked around the room shaking hands with everyone. Shaikh Hamed gestured to the empty chair beside him and Fitz walked over to the old shaikh, who looked to be well over seventy, and when the Shaikh reached his hand forth Fitz took it gently in his own hand. This was the shaikh he'd heard of who only ten years before used to amuse his guests by bending a coin between his fingers. Indeed, Shaikh Hamed had not lost all of his strength, for the grip he pressed on Fitz's hand was a startlingly strong one.

Beside the Ruler of Kajmira sat a man who looked to be in his mid-thirties, his round face framed by the white *kuffiyah* and a black beard. Fitz was introduced to Shaikh Saqr, one of Hamed's sons and the emirate's Minister of Foreign Affairs. Saqr could speak English.

Saqr, Fitz thought. The word meant falcon, but this was the face and mien of a rather spoiled, city-bred Arab, unlike the magnificent presence of Zayed. Fitz shook hands with Saqr, and after the usual amenities Shaikh Hamed patted the empty chair beside him and Fitz sat down.

He began to tell Shaikh Hamed how happy he was to meet him and how well Shaikh Rashid and Shaikh Zayed had spoken of him, Shaikh Zayed only the night before. Fitz dropped Majid Jabir's name into the conversation briefly as well.

Although it was disconcerting to have so many people listening to their conversation, Fitz was used to this, and where many Americans would not have known how to handle the situation, Fitz realized that he must push on with his discussion, and if Shaikh Hamed felt a sensitive point was being brought up, it would be his prerogative to suggest retiring to another room to complete the conversation.

"It makes me happy to hear that you are contemplating vast improvements on the Creek in Kajmira, Your Highness," Fitz began with a combination of tact and pointedness.

Hamed warmed to the subject of improvements in his country. "Kajmira is a poor state, I'm sorry to say. We do not have oil." Hamed gave Fitz a searching glance, but Fitz said nothing, waiting to see if the Shaikh had finished.

"It is true we have many improvements that must be made in

Kajmira. I owe it to my subjects to develop trade facilities wherever possible. As you know, that is why I'm here now seeing my old friend Zayed, who has been much more fortunate in finding oil than I have."

Shaikh Hamed peered out from under his *kuffiyah* at Fitz, inviting him to make the expected proposition. Fitz took advantage of the opportunity. "Your Highness, it is my hope and the sincere desire of my associates to serve Kajmira on that matter. We understand the concession with the Texas group expired two years ago, and although you have been approached, you have not yet decided with whom you will sign a new exploration concession. It is my firm belief that I and my group can do the best job for you. Not only do we wish to explore in some areas where recent new seismic information indicates we might find oil, but we are ready to actually drill the wells and produce the oil ourselves. What we want is three years to explore and drill our first well. In point of fact, we expect to be drilling our first well within a year. I feel certain, Your Highness, that if anybody can produce oil in Kajmira or the territorial waters of Kajmira it is our group."

"If you are so certain that you will be drilling within a year, why do you ask for three years?"

"It is our intention, Your Majesty, to check out the seismic information we have on the underwater shelf about nine miles off the coast of Abu Musa Island, well within your territorial waters. This should take us about three to four months. If our geologists confirm the information we have been given, we will start drilling as soon as the equipment can be acquired. If, on the other hand, the geology we discover does not seem favorable to finding oil, we will have to start looking anew with no previous seismic information to go on and this is both costly and time-consuming. But if you want oil raised in Kajmira, we are the best people to do it for you. As you well know, I'm an American dedicated to the Arab cause. My associates are all highly successful oil men. And of course no man in the Trucial States is more shrewd negotiating with Arabs, British, Americans, French, and Germans than Majid Jabir."

Hamed leaned forward, obviously intensely interested in what Fitz was saying. "What terms do you offer me for this concession?"

"Your Highness, we propose a signature bonus of a half million dollars when we sign the three-year exploratory concession. We will pay one hundred and fifty thousand dollars a year for the three years we have exclusive rights to drill in Kajmira and Kajmira's offshore waters."

"But Shaikh Rashid of Ajman was paid seven hundred fifty thousand dollars as a signature bonus."

"That is true, Your Highness, but Ajman is in control of the territorial waters only fifteen miles from the Fatah Field, where oil has been discovered and will soon be produced."

Hamed shook his head. "You yourself said that the seismic information, which I have also seen, gives strong indication of oil in our territorial waters off Abu Musa Island."

"Your Highness, our group are not commission seekers. We do not come to you and ask you for a chance to go out and peddle your concession where we can. We ourselves will put up large sums of money to go beyond acting as middlemen and actually be oil producers."

Fitz looked into eyes that gleamed like black gold. He decided to retreat slightly. "Your history with entrepreneurs such as the Texas group and others has been unfortunate. However, we must all be content with whatever arrangements are made. If it will make you feel more kindly disposed toward our operations, we will pay you a seven-hundred-fifty-thousand-dollar signature bonus. We want very much to work with you, we want to develop oil in Kajmira for the benefit of Kajmira, and of course we are looking forward to making profits for ourselves with you. But considering the large amounts of money we ourselves will be spending, seven hundred fifty thousand dollars is the highest we could go in respect to a signature bonus."

To himself Fitz wondered what he was doing talking this way. Here he was virtually a pauper compared to the others in this league. He was gambling heavily of course on the success of the gold-re-exporting venture with Sepah. If anything went wrong all this talk would be academic anyway. Neither he nor Sepah would be able to put up any share of the signature bonus in that eventuality. And then there was the rental on the concession and some share of the exploration and eventual development that would be overseen by Fender Browne using the equipment from his own field supply warehouse on the Creek.

Fitz knew that a seven-hundred-fifty-thousand-dollar signature bonus would be of great value to Hamed and would considerably strengthen the old shaikh's hand in applying to Zayed for the rather large loan—the exact figure Fitz did not know, but he felt it must be in the area of five million dollars—to dredge out and shore up the Creek in Kajmira.

After a few moments of whispered conversation with his son Saqr, Shaikh Hamed looked squarely into Fitz's eyes. "Please send your written proposal and a sample lease as soon as you can to my son in Kajmira. I will discuss it with my other sons and with our Minister of Finance." Shaikh Hamed gestured toward three other black-bearded Arabs in full robes sitting at one side of the majlis. "They have heard what you have had to say and I'm sure already are forming opinions in their minds. We will let you know very quickly once we receive your proposal."

The formal portion of the meeting was over. Fitz watched the coffee pourer fill his cup again and he sipped it as Shaikh Hamed talked in his creaking tones to some of the aides sitting about the majlis.

"Your Majesty," Fitz said, and turned to Hamed's son, "Shaikh Saqr, this has been a valuable meeting. I will be looking forward to seeing you again in Kajmira. We will send the documents to you within the week." He stood up. Shaikh Hamed raised his hand, which Fitz took in his own, this time giving the Ruler a much stronger grip, which was returned in kind. This was a tough old bird, Fitz thought to himself. It's a good thing he needs our proposition. Hamed could probably get a million-dollar signature bonus if he held out and went to one of the other oil companies anxious to get a concession on the Gulf. But it would require long negotiations with people the Shaikh didn't know. Also, Shaikh Hamed did not seem to have absolute confidence in Saqr or his other sons. Obviously Shaikh Hamed would do better to be dealing with friends and people he trusted right from the start. As Fitz turned from the Ruler and left the majlis, he shook hands with each of the Arabs as he left the room.

Back at the stud farm Fitz found Laylah, John Stakes, and

Thornwell waiting for him, their bags on Sir Harry's front veranda.

"Sir Harry," Fitz began, "I had a thought on the way over here
from seeing Shaikh Hamed this morning. Why wouldn't it be
quicker for us to drive back to Dubai in a straight line across the
desert? I hear that there are routes through the desert paralleling
the mountains and a lot of traffic goes between Al Ain and Dubai
that way."

Sir Harry appeared to give consideration to the thought. "It
would of course be going the straight route instead of the two
long sides of the triangle first from here to the Gulf and then up
the coast to Dubai. I know the camel caravans go that way. Personally I've never made the trip, so I can't tell you how it would
be. Only that it would be half the distance to Dubai that way."

Sir Harry walked over to the Land Rover and inspected the
tires. "You have the right kind of equipment for trying it that way.
If you're looking for an adventure I suspect you'll find it, although
it might be uncomfortable for Laylah."

"Don't worry about me," Laylah said.

"Why don't we give it a try then?" Fitz proposed. "One never
knows when it will be convenient to know a route between Al Ain
and Dubai without having to go through those checkpoints. Besides, even if we have to go a little slower it's still half the distance."

"Be sure you have plenty of water just in case," Sir Harry advised. "I've got a plastic five-gallon container I can let you have."

Sir Harry went back into his house and emerged a few minutes
later with the container full of water. Fitz took it from him,
thanking him, and put it in the back of the Land Rover.

Fitz drove out of Shaikh Zayed's stud farm and headed out toward the desert with the mountains of Oman at his right shoulder. The first ten miles of the trip were very little different from
driving along the hard-packed sand roads in Al Ain. Then the
sand became softer but the big sand tires floated the Land Rover
as they pushed on. The fine desert sand began to seep into the interior of the Land Rover, coming in under the tightly tied canvas,
and while the sand did not bother the occupants of the front seat,
both Thornwell and Stakes couldn't help but get a continual fine
coating of sand settling over them. Still the driving was not too

difficult and there was the comforting sight of the ruts of other vehicles in front of them.

Laylah looked up at the mountains to their right. "You know
I've always had a yen to see Oman. I understand it's the last of
the really feudal Arab countries run by a despot sultan."

"There's a hot insurgency going on there which is only going to
get worse year by year," Fitz replied.

He followed Laylah's gaze up into the rugged mountains. "This
reminds me of two insurgencies I've seen. The Kurds in Iraq and
the Vietcong in Vietnam. That's perfect terrain for guerrillas to
build up the strength to attack government installations and actually take towns and even whole countries. The Communists have
a big stake in the insurgency going on there in Oman and they
have just what they need to attract dissidents from all these Arab
countries to their side. Rich absolute dictators whose friends and
associates are making fortunes while the poor seem to receive no
part of the riches pouring into the coffers of the shaikhs."

"I thought Zayed was doing a fine job of providing for his people," Laylah said.

"Oh, I agree with you. However, there is just enough truth in
what the Communists tell the people to make their story believa-
ble."

Fitz half turned from the ruts in the desert in front of him toward Thornwell in the back seat. "Now Courty here, with his presentation, has done in the most professional fashion I've ever seen
precisely what the Communists do. He has taken certain facts,
certain little pieces of truth, and strung them together into a very
compelling and persuasive piece of propaganda which taken in its
entirety and examined coldly by a disinterested investigator would
prove to be as false as the Communist line being preached to the
insurgents along the Oman border and in the Dhofar province to
the south." Fitz turned back to his struggle with the sand.

From the back seat of the car Thornwell said in muffled tones,
"I'd like to reply to that, Fitz, but if I open my mouth it's going
to be filled with sand. I don't think your idea of driving across the
desert was so great."

"I'm sorry, Courty, but we should get back to Dubai quicker
this way than we would the other way." There was no reply from

the back seat. Both Stakes and Thornwell were holding handkerchiefs over their faces.

One hour and twenty-five miles later, still following the ruts of the other vehicles that had made the trip, they reached the first sign of civilization, a group of mud huts on the Oman side of the tracks. Although they could see no people anywhere, they had the feeling that women and children were looking out of windows at them.

An old man wearing a Pakistani-type turban and a gray-brown smock down to his knees came out of one of the houses and looked at them in a not unfriendly manner.

Fitz addressed the old man with some amenities and then asked if he was on the road to Dubai. The old man replied he was, and pointed along the tracks in the direction which the Land Rover was headed. He looked at Fitz in some surprise, perhaps never having seen a Westerner out in this desert before. Then in a warning tone of voice he said to Fitz to beware of the big hills of sand which the Land Rover would soon encounter. Sand dunes, Fitz thought grimly to himself.

He thanked the old man and they were off again. True to the old man's prediction, within another seven or eight miles they reached the sand dunes. At this point the tracks diverged widely as drivers had tried to figure how to make their trip across the sand dunes a little easier.

Fitz clenched the wheel with his hands, his fingers whitening as he stared ahead at the first of the sand dunes, knowing that worse was to come. He followed the middle tracks and the four-wheel-drive Land Rover easily climbed to the top. He shifted to a lower gear as he started down the other side of the steep dune. Fitz continued to follow the tracks and climbed another dune, descending the far side. For twenty to twenty-five minutes he continued climbing and descending the hills of sand as they became progressively higher and steeper. The tracks he was following now began to circumvent the hills, going off toward the mountains and around one enormous dune, then coming back again to attempt to stay on course. Now the dunes were so steep and so long that it was impossible to drive around them and grimly Fitz gunned the Land Rover straight up the dunes, and down the other side. The slightest deviation from a straight up and down course could end up with the vehicle turning over.

Every dune was a tense ordeal of a climb culminating in a threatened summersault as the vehicle descended the other side. Over and over again as the Land Rover went down the dunes, sometimes at a forty-five-degree angle, the center of gravity of the vehicle could be felt to converge on the point where the Land Rover would flip over its engine and land on its back. There was no time for self-remonstrances. Fitz had to concentrate everything he had on getting the Land Rover and its occupants safely through this empty quarter of sand dunes. Yet still there were the tracks of other vehicles ahead.

Laylah was gripping the handles on the front of the dashboard of the Land Rover and both Stakes and Thornwell were holding tightly to the rail that ran around the back of the front seat. Glancing down at the instrument panel in front of him, Fitz saw that the oil-heat-indicator needle was way beyond the red line which signified danger. So intensely was he concentrating on the moment-by-moment dangers that two hours passed without him realizing it. To their right the mountain range on the Oman side was coming to an end, submerging itself in the desert sand ten or fifteen miles ahead.

Far beyond the mountain range they had been paralleling, another range lofted from the desert floor, leaving a pass through the mountains as a natural entryway into Oman.

To Fitz's relief the sand dunes now seemed to be neither as high nor as steep as those behind them. Other tracks indicated vehicles going sometimes directly over the dunes, sometimes trying to go around them and find a way to avoid a direct confrontation with these awesome obstacles. All we need is a sand storm now, Fitz thought.

For another hour the Land Rover struggled over and around the dunes, frequently on the verge of being flipped over frontwards or sidewise. Not a word had been spoken in over two hours when finally, almost as abruptly as they had entered this treacherous sandy waste, they came out on stony gravel terrain.

Audible sighs of relief emanated from the back seat. Laylah turned to Fitz, her eyes shining. "You were magnificent, Fitz."

"I never should have gotten us into this in the first place."

From the back seat Stakes and Thornwell agreed.

"Well, at least it's behind us now," Laylah said.

"You want me to stop and let everybody out for a little stretch?" Fitz asked.

From the back seat came the muttered yes of Thornwell. Fitz pulled to a stop and everybody piled out and stretched their legs. Fitz put his arm around Laylah. "I'm afraid the only facilities I can offer you, darling, is for the three of us to take a little walk."

"I'm all right. I had no water or coffee for breakfast but I sure am thirsty now."

"My guess is we're about an hour and a half out of Dubai now." Fitz looked back at the mountains and then ahead. "There should be a little oasis town ahead of us and then it's a straight twenty-mile shot across to Dubai. Actually I think we'll probably make it in an hour if we don't have to stop."

"In that case, I'll just take a mouthful of water and wait until we get home before I drink a lot. I really can't see myself squatting out here in the sand."

"Let's go, fellows," Fitz called to Thornwell and Stakes, who had been drinking water from the plastic container. Laylah took a sip of water and Fitz recapped the container and put it into the rear of the Land Rover and climbed aboard.

Fitz started the engine, put the Land Rover in gear, and noticed to his relief that the oil-heat indicator showed exactly danger but not above. He started off on the last lap for Dubai.

It was four o'clock in the afternoon when Fitz pulled up in front of his house on the Gulf. He jumped out of the Land Rover, ran around and opened the door, and helped Laylah out. "Thank God, or should I thank Allah?"

"In any case, we made it!" Laylah exclaimed as she descended from her seat.

Fitz helped her down. "Actually, it was a very interesting and instructive trip."

"I'm glad you learned something," Thornwell said. "From now on I'll charter a plane and fly."

John Stakes's comments were a little less dour. Peter opened the door to the house and welcomed Fitz home, taking orders for drinks.

"I'm going to have a swim," Laylah declared.

"I'll join you, Laylah," Thornwell said eagerly.

"We all will," Fitz pronounced.

One hour later, after a swim and a shower and sitting with drinks in the air-conditioned living room, all four were talking animatedly about their desert adventure. They now had new respect for the dangers and difficulties inherent in desert travel. To try and make amends for the grueling experience he had put them through, Fitz invited Stakes and Thornwell to join him and Laylah for dinner. His invitation was instantly accepted. It was not until ten-thirty in the evening that Laylah and Fitz were alone at last.

"We've got a lot of making up to do for the last twenty-four hours, my love," Fitz whispered.

Laylah stuck the tip of her tongue out. "What are we waiting for?"

CHAPTER 17

The morning after their return from Al Ain, with only two more days and nights left to them, Fitz and Laylah swam in front of the house after their morning lovemaking and were just in the midst of having breakfast when Peter came into the bedroom where they were eating.

The Pakistani houseman explained to Fitz that for the last two days an American had been coming around to see him. Fitz asked him the man's name and what his business was. Peter was unable to answer the question other than to give Fitz the intelligence that the man was here at the front door right now.

"You mean you have him standing outside in the heat?"

"Yes, sahib. I thought you or memsahib might come into the living room." Peter looked at the abbreviated dress both of them were wearing as they finished their breakfast. Fitz and Laylah chuckled to each other. Fitz stood up and pulled a robe over his naked shoulders. "This is his third visit?"

"Yes, sahib."

"O.K., tell him to come into the living room. I'll be out in a minute."

Peter left the bedroom and Fitz shrugged at Laylah's questioning look. He pulled on a pair of slacks, thrust his feet into sandals, and leaned over to kiss Laylah. "Be right back. Whoever this fellow is he might have something of importance to tell me or he might be somebody I should talk to."

Fitz walked out into the living room and found a short, lean young man with rather long dark hair, an inquisitive look on his face, waiting for him. The newcomer was wearing the standard open-necked, short-sleeved sports shirt hanging loosely past the waist of his slacks.

"Good morning," Fitz greeted his visitor.

"Good morning, Colonel Lodd. My name is David Harnett. I'm a reporter for several U.S. newspapers, including the *Army Times*. I'm also the Associated Press stringer in the Persian Gulf area. I work out of Lebanon mostly."

"What is it you want of me, Harnett?" Fitz asked, trying to keep the belligerence he felt for all newsmen out of his voice.

"I've been here in Dubai almost three days now. I am following up a story for the *Army Times* about your activities since you retired from the Army in Iran."

"I don't know why the *Army Times* would be interested in what I'm doing now. It certainly has nothing to do with military activities."

"Actually the *Army Times* initiated the request and when I queried AP they also expressed interest in the story. I came to see you first two mornings ago but you had just left. Your manservant told me you would probably be back in two days, so I decided to stay here in Dubai and wait to see you. Naturally, since I was going to be here for two days I poked around a bit, asked questions, talked to a number of people about what's going on in Dubai and how Americans are operating here. I talked to Jack Harcross, the police chief, and Brian Falmey, the Britisher here who seems to know what's going on. I discussed American businessmen on the Gulf with the banker here, Tim McLaren, and Mr. Fender Browne who supplies oil field equipment was also helpful in making me understand the situation in Dubai and Abu Dhabi."

"Well, if you've talked to all those people, there's certainly nothing more I can tell you," Fitz said, a discernible note of irritation in his tone.

"On the countrary, Colonel, there's a great deal you can tell me. I guess a lot of your military friends are interested in what happens when a lieutenant colonel retires under circumstances such as yours. I understand from the people I've been talking to that you are involved in a shipping syndicate."

Harnett paused as though expecting a reply, but none was forthcoming. "Everyone I talked to, including the Arabs, said that it was very unusual that an American or any Westerner would be accepted into one of these syndicates here. They are tightly knit organizations that do not take to outsiders. What I'd like to

know, sir, is how you were able to become involved so quickly in
the commerce of Dubai. You seem to be a fairly well-known figure
on the Creek already."

"Well, quite honestly, Mr. Harnett, I don't know. I was asked
to become part of a group, perhaps because of my interest in boatbuilding. Also being able to speak Arabic is very helpful in doing
business in this country. I could see no future for myself back in
the United States at this time and a number of my Arab friends
came to my financial rescue when I was so suddenly forced to
leave the military because of the false and misleading stories
printed about me in the press of the United States."

"Naturally I'm well aware of the stories alleging your anti-
Semitic remarks. Of course Sam Gold is a little hysterical on the
subject of Zionism anyway. I myself try to be objective. I'm not
Jewish. My assignments happen to have been in Arab countries,
although I'll track down a good story anywhere in the world if
given the opportunity. The point is, Colonel, as you must be able
to see, there is a fascinating story here about how you have pulled
your life together. That Brit, Falmey, indicated very strongly that
you were in the gold-smuggling business."

"I would never have anything to do with anything illegal, particularly smuggling."

"I almost forgot, of course," Harnett said. "There is nothing illegal about buying gold from the banks and dealers here and taking it out of Dubai. The illegality of these operations begins when
the boat crosses the twelve-mile limit around India. This in itself
is not exactly a new story. What is new is why would an Arab syndicate accept you into their midst?"

Again the pause, met by stony silence on Fitz's part. "The
strong suggestion seems to be that your military background, your
experience in weaponry and insurgency, has equipped you to perhaps find guns and arm a gold-smuggling dhow. You know I could
write a most sympathetic story about you and your life here in
Dubai. Certainly there could be nothing wrong with a story which
describes how you are helping the Dubai shipping merchants protect themselves from piracy on the high seas. I'd like the opportunity to make a real hero out of you, Colonel."

Fitz had not invited the reporter to sit down. He regarded Harnett with intense suspicion. He was well aware of the fact that a

reporter had caused his present ills. He also perceived that Harnett was an ambitious young reporter who would have to justify
his trip to Dubai in some way, and certainly if Fitz did not give
him some explanation for what he was doing living in Dubai, the
reporter would probably plaster all over the U.S. press conjecture
about retired Colonel Lodd in shady business deals operating out
of the wide-open port of Dubai.

"Look, Harnett," Fitz began, "I know nothing about gold
smuggling. I am trying to make a living. As I told you, I speak
Arabic and it seems to me that the Arab countries are the new
lands of opportunities. I am interested in any legitimate enterprise
I can become part of. The port of Dubai is the most important on
the Arabian Gulf. And it is becoming even more important every
day.

"Merchandise from all over the world comes into Dubai and is
redistributed throughout the Gulf and, yes, into India and Pakistan. The tariffs are unusually high in both of those countries.
Therefore trade is limited with them. As you probably discovered,
more gold and more Swiss watches come into Dubai than into
any other port in the world. Obviously this tells you something
about the shipping from here."

Fitz walked over to the picture window and looked out at the
deep, clear blue water of the Gulf as he turned over in his mind
what next to say to Harnett. "If I could get the agency in Dubai
for American products and in turn sell these to the shippers or
take the risk of consigning them to the shippers and receive a
larger share of what they are sold for in foreign ports, I certainly
would do it. But I'm not in the business of smuggling goods into
countries that impose high import duties. I'm also extremely interested in the oil business at the present moment. You can honestly
say that Fitz Lodd is actively in business on the Arabian Gulf and
would welcome correspondence from any and all American businessmen who need a good connection here to help them trade in
these parts. I anticipate that five years from now Dubai will be
the biggest boom town in the world."

Fitz decided to bring the interview to a close. "Now if you'll
leave your card I will certainly inform you of any interesting progress I may make. But as for smuggling gold into India, I know
nothing about it."

At that moment Laylah chose to make her entrance and the reporter looked up at her, surprised and perhaps somewhat dazzled. Fitz walked over to her. "Laylah, meet Mr. Harnett, a newspaperman visiting in Dubai. Mr. Harnett is just leaving. We've had an interesting talk about business opportunities in Dubai."

Fitz turned to Harnett. "Mr. Harnett, meet Miss Smith. She works in Tehran."

The reporter reached his hand out and took Laylah's. "It's a pleasure to meet you, Miss Smith. May I ask what you do in Tehran?"

Laylah turned to Fitz. There was a questioning look in her eyes. Fitz nodded. "It's all right to talk to Mr. Harnett. He represents the *Army Times*, the Associated Press, and I assume other periodicals in the United States. I've been as open with him as I know how about my intentions and ambitions here on the Gulf."

"Well, Mr. Harnett, since Fitz puts it that way, I am employed by the American Embassy in Tehran. Part of my job is being conversant with all activities along the Gulf. As a former employee at the Embassy and a loyal American, Colonel Lodd has been of assistance to me in learning as much as possible about the Trucial States." She smiled sweetly and indulgently at the reporter. "Does that answer your question?"

"Yes, it does, Miss Smith. Thank you very much for your forthrightness. Not that I'm planning to put this in any story I'm writing, but it is also my job to acquire as much knowledge about this area of the world as possible."

"I understand, Mr. Harnett. Should you be in Tehran, why don't you call at the Embassy and ask for me? I'll be glad to make all unclassified material at my command available to you."

"That's great, Miss Smith. May I ask your first name?"

"Yes, Laylah. Laylah Smith. I work in the intelligence section."

Harnett shook his head. "You're the first American over here that's ever admitted to being in intelligence."

"Mr. Harnett, there is nothing covert or mysterious about intelligence gathering. It happens that I can speak and read Farsee and Arabic. My chief job is to read all the newspapers every day. Anything I think might be interesting to our ambassador I cut out and file for him. It's as simple as that."

Fitz admired the adroit handling of Harnett by Laylah. However, he could see no gain in prolonging the interview, which had been an annoyance to him from the beginning. "Mr. Harnett," Fitz said, "if there is anything more I can do for you don't hesitate to call on me. At the moment, however, Miss Smith and I have several meetings which we have to get through. She leaves to go back to Tehran in just another day. So if you'll excuse us for the time being."

"Of course, of course, Colonel. Miss Smith, it was a pleasure meeting you. When I get to Tehran I will certainly accept your invitation."

"Fine. I'll look forward to your visit, Mr. Harnett," Laylah said pleasantly but formally.

Fitz walked toward the door. Harnett took the hint and went with him. Fitz opened the door, shook hands with Harnett, and closed the door behind him. Then he went back into the living room. He looked at Laylah and shook his head. "Son-of-a-bitch newsmen. Will they ever leave me alone?"

"The only way to handle them is to at least appear to be helpful."

"I know that, Laylah. But the son of a bitch intimated that I was involved in arming a dhow to smuggle gold into India. That God damn Brit, Brian Falmey, told him. I'll be even happier than the Arabs when they get the Brits out of here."

Fitz started back to his bedroom. "Guess we'd better get ready for Sepah and Sira's luncheon."

"Then we'll have to come back here so I can start to pack. Here it is almost time to go home. I can't believe it."

"Believe me, as soon as I finish this job for Sepah I'm heading right for Tehran to see you."

"What about this job you're doing for Courty and John Stakes?"

"I'll do the job for them as best I can. But I'm not going to let any more than a week or two go by before seeing you. You know I'm in love with you, Laylah. I want you to marry me as soon as I hit it on this deal with Sepah."

They embraced, Fitz kissed her, and finally after many moments he whispered, "You will marry me, Laylah?"

"Let's talk about it when you get back to Tehran, darling. I love you too."

CHAPTER 18

The heat, if possible, was more oppressive than it had been all summer, Fitz felt as he watched Laylah's Iran Air jet taxiing out to the runway at Dubai International Airport. His eyes never left the plane, his thoughts hovering around last night with her as the jet engines whined their way into takeoff position. The jet seemed to crouch as the pilot, holding the brakes, gave the engines full blast. Then the long, sleek airplane released, moved down the runway, slowly at first, finally streaking toward the end of the cement strip. Soon it was angling upward and then it left the ground and soared over the desert and out toward the Gulf.

Sadly Fitz turned from the balcony. He walked back into the airport and out the front doors to his parked Land Rover. It was almost noon and few people were out in the sauna-like heat. Fitz climbed into his vehicle, started it up, and drove away from the airport.

Forty minutes later he was pulling up into his driveway, where, as he expected, John Stakes's sedan was parked. Morosely Fitz let himself in his front door and walked into the living room. He stood staring out over the blue waters of the Gulf, paying no attention to Thornwell and Stakes, who were sitting waiting for him.

Peter walked into the room and, seeing the mood his master was quite understandably suffering, he stood quietly but attentively. Fitz noticed him, nodded, and then looked back out the picture window. Peter scuttled back into the kitchen, appearing moments later with a gin and tonic, which he handed his master.

Fitz took a few sips of his drink and then, resigned, turned from the window and looked back into the room at his two guests. John Stakes broke the silence. "I've made all arrangements for our meeting with King Faisal's Finance Minister in Riyadh the day after tomorrow. If this shaikh is impressed, Faisal himself will see the presentation and talk to us."

"We've got the best product their money can buy," Thornwell declared. "The hearts and minds of the American people through our communications systems."

"We probably ought to fly over to Riyadh tomorrow evening," Stakes said.

Fitz didn't answer. He finished off his drink and started toward the hallway to the back of the house. "I'm going to have a swim. Anybody like to join me?"

"I'll take a dip with you, Fitz," Thornwell volunteered.

"We'll all go in," Stakes said briskly.

It wasn't like the last eight days when he and Laylah had splashed around in the Gulf nude. But after a vigorous swim of a few hundred yards out and the same back to the beach Fitz felt better physically and mentally. Everything was going to work out well. He would be going to see Laylah in Tehran just as soon as he returned from the mission to India and for the first time since he'd known her he felt completely confident and at ease with her. Now he could seriously contemplate her accepting his proposal and sharing his life. But the first step was to make the big stake on the India voyage and then get into as many other potentially profitable deals as possible. After that he would expand his influence into political matters. As Fitz had first learned in political science at Ohio State and then seen demonstrated many times throughout the world, money is freely convertible into political power and vice versa. Fitz's goals and ambitions were clearly laid out now. It was just a question of using all resources available to him to their fullest extent in order to realize these ambitions.

Stakes and Thornwell followed Fitz back into his house, where they all changed and then sat down for lunch.

"You haven't said anything about the Riyadh trip since I brought it up a half hour ago, Fitz," Stakes said. "Is everything all right?"

"I don't honestly know, John. I have to check with my associates again this afternoon. As I told you, I have a commitment which supersedes everything else. It may well be that in two days I will be obliged to meet this commitment. In which case it will not be possible for me to go with you to Riyadh."

"We can't go without you, Fitz," Thornwell protested. "You're the American they all believe in. And you speak their language. I sure don't."

"You don't need me for an interpreter. John here speaks Arabic better than I do, although he wouldn't let on unless he had to." Fitz turned to John Stakes. "Isn't that right, John?"

"You're the main attraction, Fitz. That's what's important." A worried look came across John Stakes's face.

"Look, I'm sorry. You know I'd be with you if I could. But if I went off with you to Riyadh and failed to meet this obligation I have taken on, I'll be no good to anybody in these countries again."

"So what are we supposed to do, just sit around here with nothing to do and wait for you to come back?" Thornwell complained.

"It's that presentation of yours that does the selling job, not me," Fitz replied.

"That's part of it," Thornwell said, "but a great big important point is that these Arabs trust you."

Fitz merely said, "I'm sorry, but I told you right from the beginning that I had to do this thing."

John Stakes sighed. "O.K., Fitz, we understand your position. Maybe what we should do is to go to Riyadh anyway, see how far we get, and by the time we've gone from Riyadh to Kuwait and back here, you'll be back from whatever it is you're doing, I won't ask, and if we need you to shore things up you can come with us at that time."

"That's the best thing I can suggest, John. By the time we get back maybe we'll have heard from Zayed. We'll try to arrange to see him in Abu Dhabi next time so that we don't have to make that trip to Al Ain. Then we can follow through from one ruler to the next and at least I will have this one thing behind me."

There was a long pause and finally Thornwell, obviously disgruntled, said, "Well, if that's the way it has to be, that's the way it will be. Christ, I wish there was something to do around here at night. This whole goddam Arab world is deadsville."

"You may see some changes in a year. I have some ideas of my own."

"Are you really going to build that bar and restaurant we were talking about?" Stakes asked.

Fitz grinned. "With the right full-time partner I just might. I just might."

"I'd sure like to be a partner with you on something like that, Fitz," Thornwell said, suddenly getting over his pique. "The number-one club in any city is a power base almost as influential as the mayor's office. And it is sure a hell of a lot more profitable. Unless the mayor's a crook, of course," he added as an afterthought.

"I appreciate your interest, Courty," Fitz said affably. "Of course, when I said partner I had in mind someone with a different configuration than yours or John's here or mine."

"Well, good luck, old boy," Stakes boomed out jovially. "I hope it works out that way. She's a wonderful girl. Of course, Dubai might not be interesting enough for her over the long haul."

Fitz was silent a few moments. Then he said, "Yes, you may have a point there, John. I've thought about that."

Peter brought in a platter of lamb and put it in front of Fitz. "Everybody dig in," Fitz said, "the wine's on the way."

At four o'clock that afternoon, after Stakes and Thornwell had left, Fitz drove to Sepah's home. Sepah was anxiously waiting for him. "This is it. We got the final consignment of gold we needed to make this the big shipment I wanted. Everything's ready in India and certain other profitable arrangements have been completed which you will observe during the course of the trip. We wait no longer. Be at the dhow tonight, ready to leave."

"Good!" Fitz exclaimed. "I'm ready to go. How about the follow-up with Shaikh Hamed?"

"My lawyer is drawing up the agreements now. He is conversant with oil leases and the preliminary documents for use in negotiation will be delivered to Shaikh Hamed within the week."

"We'd better get back to him as soon as we return from this trip," Fitz said urgently. "I don't want to find ourselves bidding against four or five other parties."

"When we leave Dubai we will see Kajmira before we're back in the Creek again."

Fitz returned to his house and packed up the few articles of clothing he would need for the six- to eight-day voyage. Then he sat in his cool living room, looking out over the Gulf, and sipped a cold gin and tonic which Peter brought him. He fought down the temptation to throw in a box of cheroots, those long, slender black cigars he had given up smoking about the time he first met Laylah. On his first dinner date with her Laylah had made a tactful remark indicating she didn't like the smell.

He stood up and Peter appeared from the kitchen. "Peter, I'll be away maybe eight days. You take good care here. I'll leave you a bottle of gin; the rest I locked up. You make the gin last, don't drink it all at once."

Peter grinned. "Me not drink gin, sahib. You see. All here when you get back."

"That'll be the day I have to break ice in the Gulf to swim," Fitz snorted. "O.K., take care. If you don't see me again, too bad. Nice to have had you working for me."

"I see you, the sahib Sepah, the memsahib Smith very soon." He nodded optimistically. "Very soon."

Fitz turned, picked up his bag, and left the house he had enjoyed so much during the time Laylah had been with him. He tossed the bag into the Land Rover, climbed in beside it, and headed for the Deira side, where the dhow was pulled up to Sepah's wharf close to the mouth of the Creek.

There was a great deal of activity about the unnamed dhow. As was customary, Sepah would wait until the first trip was finished before naming it. Fitz saw Sepah standing on the wharf supervising the loading process.

"Fitz," the ship's master greeted him. "Go below and make sure the ammunition is all there." Fitz threw Sepah a salute and climbed down a ladder through the hatch and into the hold. From his belt he pulled a flashlight and began examining the crates. Finally he found the boxes he was looking for. Five crates packed with a hundred rounds each of 20-mm. cannon shells. Although they were the same boxes he had personally seen loaded aboard the weapons carrier in northern Iran five or so weeks ago, he opened each box and examined the ammo. Just as he'd last seen it. Five hundred rounds of explosive smokeless shells in the hold of the ship, another five hundred rounds for future use in Sepah's warehouse. He inspected the twin cannons once again, pulling back the bolts and letting them go. Firing pins were O.K.

He snapped an empty drum into the breech of the gun. It fit snugly. One of the first jobs when they were out to sea would be to fill the drums with shells. His only worry was that they hadn't actually test-fired the weapons when they first arrived, but Sepah had refused for fear of attracting attention, even out on the desert.

Fitz looked around the hold until he located the two boxes of .30-caliber machine-gun ammunition. Once again he opened the boxes and looked over the bullets, each round linked to the next by metal clips. Later, when they were at sea, he would have them brought up to the wheelhouse. The two thirty-calibers and their mounts were safely stowed below where no prying eyes would see them. It would be a simple task to knock down the wheelhouse and reinstall them for use after the dhow was safely on the Gulf, out of sight of land. Then Fitz located the crate with the two hand-held machine guns. He checked the .223-caliber ammo for the Colt M-16 Armalite and .45-caliber bullets for the grease gun and .45-caliber pistol. Everything was in order.

With his own responsibility discharged for the moment, Fitz watched in wonderment as the boxes of gold were loaded aboard. By now he was familiar with the process. Each cardboard box, weighing forty-seven pounds, was clearly marked with the name of the bank which had shipped the gold to Dubai, and contained two hundred ten-tola bars. The ten-tola bar was the currency of gold smugglers, weighing 3.75 ounces of 99.9 percent pure gold. The human conveyor belt loading the boxes of gold from the trucks, onto the deck, and down into the hold was made up of ragged Indians as casual about the burdens they passed along as though the boxes had contained soap. There was not a sign of an armed guard that Fitz could see, yet the value of the cargo right here in Dubai was in excess of twelve million dollars. Each box being swung down the line of loaders was worth just over twenty-seven thousand dollars and three times that offloaded in India. It was a staggering concept that such valuable cargo could be openly loaded into a ship without the necessity of a platoon of heavily armed guards. A thousand years of Islamic eye-for-an-eye law, where the slightest infraction entailed the chopping off of hands, legs, and heads, mitigated against theft on any scale.

Fitz jumped off the boat onto the wharf and went up to Sepah.

"How long before we leave? I want to put my Land Rover away safely."

"I'll have one of my drivers take care of it for you, Fitz."

"I'm going to drive up the street for ten minutes, O.K.?"

Sepah grinned. "Everything in your department O.K.?"

Fitz nodded. "Soon's we get to sea we can break out the guns."

Fitz drove his Land Rover alongside the Creek to the new Carlton Hotel. It had been originally designed as an apartment house, but the owners agreed with Shaikh Rashid, the ultimate owner of the Carlton and everything else in the Shaikhdom, that a hotel would be more profitable and useful to the state, so in the final stages of completion it became a hotel. And since a hotel needs a liquor bar the Carlton was one of the first licensed bars on the Arabian Peninsula mainland.

It was a five-minute drive to the Carlton. Fitz parked directly in front of the hotel entrance. He strode inside and back to the well-concealed bar. It was a small, rather dingy place, the kind of bar a man would go to only because he needed a drink. There were only four other men in the place, all Westerners, hunched morosely over the drink in front of them. The bartender might have been a slave in bondage for all the happiness he showed at the entrance of another customer. But at least it was a bar. Fitz repeated his order for a double gin and ice three times before the doleful Baluchi, or Indian, or Pakistani, or whatever he was laboriously measured the drink, begrudgingly dropped in a sliver of ice, and slid it across to Fitz.

As he sipped the drink it once again became apparent how badly a really good bar and restaurant was needed in this part of the world. A place with music where the burgeoning oil community could go for fun and action, an attraction for the visitors and the men who would be coming in to hustle the oil money that would soon be pouring into what had to become one of the world's great boom towns. Fitz was mentally building such an establishment when he suddenly came to the part about paying for the construction and this made him look at his watch. He'd been in the silent bar, dreaming over his short-measure double gin, for thirty minutes.

He pointed to his glass but it required a negotiation to get a refill. What a few sharp bartenders could make for the house, and

what they could steal for themselves, he thought. Maybe he could
teach some Arabs to mix drinks. At least they wouldn't steal. No,
not this year, or even next, but the call of the West would get to
them and corrupt them eventually.

Fitz finished his second drink and, paying for it, he left the bar.
Not another customer had entered, and the four patrons hadn't
moved or spoken. He walked through the hotel and out onto the
street, where the hundred-degree heat and wilting humidity hit
him after the mere ninety-degree temperature inside the hotel
lobby and bar, not yet air-conditioned but electrically fanned.
Even the soggy-looking turbaned man sitting inside the front door
didn't walk outside to let Fitz into his car, despite the fact that
Fitz was still holding the paper change in his hand from paying
for his drink.

Fitz started up the Land Rover, made a U turn in the street,
and headed back the way he had come, parking beside the wharf.
Sepah's dhow was still being loaded. All the gold was apparently
aboard, Fitz noted. It seemed that the provisions for the trip were
going aboard now.

"Colonel Lodd, I was wondering when you'd get here."

Fitz whirled around. There was the reporter, David Harnett,
who had apparently been observing all the loading proceedings.
With some effort Fitz managed to stay cool. "Well, Harnett,
what are you doing, taking a stroll along the waterfront of the
Creek?"

"No, I just always had a yen to actually watch a gold-smuggling
boat head out to sea."

"What do you mean gold smuggling?" Fitz countered sharply.
"There's no such thing as smuggling out of this country."

"All right," Harnett acknowledged. "Re-exporting, I believe, is
the word they use around here."

"In any case, this ship, which belongs to a captain I've made
friends with, is heading for Kuwait. They promised to take me
along to get the feel of a ride in a dhow."

"Oh, really?" the reporter sneered. "Well, I'll be up in Kuwait
the day after tomorrow. Maybe I'll see you."

"Not if I see you first."

Sepah, standing on the rear poop deck of the dhow, was

searching the embankment, obviously wondering where Fitz was. Then he spotted Fitz and cried out, "Fitz, we go."

"Right," Fitz shouted back, and started down the dock. "Next stop Kuwait," he shouted even louder. He knew of course that Harnett did not believe him but there was nothing the reporter could prove. As Fitz walked up beside the boat Sepah asked, "Is everything O.K.?"

"Oh, sure," Fitz replied. "Everything's fine except there's a reporter up there, David Harnett, from the Associated Press. He's looking to do a story on gold smuggling, I think."

"Well, he can't prove anything and there's no law against taking gold or anything else out of Dubai."

"When do we get out of here?"

"Maybe one more hour. The crew is all here, and now provisions are aboard."

"And I'm ready." Fitz jumped over the gunwale and walked aft to the steps going up to the poop deck on which he had so carefully helped assemble what looked like a sturdy wheelhouse.

Inside the wheelhouse he leaned against the spoked wheel, put one of his feet up on the machine-gun pedestal, and waited for the final loading and boarding process. Now he wished he had brought the cheroots with him. This was the time to have a smoke. But he had kicked the habit once and nine days aboard ship with nothing much to do except smoke would have gotten him into the habit all over again. Laylah wouldn't like that.

CHAPTER 19

One hour later the three diesels down in the engine room began turning over and Sepah entered the wheelhouse. "I'll take her out from up here, Fitz."

Fitz nodded and watched the ropes being thrown aboard one by one as Sepah authoritatively called out orders. He took one last look at Harnett standing on the embankment and then studiously ignored him. Briskly the hundred-foot dhow slipped away from its mooring and headed into the Creek. Thirty minutes later they were leaving the mouth of the Creek behind them and steering out into open water.

Fitz thought, "What in the hell am I doing here? I was supposed to be a responsible light colonel, U. S. Army, not some smuggler, armed to the teeth to fight it out with the authorities." He put his head out the side window and looked behind the ship. A heavy wake churned from the three propellers and way behind the phosphorescent wake were the weak, twinkling lights of Dubai. Shit, why hadn't he at least brought one bottle with him? "Just because you might have drunk it," he told himself.

"I'll introduce you to the crew in the morning," Sepah said. "As soon as we're on course I'm going to turn the wheel over to my regular *nakhouda* and we'll bunk out in the captain's quarters below here. Tomorrow we really get the crew working."

The lights from shore had completely disappeared when the sturdy young Arab named Issa came into the wheelhouse. He was wearing the loose pantaloons and smock of seafarers rather than a *dish dasha,* and his red and white checked head covering was wrapped turban style around his head. Issa, who seemed to be in his thirties, nodded at Fitz and took the wheel from Sepah.

"Let us leave the ship to Issa," Sepah said to Fitz. "He is the best man I have. We'll go below."

The next morning Fitz woke up pleasantly to the smell of coffee and, opening his eyes, he saw a crewman standing in the cabin holding a long-beaked copper coffeepot in one hand and a cup in the other. When he saw Fitz was awake, he poured coffee into the cup and held it out to him.

After finishing two cups of coffee Fitz pulled on his pants, shirt, and shoes and stepped out of the captain's quarters onto the poop deck. Off to starboard he saw black mountains rising directly out of the water. Since he could see the sun rising above the ocean directly ahead of the dhow, they had to be just rounding the Musandam Peninsula, which jutted out into the Gulf creating the Straits of Hormuz. In another hour they would be sailing into the Gulf of Oman.

"Quite a sight from the sea, no?" Sepah asked, coming up to Fitz. They both studied the massive rock cliffs. "Until fifty years ago, despite the treaties with the British, the pirates used to come out of coves hidden in those mountains and attack the ships that ventured through the straits. At least now we're safe until we get into the Arabian Sea and halfway to Bombay."

"It's obvious why the Communist insurgents would like to control Oman. The Musandam Peninsula really commands these straits."

"It wouldn't be hard for a small launch to come out and drop a few mines into the straits in the path of the oil tankers," Sepah agreed.

"If ever I saw a Communist insurgency waiting to happen, it's right there, at the tip of Oman."

"Have some breakfast and we'll start to work," Sepah suggested. A bowl of rice with grilled fish and more coffee were brought to Fitz. He ate out on the deck and then followed Sepah from the poop deck down to the main deck, which was already a very active place. All over the deck the crew had spread out white canvas vests with rows of small pockets sewed into them. They looked something like hunting jackets with shell pockets distributed all around them. In front of each crewman was a black tray full of gold ten-tola bars. The men were tucking these matchbox-size gold bars into a pocket and then sewing them in. They worked swiftly, with dexterous fingers, at about the rate of one gold bar sewn into a pocket per minute. It appeared to Fitz as though each

vest contained about one hundred ten-tola bars, which would give
it a weight of twenty-four pounds. A convenient way for gold
smugglers and merchants in India to transport their wares.

"It will take the entire three days between here and Bombay for
the crew to sew all the gold into these vests," Sepah said. A note
of pride, perhaps not unmixed with fear, came to his voice. "This
is the largest single shipment of gold ever attempted out of Dubai,
probably out of the Arabian Gulf." He stared at the men sewing
up gold bars for a few moments. Then he started for the open
hatch. "Come, let's look at the reason so many traders joined this
syndicate."

Fitz followed Sepah down the hatch and into the hold. Although this was a large shipment, the boxes of gold took up only a
relatively small area of cargo space. The huge fuel tanks were distributed throughout in order not to put the full weight of the diesel oil in one part of the ship. The twin 20-mm. cannons domi-
nated the area belowdecks. It was as though these majestic
weapons demanded the respect of being accorded an entire cargo
hold all to themselves. "You've really got a hell of a lot more
space than you need for this kind of work," Fitz observed.

"So it might appear," Sepah murmured as they walked over to
the weapons. "Let us see how they work."

Fitz turned from the guns as three young men dropped down
through the hatch and approached him and Sepah.

"These three, Mohammed, Juma, and Khalil, are the best young
men with rifles I have discovered." A momentary twinge of pain
crossed Sepah's face. Fitz knew what hurt his friend and partner
but there was nothing anyone could do. Sepah had three daugh-
ters. His only son had died as a child.

"I'll make them proficient on this ship's armament in the next
two days, and if we get into a fire fight they'll become experts—if
we all live." He gave each of the young men a confident smile,
which they returned with forced, sickly grins.

"Come over here, watch what I do," Fitz said in Arabic. "And
learn well or you and Allah will meet face to face much sooner
than you expect." While the statement didn't add to the san-
guineness shown by the youths, they jumped into place around
Fitz.

"First you've got to learn what these weapons look like inside," he went on. Fitz slid up the backplate of the 20-mm. cannons, exposing the inner workings of the guns.

By the end of the morning all three would-be gunners had learned how to field-strip a 20-mm. cannon and were familiar with the most important moving parts of the weapon. When they had filled each of the drums with sixty 20-mm. rounds and learned how to insert the drum into the breech of the cannon, Fitz let them go up to the cool breeze blowing across the main deck.

After lunch of dates, lamb, and rice, Fitz took his three students back down to the hold. Sepah, who had left them during the morning to supervise the sewing of the gold into the vests, accompanied them into the hot cargo area belowdecks. "Now we're going to shoot these things," Fitz announced. "But we're not going to do much shooting because we need all our ammunition for the real thing. First I want you to watch me load, lock, and fire." He said the last three words in English, the language of modern war in all modern Arab countries.

Fitz fitted the drum into the breech of the left-hand weapon, locking it into place.

"To save ammo we'll only fire one gun today," he explained. Then Fitz turned to Sepah. "Open the firing strip."

Sepah went over to the bulkhead and, starting aft, he walked forward pulling out fastenings until he had reached the forward end of the strake, which he then, with the help of Fitz at the aft end, raised. The three neophyte gunners gasped in surprise as they looked out over the expanse of blue ocean outside the boat through the slit, eighteen inches wide and twenty feet long. There were two steel-reinforced ribs at each end of the strip. Fitz had importuned Abdul to figure out some way so he could have an uninterrupted thirty-foot firing slit but twenty feet was the best he could do and still guarantee that the boat would hold together.

Now Fitz explained to the student gunners the reason for the steel tubing that had been anchored into place around the barrel of the cannons. It would be impossible for them to shoot out the side of their own boat. He demonstrated the control the steel tubing exercised over the weapon. It could not be trained on the bulkheads. This gave Sepah's future combat force some measure of confidence. They had noticed and worried about how deeply inside the boat the end of the gun barrel was positioned. Fitz tried to explain to them that the reason for this was so that the enemy wouldn't perceive that the dhow was firing at them until their ship was sinking.

With the cannon ready to shoot, Fitz reached forward with his right hand and hauled back the charging lever, pulling the first shell in the drum into firing position. He flipped off the safety catch, bent his knees to bring his eye on a level with the ring sights, and then, finger on the trigger with a gentle caress, he fired a burst of three rounds. With a broad grin on his face Fitz turned to Sepah.

"How do you like that? She's beautiful, no? Did you ever hear anything so quiet that could do so much damage?"

Sepah laughed happily. "Yes, beautiful, Fitz. You did it. I couldn't believe that such a weapon could really exist."

"Wait until you see what those rounds do to the Indian patrol launches." He beckoned to Mohammed.

"Now I want you to shoot just three rounds like I did. For sweet Allah's sake, don't jerk or pull the trigger, touch it gently. Understand? Gently."

Mohammed nodded and stepped up to the cannon. He sighted out to sea and stuck his finger on the trigger. Eight or nine rounds were discharged before he could get his finger off it.

"Burst control!" Fitz cried in English. "Burst control, by Allah." Then in Arabic he cried, "Gently!" six times. The other two boys laughed loudly at their hapless comrade and Fitz called Khalil over to the gun. He succeeded in only firing six rounds. Next it was Juma's turn. He had enjoyed the advantage of watching his two fellow gunners and he had closely observed the action of Fitz's finger on the trigger.

Confidently he stepped up to the gun, bent his knees, sighted, and with a delicate sliding motion of his trigger finger allowed only three rounds out of the muzzle.

"Good, very good!" Fitz exclaimed. "Now we'll all try another burst." The last word he said in English. Someday, he thought, Colonel Buttres would thank him for sending the Trucial Oman Scouts three machine-gunners who understood combat English.

Another hour of patient instruction and he had his three students firing bursts of three rounds, one after the other, and swinging the guns as they fired.

"We're going to have a good gun crew," Fitz called up from the hatch as he gained the deck to stand by Sepah. I hope we didn't shake up the boys on deck here too much."

"They were hardly aware of what was going on," Sepah replied. "Now how about the thirty-caliber machine guns?"

"I thought we'd spend the day on them and the light machine guns tomorrow. I assume there's no chance of the Indian Coast Guard hitting us a thousand miles from the coast."

"They come out further all the time," Sepah replied. "But I would say we're safe tomorrow. It's going to be the following two days we have to worry about."

"They're all good boys," Fitz said. "How do you want to handle combat stations if we're hit?"

"You take the twenties, I'll take the wheel and the thirties, Juma and Khalil will stay below with you to learn the cannons in action, and I'll keep Mohammed on the thirties with me. For some reason I feel that when killing ceases to be abstract and becomes a case of gunning down men, Mohammed's our best boy. Did you see how he went after that cannon, even if he did squeeze off too many shots?"

"Have you had experience with a thirty-caliber machine gun?" Fitz asked. "That's going to be an important position when we close with the patrol launch."

Sepah smiled. "I have used that machine gun during the Abu Dhabi war. Naturally I could use a refresher course tomorrow but I have manned a thirty-caliber in combat, and most successfully."

"Good. Now about the two light machine guns, they will be needed if we get into close combat. They'll give us another angle of fire to pick off the Indian fifty-caliber gunner."

"I have an excellent man aboard who is expert with all hand-held weapons. I believe I told you about him. We're sending him ashore with the gold to destroy a certain trustee who has been dishonest with the syndicate. As long as he is aboard, since he is being so well paid, we will use his skills if they are required."

"Where is he?" Fitz asked.

"I will call him." Sepah went to the forward section of the dhow and returned a few minutes later with a gaunt, dark-skinned Indian wearing shorts down to his knees, the traditional smock, and a loose turban wound about his head. The deep lines that cut

through his face and the burning eyes gave him an evil appearance. Here was what Americans would call a "hit man" if Fitz
had ever seen one.

"This is Haroon," Sepah said simply.

Fitz and the Indian nodded to each other. "What's his language?" Fitz asked Sepah.

"Whatever you are most comfortable in, sahib," Haroon answered with a bow.

A high-class hit man, Fitz thought. "O.K., Haroon, you know
the forty-five-caliber grease gun?"

"For sure, sahib. My favorite weapon. But too big for this job."
His eyes lit up. "You have on this ship?"

Fitz nodded. "I also have a machine gun you have probably
never seen, the Armalite. The U. S. Army calls it the M-16."

"You have here?"

Fitz nodded. "You know what we do if an Indian Coast Guard
launch tries to stop us?"

Haroon grinned broadly, showing several gold teeth.

"Good. I will go down below and bring up the weapons. You
follow and bring the ammunition. We'll let you do some firing."

Eagerly Haroon followed Fitz down into the hold and in a few
minutes they reappeared on the deck, Fitz carrying the two machine guns, Haroon hauling up a box of ammunition. They put
the weapons and ammo on the deck amidships and Haroon paid
careful attention as Fitz took up the lightweight grease gun and
handed it to him. Then Fitz turned to Sepah. "Have you got
something I can throw into the water to use as a target?"

Sepah looked about the boat. "How about an empty ten-tola
box. It isn't very big."

"It's big enough and we have plenty of them. Let me have a
few."

Sepah shouted a command and a crewman ran forward to
where the men were sewing gold bars into vests and brought back
several of the boxes, each about the size in which a half-gallon
bottle of liquor is packaged.

"Tell him to take them forward," Fitz ordered. "When I yell
have him toss two boxes overboard."

Sepah relayed the instructions.

"Now, Haroon, let's simulate a combat situation. You're firing at men on the deck of the launch who are trying to get to the fifty-caliber machine gun. We've killed one gunner." Fitz reached down into the ammunition box and brought out two long steel magazines, each holding twenty .45-caliber bullets. He handed the magazines to Haroon to hold and, reaching down again, he brought up a roll of black friction tape. He started to pull out a strip of tape and when six inches or so was dangling from the roll, he handed the tape to Sepah and took the two magazines from Haroon.

"Do you know what I'm going to do?"

Haroon shook his head as Fitz placed the butt ends of the magazines together and handed them back to Haroon to hold in that position. Then, taking the roll of tape back from Sepah, he taped the two magazine butts securely together and tore off the tape. Dropping the roll in the ammo box, he picked up the submachine gun and plunged one open end of a magazine into the breech from the bottom and pulled back the bolt, sliding a round into the chamber. The two magazines taped together protruded about two feet down from the weapon as Fitz held it at a semi-ready position. He advanced to the edge of the gunwale of the dhow, which was cutting through the water at its fifteen-knot cruising speed.

"Toss 'em!" he shouted.

Two white boxes went out over the side and as they hit the water Fitz sighted and squeezed the trigger. A pattern of bullets stitched the water and then crumpled one of the boxes. As the other box was rushing past the middle of the boat Fitz thumbed the catch on the machine gun, pulled the magazine out, twirled it in the air, jamming the end of the second magazine into the weapon, and another line of bullets cut through the water and destroyed the second box before it could shoot beyond the end of the fast-moving dhow.

Haroon drew in a sharp breath. A shout of surprise and admiration came from him. Sepah also cried out. Fitz lowered the machine gun. "If we get into a fight that's the way you're going to have to use this weapon. You'll have forty rounds of fast fire instead of twenty."

Khalil, Juma, and Mohammed had watched the demonstration open-mouthed and stood staring at each other helplessly. Could they ever learn to do that? they seemed to be asking each other. Fitz smiled at them, reading their minds. "You can do this," he said in Arabic. "It only requires practice. It also requires a lot of ammunition, which we do not have. Maybe after we get close to home when this trip is over and we don't have to worry about the Indian Coast Guard, if we have any bullets left over I'll teach you to fire a submachine gun that way." Fitz removed the magazine and handed the weapon to Haroon.

"O.K., Haroon. Here it is." Fitz handed him the two magazines taped together. For the next half hour Fitz drilled Haroon in the fine art of inserting and reinserting the magazine into the breech of the weapon. When Haroon had the technique working for him Fitz called for two more boxes to be thrown over the side. The Indian assassin stitched the first box neatly enough but in pulling out the magazines, fast twirling them and sticking the other end back into the gun, Haroon completely missed the second box. Now he looked at Fitz with real respect.

"If they sent me to kill you I would be afraid and refuse the job." This was the highest praise Haroon was capable of expressing.

Fitz gave the Indian an encouraging pat on the shoulder. Then he held up the M-16 rifle. "Tomorrow we'll go into this baby, but I think we've all had enough to think about for today."

"Right," Sepah agreed. "Come up to quarters and we'll have tea."

Fitz reached for the box with the two submachine guns and ammunition and, carrying it, followed Sepah along the deck aft to the captain's quarters.

Over the sweet herbal tea Sepah exultantly talked about the shipment of gold aboard the dhow. He had never felt as confident about the trip on which his entire fortune and reputation rested as he did now. "You'll be interested to know, Fitz, that the last day before we set out to sea I took on an extra hundred boxes of ten-tola bars. Because there hasn't been a gold shipment successfully taken into India for six months, the agents are desperate for it. There is perhaps one hundred million dollars in foreign currency and silver waiting to be translated into gold at one hundred and ten dollars an ounce. The syndicate's gross profit on this trip should be about thirty million dollars. The payoffs come to twenty-five percent, so we net about twenty-two and a half million dollars. This will not only pay for all my past losses but make me a rich man again."

Sepah finished his cup of tea. "Your percentage will be even higher than you or I thought when we first planned this voyage."

Fitz reached into his pocket and pulled out his red worry beads, which he twisted and kneaded in his right hand.

Sepah, observing Fitz fidgeting with the beads, chuckled. "You are becoming like an Arab."

"No drinking on this trip, you have to relieve the tension some way," he answered.

CHAPTER 20

The third day out brought them within range of the Indian Coast Guard patrol launches. Now a man was placed in a lookout station atop the mast. The radar screen was under perpetual surveillance and three radios were tuned to the different frequencies known to be used by the Indian Navy and Coast Guard. The dhow proceeded at cruising speed on a southeasterly course toward Bombay, two days away.

On deck the crew was still furiously sewing the gold bars into vests. Every member of the crew knew that this trip would mean a relative fortune for him personally. Each man knew what his share would be and it was with great enthusiasm that box after box of ten-tola bars was sewed into the vests. The excitement, heavily tinged with apprehension, could be felt on deck. The crew had all witnessed the shooting practice and realized that this was a life-or-death attempt. Every man on the ship would be rich or dead soon.

Toward the end of the day with still no blips on the radar signaling an approaching ship, Sepah relaxed somewhat over tea in his quarters, where he could keep a constant vigil over the greenish round scope. Finally darkness settled over the ocean and the entire crew became less restive.

"We will take turns watching the radar screen tonight," Sepah said to Fitz. "I'll take the first watch since you had a busy day with your apprentice assassins." He laughed.

Fitz was tired and he quickly dozed off. He was awakened after midnight by Sepah. "Your turn to watch the green eye." Fitz nodded and took a chair opposite the radar screen, busily twisting the red beads in his right hand. The *nakhouda*, Issa, was steering from the collapsible wheelhouse above them as they plowed through the water at a steady fifteen knots, all three Rolls-Royce diesels humming smoothly. Mentally, as he kept an eye on the screen and listened to the crackling of the three radios, he began designing his bar in Dubai. It would be his power base and listening post. If this trip were successful, not only would he have the money to build the bar and small hotel, he would have the gratitude and respect of the Ruler and his advisers. It would require the Ruler's grant of a piece of land on which to build his place as well as the Ruler's permission to sell alcoholic beverages.

He pictured himself walking through his bar, checking on new arrivals in Dubai, gathering information which could be traded for more information. He laughed to himself. He was still an intelligence officer at heart. Then, about three-thirty in the morning, he noticed a small white blip on the radar screen. It denoted something to the southeast of them, coming from the direction of Bombay. He watched the blip move very slowly toward them and when the radar indicated it was eight miles away, he woke up Sepah.

In an instant Sepah was alert, studying the spot on the green tube. He ran outside onto the poop deck and called up to Issa that he would take over the wheel and then back in his quarters he reached out and took two spokes of the wheel in his hands and veered the dhow onto a course away from the oncoming vessel. "If we can run around them we will, even though it will delay our arrival."

Sepah eased the three throttles on the pedestal forward, increasing the speed of the dhow from fifteen to twenty-two knots as it maintained its new course, trying to make an end run around the approaching vessel. By four-thirty it was apparent that the other blip was also changing its heading onto an intercept course with the dhow.

"They've got a radar fix on us too," Sepah announced.

"With twenty tons of gold in the hold I shouldn't wonder," Fitz remarked dryly.

"There's no point in trying to get around him if he's a patrol launch," Sepah said. "I'm going to head back toward Bombay." He looked out the port window to the east, where the first faint glow of sunrise was beginning to appear on the horizon. "We'll just go on about our business and raise sail as though we were an

ordinary trading dhow." He pushed the glass window in front of
him down and shouted for all hands on deck to raise sail.

As the sun rose over the Arabian Sea the dhow was sailing along
under its large lanteen sail hanging from the gaff-rigged yardarm.
Sepah had cut back the three diesel engines to idle and the small
amount of exhaust smoke which was released underwater could
not be seen. Now the dhow looked like a simple trader plying the
ancient Arabian Sea routes.

"If that launch tries to stop us on the high seas it is a simple
and open case of piracy," Fitz said with some satisfaction. "Any
ship is entitled to defend itself against pirates." Out on the horizon the ship on a cutoff bearing was looming larger as it approached the dhow proceeding under sail.

"I would have expected to hear radio calls," Fitz said as he ex-
plored the shortwave frequencies on one of the radios.

"They know they don't need help capturing an unarmed
dhow." Sepah watched the fast-approaching patrol launch. "If we
should happen to have gold aboard, they'll never have to tell their
superiors. They'll smuggle it back to India themselves."

"Time for battle stations," Fitz said grimly.

"Tell Issa to take the helm until I can get up to the wheelhouse," Sepah replied.

Fitz ran out of the captain's quarters and mounted the steps to
the poop deck. Mohammed was already in the wheelhouse. "Take
the wheel until Sepah gets up here," Fitz shouted at Issa, then he
ran down to the main deck, where Khalil and Juma were already
tumbling down the hatch to reach the cannons. Before he followed them he looked to make sure Haroon was in his position
lying concealed in the bow of the boat, the grease gun cradled in
his arm, two taped magazines by his side, and a canvas bag of
magazines beside him. Fitz gave him a wave and a reassuring grin
and then swung down the ladder to the hold. Juma and Khalil
were standing at attention, one on each side of the twin cannons.
A drum had been inserted in the breech of both guns.

Fitz motioned his gunners to raise the strake on the port side of
the boat. In moments he was looking out through the twenty-foot-
long slit at the ocean. The patrol launch moved inexorably toward
them. Fitz reached for the binoculars hanging above the cannons
and trained them on the approaching ship. It was flying no flag,

he noticed. As he stared through the glasses he saw two sailors run forward along the deck of the launch and take up their station beside the fifty-caliber machine gun mounted on the bow.

This Fitz interpreted as a hostile act. He charged first one, then the second of the twin twenties and trained their sights just below the bridge of the launch, which he now estimated to be nine hundred yards off and closing fast. The fifty-caliber machine gun would become deadly effective at six hundred yards, the twenties had an accurate range of over fifteen hundred yards.

Squinting through the sights, his knees bent, Fitz started easing off bursts into the oncoming launch and suddenly the Indian ship started to crumble in the middle as the heavy shells wreaked destruction on the launch. He laughed aloud at the shocked surprise the crew of the Indian Coast Guard boat must be experiencing. They could see no signs of any hostile action from the small sailing dhow, no guns blazing, yet their ship was being violently torn apart. Fitz swung the twenties and took aim at the fifty-caliber gun on the bow. The gun crew was so shocked and amazed at the sudden collapse of their boat that they weren't even looking at the dhow. Perhaps they thought their twin engines had blown up. And so they had of course, but not by themselves.

Several bursts from the cannons tore the fifty-caliber machine gun from its mounts and both gun-crew members seemed to disintegrate.

Fitz stopped firing. He turned to Khalil. "Five short bursts and then we'll let Juma finish the job. Aim for the bridge, that's where the radio is."

Eagerly Khalil flexed his knees, took careful aim, and let off his allotted five bursts of three to five shells each. The bridge splintered to pieces.

"Good," Fitz said. "No more radio. O.K., Juma."

Enthusiastically Juma took the handles of the cannon mounts, sighted at the stern of the boat and began firing. The patrol launch suddenly blew up with a great geyser of red flames and smoke as Juma's rounds found the ammunition locker.

Fitz patted him on the shoulder. "O.K., O.K., no more. Save ammunition."

Fitz climbed jubilantly to the deck and was greeted by an awed crew. They had no concept of the firepower of the 20-mm. cannon

until before their eyes the hated patrol launch had been destroyed. He continued up to the poop deck and entered the
wheelhouse. Sepah seemed as awed as the rest of the crew. He just
kept shaking his head and staring at the flaming wreckage floating
seven hundred yards away from them. Suddenly he seemed to get
hold of himself, pushed up the throttles, and headed for the sinking ship. As they came closer they saw two men in the water trying to hold on to some of the still floating portions of the ill-fated
patrol launch.

"I'm damned," Fitz exclaimed. "I never thought anyone would
live through that. We'd better take them aboard. Wouldn't want
them picked up by anyone else."

The words were hardly out of his mouth before the staccato
burst of machine-gun fire sounded from the bow of the boat. The
two survivors twisted in the water as blood came to the surface.
Haroon had added two more men to his score.

"We could have saved them," Fitz protested. "There was nothing they could have done to hurt us and we might have learned
some valuable information from them, like the radio frequencies
they transmit on."

Sepah shrugged. "Too late. Next time I'll tell Haroon not to
fire on survivors without orders."

"I just wish we could know if they got a radio message out before that last burst of ours." Fitz turned and left the wheelhouse.

The crew dropped the yardarm and sail on orders from Sepah,
who revved up the three engines until the dhow was cruising at
eighteen knots, and as the morning wore on the boat pushed its
way southward toward Bombay. Fitz instructed Khalil and Juma
in cleaning the two cannons.

Fitz's personal submachine gun, the M-16, hung above the
20-mm. cannons and he removed the clip from it and dropped it
into the canvas bag of .223-caliber ammo magazines. Then he
went back on deck and strode forward to where Haroon was still
seated, cradling his submachine gun in his arms.

"Did you clean it yet?" he shouted harshly. Haroon, who considered he had just performed valorous service, looked up questioningly at the American he thought should be proud of him.

"No, sahib," he confessed. "I only shot ten rounds," he added
proudly.

"You don't keep that weapon clean it will jam on you." With that Fitz walked away from the Indian assassin.

For the rest of the day Fitz or Sepah alternately monitored the radios and radar. In midafternoon, as Fitz was searching the various shortwave dials, he came across some garbled conversation which included words in English and another language unintelligible to him. The English words were all concerned with compass bearings, speeds in knots, and nomenclature of military hardware. He knew he had a Navy or Coast Guard transmission and called to Sepah to help him listen. Sepah climbed down from the poop deck and joined him, listening to the radio.

"Sounds to me like they're trying to raise one of their boats," Fitz offered. "Probably the one we destroyed."

Sepah nodded as he concentrated on the voices crackling over the radio. "Yes, that is what they are trying to do, get a patrol launch to answer. Let me see if I can get a bearing on the signal." Each of the radios was equipped with a direction finder and as Sepah plugged in earphones and slowly turned the calibrated disk on top of the radio, the signal became stronger and then weaker until he zeroed in on the direction from which it was emanating.

"The signal is coming from a naval vessel in a direct line between our position and Bombay," he announced, glancing at the radar dial, which showed nothing as the white radius line ran round and round the tube without leaving a blip. "We'll change course to west of its position. That will delay our arrival but anything that puts out that powerful a signal has to be larger than a patrol launch. We'll have to keep a sharp eye on the radar from now until we make delivery."

Veering slightly off course, Sepah continued to run the dhow at cruising speed and as darkness fell he turned over the wheel to Issa. "You take the first watch until midnight and then wake me up," Sepah instructed Fitz. "Keep running the dials on the other two radios. If you get anything wake me up."

"Aye," Fitz responded. "Get some sleep. We may have a tough day tomorrow." After coffee and shish kebab with rice Sepah walked around the ship a few times inspecting everything and then returned to quarters and lay down on his bunk. He was soon asleep. For the next few hours Fitz twirled the dials of two of the radios, leaving the third tuned in to the frequency over which they had heard the transmission earlier in the day. About midnight a distinctly British-sounding voice crackled over the Indian naval frequency they had been monitoring. Probably one of those Sandhurst-educated Indian officers who are more British than the Brits, Fitz figured. Most of the senior officers of the Indian Navy and Army were English-speaking.

"Still no response from PL 6," the voice crackled. "Send out two patrol launches to last known position of PL 6. Command frigate bearing north-northwest from Bombay to assist in search."

Fitz took a bearing on the signal and pinpointed its position as comfortably southwest of their heading, well out to sea of them from the Indian coast. He certainly didn't want to tangle with a frigate whose guns could blow them out of the water at a three-mile range, although it was highly unlikely a vessel of that size would fire on a dhow in international waters without investigating first.

As Fitz was examining the chart, Issa, the *nakhouda*, came into the captain's quarters and walked up behind him. He pointed out their present position, having just taken a celestial fix with his sextant. By morning they would be just over two hundred miles from Bombay, which meant they should be making their rendezvous with the Indian smuggling boats about twenty-four hours from now. The situation seemed very good to Fitz. With a frigate and two launches out looking for the missing ship, there would be that much less chance of running into another Coast Guard or Navy vessel.

He waited until almost two in the morning, when his eyes were getting heavy and he could no longer concentrate on the radar screen, to wake up Sepah. Giving Sepah a report of the radio message he had intercepted, he went to his own bunk and fell into it, asleep as his head touched the pillow.

When he awoke in the morning it was to the smell of steaming aromatic coffee. Sepah's server was standing beside the bunk and as Fitz's eyes opened, the server poured a cup of coffee and handed it to him.

Fitz made a mental note that when and if he made it home Peter would wake him this way unless he had more alluring company with him. Sitting up on the bunk, he sipped the coffee. Finishing it and shaking the cup, he stood up and looked around the quarters. Except for the coffee server who took his cup, he was alone. No one was watching the radar tube although he saw that it showed no blips. Did this mean, as he fondly hoped, that they were safe? A crewman brought him a basin of water and he washed his face and brushed his teeth, using the cup of water beside his bunk, and went out on deck. It was a clear, bright, hot day but the speed of the dhow plowing through the water provided a comfortable breeze on deck. He ambled up to the wheelhouse, where Issa was steering. He was surprised that Sepah wasn't either on the poop deck or in quarters and he padded back to the main deck to find the master of the ship.

Finally, down in the hold, where it was hot and airless, he found Sepah painstakingly counting each vest and checking each pocket, making notations in a notebook. He looked up as Fitz dropped into the hold.

"Tonight, as soon as it is dark, we'll start carrying these vests up on deck. All-lah!" he exclaimed. "This is a monster load of gold. Never again will I try to move so much on a single run. The nervous strain is too much for a man."

"Any problems with the tally?"

"None at all. In this business every man must be honorable. There is too much at stake. And, moreover, nobody wants Haroon after him."

"No one is monitoring the radar," Fitz said.

"I checked it just fifteen minutes ago before you woke up. And we have a man at the top of the mast, as you may have seen."

Fitz nodded. "But radar sees further."

Back in Sepah's quarters they took a look at the radar tube and then sat down. "I think we're going to be lucky," Sepah said. "I just feel that we won't see any more Coast Guard boats."

"I hope you are right." Fitz glanced at the radar. "I'll keep my eye on the tube, you do what you have to do."

After watching the radar screen for an hour Fitz left the cabin and walked out on deck. Seeing Haroon sitting on the deck up forward, the machine gun still cradled lovingly in his arms, Fitz went up to him. Professionally he was curious about the killer's methods.

After greeting the Indian, who assured him that he had thoroughly cleaned the submachine gun, Fitz asked him what sort of weapon he favored for killing errant trustees.

A grin of sheer malevolence spread across Haroon's face and gold flashed from his teeth. He pushed aside the folds of his jacket to reveal a long leather sheath strapped to his chest. From the sheath he pulled a wicked-looking thin blade.

"For this job the knife is best. It is silent and a man whose life flows from a cut throat and belly is the best warning to others what must happen to them if they cheat the gold syndicate."

Fitz shuddered slightly. "I quite agree, Haroon."

CHAPTER 21

When, in the early evening, they had not sighted another ship and the sun was dropping closer to the rim of the ocean, Fitz began feeling as high as though he had been drinking. They were heading southeast, paralleling the Indian coast fifty miles away. The rest of the crew seemed equally euphoric, laughing, pushing each other about the deck, no doubt dreaming how they were going to spend the money they would make on this trip.

Issa, the *nakhouda*, was at the helm heading the dhow in toward a coastline he knew as well as the Creek at Dubai. He was a veteran of many such trips and several "accidents" when it had been necessary to drop the gold overboard as an Indian patrol launch bore down on them.

Fitz and Sepah were having their coffee in quarters just before dark when Fitz, his eyes never far from the green tube, let out an exclamation. Sepah followed his glance and jumped to his feet. The blip was a larger one than the patrol launch had made and was coming on a direct heading toward them.

"I was afraid this was all too good to be true," Fitz groaned.

"Let's not worry until we see what it is," Sepah answered. "It won't be long before we'll get a look."

"At night?"

"It won't be completely dark for another hour. The sun hasn't touched the sea yet. We'll maintain our heading for the rendezvous twenty miles north of Bombay. I'd like to make it tonight."

"And if we don't?"

"My receiver will also be there tomorrow night with boats and men ready but it is dangerous to have a reception party in the same place two nights running."

They continued their course, steering east of southeast, closing the distance between them and the coastline and watching the blip on the radar tube. Issa was steering the dhow, standing beside Sepah in his quarters. Fitz and Sepah were both sweeping the ocean ahead of them with binoculars. Finally, at a range of six miles, Fitz let out an exclamation. "It's a big gunboat. A hell of a lot more than we can handle."

Sepah ordered Issa to swing the dhow on a course off to the right, almost due south, away from the oncoming gunboat. "They probably can't see this little dhow visually yet. Let's see how they react to our change of course."

After ten minutes running away from the head-on course with the Indian naval vessel, Fitz saw through his glasses that the large ship was turning westerly to its left to cut them off. The blip on the radar also showed the change of course.

"Change course to northeast," Sepah snapped. "Full throttle!" Issa abruptly spun the wheel and the dhow turned sharply in an acute angle on itself to the left, heading back north away from the oncoming Indian ship and east toward the Indian coast. Once on course Issa pushed all three throttles full forward and the wooden boat shuddered and seemed to leap forward as the three powerful diesels ground out their full power.

"Now you see why we spend so much money on the best diesel engines." Sepah watched the Indian ship change course once again as the dhow fairly flew away from it. "Fitz, work the radio and see if you can pick up any signals."

Fitz played the frequency dial on the receiver, trying to pick up some radio signals from the ship vainly pursuing them. At the end of thirty minutes the gunboat was out of sight behind them and the blip on the radar screen was fast receding to the edge of the tube. With darkness now covering the ocean the dhow was once again safe, at least temporarily.

"I can't pick up any signals," Fitz complained. "God damn, I wish we'd picked up those two men. Haroon could have had his jollies torturing the Indian Coast Guard SOI out of them." He noticed Sepah's lack of comprehension. "Signal Operating Instructions," he explained.

"You can be sure that the radios are calling out all over the Arabian Sea to look for a smuggler heading on a northeasterly course at high speed," Sepah answered. "We'll fool them."

He continued on his course for another half hour, long after the

Indian war vessel had faded from the radar screen. Then he checked his watch. "It's twenty-two hundred hours, two hours to midnight. We change course here and in four hours we'll be right off our rendezvous point, Bassein, twenty miles north of Bombay. Hopefully the entire Coast Guard and Navy will be expecting us to continue on our runaway course and searching the sea north of here."

Sepah gave the orders to Issa and once again the dhow swung around sharply, changing from a northeast to a southeast bearing in a direct line for the point where the gold would be turned over to Sepah's Indian reception organization. There was no thought of trying to sleep now. Fitz watched the radar tensely as the *nakhouda* held the dhow on course toward Bassein. Occasionally he walked out on the main deck in front of the main wheelhouse and captain's quarters, where the speed of the boat created a brisk breeze outside.

"By God, you're really using the diesels, Sepah," Fitz remarked as they went into their third hour on course to the rendezvous north of Bombay.

"This is what they're for. Now you see why we carry such large tanks. Even so, on the way home once we get away from the Indian coast, we'll proceed under sail. We'll have used up more than half of our fuel by the time we make contact with my people."

They were well into their fourth hour when Fitz was able to make out lights in the distance and south of their position a yellowish glow tinged the horizon. "There's Bombay." Sepah pointed at the glow.

Issa seemed to be heading directly toward the lights ashore, about ten miles off, Fitz figured. He wondered when the small fleet of boats would be coming out to meet the dhow and relieve it of its multimillion-dollar cargo of gold. As they approached the hulking land mass at almost forty miles an hour, Fitz kept expecting they would stop. In ten minutes they were within five miles of land and still speeding toward it.

"When do we stop?" he asked Sepah uneasily. For the first time Sepah failed to answer a question. He merely stared grimly ahead. Every two minutes the dhow was a mile closer to shore. Certainly they were unalterably within Indian Coast Guard legally controlled waters now and still rushing closer to land.

Slowly the *nakhouda* began throttling back and the dhow settled into the water as it slowed down to twelve knots. They were
no more than two miles from land now and still going in.

"Hey, Sepah." Fitz made no effort to conceal his agitation. "I
thought we stayed outside of Indian territorial waters and the
boats came out to us."

"Not this trip, Fitz." Sepah continued to stare ahead into the
darkness. Then a light began to blink ashore and Issa veered the
dhow so it headed straight into the flashing light. Now he had
throttled down to a crawl. The dhow continued ahead and Fitz
saw that they were coming into a cove. Land rose up on both
sides of the ship. They were right inside the Indian subcontinent.
This would be a deadly place out of which to fight. Fitz was
unabashedly frightened. It was one thing to die at sea fighting,
but another to be captured right on Indian soil in the act of smuggling and no doubt the Indian Navy would tie the heavily armed
dhow to the disappearance of the patrol launch. Nevertheless,
since there was nothing he could do but stand by, he tried to put
his fears aside and watch what happened.

The dhow came to a complete stop and drifted in the cove. Issa
did not order the anchor to be dropped, rather he held his position by jockeying the throttle of one of the engines from forward
to reverse. At least they could run for it when the time came, Fitz
thought approvingly. A small boat came alongside and a man
bounded up onto the deck of the dhow. Sepah went to meet him.
The two shook hands and talked in English, still the universal language of diplomacy, war, and thievery. Sepah didn't bother to introduce Fitz, and the crew of the dhow immediately began shift-
ing the gold-laden vests from the deck to the small boat as Sepah
and his receiver talked.

The receiver called to two of his men and they hoisted up an
enormous steamer trunk from the boat to the deck of the dhow.
"You will find that the checks and currency in here cover about
half the price landed in India of your cargo," the receiver said.

"The rest will come through normal banking channels from our
trustees," Sepah explained in an aside to Fitz.

"That is true," the receiver said. "However, it happens I have
here, on the beach, forty tons of silver bars it would be convenient
if you would take aboard. I realize it is unusual for you to return

with anything, but this would save perhaps three months getting payment back to you."

"You have the men to load it before daylight?" Sepah asked.

"Certainly."

"Then get started. We'll offload gold on the starboard side and take the silver bars aboard to port."

"I'm in no hurry for my money," Fitz said. "Why don't we just get our asses out of here while they're whole?"

"We can easily carry forty tons of silver bars and for this particular trip it will make me very happy to return to Dubai with the largest amount of our profits aboard. The cream, so to speak, will come through later. But within days of the time we return every investor will be paid back in total as well as receiving at least half his profit, which already is a bigger return than he could have hoped for putting his money in any other business venture."

Sepah gave Fitz a meaningful look. "You make sure your guns are ready. We still may have to fight our way out of here. Even if we have offloaded the gold the Indian Coast Guard would confiscate the boat, cargo, and negotiable paper we've picked up and imprison us for a long stretch if they could catch us." Sepah went back to supervise the offloading of the gold and simultaneous taking aboard of silver bars.

Fitz found his three gunners standing behind him waiting for orders. He sent Mohammed and Khalil up to the wheelhouse to stand by the thirty-caliber machine guns and he and Juma went below, pushing their way through the boat crew carrying up the gold-filled vests. With Juma's help Fitz opened the firing slits on both sides of the dhow, which had the effect of cooling off the hot cargo hold to the comfort of the crew members pitching up the twenty-four-pound vests of gold ten-tola bars. He snapped a magazine drum into the breech of both weapons. All it would take was a manual pull on the charging bolts and they would be ready to level destruction at any attackers.

Leaving the hold, Fitz dashed up to the poop deck and saw that Mohammed was standing by the thirties. He threaded the two belts of ammunition into the machine guns and they were ready now if needed. "All yours, Mohammed," Fitz said. "But whatever happens, don't knock down the wheelhouse and start firing unless you get orders from the captain or myself. Someone will be up to

stand by with you." Mohammed nodded, elated at being given the
responsibility for these powerful weapons. Fitz dropped back to
the main deck to find Haroon and retrieve the grease gun with
which the Indian was having an obvious love affair. He found
Haroon in his accustomed position up in the bow of the boat, the
weapon cradled in his arms, waiting for his orders to disembark.

Tactfully Fitz relieved the Indian assassin of the machine gun.
After all, he pointed out, a man couldn't walk into Bombay with
an American submachine gun slung over his shoulder and there
was no way to conceal it. Besides, Fitz insisted, Haroon was a
dagger man. A slit throat or knife in the back was his feared trademark, not a mere bullet in the head, which any thug could admin-
ister. Having built up Haroon's pride in his accomplishments, Fitz
walked away from him carrying the weapon.

It took the rest of the night to complete loading forty tons of
silver bars onto the dhow, although unloading the gold, a process
in which the crew and reception party was highly practiced, was
accomplished in just over an hour. Fitz stayed near Sepah at all
times and learned a little more about the gold-smuggling trade.

Along with the silver bars being stacked up in the hold of the
dhow Fitz noticed that many burlap bags, stuffed almost to the
bursting point, were being thrown aboard. He estimated that a
minimum of sixty, perhaps as many as a hundred of these bags
were being stored below with the silver.

Sepah, as he strode back and forth across the deck, noticed Fitz
eying the last of the bags coming aboard. The smuggler laughed.
"I told you, Fitz, that I had managed to make some arrangements
to increase the profit on this trip."

"I sure didn't expect I was getting into dope," Fitz replied
hoarsely. "Hashish?"

"The finest," Sepah confirmed. "Sent down from Katmandu especially for this voyage. It is worth well over its weight in gold in
Europe and America."

The receiver and Sepah discussed the place where the twenty
tons of gold which had just been offloaded would be hidden. It
was to be in the excavated basement of a warehouse outside of
Bombay, one of many such caches Sepah had set up during his
year in India organizing his gold smuggling and distribution organization. This particular one had never been used before.

Once the receiver had delivered the gold to this hiding place it was his mission to contact the trustee, usually a lawyer or respected Indian businessman interested in making big money illegally. The trustee might change the hiding place of the gold shipment before disposing of it or perhaps keep it in the same place if he felt it safe there. In any case, with the trustee reposed the knowledge of where the gold was physically stored and the key to the vault in which the gold rested.

Sepah, as was the case with the other major smugglers, had retained half a dozen trustees and each load was entrusted to a different one on the assumption that even the corrupt, inept Indian authorities would catch up with a trustee if he constantly dealt in large sums of money. It was the responsibility of the trustee to contact the Indian gold agent who would actually take the gold around the country, his men wearing the vests, and sell it. The agent took the money he received from the gold-hungry ordinary Indian citizens and businessmen whose faith in the rupee was nil and turned it over to the trustee, who in turn converted it to negotiable paper and sent it back to the original gold smuggler in Dubai.

The money collected by the trustee from the agents generally came in the form of American traveler's checks collected by tradesmen and in personal checks for pounds sterling and other foreign currency sent home from Britain and the many other countries where immigrant Indians and Pakistanis worked. The Indians at home knew that any foreign currency could be sold at double the legal rate in rupees and millions of dollars a week in foreign-trade credits were lost to the Indian Government, the money going out of India without ever having been processed through the economy. Thus the desire of the Indian Government to put a stop to gold smuggling.

It was the job of the trustees to collect this heterogeneous horde of foreign money credit from the agents and send it to Dubai. It was easy enough for couriers to board an airplane in Bombay and carry these paper instruments in a briefcase to Dubai.

The only problem to Sepah and others like him occurred when a trustee was dishonest and failed to send back the money or claimed they had sent it back "but something must have happened to the courier." The disembowelment of a lawyer or businessman known by others in the field to be a trustee of a Dubai gold smuggler was the most effective countermeasure to cheating that Sepah had been able to discover.

Sepah and Fitz watched Haroon leave the dhow with the last load of gold. "It really doesn't pay to cheat on me," Sepah commented, "but corruption and dishonesty are such a part of daily life among Indian Government officials and businessmen that my people have to be reminded of this once or twice a year."

The sun was climbing over the hills behind the cove when the silver-laden dhow motored cautiously out of the secret reception area. Issa, at the wheel, standing in front of the twin thirty-caliber machine guns, hugged the southern coastline to give himself the optimum range of vision northward possible before turning north and west for the Gulf of Oman and safety. All eyes strained northward and the lookout on top of the mast swept the seas with binoculars. The radar was useless until the dhow gained the open sea since the signal operated only in an unobstructed line of sight and the cliffs at the mouth of the cove bounced the radar beam back.

With the sun behind them, some slight advantage at least, the dhow popped out of the mouth of the cove into the open sea and simultaneously blips appeared on the radar screen Fitz was studying and warning shouts came from the crow's nest.

Coming at the dhow from both north and south were patrol launches. An Indian Coast Guard frigate was steaming toward them from Bombay to the south. "Right into the middle of the sons of bitches!" Fitz exclaimed. "We're lucky they didn't come into the cove after us and bottle us up."

"There are ten or fifteen coves just like the one we used along this coast," Sepah explained. "They had to wait until we hit the open sea." He turned to his *nakhouda*. "Give it full throttle, northwest!" he ordered. Then to Fitz: "We can outrun the frigate but we'll be taking on two patrol launches."

Fitz held the glasses to his eyes. The calibrated range-finding hairs showed him that one launch was about three miles south and the other about the same distance north, both headed on an interception course with the dhow. The frigate, five miles south, could be seen already uncapping its heavy cannons.

"Better take evasive action," Fitz warned.

Sepah shook his head. "We've got to make a straight line northwest out of here." He grinned wryly. "Besides, we have a better chance of not getting hit if we let them aim at us. The Indians can't shoot. We're more apt to take a round by accidentally running into it than maintaining course."

Through his glasses Fitz saw the flash of the cannons mounted in the forward turrets of the frigate. Moments later first one, then a second shell exploded in the water behind them, sending up geysers of smoke and water. The next salvo sent up sprays of ocean water a couple of hundred yards off the port side of the dhow.

"I hope to hell you're right about their shooting," Fitz muttered worriedly. "The patrol launches seem to be standing off to give the big ship a chance to hit us."

"We're just out of its range," Sepah replied, looking back at the plumes of water sent up by short-falling shells. "And we're already at the three-mile limit, not that that means anything now."

The patrol launches, seeing their quarry was out of range of the frigate, bore down on the dhow from north and south. The best he could hope for would be many years in an Indian jail, Fitz thought to himself. Certainly no life ahead of him with Laylah if they didn't get out of this trap. Fitz thought about the load of hashish they were running. He also thought about the fact that he had actually been involved in putting contraband directly onto Indian soil. A lot different from helping a friendly shipowner protect his ship and cargo from hijacking on the high seas. And then Fitz remembered Brian Falmey's warning that British officers frequently rode aboard these Indian Coast Guard patrol launches as advisers.

"We're going to have to fight," Sepah cried.

"I'll consider we're on the high seas when we're beyond the twelve-mile limit," Fitz replied steadily. "Until then I won't fire a shot. After that I'll happily blow the pirates to pieces! Any British adviser who engages in piracy deserves what he gets."

Sepah stared at Fitz, dumbstruck. "You must be crazy, Fitz! If they stop us with the guns on board we'll be in prison for life."

"Maybe. But you didn't tell me we were going to actually sail inside Indian land territory. And you certainly never mentioned we'd be taking back a load of hash! I signed on to fight off pirates on the high seas."

Sepah compressed his lips and then stared out at the patrol launch approaching from the north. "He'll be able to rake us with his fifty-caliber machine guns in five minutes."

"Then turn south away from him. At flank speed you can make it out ten or fifteen miles from shore before the patrol launch catches up."

"We'll be heading into the other patrol boat and put ourselves back in range of the frigate's three-inch guns!" Sepah shouted. "Fitz, for God's sake, man! This is it! Look at those patrol launches coming in from north and south to cut us off. If you don't want us to lose everything, including our lives, because of some meaningless principle, you'll get down below and start shooting."

"It's not meaningless to me, Sepah. Legally they can stop us inside of twelve miles. After that it's piracy. We are in our rights to fight back. And as long as the frigate is firing at us the patrol launch to the south will hang out of range."

Sepah gave Fitz a cold look. "If I felt your three gunners could do the job alone—" He left the rest unsaid and dashed into the wheelhouse, grasping the wheel from Issa, wrestling it around so that the dhow was now heading out to sea on a southwest course, away from the intercept course with one patrol launch but directly back into range of the three-inch guns booming away from the Indian Coast Guard frigate.

Turning the wheel over to Issa again, Sepah stalked out of the wheelhouse. In cold fury, his voice barely controlled, he clipped off the words, "Now will you go below and ready the guns? On our present course we'll pass back through the range of the frigate." He looked to the north and then south. "The two patrol launches are already changing their course, as you can see, to cut us off after we come out of the frigate's range again, so that if by some chance the three-inch gun doesn't get us they will. At that point by my calculations we will be beyond your precious twelve-mile limit, more like fifteen miles off the coast. Does that satisfy your sensibilities, Colonel?"

Fitz nodded. He turned and even as he ran down the deck toward the hatch leading to the hold a shell from the gunboat fell close enough to rock the dhow. Fitz dropped down the ladder and ran to the twin twenties aft. Khalil and Juma were standing by. He put a hand on their shoulders. "Stand steady."

As the high-speed dhow cut through the Indian coastal waters into the Arabian Sea and across the range of the frigate's guns once more, shells began falling close again, now bracketing the dhow. Sepah held a steady course despite the shells hitting all around him. He was too tense and occupied in steering the dhow to rage at the extreme danger Fitz had forced him into. Minute by minute as the slower frigate's heavy engines propelled it into closer range of the elusive dhow, Sepah was approaching the twelve-mile limit.

Sepah's assessment of Indian gunnery was valid. Shells fell all around the dhow, in front of it, behind it, on both sides. But even now, with the dhow pinpointed in accurate firing range, the Indian frigate hadn't scored the direct hit which would have instantly destroyed the relatively fragile wooden craft.

Sepah maintained a direct heading, his eyes alternating from the chronometer to compass, then to the sea and back to the ship's clock. A shell fell close enough to the dhow to rock the ship violently. Then another shell threw it over in the opposite direction.

Below, Fitz and his gunners held on to the steel guardrails, their legs buckling as the small ship lurched from side to side.

Sepah, staring at his chronometer, began to ease the wheel over, changing course to northward again, pulling slowly out of range of the Coast Guard frigate once more and into a line of direct confrontation with the patrol launch to the north. It was exactly eight minutes since he had changed course to avoid firing on the patrol boats within the twelve-mile limit. As he pulled away from the frigate, a shell fell directly where the dhow would have been had Sepah not changed course. He breathed deeply. He had succeeded in putting the dhow on a tack which would intersect with the northern patrol launch's course approximately twelve to fifteen miles offshore.

A series of shell bursts in the water walked across the surface toward the dhow as it sped to get out of range once again. Sepah swore as he watched the high sprays move inexorably toward him.

Some British adviser, frustrated at the Indian's ineptitude, had taken over as fire officer, he thought to himself.

Down below, looking out the firing slit, Fitz watched the patrol launch speeding through the water at them from the north. The sun glinted off the small, fast Coast Guard vessel streaking in to cut off the dhow's escape course. The target was a small one since the launch was coming bow on at them. Already two Indian gunners had worked their way forward on the bucking deck of the launch to man the formidable fifty-caliber machine guns.

Never again, Fitz told himself, would he let himself get into a situation like this. He, an American, a retired lieutenant colonel from the U. S. Army on a pension, on the verge of losing everything. Through the binoculars he estimated the range of the launch at three thousand yards. He handed the glasses to Khalil. Then he glanced at his watch. In ten minutes they would easily be beyond the twelve-mile limit at the moment of confrontation with the first patrol launch. Suddenly the dhow swung sharply off course as a shell burst beside them, showering the men below with splinters from the beam.

The dhow righted itself. "We'll open fire when they're within range," Fitz commanded. Several members of the crew had been wounded by the splinters. The first patrol boat, believing it was coming in for the kill, churned through the water toward them. As Fitz was about to lean over the weapons and blast at the launch an idea suddenly hit him. If he didn't want to have to go on another of these trips he'd better let everybody see that Khalil and Juma were perfectly capable of taking care of the enemy with the twenties.

He tapped Juma on the shoulder. "Take the cannons!" he commanded. "When Khalil tells you to fire, let 'em have it!"

An ecstasy of killer instinct breaking loose in him, Juma took the handles of the mount in his hands, forefingers going to the triggers. He squinted through the calibrated ring sight at the oncoming Coast Guard launch.

Fitz sensed that in Juma's excitement he might fire prematurely, wasting precious ammunition. He placed a steadying hand on the youth's tense shoulder.

"Range?" he called to Khalil.

"Two thousand five hundred, sir."

Fitz smiled. The lad was coolly keeping account of the enemy's distance. Suddenly the dhow heaved over and the sea water poured in through the gun slit. A rent opened in the bulwark behind the gun. One of the crew members watching the guns sprawled forward, bleeding from splinter wounds in the back of his head.

"Steady!" Fitz shouted. The Indian gunboat falling behind them had finally managed to lob a shell almost into the dhow. Another few feet, Fitz judged, and they'd be sinking.

"Range!" Khalil shouted exuberantly as the dhow righted itself. Neither he nor Juma had paid the slightest attention to the attack from the other side of the dhow.

Fitz gave Juma a vise-like squeeze on his frail shoulder and the Arab lad began caressing three- to five-round bursts out of the two cannons. The weapons bucked in their mounts but Juma kept them trained on the oncoming launch. There was so little noise and no smoke that even in the hold of the dhow the destructive salvos pouring forth from the cannons were hardly discernible. As Fitz watched he could see with his naked eye the patrol launch shudder as it took the explosive shells. Yet still it came on at flank speed toward them.

Again Fitz wondered what the skipper of the oncoming vessel must be thinking. There was no sign of hostile action ahead of him. There wasn't a chance in the world that the Indian officer in command had ever been warned against such a circumstance as he was now facing, so there was no way he could fathom what was happening to his boat as Juma exultantly fingered off burst after burst into the bow of the oncoming ship.

For an instant Fitz looked through the slit behind him and saw that the launch approaching from the south was coming within range. Now he wished more than ever he could pick up the radio communication between the two launches and the command frigate. Other than the one shell which had almost sunk them, there had been no further near hits. Fitz figured that the dhow had outrun the range of the gunboat. But the two launches posed a dire threat to the dhow. Turning back to Juma, he noticed he was still firing at the oncoming launch, now a thousand yards away and impotently firing the fifty-caliber machine gun, which Juma hadn't knocked out even though the launch itself seemed to be slowing down.

Fitz, for an instant, thought of taking over long enough to wipe out the fifty-caliber before it got in range but thought better of it. If these boys did it all, then he certainly would never have to make another run. He held Juma by the shoulders in a steadying gesture. "Get the fifty-caliber," he called into his ear. "Take your time, aim carefully, range eight hundred yards, knock out their machine gun."

Juma nodded and seemed to sigh and pull himself together. Then calmly he squinted through the sights again a few moments and gently squeezed off a series of five-round bursts.

Khalil, staring through the glasses, let out an exuberant shout. Fitz snatched the binoculars from him and peered through them. There was no sign of the two gunners who had run out to the heavy machine gun and the weapon itself had been torn from its mounting, lying on the deck askew, attached, it appeared, by only one of the three bolts in its pedestal. Fitz patted Juma on the shoulder. The launch was noticeably slowing down, but it was still moving toward them.

Through the gun slit behind him Fitz saw that the second launch was now coming very much in range from the south but well aft of the dhow. It would be difficult to get a shot at it from the side gun slit. He patted both Khalil and Juma on the shoulder and pointed out their other pursuer. The two Arab youths gauged the problem and then looked at Fitz questioningly.

Now that the dhow was again out of range of the frigate the second patrol launch was pursuing them from behind, slowly but steadily catching up with them. While it might have been tempting to slow down, let the launch dash into range and blast it, the gunboat would gain on them and start hurling shells once more and the most important thing at the moment was to get away from the big boy. Perhaps the two patrol launches were in radio contact with each other and both realized that in some mysterious invisible manner the dhow was armed and shooting at them. Still it must be hard for the Indian captain of the second launch, streaking after the dhow, to believe that the wooden ship could shoot back at him when, sweeping the boat with his binoculars, there was no sign of guns aboard.

Fitz pointed at the rear gun port in the square aft end of the boat. Then he tapped the guardrail. This was all the direction he needed to give. Khalil pulled the fastening bolt out of the corner angle of the guardrail, lifting the steel tube up so that the silencer-covered barrels of the 20-mm. cannons could be swung upward out of the protective cage which kept them from being aimed at the inside bulkheads of the boat. Then he pulled the bolt at the upper angle of the rear cage, pulled up the rail, and Juma depressed the barrels into the rear cage, which Khalil refastened. Now Juma was ready to give the pursuer a lethal dose from the rear stinger.

Khalil watched the oncoming patrol launch through his glasses and when it came within range he shouted. Juma stroked the triggers and the two 20-mm. cannons spewed destruction from the back end of the dhow. Again the target was a small one, the oncoming bow of the patrol launch, but Juma poured explosive cannon shells into it and across the deck, catching the fifty-caliber machine gun in a crushing deluge of heavy bullets, knocking it off its mount, slamming the shattered bodies of the gunners back into the ship's bridge. Juma kept firing into the oncoming boat until it seemed to rear up on its end and settle back into the water.

With both patrol launches disabled Fitz ran up to the main deck in time to see the mainmast fall forward on its cables and the wheelhouse collapse, revealing the twin thirty-caliber machine guns. Sepah changed course and headed directly at the launch that had been pursuing them and was now sinking. At a command Mohammed raked the decks with thirty-caliber machine-gun fire, killing several coastguardsmen who were trying to abandon the wallowing, broken vessel. The second patrol launch was making a feeble effort to turn from the dhow and run, but as soon as Sepah was convinced that there could be no survivor of the second launch that had attacked them, he wrenched the wheel over and gave chase to the first. In moments he was close enough for Mohammed's withering fire to be effective as the twin pattern of bullets searched through the wreckage of the bridge for the helmsman and captain. The Indians didn't even try to man their own thirty-caliber machine guns, which were exposed to the fire from the dhow.

Sepah circled the patrol launch as it began to sink, searching for any sign of survivors. But there were none, or if there were they had chosen to go down with the ship rather than be strafed to shreds in the water.

Slowly Fitz walked across the deck and up to the poop. Sepah was shouting some victory chant at the sky, holding the exposed wheel in front of the machine guns. Mesmerized, Mohammed was still shooting off bursts into the wreckage.

"Sepah!" Fitz shouted harshly. "The frigate will be in effective range of us any minute. Get out of here!"

Sepah's glare at Fitz was hostile. "We want no survivors to give away our secret, do we?" Quickly he spun the wheel around, again resuming his northwesterly course, pushing up the throttles to flank speed. Then Fitz went below and watched as Khalil and Juma very efficiently began the laborious and crucial task of cleaning the 20-mm. cannons, covering them with oilcloth and putting up the firing slits.

The man who had been wounded by splinters was lying comfortably on the deck, his fellow crewmen having bandaged his wounds. Except for the torn area of the deck the dhow was in good condition and smoothly plowing across the Arabian Sea away from the Indian coast. In open sea there was little chance that anything bigger than the patrol launches could catch it and the crew of Sepah's dhow had proved they could destroy the present Indian Coast Guard patrol launches handily.

Gradually as they fled deeper into the Arabian Sea, Sepah eased back on the throttle. Diesel fuel must be conserved. Speed was no longer of the essence unless somewhere out at sea they were threatened by another patrol launch.

Fitz and Sepah had neither talked nor faced each other the entire day since Fitz's refusal, just at dawn, to fire on the Indian Coast Guard vessels inside the twelve-mile limit. Now, with darkness falling and the dhow under the command of its regular *nakhouda*, Issa, the inevitable confrontation must occur, since they shared quarters.

Fitz felt nothing but relief at getting out of a near-fatal situation. He also enjoyed a sense of justification. He had played strictly by international law even at the risk of the loss of the fortune they had amassed on the trip and their lives and those of the crewmen. It would have been so easy to have stayed out of range of the frigate and blasted the two motor launches out of the water.

"Good evening," Fitz said as he entered quarters. Might as well get it over with, he thought.

Sepah nodded silently. The coffee pourer approached Fitz and offered him a cup. Fitz took it and sipped the hot fragrant herbal liquid. Sepah still regarded him silently. Finally, to break the uncomfortable silence, Fitz said, "It had to be my way. Neither of us are murderers—I hope," he added. Sepah nodded. Some response at least.

"I should think you would be as relieved as I am that we made it out of their territorial waters and only because they illegally continued pursuit and had their fifty-caliber machine guns trained on us with the obvious intention of firing did we, of necessity, fire first."

A wry smile crept across Sepah's face. "Since we are safely away, all we worked and fought for secure, I can see your point even though they don't have any laws other than their own. You saw how the first patrol boat tried to stop us in international waters."

"True. But at least now I can use my share of the money knowing within myself that I murdered no one to get it. If there was a Brit on either of those last two boats he should have stopped the Indians at the twelve-mile limit."

"As I said, Fitz, I can afford to agree with you now." A bleak expression crossed Sepah's face. "Just how I might feel if we were in an Indian prison at this moment, our fortune lost, is something else."

"It is my determination that we wouldn't have lived to see a prison," Fitz replied.

"You see? A man of your sensibilities shouldn't be in our trade. And, Fitz, I have yet another little surprise in store for you."

Fitz looked up in alarm. "What are you talking about, Sepah?"

"You'll see. Just a little further profit added to this venture."

"Which reminds me," Fitz said, looking at Sepah steadily, "you can deduct any portion of the profits deriving from that load of hash from my share."

"With pleasure," Sepah replied mockingly.

CHAPTER 22

In a state of extreme agitation Brian Falmey strode into the office of Jack Harcross, chief of the Dubai police force, an old-time British colonial police officer now on contract with Shaikh Rashid to run the Emirate's law enforcement. Harcross was not a man who was easily ruffled and seemed hardly to notice the almost apoplectic condition of the Political Agent. "Hello, Brian," he greeted his fellow Brit genially, "come sit down. I wasn't expecting you."

"Sorry I didn't call first but I've just gotten some most distressing intelligence from Bombay. Seems that two Indian patrol launches have disappeared off the high seas. The first just vanished without a signal. Then yesterday another patrol launch myteriously sank. It had radioed in that it was bearing down on a fishing dhow, when suddenly its hull shattered. The Indian crew could see no armament on the dhow whatsoever and yet the captain radioed that their ship was coming apart. That was the last word that came from the patrol launch."

"Too bad, Brian. But I really don't see what that has to do with the Dubai police force."

"What it has to do with the Dubai police force is that the dhow that destroyed two Indian patrol launches came out of the Dubai Creek."

"And just how do you know that, Brian?"

"I can't prove it, yet. But I believe that this former American colonel, Fitz Lodd, is behind the whole thing."

"But, Brian, didn't you say that these two launches disappeared off the high seas undoubtedly well beyond the twelve-mile limit?"

"That would appear to be the case."

"Haven't I also heard that Indian patrol launches are preying on the Dubai dhows way outside the territorial limits?"

"I suppose that does happen."

"Then wouldn't an enterprising dhow captain be quite justified in protecting himself from hijacking on the high seas?"

"Now you're getting into technicalities, Jack. The point is that this American has come to the Creek, arranged for weapons to come in, and armed a fishing dhow. Surely this is against the law."

"Oh quite, Brian. His Highness has very definite views about any armaments coming into the Creek unregistered with us and the Trucial Oman Scouts. Funny, I never heard anything about Sepah arming his dhows."

"Jack, I want you to arrest this American. Take him off Sepah's boat. Search the boat when it comes back. I'm sure you'll find the guns mounted aboard."

"You know Sepah is very close to Shaikh Rashid. The Ruler is a partner in all commercial enterprises on the Creek. I don't know as it would be wise to get involved in Sepah's business."

"We can't let this sort of thing continue. The American will go from one illegal scheme to the next. He must be stopped and deported."

"But I was under the impression, Brian, that Colonel Lodd is a personal guest of His Highness. What have you got against him anyway? If you're so worried about the arms business why don't you do something about Jean Louis Serrat. We all know he is selling French guns and ammunition to any buyer in the Arabian Gulf with the money. He's the man I'd like to catch bringing arms into the Creek. But of course he'd be too smart to do that. Nevertheless, Serrat makes his arrangements here, I know that."

"Are you telling me," Falmey snapped irritably, "are you telling me, Jack, that you refuse to search this dhow when it gets back and arrest the American when you find the guns aboard?"

"Let me think about it, Brian. I really would talk to His Highness first." Harcross smiled benignly. "I'll see what I can do and get back to you."

Falmey stood up. "I'll call you tomorrow and if I get new intelligence I'll call you sooner."

"Yes, you do that, Brian."

Entirely unsatisfied with the attitude of Jack Harcross, Falmey left the police station and drove back to his office on the Dubai side of the Creek.

When Brian Falmey returned to his offices he found the re-

porter David Harnett waiting for him. Falmey had talked to Harnett on several occasions when the reporter was researching a story
and the British Political Agent well understood the value of good
press relations, particularly in a period of such flux as was now
being experienced with the imminent evacuation of British troops
and military influence from the entire area of the Trucial States
and the Sultanate of Oman. Sometime in 1971 the Trucial States
would be an independent Arab country and it was necessary before then to establish permanent firm British influence here.

"Hello there, Dave," Falmey greeted the reporter, "what can I
do for you?"

"I'm just following up on a story, Mr. Falmey, checking all
leads. The same story we discussed a few days ago."

"You mean that cashiered American lieutenant colonel, Lodd?"

"Exactly, sir. Five nights ago I saw him get aboard a dhow tied
up to the dock on the Deira side of the Creek. This was a dhow
owned by Sepah. In talking to you before, you suggested to me
that perhaps Lodd was working with Sepah in the re-exportation
of gold. It was also your opinion that Lodd had somehow arranged for guns to come into Dubai and had armed the dhow."

Falmey nodded encouragement and Harnett continued. "Just
before Lodd left I had a word with him. He told me that the
dhow was going up to Kuwait and he was going along for the ride.
Naturally I didn't believe this. I was sure he was going directly to
Bombay or some smuggling port near Bombay to unload gold.
However, to be on the safe side I flew up to Kuwait, went down
to the docks, and for a full day I looked at every dhow in port. I
can tell you definitely that this dhow that Lodd shipped out in
did not go to Kuwait."

Falmey laughed aloud. "Of course he didn't go to Kuwait or
any place else but the Indian coast. And furthermore—"

Falmey was interrupted by his deputy, John Brush, who came
into the office in a state of excitement. "Mr. Falmey, we just got
word from Bombay—" The Foreign Service type gave a wary look
at Dave Harnett.

"Mr. Harnett," Falmey began. Before he could go any further
Harnett stood up.

"I'll wait outside for you until we can finish this conversation if
that's all right with you, sir."

"Certainly, Harnett. I'll call you in as soon as I'm free." He watched as Harnett left his office and closed the door behind him.

"You know for an American and a news chap at that he's not such a bad fellow.

"Now, Brush, what is the signal from Bombay?"

"We just got word that a third Indian patrol launch was destroyed by gunfire while in pursuit of what appeared to be an unarmed dhow just off Bombay."

Falmey slapped the table with the palm of his hand and stood up. "Another one!"

"There was a British ensign aboard, sir. It is a great mystery to our people in Bombay exactly what is happening. And the radio signals from the patrol launches never seem to be definite on the fact they're being fired on."

"No, of course not," Falmey muttered. "That bugger Lodd, he's an ingenious devil. I've been able to get some information on him. He was a top American expert on guerrilla-warfare tactics. But to be responsible for the death of a British naval officer, that is going too far. Send that reporter chap back in and see what more you can learn from Bombay."

Brush left his superior's office, walked out and told Harnett he could go in, and returned to the signal room.

"Sit down again, Harnett. I think I can give you some further information on this fellow Lodd."

Harnett took out a pencil and notebook and listened carefully as Falmey told him the new information. "I'd say he and Sepah are obviously in this thing together," Falmey concluded. "You know how costly it is when they have an accident—that's how they refer to an incident in which they have to jettison the gold rather than get caught with it by the Indian Coast Guard. Sepah has had two such accidents. Obviously he hired your Colonel Lodd—"

"Please, Mr. Falmey, don't refer to this particular person as *my* Colonel Lodd. Just because he's American he's not mine."

Falmey warmed up to the American reporter immediately. "Sorry, Mr. Harnett. I expect I am a bit agitated over this latest turn of events. This Lodd is obviously a renegade. An international renegade. In any case, he has murdered God knows how many Indian crewmen and one British officer in the last four days on the Arabian Sea."

"Can I print it, Mr. Falmey?"

"Suit yourself. I know it to be true. I warned Lodd not to get himself involved in a shooting match with the Indian Coast Guard. I told him there were British officers aboard these boats. Yet it would seem that he has completely disregarded the advice. Of course print it. And if you want to follow up on this story just stay around here in Dubai, keep in touch with me, and when this high-speed smuggling dhow returns you will see the boat searched, impounded, and Lodd arrested."

"I wouldn't leave now for anything," Harnett replied. "I'll be keeping a watch out also. I would appreciate it, sir, if you would call me at the Carlton Hotel with any new information you may receive. In the meantime I will file the story from here."

"I have a good idea for you, Harnett. When you have filed your story and given them enough lead time so that they have the scoop, is that what you call it?"

"Yes, scoop."

"Then why don't you call Reuters bulletin here and give them a crack at releasing the story locally."

"Thank you, sir. I will certainly take your advice. Now if you'll excuse me I'll get cracking on the story."

"Right-o, Harnett. Anything more you need, call me. You have the number here."

CHAPTER 23

Three days cruising, alternately sailing and running the diesels at low speed, brought Sepah's dhow into the Gulf of Oman. The crew labored industriously to repair the damage inflicted by the three-inch gun and the dhow was beginning to look like new. Fitz was growing increasingly more apprehensive about Sepah's promised surprise. At first he actually wondered if he was to get a bullet in the head and be tossed overboard. But Sepah was not a murderer; in fact, Fitz strongly suspected that Sepah too had been relieved not to have fired on the patrol boats in their own waters.

"Someday soon, Sepah," Fitz warned, "you must realize that the Indian Navy and Coast Guard will get onto what you've got here and take steps accordingly. They'll be armed with forty-millimeter cannons mounted in quadruplex. You better go back to the old way of handling your cargoes and let the Indian receivers come out to meet you beyond the twelve-mile limit and take the gold. Or if you're about to get caught, salvo it."

"I will, Fitz. Of course I will." Sepah laughed. "But this time, this one time when we had surprise on our side, I wanted to go all the way in, talk to my receiver, and pick up payment right away. No one will ever again try a single gold shipment as big as this was. And we're home with half of our profits in the dhow. You realize how much money you will be paid before a week is up? You won't wait three or four months for it, you'll get it now!"

Fitz was still worrying about Sepah's surprise as they approached the Straits of Hormuz. Quoin Island appeared off their port bow. To their right was Iran, to their left Arabia. What Fitz wanted now was to see Laylah as soon as possible. He was rich. His share of just this voyage would come close to three hundred thousand dollars, he and Sepah had tentatively calculated, perhaps more, even without a portion of the huge profits that the hashish would bring in. He had taken his chances and become a different man. He was ready to expand his life style. There was oil, finance, and diplomacy ahead of him now that he had made his basic stake.

It was midmorning when they entered the Arabian Gulf. "Now," Sepah finally explained, "one hundred kilometers from here is the island of Abu Musa. We're going to pay it a visit."

"I understand." Fitz was happy. "Nine miles off Abu Musa in the Kajmira offshore waters, existing seismic information indicates we'll find oil."

"Correct. I thought you'd like to see the island itself."

"You had me worried for the last three days. I thought there was some sinister aspect to that surprise you mentioned."

Sepah smiled inscrutably. "It's an interesting island." He called for a little more speed from the diesels, now that he was positively safe from having to outrun a patrol launch, and by late afternoon they were putting into the small harbor at the southwestern corner of the square island. From a distance they had been able to see the rocky four-hundred-foot-high hill at the northeastern tip of Abu Musa.

"Sort of a barren place," Fitz commented.

"There's only one industry on the island," Sepah replied. Then he chuckled. "Two, I guess I should say. On the western side of the island is a red-oxide mine. The people of the island run the machinery to produce about sixteen thousand tons a year, which is shipped off to a paint and a lipstick factory in Iran."

The crew was making the boat fast to the small wooden dock. "Want to go ashore?" Sepah asked.

"Might as well. Doesn't look like there's much to see." Fitz stepped over the thwarts and onto the dock. It was now about five in the evening, the sun was slanting low across the Gulf as Fitz walked among the crumbling mud houses. The one sign of authority was the police station in a sandy square with a flagpole flying the flag of Sharjah, the Trucial state which claimed sovereignty over the island.

Veiled women walked to and from shallow wells at the outskirts of the village, where they scooped water up in buckets. A more dismal, drab place Fitz couldn't imagine. Yet he could picture the changes that would be occurring here when oil began flowing nine miles off the island's coast. The water around the island was deep and a good port could be established. All in all, the island would make an excellent oil terminal. Offshore pipes could be laid the nine miles from the pumping rigs to a tank farm on the island. Studying the charts and the geological information, Fitz knew that there should be fine fishing out here also, one of his favorite pastimes, though of late he had not had time for this indulgence.

Fitz wandered back to the dhow, where, to his surprise, he saw a line of men, Pakistanis and Indians, each carrying a small bundle, straggling aboard. As Fitz watched, the men filled the hold and crowded the deck. The dhow must have taken on a hundred men. By the time the boat was loaded there was barely room for Fitz to get through to the steps up to the poop deck, where Sepah stood.

"I guess I misjudged when I decided there was no sinister purpose for stopping by Abu Musa." Fitz shook his head as he looked over the crowded deck.

"These men can't get work at home," Sepah explained. "The Indian and Pakistani governments are both delighted to get rid of them, and in Dubai and Abu Dhabi labor is badly needed. The fact that it is illegal for these men to enter is a technicality from which great profit is derived."

"There must be a reason why it's illegal."

"An old law. The British think that Communist agitators will come in with these men, but who is there for them to agitate except themselves? Abu Musa is a sort of halfway house for them. Indian boats bring them that far and then Dubai boats, with the right contacts, put them ashore." He turned to Issa. "Cast off. We want to reach Kajmira well before daylight," he ordered.

The creek of Kajmira, specially lighted by Sepah's men, who had been waiting for two nights, shimmered in the land mass before them at about three in the morning. Slowly Issa guided the dhow into the heavily silted stream and up to a dock in front of Sepah's warehouse. Sepah's operations here contributed heavily to Shaikh Hamed's income.

The illegal immigrants were herded from the boat and onto the dock, the process taking a short time. The men were eager to

reach their destination. Trucks were ready to transport them to
Dubai and Abu Dhabi, where virtual slave-labor camps were waiting for them. In two days they would be working on the roads and
the various construction projects of the Trucial States.

"What is it worth to take a load like this into the Trucial
States?" Fitz asked.

"In your money? About a hundred dollars a head. So you see,
we made an extra ten thousand dollars on that little detour."

"They don't look like they had one dollar, much less one hundred," Fitz commented.

"They don't. Every last rupee they had went into getting them
to Abu Musa. But we get paid by the construction companies.
They take the passage out of the men's salaries. Actually everyone
profits. These people have work and can send home money, construction booms in the Trucial States."

After the illegal immigrants had been unloaded, a four-man
crew from the warehouse pitched in with the men on the ship to
unload the silver bars and bales of hashish.

"One of the things that Shaikh Rashid will absolutely not allow
to be unloaded in Dubai is any sort of narcotics," Sepah said.
"Fortunately Shaikh Hamed has no such qualms as long as the
requisite amount of money flows into his coffers."

"How do you get rid of the hash?"

"By tomorrow night it will all be gone. I'll make one call to
Beirut and an airplane will be here to pick it up. There is a small
area near here, about a square mile of hard-packed sand, where
the airplanes come in and out when it is worth their time. And
they pay cash right there. It appears they can absorb as much as
we can send them."

By the time the sunrise glowed in the mountains behind Kajmira, all the silver and bales of hashish had been stored in the
warehouse and Fitz was discussing the possibility of driving back
to Dubai instead of going on the dhow when a car drove up to
them. Fitz's old friend Ibrahim stepped out, his white robes blowing behind him as he strode toward Fitz and Sepah.

"My friends," he said, "I am thankful I found you. I have very
important news to tell you. It seems that word of the results of
your recent trip to India has already reached the British. The
mua'atamad has persuaded Jack Harcross and a detachment of the

Trucial Oman Scouts to meet you when you sail into the Creek. They will inspect the boat and if they find anything that looks like firearms aboard, the American, Fitz, will be arrested. They know that three Indian Coast Guard ships have been destroyed by gunfire and they blame Fitz for this business. It seems that one British officer was killed in the fighting."

"How do you come by this intelligence?" Fitz asked.

"I heard it at the palace."

"Thank you, Ibrahim," Fitz said. "You have done me a great service."

"And you have served me well too by letting me know in advance what to expect in the Creek," Sepah echoed.

Ibrahim bowed before them and turned back to his chauffeured Mercedes-Benz with wide sand tires. "I'm glad I could be of service. I know you will be careful. The Ruler wants only the best for all of his friends."

Fitz and Sepah watched Ibrahim drive off. "Even though he's not expecting me this would be a good time to call on Shaikh Hamed," Fitz said.

"Very fine idea, Fitz," Sepah agreed. "I have an extra Land Rover you can use to drive back to the Creek. I will drive back also and tell Issa to remove all signs of the guns and mountings before bringing the dhow into Dubai Creek. Can you find your way back to Dubai along the beach?"

"I'm sure I can. The only problem is getting around the Khor beyond Sharjah. I'll just have to wait until dead low tide and drive across. I'll see Shaikh Hamed now and then come back and help take the guns and mounts out of the boat."

"Come over to my house tonight." Sepah bestowed on Fitz a conspiratorial grin. "We will begin going over accounts then."

"That will be a pleasure, Sepah."

At seven-thirty that morning Fitz arrived at Shaikh Hamed's residence and was welcomed by the Ruler's steward. He was led into the majlis, where Shaikh Hamed was sitting in an armchair, a table at each side, and sipping a cup of coffee. Hamed showed no surprise when Fitz walked in. He gestured at the chair next to the table on his left and Fitz sat down between Hamed and his son Saqr, with whom Fitz shook hands and exchanged amenities. For some reason—he couldn't isolate it from general impressions—Fitz had taken a dislike to the pudgy son of old Hamed. Perhaps it was the sullen air about him, or a general feeling of mistrust. In any case, Fitz was glad he was dealing with the old Ruler and not the son.

After the customary greetings and sipping another cup of coffee, Fitz asked the Ruler if he had yet received the oil-concession documents. Shaikh Hamed assured Fitz that he had received them, that he had read them, as had his sons. Their Finance Minister was currently studying the lease and they hoped to proceed with final negotiations as soon as possible.

"It would be a great help if we can work out something with Abu Musa to use part of the island for oil storage and as a terminal," Fitz suggested.

"This I'm sure we can do," Hamed replied.

There was no more business to discuss but Fitz wanted to be able to say he had been in negotiations with Hamed, so he and the Shaikh talked in generalities regarding the oil business. Finally, with nothing else to talk about and the Ruler obviously wanting to get on with other business, Fitz took his leave of Shaikh Hamed and shook hands with Saqr and then the other Arabs along the two sides of the majlis as he left.

Fitz returned to the dock and found his three gunners dutifully waiting for him. Mohammed, Juma, and Khalil had managed a few hours' sleep on the dhow between the time it had been unloaded and now. For the next three hours they removed all the guns and mountings from the dhow. By noontime, when they had finished, there was no indication left on the dhow that it had ever been armed. The guns, ammunition, and mountings were all stored in a corner of the warehouse and Fitz was ready to make the drive over the desert sands and along the beaches back to Dubai, about thirty-five miles along the Gulf. Fitz went to look for Sepah to make final arrangements for their meeting on the Creek before starting out.

Sepah was standing outside the warehouse watching the loading of the bales of hashish into a truck. Even as Fitz was walking up to him the sound of an airplane could be heard overhead circling. Fitz looked up and saw the venerable old DC-3 looking for a place to put down, finding it, and straightening out for final approach and then touching down. "You don't waste any time moving that stuff, do you?"

"This cargo I don't like to store at all if possible," Sepah confirmed. "It happened that the people we use had a plane in Kuwait already and were able to get it down here today."

"I'm off, Sepah. I'll see you either tonight or sometime tomorrow." Sepah and Fitz shook hands.

"It's been a most successful voyage, Fitz."

"Good, Sepah. I want to be able to put up my share of the signature bonus when we sign with Hamed. I don't think it will be much longer before we'll have that concession."

Fitz started off in the Land Rover he had borrowed from Sepah's well-stocked warehouse. After two hours he reached the Maktoum Bridge, which crossed the Creek. He was about to go over to the other side and drive to his house when a mischievous thought came to him. He turned the Land Rover toward the sea and drove along the Deira side of the Creek to the Carlton Hotel. According to Ibrahim, there should be a reception committee waiting for the dhow to enter the Creek. The obvious place to wait for a dhow to come into the Creek in some comfort, since there was no predicting the dhow's arrival time, would be the Carlton Hotel. The lobby was reasonably cool and there was of course the bar there. Fitz parked about a half a block from the Carlton Hotel and walked along the edge of the Creek looking at the dhows tied up two, three, and sometimes even four abreast. Once opposite the hotel he crossed the street and walked in the front door, as though innocently heading for the bar and a cold drink, when as he expected he saw Jack Harcross, Brian Falmey, Colonel Ken Buttres, and, what did surprise him, the reporter Dave Harnett with them.

Fitz greeted them casually, said he was just going in for a drink, and asked if anybody wanted to join him. He gave the reporter a baleful look. "Even you, Dave."

It was the first time he had called the newsman by his first name, but this seemed to be a good time to begin. Falmey stalked across the lobby of the Carlton Hotel to Fitz. "And where have you been, Lodd?"

"Oh, I've just been up in Kajmira to see Shaikh Hamed. As you've probably heard, since you hear everything, I'm hoping to

work out an oil concession with Kajmira." Fitz looked from Falmey to Colonel Ken Buttres to Jack Harcross and Harnett again.
"And what is this powerful group all doing together in the lobby
of the Carlton Hotel?" He looked down at his watch. "Well, it is
almost five. How about that drink? I'm buying, if you'll allow
me."

Falmey, red-faced and enraged, sputtered, "Don't try to fool us,
Lodd. You got off that dhow in Kajmira or someplace, took the
guns off and hid them, and then drove back here to Dubai. We
know your boat is about somewhere."

Fitz looked at Falmey in dismay. "But, Brian, I've just been
working on these oil deals. Sure, I was out with Sepah for a couple
of days on his new dhow. But all we did was cruise. You know I
love boats. Did a little fishing." Fitz looked at Harnett. "As Harnett probably told you, we put out for Kuwait. Sepah decided to
drop in on Abu Dhabi on the way and as a matter of fact I left
the dhow there. I was anxious to get on with the oil negotiations,
you know."

Jack Harcross could hardly conceal his amusement at Falmey's
anger. Harcross had never wanted to search Sepah's dhow and,
knowing that Shaikh Rashid admired Fitz, he certainly didn't
want to have to explain to the Ruler why he had discommoded his
American friend. He strongly suspected that anything Colonel
Lodd was doing was at the behest of high-ranking Arabs close to
Shaikh Rashid.

Falmey, stammering in a rage at the way Fitz had blithely re-en-
tered the Dubai scene, his voice rising an octave, cried out, "For
your information Mr. Cashiered Colonel, in the last week you've
killed twenty-six Indian Coast Guard crewmen, including one
British adviser on a patrol launch out of Bombay, and all for gold.
Don't think we're going to forget it, sir."

Fitz looked at Falmey lazily. In his best British imitation he
drawled out, "My dear sir, I really don't know what you're talking
about. I told you I've been negotiating oil leases in Kajmira and I
went up to take a look at Ras al Khaimah. This business of guns?
You're absolutely off the wicket, Falmey." Falmey trembled in
speechless rage.

Jack Harcross, who had remained silent, now handed Fitz a
copy of the mimeographed Reuters daily news bulletin. It was the
nearest to a newspaper that Dubai could boast. "Colonel Lodd,

would you mind taking a look at this story. It certainly reflects the belief of most of us active here about the Creek."

Fitz took the bulletin and began reading. He got through only the lead, which began, "Ex-American Army officer James Fitzroy Lodd, who was forced to retire prematurely after being quoted widely in newspapers around the world for making anti-Semitic remarks in regard to the Arab-Israeli conflict, is believed to have armed a gold-smuggling dhow on the Arabian Gulf and shot up three Indian patrol launches which tried to stop his boat." Fitz noticed the story carried an Associated Press identification.

Apparently unruffled, Fitz turned to Harnett. "Dave, you better be able to prove that story because I'm not going to let the news media hang me a second time with false statements. I let it go by once. I won't again. I promise you, and I have the means to do it now, that I will sue not only you but the Associated Press and every newspaper in the United States that carried that story. You'll be lucky to get a job as a copy boy on a country weekly after this."

Harnett was somewhat shaken by the calmness in Fitz's tone. "But everybody knows that you brought two twenty-millimeter cannons out of Iran, put them on Sepah's dhow, and then went with him to show him how to use the armament," he argued weakly.

"Everybody knows?" Fitz looked at Jack Harcross. "Do you know, Jack, that Sepah and I shot up three Indian boats? Do the police have any proof of this?"

Harcross shook his head. "No proof, Lodd. Just belief."

Fitz looked at Colonel Ken Buttres. "And, Ken, what proof have you got that there is any truth in this story Harnett wrote?"

"Just what Jack says. Nothing anybody can prove. But there's no doubt in our minds what happened."

Fitz turned to Harnett. "Dave, you can do one of two things. You can get absolute proof of what you claim I did and get it in twenty-four hours or you can run a detailed denial from me of the story, because if you can't prove that story I'm going to start suit in twenty-four hours."

"I tried to find you before I ran the story," Harnett protested. "I even went up to Kuwait looking for the dhow. Naturally it never showed up there. We know where it went."

"Well, if you know, then you can prove it."

Harnett backed down somewhat. "Naturally I will send your denial out on the wires. Just write it for me or give it to me verbally now. If I could have found you before I ran the story I would have put the denial in the second or third paragraph. But I assure you, I would have run the story anyway."

"O.K., Dave, come on up to the bar with me. I'm going to have a drink and I'll write out my denial and hand it to you. How's that?"

"You go on up and write the denial. I'll be waiting right down here," Harnett replied. Fitz walked over to the main desk, took out a telegram form, and wrote out: "Former Lieutenant Colonel James Fitzroy Lodd categorically denied that the story was true. There is no proof that he was involved in any type of smuggling activities or the use of firearms against Indian Coast Guard ships. Colonel Lodd is engaged in the oil business in various states along the Arabian Gulf."

Fitz walked over to Harnett. "You can start out by putting this in tomorrow's Reuters bulletin and filing it right now with the AP." Then, with the security of the riches to come, he tried a bluff. "I will alert my lawyers in Washington by telephone at nine o'clock in the morning their time tomorrow to be looking for the wide publication of this denial."

Harnett took the telegram form, read it briefly, and said, "I'll do the best I can. I can't promise the AP will run the denial."

"Then you'd better tell them what I just told you. This is not a threat, I'm merely telling you what will happen. A suit for heavy damages and punitive payments will be filed within three days if the AP does not heavily encourage its member newspapers to run this part of your story which was missing." Fitz turned to Jack Harcross and Ken Buttres. "Now I am going for that drink. The invitation is still open."

"I'll join you, Fitz," Ken Buttres said.

"Yes, it's about that time," Jack Harcross agreed.

The three walked around to the bar at the back of the lobby and sat down together. Harnett went to the telephone to call his AP office in Beirut. Brian Falmey, still livid, stormed out of the lobby of the hotel.

CHAPTER 24

Fitz and Sepah arrived together at Shaikh Rashid's majlis. Sepah was wearing the Arab *dish dasha* and *kuffiyah* and Fitz had on a seersucker suit and tie. The searing heat of summer had been replaced by moderately hot days now that autumn had arrived. They walked into the business wing of the palace and proceeded down the corridor to the majlis. This was a different room from the one in which Fitz had first met Shaikh Rashid upon his arrival in Dubai. The Shaikh's majlis looked like the bullpen of an insurance company. The walls were glass from about three and a half feet up to the ceiling. Shaikh Rashid sat at the far end of the glass-enclosed room in a comfortable-looking armchair. Beside him was a table with a white telephone on it. Retainers and advisers were seated on both sides of the room on chairs and some were walking around behind Rashid's chair.

The coffee server was busily attending to Rashid's supplicants as they came in and sat down. There seemed to be about an equal number of Arabs and Westerners. The Arabs talked with each other in low tones, played with the worry beads in their hands, and sipped coffee, waiting their turn to approach the Ruler with their business.

Majid Jabir was sitting at the Ruler's right. He was acting as both adviser and interpreter. A few of the Westerners spoke Arabic and most of the rulers either did not or would not speak English on their own home territory. Fitz noticed that Fender Browne and Tim McLaren were sitting near the Shaikh and that there were two empty seats next to them. Shaikh Rashid and Majid Jabir were talking to Ted Sommers, president of the newly formed Dubai Oil Drilling Operations. With the first offshore oil shortly to be produced, royalties would soon be accruing to Dubai, and in the Emirate of Dubai, Ted Sommers was the most important single person after the Shaikh himself. It was Ted Sommers, Fitz had learned, who had made the seismic information available to Fender Browne indicating that there was another oil field which could be tapped off the island of Abu Musa in the territorial waters of Kajmira.

Fitz and Sepah walked into the majlis nodding and shaking hands with the Arabs and Westerners sitting around the edge of the room. They made for two empty seats and sat down, Fitz beside Tim McLaren. Shaikh Rashid caught Fitz's eye, smiled and nodded to him, and then went back to finishing up his business with Ted Sommers. The coffee server came over to Fitz and Sepah, gave them each a small cup, and filled them with hot black coffee from the pelican-beak copper coffee pourer.

After Fitz had taken a couple of sips of his coffee, McLaren leaned over to him. "Congratulations, Fitz."

Fitz looked at the banker innocently. "On what?"

"Oh, come on, Fitz." McLaren looked over at Sepah and they both grinned at each other as though sharing some secret knowledge. "Who do you think is processing all the paper Sepah has suddenly acquired? Between the British and American money orders and traveler's checks, the currency from about five different countries, and the personal checks which if they all clear come to about three million dollars, I'll be putting about ten million into Sepah's account with us. You are now a man of considerable wealth and position."

Fitz smiled inwardly. The final accounting had exceeded his expectations, reaching three hundred and fifty thousand dollars. It would have been more had he accepted a share of the profits from the hashish. He could also look forward to approximately one hundred and fifty thousand dollars from each of the next three shipments. Of course, that was not something he could bank on at this point. Any one or all of the succeeding shipments could be lost. Fitz had grave doubts as to the chances of the next three shipments being successful. The Indian Navy and Coast Guard were on to them now.

"If things work out today as I hope, Tim," Fitz said, "I'll be around to see you before you close. I may be in the market for a loan."

"If it's after hours I'll open for you. I've got to take care of our top customers, you know." Tim's statement pleased Fitz. He had never been a "top customer" of a bank before and had never expected to be.

Ted Sommers stood up and left his seat beside the Ruler. He and Shaikh Rashid shook hands and Sommers left the majlis as Rashid looked over and gestured to Fitz and Sepah to come and sit beside him. Once more McLaren leaned toward Fitz. "Looks like you're number-one boy with the Shaikh these days," McLaren said enviously.

Fitz and Sepah approached the Ruler and each in turn shook his hand and sat down with him. After the customary amenities the Ruler said, "Your business flourishes, Sepah."

Sepah nodded. "I have had good fortune recently."

"Your good fortune is the good fortune of all of us." That was true of course, Fitz thought. Sepah had mentioned to him briefly that the Ruler was a twenty percent partner in all enterprises. Fitz had commented that that was still about half of what corporations in the United States paid in taxes, so they were really all very much ahead of the game.

Rashid turned to Fitz. "And you, my friend, how is living and working in my country? Agreeable to you?"

"Your Highness, I will always be grateful to you for inviting me to come to the Creek. I can think of no other place I'd rather call home than right here."

"Your ventures have been successful, I take it."

"Indeed, Your Highness, they have. I am sorry that some American reporter saw fit to come out with a lot of concocted sensationalism about me. I hope it has not embarrassed you."

Shaikh Rashid looked down at a page in Arabic in front of him. "I have before me the report of the newest story, which presents your denial of all the adventuresome antics of which you have been accused. Since there is absolutely no shred of proof to substantiate what this American reporter says, he has been politely asked to leave my country and not come back."

"Your Highness has acted with wisdom and dispatch," Fitz murmured. "Thank you." Fitz looked at the report in Arabic and, sitting across from Rashid as he was, the Arabic characters were right side up for him. He looked up at Shaikh Rashid. "Your Highness, you have the report upside down."

Rashid laughed. "Yes, I long ago learned to read upside down. It confuses visitors who come around behind my chair and read over my shoulder."

Rashid looked up and caught the eye of Fender Browne and motioned him and Tim McLaren to come up and sit near him. Chairs were immediately produced as the two sat down. Majid Jabir, who had been talking to other attendants at the majlis, also now walked back to the side of his Ruler and the conference began. Although Tim McLaren realized the importance of being able to speak Arabic and was industriously working at learning it, he was still a long way from being able to carry on a business conversation in the language, so Majid Jabir translated for him as they went along.

Shaikh Rashid opened the conversation declaring his sincerest wishes for the prosperity of his friend and old ally, Shaikh Hamed of Kajmira. Rashid went on to say that of course neighboring Sharjah would claim rights to any oil found offshore of the island of Abu Musa. Majid Jabir pointed out that the island of Abu Musa could only claim oil within three miles of shoreline. This promising structure was nine miles away from the island of Abu Musa and very definitely within the territorial waters of Kajmira. Shaikh Rashid, looking very wise, his usual benevolent expression disappearing, indicated his feeling that the current Ruler of Sharjah was not beyond anything.

Fitz was well aware of the old adage in the Arab world, which undoubtedly had started right here in the Trucial States, that "your neighbor is your enemy and your neighbor's neighbor is your friend." During the meeting Rashid gave his blessing to this first group of Trucial States residents to start a company for the purposes of exploring and drilling for oil. Sepah, Majid Jabir, Fitz, and Fender Browne would find the financing, perhaps with the help of Tim McLaren's bank, to pay the seven-hundred-and-fifty-thousand-dollar signature bonus to Shaikh Hamed. Then they would have to get into the truly expensive business of exploration and the actual drilling of the offshore wells. Rashid promised full support to the effort. This sort of oil deal would be of benefit to both Kajmira and Dubai as well as to these brave individuals who are financing on an independent basis in a very competitive situation the formation of an oil-producing company.

With the oil business now behind them Rashid looked at Fitz and asked what had happened to Harcourt Thornwell. He had been impressed with the presentation and had heard twice from Zayed that this was something worth pursuing. Fitz said that business had taken him away for the last two weeks but he understood Thornwell had gone back to see Zayed again and was presently in Kuwait. He promised to keep the Ruler informed of the progress Thornwell was making in putting together his communications syndicate in the United States.

Rashid seemed in unusually good spirits this day and he asked the question Fitz was hoping he would hear. "Colonel Lodd, your experience in Dubai seems to be a successful one. Is there anything more I can do to be of assistance to you?"

"Your Highness, there is one thing I would like. More and more Westerners are coming into this part of the world, particularly Dubai. Surely Mr. Sommers is telling you how many more Americans will have to come in to help with the oil production. Businessmen come in and out of Dubai every day. One thing is missing here. There is no place for Westerners and those Arabs that feel so inclined, to meet, have good conversation, and drink the alcoholic beverages that we have become accustomed, indeed addicted to. We need a place where we can have entertainment Western style. I would even like to bring in Western women to help entertain."

Fitz saw a slight frown crease Rashid's brow. Hastily he amended this last statement. "What I meant, Your Highness, was women singers and entertainers. I certainly didn't mean that we would be in any way interested in anything resembling prostitution. What I am asking for, Your Highness, is the permission to build a bar and restaurant." Fitz looked at Rashid anxiously.

Finally Rashid asked, "Where would you build such a place?"

"Somewhere on the Deira side of the Creek near the airport. Frequently businessmen take a plane to Dubai just to have meetings and then get on a plane and go on to Kuwait or perhaps Iran."

"Yes, I believe the Deira side would be the best place for such an establishment. My next business is with Jack Harcross, our Chief of Police. I will discuss it with him and ask him to make out the necessary papers to license you to build such a place and to sell fermented beverages." The Shaikh sighed. "How in just my lifetime we have changed our centuries-old Islamic traditions. If we allow it you Americans and British and French and Germans will de-Arabize us. We'll find ourselves merely Westerners in *kuffiyah* and *dish dasha*."

"No, Your Highness, I don't believe that will ever happen. It certainly would be tragic for us to see such a thing occur."

"My father played on just such fears to make the Creek the number-one trading port on the Trucial Coast. When the Westerners wanted to start shipping goods into Sharjah creek, my father sent his agents to the Ruler of Sharjah to say that Shaikh Sa'id al Maktoum of Dubai was very happy that all the Westerners were going to go into Sharjah and not Dubai, let Sharjah have the infidels drinking, carousing, and infecting its young men with their customs. Dubai certainly didn't want that. The old Shaikh of Sharjah was so incensed that he refused to allow the British trading companies to use the Sharjah creek and they came to my father, who welcomed them to Dubai. This was fifty years ago and ever since Dubai has been the most important seaport between Kuwait and Hormuz."

Rashid smiled at the memory of his father's cleverness. Then he turned back to Fitz. "It is a new world with new customs. If Dubai is to progress, if the Creek is to be the great port I envisage with great new hotels, office buildings, and commercial facilities, drydocks, a true deep-water port that can take in twelve or fifteen ships at a time, if my dreams for Dubai are to be realized, we will have to sacrifice some of our old attitudes." He paused contemplatively and then, smiling at Fitz, asked, "Do you have a name in mind for your new—" Then he switched to English to the great surprise of all of them. "Bar and restaurant?"

"Your Highness is indeed conversant with certain American customs," Fitz said, smiling. "Yes, as a matter of fact I do have a name for my place. I want to call it the Ten Tola Bar." At this Rashid actually laughed aloud, as did Sepah and Tim McLaren. "Very fitting, most appropriate for you, Colonel," Rashid replied.

Rashid indicated that the meeting was over and all of them stood up, shook hands with the Ruler, and then turned to leave the majlis. On the way out Fitz went over to Jack Harcross, who was just being summoned to the Ruler's side.

"Can I come up and see you sometime this afternoon, Jack?"
Fitz asked.

"What's it all about?"

"The Ruler will tell you. Would about three o'clock be all
right?"

"Certainly, I'll be there."

Fitz left Rashid's majlis feeling highly satisfied with his new career in Dubai to this date.

Part III

OIL
1969

Fitz was beginning to know the seascape below by heart. He always sat on the left side of the Air Iran jet from Dubai to Tehran via Bandar Abbas and Shiraz so that he could look out the window five minutes after the climbing aircraft passed over the coastline and see way off in the distance the tiny island of Abu Musa. From the air it was possible to see how the shoal water around the island dropped off to the underwater shelf. And nine miles out they would soon be setting up the offshore drilling rig.

This was Fitz's fifth trip to Iran since he and Sepah, along with Fender Browne and Majid Jabir's designated surrogate, had signed the exploration and development lease with Shaikh Hamed. It had been a solemn and exhilarating occasion. Fitz's share of the signature bonus had been one hundred and fifty thousand dollars, just under half of what he had been paid by Sepah when the profits of the voyage had been divided. Now more than ever he felt like a man of property. The day after the impressive ceremony at Shaikh Hamed's residence in Kajmira, Fitz had made a flight to Tehran. He arrived on Thursday afternoon, met Laylah at the Embassy, took her home, and from then until Saturday morning, the end of the Moslem weekend, they had indulged in lovemaking interspersed with caviar and iced vodka. He had hated to leave her but now he was truly a very busy man. Just a week after his return Fitz supervised the ground breaking of the hundred-and-fifty-thousand-dollar structure that would be the Ten Tola Bar. He had borrowed half the cost of the building from Tim McLaren's bank and prayed that Sepah's second gold-re-exporting venture would not result in an accident.

Shortly after ground breaking, with a British-supervised construction company hard at work on the building, Fitz had joined Fender Browne on the seismic boat he had chartered. The

150-foot diesel-powered ship was a symphony in luxury contrasted
to Sepah's dhows. The quarters were spacious and the ship contained a modern galley with two Pakistani cooks. For several days
they cruised over the site of the favorable geological formations at
the edge of the shelf two hundred feet below. Trailing almost a
mile of copper cable and the torpedo-like electronic thumper creating shock waves in the water which plumbed the depths and
brought up the seismic information they needed, it was determined that they had indeed made the investment of a lifetime in
securing the oil concession for Kajmira. The next step was for
Fender Browne to assemble the huge offshore rig that would be
needed to drill into the shale surface below the Arabian Gulf.

Returning from the seismic trip and checking on the construction of the Ten Tola Bar, Fitz once again made the weekend
trip to Tehran to be with Laylah. He was acutely aware of the extent of her popularity in Tehran. She knew everybody and everything that went on. As always, he proposed to her before leaving.
And as always, she had said they could discuss it more seriously
after his divorce. Fitz was so busy with all of his projects that
there was no time for him to take a month off and go back to the
States.

Laylah confessed that she frequently heard from Harcourt
Thornwell and sometimes saw him. He was trekking through the
Arab states in his quest for the many millions—half a billion, he
estimated, in petrodollars—to put his communications empire together. Fitz realized, not having heard from either Stakes or
Thornwell since returning from the gold trip, that they had decided they could dispense with his services and had quietly terminated their informal agreement with him.

Fitz had begged Laylah to come to Dubai and help him run his
interests. But she was currently much involved and excited with
her work at the Embassy and had no desire to give it up at the
moment. On one of Fitz's weekend visits Laylah did produce for
him an accomplished restaurateur, an Iranian with the improba-
ble name of Joe Ryan who, like Laylah, was the product of an
American father and an Iranian mother. Joe was willing to come
to Dubai and see to the day-to-day operations of the Ten Tola
Bar.

During this trip Laylah gave Fitz one interesting piece of infor-

mation. Brian Falmey had been in Iran as part of a British delega-
tion received by the Shah. With Britain getting ready to leave the
Arabian coast of the Gulf, many compromises were in the mak-
ing. Two weeks after Fitz's return, Falmey's motives became clear.
The Shah of Iran, who had claimed and taken from Ras al
Khaimah by force two islands in the Gulf, Greater and Lesser
Tumbs, strategically located at the mouth of the Straits of Hor-
muz, now claimed the island of Abu Musa.

Somehow Falmey had persuaded the Ruler of Sharjah to compromise with the Shah. Sharjah would control the half of the island facing its coastline and Iran would control the other half.
Any oil revenues that might derive from future development
would be divided between the Shah and the Ruler of the Emirate
of Sharjah. There was little or no chance that oil would be found
within the three-mile limit around the island, so the division of oil
royalties seemed academic.

The Shah's interest, according to Brian Falmey when he announced the decision, was to have another military and naval base
out in the Gulf. Later Fitz would berate himself for not figuring
out the full extent of Brian Falmey's planning. Mostly his mind
was on Laylah.

A month after his third trip to Iran, Fitz once more returned. A
month away from Laylah, not seeing her, was painful emotionally
and physically. To his distress he found that Harcourt Thornwell
was in Tehran, having set up headquarters in this centrally located Middle East city which although not Arab was still
Moslem. Courty was seeing Laylah a great deal, a fact deeply disturbing to Fitz although she was as loving and tender with him as
ever. On his last trip Fitz had offered to stay longer than the usual
weekend, but this time Laylah said she was going to be very busy
and wouldn't be able to see him. So it was with a heavy heart that
he took Joe Ryan back to Dubai with him, leaving Laylah in what
he now considered a city treacherous to his future with her.

Joe Ryan had indeed been a find. He had much experience in
bar and restaurant management both in Tehran and in Beirut. He
was an easygoing young man as far as his personal life was concerned and had never saved much money. Although he was in
demand as a maître d' and headwaiter, no restaurant owner was

actually willing to put him on a generous profit-sharing system, make him a partner, so to speak.

Joe's father had been one of the early tool pushers from the United States to come to Iran and start developing the oil wells. He already had a wife at home when he married Joe's mother and when he retired he merely walked away from his Iranian sweetheart and ten-year-old son, giving them ten thousand dollars, all he had saved in Tehran, and saying goodbye.

Joe could have passed for an Iranian or American. He was handsome with heavy black hair combed high on his head, ducktailing behind his ears. He wore strictly American-style clothing and spoke English, Farsee, and Arabic with a smattering of French and German. Fitz offered him a reasonable salary against one fourth of the profits, which were computed after finance charges amortizing the entire cost of construction and furnishings over five years. It was a good deal for both of them.

Laylah had vouched enthusiastically for Joe's honesty and ability if not for his life style. He liked gambling and women.

"You'll have to do without women temporarily," Fitz had warned him. "However, I have secured permission to bring girls in to entertain and, this was a big concession, I can have four women to act as hostesses and waitresses."

As long as Joe had a hand in picking the girls the whole plan sounded marvelous to him. He knew just where to go in both Lebanon and Tehran to find the right girls. "Make sure they speak good English, that's all," Fitz had demanded.

In Dubai, Joe Ryan moved in with Fitz temporarily until quarters could be found for him. Joe proved his worth from the start, coping with the problems of construction and furnishings as well as purchasing and supervising the installation of the generator and the air-conditioning units.

Meanwhile Fitz was occupied with many of the details inherent in setting up the oil-drilling operation. From Fender Browne he received a fast and thorough education in all facets of the oil business. "What we're trying to do is pretty damned bold," Browne warned. "In fact, I haven't seen it ever done. A bunch of guys with limited capital pulling off something like this. It takes ten or fifteen million dollars for a big oil company to go in and do what we're trying to get by on for just a couple of million. Of course, I can get a rig put together for a quarter of what it would cost a major producer because I actually have the stuff, or most of it, and people like McDermott will go along with me. Everybody here on the Creek is helping me."

"For a nice piece of the action," Fitz commented.

"If we hit. Which we will," he added with determination. "I'd say we should be able to start moving our rig out into the Gulf in six months."

And now Fitz was making his fifth trip to Tehran. He was uneasy, a lump of angst sat in his stomach when he thought of Thornwell operating high, wide, and handsome—rich, old family, Laylah's type. John Stakes was always at Thornwell's side and apparently they were making a strong impression throughout the Arab states. Still, Fitz knew his Arabs, perhaps even better than Stakes. He didn't believe that it would be possible to get even three or four of the rulers who could put up the kind of money Thornwell wanted to act in concert. It just seemed to be an ethnic thing about the Arabs. They couldn't unite and put through a major undertaking like a huge multicorporate financial program such as Thornwell was proposing.

Fitz was also concerned about being away from his major interests in Dubai. Fortunately, he thought, Sepah had enjoyed another successful gold trip and had paid Fitz just over a hundred thousand dollars before he left for Tehran.

His thoughts were interrupted by the ding that signaled the passengers to fasten their seat belts and, looking out the window beside him, he saw the jet was descending into Bandar Abbas.

CHAPTER 26

The customs officials at Bandar Abbas knew Fitz well by now and his familiar one small suitcase went through inspection with the wave of a hand. Then he reboarded the plane and his heart started beating faster the closer he came to Tehran.

The timing of this flight was good. By the time Fitz deplaned at Tehran's Mehrabad International Airport, claimed his suitcase, and found a cab, he would arrive at Laylah's apartment about the same time she returned from her job at the Embassy.

Fitz bounded up the stairs of the apartment building to Laylah's second-floor flat after she buzzed the door to let him in. She was waiting for him, and as he walked into the apartment and put his suitcase down, Laylah handed him the small pony glass of ice-cold vodka. He took it, she picked up one herself, they clinked glasses and sipped. But he felt something was amiss. Usually Laylah was waiting for him to take her into his arms and they would be making love within minutes of his arrival. Only after the first lovemaking did they have vodka and caviar.

"Come sit down, Fitz." She gestured at the sofa. He sat down on it and Laylah sat on a chair facing him across the coffee table. More than ever now he began to sense something was wrong. That old angst returned. He swallowed the rest of the vodka.

"Something the matter?" Fitz asked anxiously.

"Oh, not really," Laylah replied. "I'm taking you out to a party in about half an hour."

"The only party I want is here with you."

"This is important for you and me. It's a sort of diplomatic party. At the Embassy. You'll see your old friend General Fielding."

Fitz made a face. "I know," Laylah went on, "but this one

you'll find interesting. Your British friend from Dubai will be there, Brian Falmey."

Fitz looked up at her, surprised. "Brian Falmey over here? What's he doing at the American Embassy?"

"He's been there several times, as I've told you. And I expect Courty Thornwell will be there."

Fitz grimaced. "I haven't seen or heard from him for months. Don't know why I should spoil the record now." He gave her a beseeching look.

"Laylah, do we really have to go?" He knew something was very wrong. What it was he could only guess but he was certain it had something to do with Thornwell.

"Take my word this is important for you, Fitz." She took a tiny sip of the vodka as though pausing to think of what to tell him next. "Through my connections at the National Iranian Oil Company I may have learned something that you ought to know."

"I guess there're several things I ought to know. Well, let's start with the NIOC."

"Brian mentioned to me that he was going to be having an audience with the Shah and Dr. Egbal, Chairman of the NIOC. I talked to a friend who is close to both the Shah and the Minister of Oil. A very handsome young man, I might add, who is trying to romance me."

"Isn't everyone?" Fitz remarked dourly.

A look of irritation passed across her face. "I'm just trying to explain how it was I learned what I'm about to tell you. But don't tell anybody where it came from or Palva—that's my friend—will be in big trouble."

"What is it?"

"Fitz, did you ever wonder why the Ruler of Sharjah so readily agreed to share Abu Musa Island with Iran?"

"As a matter of fact, I did. Although Iran could easily take it. Personally I couldn't see why they would want it. It's the most barren place I've ever seen. And certainly there's no oil within the three-mile limit of Abu Musa."

"Brian Falmey was telling me," Laylah went on, "how badly he feels about the British influence being pulled out everywhere east of Suez. He's one of the British people out here in charge of leaving things tidied up when the British leave. Naturally they want to continue to exert influence after they pull out. The British are dependent on the Gulf area for oil and they have a particular need to keep things peaceful. You'll remember that Iran tried to claim Bahrain."

"Of course I remember that. The Shah has gone a little mad, I think. He's trying to claim everything in the Arabian Gulf including what are clearly Arab islands. But Bahrain has always been Arab. I don't see how the Shah ever had any right to try to claim that."

"What he has a right to do has nothing to do with the situation. The Shah has the most powerful military in the Middle East. Now, suppose Abu Musa unilaterally declared that it owned all oil within a twelve-mile limit instead of a three-mile limit. What would happen then?"

"But they can't do that."

"Why not? If they had the backing of the British they could."

"But it's against all international laws. If they did that it would mean Sharjah and Iran and not Kajmira would own the territorial waters in which our concession lies. We paid seven hundred fifty thousand dollars for that concession. My God! That would destroy everything I've tried to do in the oil business since I've been in Dubai!"

"I know it, Fitz," Laylah said patiently. "That's why I'm telling you. The Brits traded the Shah your oil concession for no more Iranian claims on Bahrain."

Fitz thought about the situation. "I suppose if the British backed Sharjah it would certainly open our concession to question. But we signed all the documents with, as a matter of fact, Falmey present."

"Now isn't it important for you to go to this party? Wouldn't you like to ask Falmey personally what the situation is? And you'd be doing it more or less on your own home territory, the American Embassy."

"You're right. It just seems incredible that such an open and flagrant violation of international law could be contemplated by the British. Although I wouldn't put anything beyond Falmey."

"You've got to look at it from his point of view. He had to give the Shah something to make him keep his hands off Bahrain."

"And that ruins me," Fitz muttered.

"I have an Embassy car coming to pick us up here. Oh, by the way, do you still have your apartment in Tehran?"

Fitz felt the second blow of the old one-two about to land. Hesitantly he said, "Yes. I still haven't taken everything over to Dubai."

"I'm glad you have it because I have a little problem here now. My grandmother and aunt have taken to calling on me at odd hours of the night and in the morning. I think they suspect that you stayed over with me the last few times you were here. I guess some busybody saw you coming out and called them. I really don't want to upset them at this time."

With each word Fitz felt more and more miserable. He had a presentiment that something like this might be in the wind ever since he heard that Thornwell was staying in Tehran. "Laylah, why don't I get a nice suite at one of the new hotels and we can stay there together?" he suggested.

"No, darling, I can't do that either. They'll be calling me and if I'm not home at two in the morning or seven in the morning all hell will break loose." Laylah took another sip of her vodka and Fitz finished his off.

"I'm sorry, darling." Laylah stood up. "Anyway we'll go out and have a lovely dinner together. Then after dinner we'll talk things out and perhaps come home for a drink. But you've got to promise me that you won't try to stay." An utterly crushed look possessed his features. "Oh, I am sorry, darling. I can't help it. It's just one of those things." Laylah seemed really distressed. "The Embassy car will be here any minute. Do you want to freshen up or anything?"

"Yeah. Let me just go in for a minute or two."

The driver from the Embassy was one that Fitz had used on several occasions. They greeted each other and Fitz helped Laylah into the back seat of the car. Now he not only worried about his relationship with Laylah but his oil interests as well.

The cocktail party and reception was already under way when they reached the Embassy. The first person Fitz saw as they walked in was Harcourt Thornwell, who appeared to have been waiting near the door watching, impatiently, Fitz thought, for Laylah's arrival. He thought he noticed a knowing, perhaps questioning look on Thornwell's face as he caught Laylah's eye. He came over to them, greeted Laylah, and turned to Fitz, "Hi, Fitz," he said. "Good to see you again. How are things in Dubai?"

"Oh, same as ever," Fitz answered.

"I read a little bit about that trip you took when you couldn't make it to Riyadh with us," Thornwell said, just a hint of reproach in his voice. Fitz knew perfectly well that this was Thornwell's way of saying, "We could have used you but we don't need you now."

"Don't believe everything you read in the papers." Fitz smiled deprecatingly. "Particularly what you read about this part of the world."

"I don't believe *everything*," Thornwell answered, meaning precisely that he didn't believe everything but he did believe what was said about Fitz.

"Courty," Laylah interrupted, "excuse us for a minute. We've got to go over and say hello to the Ambassador, General Fielding, and a few of Fitz's old friends here. We'll join you a little later on. By the way, has Brian Falmey shown up yet?"

Thornwell looked around the room. "There he is over there." Thornwell turned to Fitz. "That ole Brit's not your best friend in Dubai, is he?"

"We do have our differences, of course. And you must realize, there is great British-American rivalry throughout the Middle East. They've been out here for two hundred and fifty years, we invaded it about forty years ago, and now they think that the Yanks are not only coming, they've taken over." Laylah steered Fitz away from Thornwell and they went around talking to old Embassy friends and acquaintances of Fitz's.

They spotted Falmey standing more or less alone in a corner of the room and Fitz and Laylah split up, Fitz heading for Brian Falmey, Laylah returning to Harcourt Thornwell.

"Hello, Brian," Fitz said genially, coming up from Falmey's left flank unobserved by the Brit.

Falmey turned and saw him. "I'm surprised you could find time from your extensive interests in Dubai to get away," he replied.

"I do have interests here in Tehran," Fitz retorted.

Falmey looked across the room and saw Laylah now talking to Thornwell. "I've observed that your interests are shared by at least one other gentleman."

Fitz followed Falmey's gaze and saw Thornwell talking intensely to Laylah. He turned from the sight and endeavored to show no reaction. "You can't blame him, can you?" Fitz remarked. "By the way, Falmey, I was at a rather important majlis yesterday and I heard a little bit about some of the bargaining you're doing over here with the Shah."

"Bargaining?" Then sharply: "Which majlis?"

"It doesn't really make much difference whether it was Shaikh Rashid's majlis or Shaikh Hamed's majlis or Shaikh Zayed's majlis or for that matter the majlis of Shaikh Khaled of Sharjah." Fitz bestowed a penetrating glance upon Brian Falmey. "The point is, the word's out that you are telling the Shah the British will back up a unilateral extension of the territorial waters of the little island of Abu Musa from three miles to twelve miles."

Brian Falmey came as close as an old-line British gentleman allowed himself to showing shock and surprise. He made several attempts to start a sentence and finally came out with "I can't understand how such a statement could have been made."

"Then it's not true?" Fitz glanced over at the American Ambassador. "Maybe we ought to go over and discuss this with His Excellency," Fitz suggested.

Falmey sputtered inconclusively. Finally he managed, "This is all hearsay. I don't understand how you could have heard anything about such discussions back in the Trucial States."

"Look, Falmey, there are a lot of people involved in this that you don't even know about. If this is the sort of connivance that is being planned, the least you could do is tell us. How about it?"

"There's nothing to tell."

"Are you asking me to go back and tell Majid Jabir that the information is wrong and he can safely go ahead with any investments he might counsel being made in the Kajmira concession?"

Falmey stared at Fitz a few moments, his jaw quivering. Fitz could see he had caught the Political Agent in the act. Something as important as this would not be Falmey's decision. It would have come from the Foreign Office of the British Government and would be backed up, if necessary, by the British Navy. Falmey was merely a sort of a waiter who carried on his diplomatic tray the goodies prepared in the international kitchen of diplo-

macy staffed by the highest representatives of British foreign policy. Fitz couldn't resist letting Falmey have one more barb. "I'll
tell Majid Jabir that there's no problem. He can go ahead with
developing certain interests he has in conjunction with Shaikh
Hamed."

Falmey slightly recovered his aplomb. "You can tell Majid
whatever you want to tell him. I certainly have no comment to
make on the rumor you just repeated to me." With that Falmey
turned and walked away from Fitz in as deliberate a manner as
possible.

Fitz realized that Laylah's source was correct. The three-mile
limit would be extended to twelve miles, the British Government
and the British Navy would back this up. Whatever pain may
come out of this trip, he thought to himself, thank God he had
made this discovery before it was too late to save the situation. He
turned toward Laylah and Thornwell and walked over to them.

"It's been a very interesting party," Fitz said. "I've seen some
old acquaintances and learned some new facts. What do you say
we get out of here?"

Thornwell appeared to be surprised and taken aback.

Fitz took Laylah's arm and turned to Thornwell for a minute.
"So long, Thornwell. Give my best to John Stakes if you see him."

Thornwell nodded uncertainly. He seemed about to protest but
Laylah shook her head slightly at him and she and Fitz left the
Embassy party. Outside the reception room Fitz looked about for
the driver he knew. "I'll find our man and get him to take us to
the Darband Hotel. We can use cabs from there."

Laylah was strangely silent during the thirty-five-minute trip
from the Embassy to the hotel. Fitz felt a sense of foreboding. He
reached for her hand, which she allowed him to take without response. "You were right about the Abu Musa thing. It's very fortunate I found out. I don't know what I can do about it but it's
better to know."

"I'm glad I was able to be helpful." Fitz could not think of an
answer and Laylah remained uncommunicative. When they
reached the hotel Fitz led her to the dining room, where they
were recognized by the headwaiter. Because of the proximity of
the hotel to Laylah's apartment, they came here frequently. The
headwaiter bowed them to their customary table in the corner.

"The usual to begin, madame?"

Laylah shook her head. "I'll just have a glass of white wine, thank you."

The headwaiter looked at Fitz.

"Make mine a martini very dry." Fitz had the feeling that he would need a martini, if not two, for dinner. The drinks arrived and they sipped silently. Finally Fitz could contain himself no longer. "What's the matter? What's happened to us, Laylah? You've never been like this before. Tell me what's wrong?" he asked anxiously.

Laylah half turned to him. "It isn't anything that's wrong exactly, Fitz. It's just that things are different."

"How do you mean different?" There was no answer for a moment. "Thornwell?"

"Well, Courty is around a lot and of course we do have much in common."

"Which we don't?"

"Of course we do, Fitz. More really than Courty and I. Courty kind of takes me back to my college days. But you are part of the real world, the world that interests and fascinates me the most."

"What do you think of Courty's scheme to raise Arab money to take over the communications industry in the United States?"

"It's a pretty brave idea. But I don't think he can do it. At least I don't think he can do it now. I've tried to help him and encourage him. I've introduced him to people very close to the Shah. The Shah's interests of course are tied much closer to the Arab world than to Israel."

"And the American press said that I was engaging in anti-Semitic discussions." Fitz laughed bitterly. "Well, Courty certainly took the most powerful leaf out of Adolf Hitler's book."

"Fitz, that's not fair and you know it. You were right in the middle of it yourself. The only reason you didn't stay with him was because of that trip you made where you killed all those Indians."

"I blew up three pirate ships, Laylah. An act of self-defense."

Fitz took a long sip of his martini. He forced himself to calm down for a few moments before continuing the conversation. Then: "I love you, Laylah. I want to marry you. I could go the route, all the way to being an ambassador to one of these Arab countries with you as my wife."

"Every time you come here you propose to me. But, Fitz, you're a married man, and you haven't done a thing about getting yourself unmarried. This is what confuses me."

"I told you that just as soon as I can spare a month I'm going back to Washington and the divorce will be granted."

There was another long silence. Again Fitz took a strengthening gulp of his martini. Laylah reached a hand across the table and put it on top of Fitz's. He felt the sudden thrill of excitement at the touch. "Fitz," Laylah began earnestly, "until all these things are worked out why don't we just be good friends. Maybe we can go back to what we were at the right time but this isn't it. I'm honestly confused, Fitz. I think I still love you but quite honestly I'm enjoying my life here in Tehran. I love my work at the Embassy, I love the parties, the contacts. I love being on the inside of what's going on in the most exciting and important part of the world now. And perfectly candidly, Fitz, I do enjoy seeing Courty Thornwell."

"Are you having an affair with him?" Fitz knew he shouldn't have asked the question but couldn't help himself.

Laylah looked at him a moment, took her hand off his. "I may be what they call a liberated woman. But I could never have an affair with two men at the same time even if I only saw my man once every month, which is the way it's been."

"I'm sorry, Laylah. I shouldn't have asked that."

"No, you shouldn't have."

Fitz put his hand up, signaled the headwaiter to bring them another round of drinks, and then they sat silently until the two fresh drinks were brought to them. Laylah had only half finished her first glass of wine but she made no objection to the order. Fitz took a sip of the second martini. He felt more objective and less emotional about their situation now. Finally, breaking the long period of quiet between them, he said, "All right, Laylah. It doesn't matter what I have going in Dubai at this moment. Nothing is as important to me as you. I'll head back for Washington next week. I'll stay there until I get the divorce. Then I'll try again with you."

Having delivered himself of this speech, Fitz suddenly felt very decided upon his future course of action.

Laylah put her hand back on his again. "For your own sake, and for hers, this is something you should do."

"What's motivating me to do this now, to leave the oil deal just when it most needs attention, what's motivating me to leave the Ten Tola Bar completely in the hands of Joe Ryan—the reason I'm doing this is so I can come back and marry you, Laylah."

"I'm not making any promises to you, Fitz. I don't know what I'll be doing or how I'll feel. I do know I care for you very deeply but our relationship confuses me now. Maybe when you're free the confusion will be gone."

"The confusion probably has something to do with Courty Thornwell being on the scene," Fitz said dryly.

"Yes, I guess it does. I'm not in love with him, not the way I loved you."

Fitz interrupted her. "I hate hearing you put that in the past tense."

Laylah smiled regretfully at him. "I guess that's all part of the confusion I was talking about."

When they returned to Laylah's apartment after dinner Fitz knew that any suggestion he made about staying with her or having her stay with him would go a long way toward killing what chances he might still have with her. Before he left her at the door, his suitcase in hand, he said, "I'm going back to Dubai tomorrow. And then I'll head on for Washington as soon as I can get away. There's one thing you could do for me, Laylah."

"Of course, Fitz. You want me to keep in touch with my friend at NIOC?"

"That would certainly be a tremendous help to me. It's not just my money, it's my reputation with my partners. I seem to have become leader of the syndicate."

"May a mere woman make a suggestion to you?"

"Please. Anything you have to say is important in my life. Both personal and business."

"All right, Fitz. We discussed your going to see my mother and father in Philadelphia about how a campaign contribution could put you in line for an ambassadorship to one of the Arab countries. Let me give you another thought. A good friend of my father's is Lorenz Cannon. He's the president and, I suppose, the majority stockholder in Hemisphere Petroleum Company out of New York. Cannon is a powerful oil man. What you are trying to do, I think, requires considerably more influence on a totally international basis than you and your group can bring to bear. I know that Majid Jabir gets more powerful, rich, and influential every day. However, even his helping you behind the scenes isn't going to change this situation. You need—to use the vernacular—some big juice, some heavy muscle. Right?"

"I'm beginning to think so. Lorenz Cannon? Hemisphere Petroleum? All right, I'll be certain to contact him if your father and mother will make the introductions."

"They will, Fitz. I'll write them tomorrow. My father has never lost his interest in the Middle East. I think secretly he was very disappointed when the State Department passed him over for Ambassador to Iran. I've always felt that's why he retired. He said, of course, that the lure of private industry and the opportunities constantly being offered to him had finally become too much to turn down."

Fitz set his suitcase back down on the floor again, put one hand on each of Laylah's shoulders, and very gently but positively kissed her for a long moment. Then he took his hands from her, reached down and picked up his suitcase, and opened the door. "Thank you for everything, Laylah. Just, please, one thing. Don't make any drastic decisions until I see you again, a free man. Agreed?"

Laylah nodded, her eyes moist. "Agreed, Fitz."

Fitz smiled at her a moment, then turned and left the apartment.

CHAPTER 27

It was a long and arduous trip from Dubai via Lebanon, London, and New York to the Twin Bridge Marriott Motor Inn on the Virginia side of the Potomac River near the Pentagon. Fitz had been on airplanes and sitting in airport waiting rooms for more than two days when he finally checked into the motel. Autumn in Washington, D.C., provided excellent weather. Much cooler of course than the temperatures he was used to on the Gulf but still warm enough so that he didn't need an overcoat. Travel-worn, weary from jet lag across eight hours in time zones, Fitz looked at the first bed he'd seen in the last forty-eight hours.

He hung his clothing bag in the closet, opened his suitcase, and neatly laid out his sparse wardrobe. He resolved to buy most of the clothes he would need in Washington or New York. After a long hot shower and a shave the temptation was to fall into the bed and sleep for a few hours. However, he shook off this urge and, taking out his notebook, he reached for the telephone. The first call he made was to his old friend and fellow staff member at Military Assistance Command in Saigon. He didn't know precisely where Colonel Dick Healey was presently assigned, merely that he was somewhere in Washington, D.C. Dick's wife, Jenna, answered the phone. She let out a whoop when Fitz identified himself. "Fitz, we thought you were somewhere out in the desert with the Arabs. You're really here?"

"At the Marriott Hotel in Virginia. Where's Dick assigned now? I want to see him."

There was a slight hesitation at the other end of the line and then Jenna said, "I'll try and reach him and have him call you. Are you going to be there for a while?"

"I expect so. If I'm not in, ask him to leave a message for me."

"I know he'll want to call you, Fitz. Isn't it funny? We were just talking about you two days ago. When all that business came out in the papers, first the Jews and then the Indians, you became the hottest topic in town among your old friends. Even the war in Vietnam lost interest beside your escapades."

"Don't believe what you read in the papers. I'll tell you all about it when I see you."

After hanging up with Jenna Healey, Fitz steeled himself to the next task. Marie would be at home waiting for his call. He had cabled her his approximate time of arrival in Washington. He dialed her number. "Hello, Fitz," she said in her flat tone. "You got here."

"Yes."

He paused on the phone but Marie had nothing more to say, so Fitz said, "I guess we ought to get together. I came a long way to see you. How is Bill?"

"Bill is doing very well now at Valley Forge Military Academy. I think his attitude has improved and he won't be as difficult any more. He really missed having a father," she added accusingly.

"I begged you to let him visit me in Iran."

"I told you I wouldn't let him go over to some half-civilized place in the desert."

Fitz was again reminded how insular Marie had always been. Her life revolved around her family in Indiana and her girl friends at the office. She mistrusted and was afraid of any place outside the continental limits of the United States. She wasn't even so sure about California for that matter. Fitz smiled indulgently at her attitude.

"I'd like to see Bill sometime while I'm here," he said. "Maybe if he and I got together he'd like to come see me on a vacation sometime."

"We have a lot to settle first, Fitz," Marie said primly. "My lawyer, Jack Ruttberg, is expecting to hear from you. His office is downtown in Washington. I'll give you his number."

Fitz took a pencil and wrote the lawyer's phone number down. "I'll call him right away, Marie. Do you want to talk to me after I've seen him?"

"Well, that's up to Mr. Ruttberg. Whatever he says."

Fitz fought down the rising exasperation. "All right, Marie, I'll

see your Mr. Ruttberg. Maybe I'll be talking to you, depending
upon what your lawyer says."

"That's right," Marie said, hanging up.

Fitz stared for a moment at the slip of paper on which he'd
written the lawyer's phone number. Before he could call it the
phone rang. He picked it up. "Fitz! We were wondering if we'd
ever see you again in this world."

"Hey, Dick, it didn't take you long to get back to me."

"No, I was at my desk, which doesn't happen very often, when
Jenna called."

"Where are you assigned now anyway?" Fitz asked.

"Tell you when I see you. You're eating with us tonight. I told
Jenna to bust the budget on dinner."

"Are you still living in the same place?"

"Right. You know how to get there. Do you have a car?"

"No, I'll grab a cab."

"I'd come get you but I know I'm going to be working late."

"No sweat. I'll get a cab. What time do you want me to be
there, about seven o'clock?"

"That'll be great. Everybody has been trying to find out where
you are. I might make a few phone calls and let them know I've
got you captured."

"O.K. by me. See you tonight at your place."

When Fitz hung up he felt much more buoyed than he had in
the last few days. He and Dick had been in the Intelligence Section in Saigon and both of them had served in Special Forces in
Vietnam together in 1964 when the Green Berets were the only
Americans fighting the war there. Then Fitz had returned for his
second assignment to the Middle East while Dick had gone to
Washington. Fitz had been pulled out of the Middle East and
sent back to Saigon for six months of special duty and then back
to Tehran. He couldn't complain. His life had been varied and exciting in the military. He had been sent to the Army language
school in Monterey to learn Arabic, but he still felt an ache at not
making full colonel and a career in the higher echelons of the
Army. Fitz picked up the phone again and reached Jack Ruttberg,
who suggested that he come over after lunch, at two o'clock.

Then Fitz made his final call, dialing the long-distance operator. He gave her the phone number of the Hoving Smiths in Rad-

nor, Pennsylvania, and said he'd talk to anyone who answered. If there was a maid he thought he could at least leave his phone number and the message that he had called. Laylah's parents would probably be expecting his call today, since she wrote to them the day after he last saw her. The phone was answered on the second ring. It was a woman. Perhaps Laylah's mother. In fact, he was sure it must be, since she had a slight accent.

"Mrs. Smith?" he asked tentatively.

"Yes. Who's this?"

"This is a friend of your daughter's. My name is—"

"Colonel Lodd," Laylah's mother interrupted him. "I've been hoping you'd call. We received Laylah's letter two days ago. How was she when you last saw her?"

Fitz wondered how to answer that question. How was she? Confused? She'd certainly sent him away a fairly confused figure.

"Fine," Fitz said heartily. "Laylah is just great. As always."

"We certainly hope you're going to come and see us, Colonel," Mrs. Smith said hospitably. "In her letter Laylah mentioned some of the things that were on your mind. Hoving and I have discussed it and he has several very good ideas for you. I'd love to have you be our house guest for a few days if you could make it."

"I'm looking forward to meeting you and Mr. Smith," Fitz replied. "I don't know just how long I'll be in Washington but I can let you know tomorrow when I can visit you."

"Today is Wednesday. Perhaps you could come for the weekend," she proposed.

"I think the weekend would work out. Can I let you know tomorrow, Mrs. Smith?"

"Certainly. Hoving has some friends who could be helpful to you in both of your endeavors."

"I appreciate Mr. Smith's interest," Fitz said. "I'll talk to you again tomorrow."

Except for Marie and the Ruttberg connection, things seemed to be going the way he hoped they would. Of course, the real reason he was here was to somehow get the divorce finished with. He thought it was all set. Now with the lawyer involved Marie was acting differently.

Later, feeling refreshed from a shower and shave and clean clothes, he took a cab down to the address of Ruttberg's office.

From the doorway to the office building he looked around and spotted a restaurant and bar across the street and headed for it.

At two o'clock sharp he was walking through the door into the reception room of Ruttberg and Quinn. Bolstered by the three straight brandies he'd consumed and the roast-beef sandwich, he felt equal to facing what would undoubtedly be a nasty conference with Marie's lawyer.

Fitz identified himself to the receptionist and was swiftly ushered into the office of Jack Ruttberg. Ruttberg wore an obvious black toupee; he had a pencil-line mustache and a rather hawk-like face. He peered over a great hook nose at Fitz, who sat opposite him. After telling Fitz that he'd been following his career in the papers, first certain anti-minority-group statements, then his latest escapades, smuggling gold and taking on the Indian Coast Guard—"to the Indians' disadvantage, happily," Ruttberg added —the lawyer inquired as to the size of the settlement Fitz was thinking about.

"You know what a lieutenant colonel's pension is, Mr. Ruttberg. That should provide you with the parameters of my capability for making monthly alimony payments."

"Oh, of course you'll be making monthly alimony payments. It's the lump-sum cash settlement that I'm interested in."

"A retired lieutenant colonel doesn't have much cash hanging around," Fitz replied.

"But a retired lieutenant colonel who's been working with the Arabs for a year and who is involved in what I'm told is a very lucrative type of adventuring—namely, smuggling gold from the Persian Gulf into India—a lieutenant colonel like this would be indeed able to pay a substantial settlement in order to get a divorce."

"That is all a lot of contrived nonsense. It is true I am trying to get into some business endeavor in the Arab world, but I have not done so successfully yet. In the meantime I'm living on my pension as a lieutenant colonel and that's it. The most I can do is send my wife a portion of my pension. I'm willing to send her half of my pension. That's the best I can do. I have to have something to go on myself."

In his own mind Fitz knew he would send Marie and his son generous amounts of money as he acquired it. But he didn't want this lawyer to think that he could be expected to come up with a large sum of money. Fitz stared at the lawyer. "As a matter of fact, as long as we are married and not separated there is no legal way I can be forced to give her any of my pension if I don't want to. Naturally I want my son to be taken care of, so I will do what's right for him. Legally you cannot attach a government pension, as you well know. I came back here to help my wife out; she wants a divorce and so do I. She's still not old. I assume she is as attractive as she was the last time I saw her. I'm sure that she has marital opportunities. Therefore it is to both our advantage to see that this divorce goes through as soon as possible."

"Your wife is of the opinion that you are possessed of substantial funds. She feels she deserves a share of whatever you've made in your Persian Gulf adventures."

"Well, if my wife wants a divorce she'd better get it now, because when I go back to the Arabian Gulf, nobody will find me and there will be no part of my pension that she will see. She's prevented me from seeing my son, she has refused to allow him to visit me; she knew I was serving the United States abroad and not deliberately staying away from home. She refused to join me in Tehran, where I was stationed, because she said it was a half-civilized desert town. I don't know my son any more. I'm perfectly prepared to go back and disappear into the Arabian desert for the rest of my life. My wife will never be free nor will she share in my pension, modest though it is."

Fitz was almost enjoying delivering his ultimatum. "So I'll give you my deal right now, Mr. Ruttberg. Half my pension to her and my son; it will be at her discretion how she takes care of him. She's never let me have any say in it anyway. And a settlement of the five thousand dollars I've managed to save over the last two years or so. I will also advance one more thousand dollars, which is not easy for me, but I'll do it toward legal fees on her side. That is my offer. That is all I can do and I will leave it to you to pass this along to Marie. You can take it or leave it. If Marie allows me to get to know my son and I am fortunate enough to achieve any affluence, I'll see that he is well taken care of. If on the other hand I am prevented from getting to know my son in the future as has happened in the past, I can perfectly easily disappear into the desert. I am a Bedouin, Mr. Ruttberg, if you know what that means. It's a nomad without roots. I have no established means of income that you can attach beyond my government pension, which is inviolate. So I suggest you pass this information along to Marie and let me know as soon as possible at my hotel, the Twin Bridge Marriott. I expect to be in town not more than forty-eight hours and not less than twenty-four. So I would suggest that you try to reach me no later than tomorrow evening, because when I go back to Arabia, my wife and the son I've never known, Bill, will have to get along on their own. Do you have any questions to ask me?"

"Mr. Lodd, you've made your point perfectly clear. I'll pass your comments along to Mrs. Lodd. It will be her decision what to do from here on in."

Fitz stood up. "Then I'll expect to hear from you before tomorrow evening."

"I will follow Mrs. Lodd's instructions."

Fitz turned on his heel and walked out of the lawyer's office. It was a relief to be out in the hall and even more of a relief to gain the street and start walking. He was back at his hotel by three o'clock. It had not been a long meeting with Ruttberg. Now he wondered whether he dared try to take a three-hour nap before going over to Dick Healey's house. He badly needed sleep.

Fitz picked up the telephone and asked for two calls—one at six o'clock and the second at six-thirty. If he slept through the first call, as could happen, the second one would be sure to arouse him. He took off his suit and lay down on the bed in his underwear and was instantly alseep. It seemed as though he had been asleep no more than a minute when the phone rang and woke him up. He glanced at his watch. He had slept an hour. It was four o'clock. Silently he cursed the telephone operator to himself as he picked up the phone. "Lodd!" he barked into the telephone.

"Fitz?" It was Marie. Fitz sighed, rolled over, took a deep breath, exhaled all the air in his lungs, took half a breath, exhaled that, and then sat up.

Anxiously. "Fitz, are you there?"

"Yes."

"Fitz, I think we should see each other."

"That's what I suggested when I called you this morning but you wanted me to see your lawyer. I saw him. I don't see as we have much to talk about. I told Mr. Ruttberg exactly what I could and could not do. What more do you expect?"

"I expect you to be a gentleman. I expect you to be decent. I expect you to do everything you can for your son."

"Oh, for God's sake, Marie. You wrote and said you wanted a divorce. I came all the way back so that we could work it out and then you send me to a Ruttberg. Why didn't you meet me yourself first?"

"Can we meet somewhere for a cup of coffee? Maybe tonight?" Marie asked.

"No. I wanted to see you and would have when I called you before. But since you told me I would have to work things out with your lawyer I've made other plans. I'll be glad to see you tomorrow morning."

"I'll come over to the Marriott and meet you for breakfast," Marie replied quickly. "Afterward we could go together to Mr. Ruttberg."

"Now that's the way I like to hear you talk. The two of us have usually been able to work things out, Marie. I'll see you in the morning."

Ordinarily Fitz would have worried the situation about in his mind for the next two hours but he was too fatigued to do so. He still could catch almost two hours' sleep before it was time to get ready to go to Dick Healey's. He fell back on the bed and once again was instantly asleep.

CHAPTER 28

At nine-thirty that evening Fitz and Dick Healey were sitting out in the kitchen, a bottle of cognac between them, each sipping from an old-fashioned glass. Fitz somehow had the impression that this was what the evening had been leading up to all along. They talked about all their old friends, Jenna asked about Marie, and Fitz had said they were getting divorced, a far from uncommon occurrence among the couples in his and Dick Healey's circle of military acquaintances. Then he had given them a thumbnail sketch of his life in Dubai.

He had carefully left out any references to Laylah or gold smuggling. During dinner Jenna and Dick had been too polite to bring up the news stories. Now, over their cognacs, all the small talk behind them, Dick came to the point. "I haven't told you what I'm doing now."

"I assume that you've gone to that happy hunting ground for former Special Forces colonels—the 'Company' in Langley?"

"A very astute assumption," Dick replied. "Yep, I'm with the Agency. Like you, I retired early and went into a very nice slot over there. I'm doing just what I've always wanted to do. Without a bunch of chicken-shit generals crawling all over my ass. Now level with me, Fitz. What are you really doing in Dubai or wherever the hell it is you're operating on the Persian Gulf?"

"In the first place, it's the Arabian Gulf. And in the second place, there are a lot of good reasons why I shouldn't level with anybody about what I'm doing," Fitz replied. "Why are you so interested?"

"Fitz, we've been good friends for a long time. We've been under mortar storms together, we both almost got it when we pulled off that operation inside Cambodia together, we sweated out promotions and we sweated out the goddam MAC-V brass

trying to do in all of us green beanies. You honestly think anything you told me that could hurt you I would use? What I'm trying to do is help you and help me too. So why don't you just level
with me?"

Fitz finished off the cognac in his old-fashioned glass. Dick
picked up the bottle and half filled the glass again. "O.K., Dick. It
would be a relief to tell one friend everything that's happened."

It was almost ten o'clock when Fitz had completely finished the
saga of his life, leaving nothing out, including his affair with
Laylah and the gold-smuggling trip to India. When he was finished Dick Healey pursed his lips and let out a whistle.

"You've really had some adventures. I'm glad you made money
anyway. So you really think someday you might get appointed ambassador to one of those Arab countries?"

"I know I'd be the best the government could find. I've heard
that when the British leave, the Trucial States are going to become something called the United Arab Emirates. Now that
would be a good place for me to be an ambassador."

"My only thinking is," Dick said, "that those news stories won't
do you any good at the State Department. Even though it was
later printed that you had denied any participation in smuggling
activities or firing on Indian Coast Guard boats, I think you
might have some hard going. But, Fitz, there is a way you could
serve your country and continue to do just what you're doing. It
seems to me that your bar there . . . what do you call it?"

"The Ten Tola Bar."

"Right. The Ten Tola Bar. It seems to me the Ten Tola Bar
would make an excellent cover for somebody who was working
with the Agency."

"Are you recruiting me, Dick?" Fitz chuckled.

"I'm merely saying you could be helpful to us. We probably
have less strength on the Arab side of the Persian Gulf than in
any other strategic part of the world. That's been the domain of
the Brits traditionally and most of the information we get comes
from British sources. But now we've had to re-evaluate our position. Studies indicate that each year the United States becomes
more and more dependent upon Arab oil, specifically oil that
comes out of the Persian Gulf and across the ocean to us."

Dick sighted through his glass of cognac, took a sip, and put it

down. "We are well aware of the insurgency problems brewing in
Oman and the Dhofar province between Yemen and Oman," he
continued. "We are also aware of the possibilities of a Communist insurgency successfully taking control of the Musandam Peninsula at the tip end of Oman which really commands the Straits
of Hormuz. We know that both Chinese and Russian arms are
getting to the insurgents in the Dhofar province and other parts
of Oman. This of course we get from our British counterparts.
When the British leave, in 1971 at the latest, who's going to keep
an eye on this insurgency?"

Dick continued in urgent tones. "King Faisal in Saudi Arabia
and all of your friends, the shaikhs in the Trucial States, Qatar
and Bahrain, have little or no knowledge of insurgency in Oman.
But as our dependence on Gulf oil becomes increasingly more
acute, we expect the Communist insurgents to step up their activities."

Dick Healey laughed in disgust. "Here we are up to our necks
in Vietnam, trying to get out, and we're already looking to another area where we may have to involve ourselves. We're pretty
sure that by the middle seventies we'll find ourselves drawn into
the Oman situation. It's a typical Communist insurgency operation. The guerrillas in Oman heading up north to control the
Straits of Hormuz are being supplied with weaponry from the
Communists. If the Communists can subvert Oman they'll eventually control Saudi Arabia and the other Gulf states."

"That's what I've been saying now for a year," Fitz replied.
"I'm glad to hear that the Agency at least is on to this situation."

"We're very much on to it. As a matter of fact, when I first
read about your exploits in the Indian Ocean or wherever it
was—"

"The Arabian Sea," Fitz corrected him.

"Right. When I heard about that I knew Fitz was up to his old
tricks and it occurred to me that perhaps if I could reach you
somehow—I was even thinking of making a trip over there to try
to locate you—we might be able to get you unofficially working
for the Company."

"Naturally, Dick, I'd do anything I can to help you and pass on
information to you. Quite honestly I would not want to be with
the CIA. I'm a businessman. All it would take would be the

slightest indication that I was actually a CIA agent to wreck all my future business plans in Arabia."

"I'm not suggesting you become an agent or even a paid employee of the Agency, Fitz. But there are ways you could be of help to us. Just keeping your eyes open, for instance. Incidentally, any services you were able to perform for the United States in an unofficial capacity wouldn't do you any harm at all if you're serious about trying to secure an appointment as an ambassador. From what you tell me and what I know about the new Nixon administration, your dream is not an impossible one. You certainly have the qualifications, you speak the language, which is rare among Americans, and frankly you have the money to go and buy an ambassadorship. We have no illusions about a direct relationship between campaign contributions to a presidential campaign and the appointment of ambassadors—and ambassadresses," he chuckled, "to attractive posts throughout the world. Most contributors would never want to go to an Arab country. In other words, what I'm saying is, you help us and we'll help you. And we can give a great deal of help at the right time. Tricky Dicky has been successful in putting his money buddies into really sensitive spots."

"Sounds interesting. Where do we go from here?"

"I told our Middle East people that I would sound you out about this tonight. I'll go back to them tomorrow and I'll call you at the Marriott about another appointment. How long are you going to be around?"

"How long do you want me around? I'm planning to go up to Philadelphia and see Laylah's mother and father this weekend. And there's the matter of finalizing the divorce between Marie and myself."

"On that I can't advise you, thank the Lord. Jenna and I have never had the inclination to explore the possibilities in that area."

Fitz and Dick finished off their cognac and then Fitz said good night and called a cab.

Back at the Marriott he went to the cocktail lounge on the top floor, from which he could look out all over the city of Washington, D.C. Here was the source of all major decisions. Here is where he would eventually have to return in order to get what he wanted. He wondered what "cooperating with the CIA" really entailed. Could it result in his getting the ambassadorship to the United Arab Emirates should such a federation really be formed? Fitz could feel the fatigue creeping through him, exerting a sort of partial paralysis over his mind and movements. By midnight he was back in his room sound asleep.

CHAPTER 29

By noon Fitz was actually buying Marie a drink before lunch. It seemed that his strategy of not having a lawyer to represent him— I trust Mr. Ruttberg implicitly—because he couldn't afford two sets of legal fees, had worked nicely. He knew that he shouldn't have paid the five-thousand-dollar settlement in advance, before the decree was final, but this naïve gesture had pleased the Ruttberg and thus Marie.

Ruttberg must have thought he was the most stupid ex-lieutenant colonel ever to have been involuntarily retired from the Army when Fitz agreed to have the pension checks sent directly to Ruttberg's office and after much argument agreed to increase the division of his pension from one half to two thirds of the money to Marie for herself and Bill. And Fitz had even condescended to a twenty-five-dollar-a-month fee to Ruttberg for handling the money.

All Fitz could think of was returning to Tehran with his divorce decree in hand. He had the right to visit his son and have Bill visit him anyplace in the United States. Fitz resigned himself to having to wait for Bill to grow up before he would see him again. But Marie had arranged for Fitz to be able to visit his son at Valley Forge Military Academy. He would have to be near Philadelphia anyway to see Laylah's parents.

"Too bad," Marie mused over her manhattan.

"We've known this was the best way for several years," Fitz said. "No point going on the way we were. You'll meet someone, if you haven't already, that will suit you better than I."

"It's not that easy, Fitz."

"You'll like Santo Domingo." Fitz made the desultory comment. "Only two days and you're back here a free woman. By the way, I appreciate your setting up the visit with Bill."

"I hope you'll try to come back and see him more often."

"I'll try, of course, but it's an expensive trip."

"Why don't you stay around here and get a job?"

"I feel more at home with the Arabs than I do here. And with only one third of my pension to live on I can get by much cheaper there. I'll get a job doing something for the Shaikh."

"Somehow it doesn't seem right, an American being a servant to one of those heathen tribesmen."

"I guess I'm different than most Americans."

That afternoon Fitz called Laylah's mother and said he could make it for the weekend if that was still all right with the Smiths. In her charming accent Laylah's mother said to please call her Maluk, not Mrs. Smith. She and Hoving would be looking forward to seeing him Friday in time for dinner. Fitz explained that he would rent a car and be driving. Then he spent the rest of the afternoon catching up on his sleep. Dick Healey had set up a big evening for him.

In all the time Fitz had spent in or near Washington he had never been in the Silver Slipper before. Dick had picked the place for their meeting, he explained when Fitz slid onto a chair beside him at the corner table, because this was a non-meeting. Just a couple of old friends hoisting a few and looking at the girls. A bosomy lovely came up to the table. She hovered suggestively after taking the drink order.

"What's your name, love?" Dick asked.

"Mia," she replied. "Theese ees my table." She had a fetching Latin accent. "I go get you scotch and soda."

They watched her as she walked away from the table. "O.K., Dick. I like the scenery but why here?"

"We're always catching hell from some congressman trying to make a name for himself with the liberals by investigating the Agency. Some of the suggestions you're going to hear might be considered improper. The Agency asking a private businessman working abroad to do a little work on the side for us, you know. This way we can always truthfully say we never had any conversations with you except for a social evening at the Silver Slipper." Dick raised his hand and waved toward the entrance to the nightclub. "Here's Abe now. He's going to be working the Persian Gulf area out of Beirut."

"Then he'd better start calling it the Arabian Gulf," Fitz commented. He turned around in his seat and saw the swarthy young man approaching them. He looked like a Lebanese, Fitz thought.

"Hi, Abe, glad you could join us," Dick Healey said. "Meet an old pal from Saigon, Fitz Lodd. Fitz, this is Abe Ferutti." Abe took a seat just as Mia returned. She put Fitz's drink in front of him.

"Hello, baby," Abe said. "I'll have one of those too."

"Fitz is with us, Abe." Dick noticed Abe's preoccupation with the Latin waitress. "How are the girls in Beirut?"

Abe turned from Mia. "Expensive. I'm going to import some French girls, I think. Those oil drillers come up with lots of money and spoil the girls for the rest of us low-paid peons." He turned to Fitz. "Dick has told me all about you. If you can get a couple of blondes into the Trucial States to work in your club, I think I can send you at least one honey, better than anything here even."

"If she speaks English and Arabic and you guys want her in, no problem."

"I'll meet you in Beirut, Fitz. When are you going back?"

"I should have a divorce coming final next week. Then if Dick doesn't have anything in mind for me I'll be on my way. I just have some oil business to clean up in New York."

Dick glanced at his watch. "Big Luke Boless, now Brigadier General Boless, is going to be joining us. He wants to see Fitz again. How the hell he got on the general's list so damn fast I don't know."

"He was always kissing ass and pimping for the two and three stars around MAC-V in Saigon." Fitz took a long pull on his drink. "That's one way of doing it."

"Fitz"—Abe's tone had a serious note—"can you still get your hands on those guns you got out of Iran?"

Fitz looked at the agent in surprise. Abe grinned. "Oh, it was in the papers, don't you remember?"

"And so was my denial to those scurrilous charges made by some half-assed reporter."

"Hey, Fitz." Dick nudged him. "Abe and I had a long talk about you, remember?"

Fitz shrugged. "Sure. I know where they are when they're not mounted on a certain high-speed smuggling dhow." He looked at Abe. "Why?"

"Just wondering for future reference. You haven't any objections to getting into an operation if we need you?"

"You can be goddam sure I have big objections to getting into operations. Information? I'll help you every way. I'll even help you plant your female spy. But overt action? I've done too much of it as it is."

"I don't think there'll be any call for something like that," Dick hastily broke in.

"It's mostly information we're after," Abe confirmed. "Once we get out of Vietnam there's another budding little insurgency waiting for us over in Oman. If the Commies are successful there, and it's going to take them quite a while, we're in big trouble. That's where our oil comes from these days. With the Brits pulling out and the Arabs happily oblivious to what the Russians and Chicoms are doing, subversion is going to escalate."

"Nothing new about that theory," Fitz remarked.

"What's new is how close they're coming. Do you know a Frenchman named Jean Louis Serrat?"

"Sure. An oil man and gun runner."

"Exactly. And he doesn't care where he sells guns as long as he makes big French arms deals. And incidentally, not that it's in our province, but he takes a hunk of his pay for the arms in morphine base. Next step heroin. Next step the veins of America's ghetto youth."

"What do you want me to do?"

"I'm not sure. We're working on strategy. You'll be informed. What we're trying to avoid is America running out of oil by 1976."

Another waitress walked by. "Lori," Abe called. "Come over here."

"It's not my table, Abe."

"So I'll move over to your side of the room." He turned back to Fitz and Dick. "Boy, if you knew some of the powers in our gov-

ernment that come here to get laid, you'd shit. Mia screwed one
of our Presidents once."

"Have you got a plant here?" Fitz asked.

"Of course. The agency can't rely on J. Edgar for its domestic
information."

"By the way," Fitz asked, "do you speak Arabic?"

In flawless classic Arabic, Abe said, "There is only one God and
that one God is Allah and Mohammed is his prophet."

"Well, they'd know you weren't a Gulf Arab."

"Man, ah kin talk suthin nigra," Abe laughed, and then
spouted off in the harsh, less-cultured dialect of the Arabian Gulf.
Fitz was impressed. This really was some sort of super spy.

He turned to Dick. "What are you getting me into? I see how I
can help you, get into deep trouble and end up very dispensable.
What do I get out of it?"

"Tomorrow noon, at the Metropolitan Club, we'll get into
that."

"And maybe I'll be assigned to your country team, Mr. Ambassador." Abe smiled. "Meanwhile"—he reached into his pocket and
pulled out a small device about the size of a matchbox which had
a long wire attached to it—"ever seen one of these?" Fitz shook
his head. "This is a tiny transmitter; the wire is the antenna. I'll
give you a demonstration." From his pocket Abe took a roll of ad-
hesive tape and then taped the transmitter under the table, the
antenna hanging down the table leg.

"A bug, huh?" Fitz murmured.

"Right. This table is bugged." He turned to Dick. "When is
Boless coming over?"

"He should be here now," Dick answered.

Abe called Mia over to the table. "Hey, baby, we're expecting a
friend over in a couple of minutes. General Boless. Seat him here
and be nice to him, you know what I mean?"

"Sì," she replied. "Eet ees early. I am not so beezy."

"Now let's take a seat over in the far corner, away from this
table." They stood up. Fitz and Dick followed the agent to an
empty table at the other end of the nightclub. From an inside vest
pocket Abe took out a miniature transistor radio. He put it on the
table in front of him as a red-headed girl came over. "You decided
to move tables?" she asked. "My name is Lori."

"Hello, Lori, I'm Abe. You don't remember me?"

"We get so many people," Lori answered apologetically. "Anyway I'm glad you came to my table. Things are slow tonight. What can I get you?"

They all asked for a scotch and soda and then sat, waiting for Luke Boless to arrive. Abe put the small transistor to his ear and listened, then smiled.

They were halfway through their drinks and Fitz was beginning to like the red-headed Lori when the hulking civilian-garbed general entered the club. "There he is. Now let's hope Mia does her stuff," Abe said. They watched Luke Boless ask the headwaiter something and then he was directed to the table they had just vacated. Mia was waiting for him. Abe handed the transistor to Fitz, who put it to his ear.

"'Allo, General," Fitz heard Mia greet him through the bug. "Your friend weel be right back. He tell me take good care of you."

They all saw the leer come across the heavy officer's face. His words came clearly over the receiver. "Honey, I just bet you could take care of me real nice."

"Anything you want, General." Mia was playing it strong and Boless was eating it up.

"What I want is a little bit of you. I don't have to wait for my friends. Can you get off early? I've only got a couple of more days in town before I have to go back to Saigon."

"I'm sorry," Mia said sadly, "but I have to stay here until one o'clock in the morning."

"I'll wait if you think it would be worth my while," Boless pitched. "Oh, what I wouldn't give for a little Latin lovely like you to keep me company."

"I don't have plans for after work. One of your friends suggested maybe he and me get together."

"Hey, honey, that Colonel Healey? He's married. He don't know what the word 'swing' means. I don't know who was with him but you'd be better off with me."

"You are one peestol, General." Mia's Latin accent rippled seductively. "You are much cuter than your friend. You want I get you a dreenk?"

"Sure. Where the hell did they go anyway?" He grinned lasciviously at her; his intentions were clear even viewed from across the room. Fitz, Dick, and Abe laughed uproariously. "Not that I give a damn," Boless went on. "You and I could have a great time tonight if they never showed up."

Dick stood up and, followed by Abe and Fitz, walked over to the table. "Sorry to disappoint you, Luke. But you can still have a great time with Mia tonight."

Luke looked up. "What? Oh, hiya, Dick. The little lady and I were just talking."

"You a peestol, General." Dick mimicked the Latin accent. "And you're much cuter than any of your friends. Are you going to order that drink?"

"What the hell, you were sneaking up on me and listening."

Without answering, Dick took a seat. Boless saw Fitz and roared, "Hey, Fitz, you old Jew-baiting, Indian-killing bastard. I've been trying to figure out how to reach you ever since I started following your life in the newspapers."

"Hello, Luke." Fitz shook his hand and sat down. "So you got the big star, eh?"

"Yeah, finally made it." He looked up at Abe, who was introduced to him by Dick. "He looks like he's out of that spookery you joined," Boless commented. Then: "Say, how did you know what my little Latin lady and I were saying to each other?" he asked suspiciously.

Dick Healey reached under the table and untaped the bug and showed it to Boless. "See, you never know who's listening in, General. A man in your position should be careful."

Boless took the transmitter and examined it. "This is a good one. I could use it when I get back to Saigon. Want to sell it?"

"Belongs to Abe."

"How about it, Abe?"

"Be my guest, General. Someday you can do me a favor. I understand you are in charge of the PX system, and you run Bien Hoa, the biggest installation in the 'Nam." Abe handed the bug and the transistor to General Boless. "Good listening."

"Thanks very much, really, Abe." Boless was delighted with the bugging device, examining it, turning it over in his fingers. "By God, I know where's the first place I'm going to plant this baby."

Fitz had never seen such a neat little spy package. A lot of new stuff had been developed since he had been involved in surveillance activities right after the Korean War. He wondered why Abe Ferutti had wanted to demonstrate the equipment for him in a nightclub. But when he thought about it a moment he realized exactly what Abe had in mind.

To Fitz, Abe said, "Keep in touch with Dick. Before you go back I'll have a briefcase full of goodies for you to use strategically in the Ten Tola Bar. It was nice having a drink with you, Fitz. Next one will be in the Ten Tola Bar."

"Where's that?" Boless asked.

"In Dubai," Fitz replied. "At least it soon will be."

"Dubai, that's what I want to talk to you about, Fitz," Boless said. He glanced furtively at Abe, who pushed back his chair and stood up.

"Fellows, I've got work to do and miles to go tonight. It was nice seeing you." With that he walked out of the Silver Slipper, giving Mia a delicate little pinch.

"Nice guys you work with, Dick," Boless said, still fondling the bugging device. "I always did like the Agency. I wouldn't mind an assignment there myself."

"If you guys don't mind I'm going to have to excuse myself too," Dick said. "Jenna wanted me to get home early tonight. I'm sure you two studs will be all right together."

Dick Healey stood up. He started to reach in his pocket but Fitz held up his hand. "Forget it, this is on me. I hope our meeting for luncheon works out well tomorrow," he added pointedly.

"I think it will, Fitz." Healey left Boless and Fitz alone together.

"Things are going good in Saigon," Boless began.

"From what I read and hear it sounds like we're getting our asses whipped," Fitz answered.

"What I mean is, well . . ." Boless paused as though to consider what it was he did mean. "Well," he repeated, "you're a businessman, Fitz. I guess I'm not out of line saying you're an opportunist?"

"I guess not," Fitz was reluctantly forced to agree.

"I really got a kind of thrill reading in all the papers how my old friend Fitz Lodd got the gold in and the money out and wasted a bunch of gooks—wogs, our British brethren call them—who tried to stop you. I said to myself when I read that story, by God, Fitz is the man I've been looking for all the time. I think I may have a good proposition for you if you're interested."

"I'm always interested. That's my business now."

Luke Boless dropped his voice to a conspiratorial level. "It happens that I have to deal with a bunch of American and Chinese and Indian and Viet businessmen over in Saigon these days. Things are a lot different since you left. We've got a smart sergeant major over there and he's put a fine bunch of good old country boys together, sergeant majors of all the units. Now there's a lot of money being generated and the question is where to put it."

"A nice problem to have."

"There are not many people I can even discuss this little problem with. Now this group I'm advising, they don't just want to put money into a Swiss bank account. In the first place, we've heard that the Swiss Government is no longer keeping numbered accounts absolutely secret. The U.S. can pressure them into revealing the owners of account numbers. Second, the boys would like to see their money earning more money. Now we've done a little research and it looks to us like this Dubai and other places in Ay-rab countries have developed unbreakable numbered accounts."

"I think you're right, Luke. I know some of the banking people in Dubai. They tell me that they've got the most unassailable system of numbered bank accounts anywhere in the world."

Boless nodded. "Now for openers we've got about twenty-five million dollars we'd like to put away."

Fitz pursed his lips and whistled. "How the hell did you manage to amass that much money?"

"There's more money coming into Vietnam than you can imagine. We've got us a little group over there of American civilians and military people and every dollar that comes into the 'Nam, some sticks to the side of the funnel. Now if one of our boys, one of our civilian boys, were to make a trip from Hong Kong down there to Dubai and wanted to transfer twenty-five million dollars, could you take care of it?"

"Well, of course we could take care of it. A good friend of mine, an American, runs the First Commercial Bank of New

York in Dubai. He can set up accounts for you that nobody could break."

"The Commercial Bank of New York? If someone was to really look hard couldn't they put some pressure on their New York head office?"

"Not according to my friend Tim McLaren. The Dubai branch is practically a separate entity. At the beginning it was financed by the New York head office but now it is not only making out on its own but sending a lot of money back to New York. Nothing can happen in Dubai without permission of the Shaikh and one thing the Shaikh will never do is give permission to any investigators to break into the numbered accounts in Dubai banks. Your money will be safe there."

"O.K., great. Now what we want to do is to move this money into Dubai and put twenty million into numbered accounts and the other five into some kind of moneymaking operations. Can you help us with that?"

"Of course. Dubai's becoming the world's biggest boom town. It all depends on how much risk you want to take with your money. Put it into gold smuggling and you can triple it in one smuggling season. Of course, you take a risk, but what they do there is put a syndicate together and then make four trips to India. If three out of four trips are successful, you've made a big profit on your money. Naturally if all four of them happen to be successful the profits run even larger."

"Unsuccessful means the Indian Coast Guard catches up with you?"

"That's right. But the fellow I deal with has been very successful at either eluding the Indian Coast Guard or discouraging it from messing with his boats. Let's just say, Luke, that if you want to move money into Dubai, I'll do my best to look out for it."

"When are you going back?"

"A week or ten days, I suppose. Why?"

"Well, you look for a guy named Tony DeMarco from Hong Kong and Saigon. Tony will look you up in Dubai in about a month. How does he find you?"

"Tell him to come to my bar, the Ten Tola Bar. It should be opening anytime now. Certainly it will be open in a month."

"The Ten Tola Bar. O.K."

"Tony DeMarco from Hong Kong and Saigon," Fitz repeated. "Is he the civilian side of your syndicate?"

"That's right. You might call him our broker. If he likes what you show him, he'll move the money down there in just a few days."

"I know it's none of my business, Luke, but what are you doing to generate this kind of money?"

Luke looked around to see if anybody was showing interest in Fitz and himself. Nobody seemed to be near their table. Everybody was paying too much attention to the waitresses or themselves. He gave Fitz an owlish look. "Well for one thing we have slot machines in the 'Nam. Remember?"

"So you're skimming the slots. Just what they were doing in Germany back in 1962 and 1963 in the 24th Division."

"That's right. As a matter of fact, we've got the 24th's first sergeant over at MAC-V now. We put a civilian group's slot machines into all camps in the 'Nam. Right now they're winning about half a million dollars a month. Then we got an even more interesting racket. The Vietnam Government charges a 250 percent duty on all civilian cars. We bring in fifty Toyotos from Japan every month, mark them for military use, keep them in military warehouses, and sell them for only 150 percent above the list price. We sell them as fast as we bring them in."

Boless was really warming to his subject. He seemed to be greatly enjoying explaining to Fitz how his military Mafia was systematically looting the Vietnamese and United States economy. Aside from the fact that Fitz didn't really want to be a part of such an operation, what disturbed him most was that Luke Boless felt he could talk freely to him. Had his reputation as a man of integrity fallen so low because of those newspaper stories? he asked himself.

"Then of course there are the enlisted men's clubs all over Vietnam," Boless went on. "There's over one hundred of them right now. And most of those clubs put on a show every night—singers, dancers, jugglers, magicians, even strippers. Each club sergeant pays anywhere from 200 to 400 or 500 dollars for the show. And of course the entertainers kick back a commission of about 30 percent. You multiply 30 percent of 300 dollars per night by 100 and you get some idea of what this sergeants' syndicate is taking in.

Take my own camp at Bien Hoa—the biggest in Vietnam. We've got what we call a massage parlor. A hundred girls right on post. Madam Phong, who runs the whole operation, pays 25 percent of the proceeds to the sergeants' syndicate and of course the buying is something else. Every mess hall has to buy equipment. Every club has to buy equipment. It's all bought through the civilians who are part of the syndicate. And then there's the currency manipulations. When you get back to Dubai you just check the way the Indians are paying for that gold you smuggle into them. All the money changers in Vietnam, the currency manipulators, are Indians. Their mosques are depositories for all the money they make fooling around with the Vietnamese piaster. They have to go through us too. So that's where it's all coming from, Fitz."

"The whole thing sounds illegal, immoral, and it stinks."

Boless's grin merely spread wider across his face. "Like the bankers say, money is money. I'm sure that in Dubai nobody will be worried about the way the money was made. Right?"

"I'm afraid so, Luke. O.K. Tell your man DeMarco to look me up. I'll put him with the right people. Now I think I'll just pay this check and get the hell out of here."

"O.K., Fitz. You'll be our man in Dubai. Naturally we expect to make it well worth your time." He laughed uproariously.

Fitz stood up and pushed his way through the growing crowd in the nightclub, heading for the front door. He couldn't get out fast enough.

CHAPTER 30

The contrast between the meeting the night before and the luncheon today was enormous, Fitz thought, as he entered the sacrosanct halls of Washington, D.C.'s exclusive Metropolitan Club. Dick Healey was waiting for him in the reception room and escorted him to the elevator that took them upstairs to the dining room.

"Let me tell you a little bit about the guy we're going to meet. Matt McConnell. He is the liaison between the Agency and the State Department. He goes back to the days when the Dulles brothers ran State and the Agency together. Matt's got more strength at State, particularly when it comes to picking overseas envoys, than hardly anyone in Washington outside the Agency knows. If Matt figures you can be of help to the Agency, he'll try to be helpful to you when and if you're ready to really make an effort to become an ambassador to some Arab country."

"It isn't just some Arab country. It's the new United Arab Emirates."

"Well, whatever, you're talking to the right man here. We might as well go over to his table and wait for him. It's the most private table in the club."

"Unless some waiter has bugged it." Fitz smiled wryly.

"Matt doesn't get bugged. He bugs." Dick Healey led Fitz through the dining room, opulent in its very simplicity, and they sat down at the round table in the corner. Matt McConnell appeared at the door, waved, and walked over to them. He was a stout, florid-faced man with close-cropped iron-gray hair, and he wore rimless glasses. After introductions Matt sat down and said to Fitz, "I'm delighted Dick could get us together. You've become a pretty colorful individual in the last year."

"Through no wish of my own," Fitz replied.

"I know what you mean, Fitz," Matt agreed. "Let's just hope it hasn't done you any irreparable harm. I don't really think so. These things tend to blow over quickly and nobody really remembers six months later what they read in the papers. As long as there aren't too many follow-up stories," he cautioned.

"I do my best to avoid the press. As a matter of fact, the reporter who did that story has been permanently expelled from Dubai."

"There will always be other reporters to take his place. But that's not why we're here. Dick has told me about your desires and ambitions." Matt McConnell paused and the three men gave a hovering waiter cocktail orders.

When the waiter had left, McConnell continued. "You know the Middle East intimately, you speak Arabic, you are a personal friend of the Arab tribal chiefs forming this new United Arab Emirates. Already you are more qualified than ninety percent of our ambassadors. Therefore, if a year from now when the question of an American envoy to that part of the world comes up and you were still interested in the job, I wouldn't hesitate to recommend you just based on what I've been able to learn from poking around the Agency files and talking to Dick and others who know you."

Matt paused, then looked shrewdly over the top of his rimless glasses at Fitz. "Of course, I've only made a quick cursory investigation. However, as you are very well aware, qualifications are by no means the chief consideration when the United States picks an ambassador. This is unfortunate but nevertheless true. Naturally there are a few career diplomats who serve with distinction and enormous capability. Of course, this type of ambassador is sent only to the critical areas, the sensitive areas where we can't afford to play politics with an ambassadorship. Much as I hate to say it, there is another even more important qualification, the ability to give financial support to the party that owns the White House. Whether you're a Democrat or Republican isn't really important. The important thing is that you have contributed a hundred thousand or so dollars to the treasury of the Republican Party, in this case, and have done so through the correct channels so that your donation comes to the attention of the President himself and those around him who are parceling out the patronage. This is a prime capability taken into consideration for an ambassadorship."

"Matt," Fitz said confidently, "I can probably qualify for the job in that respect too."

"Yes," McConnell hummed. "So Dick indicated. Fortunately the time for a decision on who will represent the United States in that new country when it is formed next year is far enough away from the present that nobody is going to question the source of our funds. If you were to make the contribution today, I'm sure the Republican Party would take it, but at the same time they would probably believe the stories in the newspapers about you and say, 'Yes, we'll take his money but we can't really have him representing the United States abroad.' A year or a year and a half from now things will be different. And of course in 1971 the Republican finance committee will be out looking for money to finance the 1972 presidential campaign. So let's say your outlook is bright. Now let's take a look at what you could do for us."

"I've talked with Fitz at some length about that, Matt," Dick Healey interjected. "He has met our man in Beirut. He understands that there is a possibility, though certainly not a probability, that he might be asked to take on an unofficial and unpaid operational assignment."

The phrase "operational assignment" was a chilling one to Fitz. However, he made no outward show of feelings at the suggestion.

As they progressed through the cocktail and their luncheon, a clear implication emerged. We can help you get what you want but in return we want you to help us. However, you will have no official capacity nor will you ever be able to be linked to the Agency. We'll tell you what to do, you do it, and if you get into trouble that's your problem, not ours.

Toward the end of the luncheon Fitz briefly mentioned that over the weekend he was going to be talking to an ex-State Department diplomat, Hoving Smith. Matt McConnell looked up from his dessert course sharply. "You know Hoving?"

"No, but I'm looking forward to meeting him and his wife. I know their daughter. She is with the Embassy in Tehran."

"That's right," Matt agreed. "She has a sort of Arab name, doesn't she? Her mother is Persian or Arab or something like that."

"Her mother is Iranian. The daughter's name is Laylah."

"That's right, Laylah Smith. Now you take Tehran. That is one place where I would fight like a steer in a rodeo to keep a political appointee from going as ambassador. It is one of the most sensitive posts in the world. I've heard about Laylah. A beautiful young woman who speaks Farsee flawlessly."

Matt grinned. "Well, Hoving certainly should be able to give you some good advice on what to do and for that matter what not to do in the pursuit of an ambassadorship. I'm also certain that more than anyone he could direct you as to how best to make a substantial campaign contribution work to your ultimate objective."

After the luncheon Fitz and Dick Healey walked a few blocks in the brisk fall Washington weather. "I get the message loud and clear, Dick."

"Yes, I expect so. Before you leave to go back to the Middle East, be sure and contact me. Abe's putting together that little basket of electronic surprises for you to take back to Dubai. We'll send somebody over to give you instructions in how to use the equipment. It's pretty simple basically. I don't think you'll have any trouble."

"I'll have trouble if I get caught using it."

"That's what our man is coming to see you about. He'll make you so proficient in the use of these devices that you will not get caught."

CHAPTER 31

In the gathering dusk Fitz drove into the town of Radnor, Pennsylvania, situated on what is known as Philadelphia's Main Line. Laylah's mother had given him specific directions to the fieldstone house set back from the road. It was exactly what Fitz had always imagined Laylah's family home would be. He parked the rented car in the large circular gravel driveway and stepped out. Reaching into the back seat, he took his one suitcase and clothing bag, slammed the door shut, and walked across the crunching gravel to the front door. Before he could ring the doorbell it was opened by a very proper-looking older woman in a black dress and white apron. The Main Line maid personified, he thought.

"You can leave your bags in the hall. Mrs. Smith is waiting for you in the drawing room," the maid announced.

Fitz put his things down and followed the maid through the hallway and back to a large room with leaded casement windows looking out over a spacious back lawn sloping down to a duck pond on which floated a family of white geese. Laylah's mother came toward him holding out her hand. Her hair was long and black without a touch of gray. She was a handsome woman and definitely possessed of the distinguished Persian features which characterized the aristocracy of Iran. She certainly was Laylah's mother. "Mr. Lodd, what a pleasure to meet you after hearing so much about you." She and Fitz shook hands.

"It's a pleasure to be here, Mrs. Smith. Laylah's talked about you and Mr. Smith so much."

"Please, call me Maluk and my husband Hoving. I planned on just the three of us having dinner this evening and getting acquainted. Hoving should be home any minute and he'll tell you who is coming over tomorrow to meet you. Laylah has told us of your very commendable ambitions. Hoving thinks he can help you

on the oil thing and on the ambassadorship. As you know, he was
with the State Department for many years."

"Yes, Laylah told me. That's how the two of you met, wasn't
it? He was on assignment to Tehran."

"Yes, we met at a diplomatic reception in Tehran during the
war. Hoving was a young naval officer at the time." Fitz enjoyed
Maluk's harmonious accent. "Now, Fitz, I'll show you to your
room so that you can freshen up. By then Hoving will be here and
we'll have a cocktail."

Maluk Smith led Fitz upstairs to a comfortable guest room
overlooking the lawn and the pond below. Fitz hung up his clothing bag, opened his suitcase, went into the bathroom, and washed
up. Twenty minutes later he descended the stairs to the living
room, where he found Maluk and Hoving Smith waiting for him.
Again, Hoving was very much what he'd expected. He was tall
and bald and wore a gold chain across his vest. Fitz had seen pictures of him, of course, in Laylah's apartment in Tehran. He wondered if he should say he'd been in Laylah's apartment. He wondered how much Laylah had told them about their relationship.
Were they looking at him as a prospective son-in-law? He decided
to play things cautiously. Hoving Smith was very much the distinguished retired State Department official. After the greetings he
said, "It was good of you to call from Washington to say you
were going to be busy for lunch tomorrow. Did you have any trouble driving up here from Washington?"

"No, Maluk's directions were perfect. I found the house quite
easily." Fitz had called to tell Laylah's mother he would be tied
up for lunch on Saturday although he hadn't said it was lunch
with his fourteen-year-old son. He wanted to approach the subject
of how much older he was than Laylah in a tactful manner and
only at the right time. Hoving announced that he was going to
have his regular martini and Fitz said that would be fine for him.
Maluk asked for a glass of sherry.

"I've got an interesting fellow coming over tomorrow night for
you to meet," Hoving said as he carefully sliced two lemon peels.
"He's chairman of the State Republican Committee. He's very
close to the Nixon administration. I think Pennsylvania raised
more money for the President's campaign than any other state
with the possible exception of the President's home state of Cali-

fornia. Hoving handed Fitz his martini and Maluk her sherry, then the three of them sat down. Maluk took the sofa, Hoving Smith an armchair beside the sofa, and Fitz sat on a straight chair on the third side of a coffee table. They all took a long sip of their drinks and then put them down.

"Well, tell us all about our little girl, Fitz," Hoving boomed. "She's very good about writing letters but we sometimes think she doesn't tell us what she's really thinking and doing." Maluk and Hoving looked at Fitz expectantly.

"Your daughter is certainly the star of the American Embassy in Tehran. I think every man there is in love with her. To say nothing of the majority of the Shah's government. If you want somehing done in Tehran, talk to Laylah Smith. She certainly was an enormous help to me both while I was working at the Embassy with her and then afterward when I retired."

Hoving looked at Fitz appraisingly. "Yes, of course, we read about you in the newspapers. A very romantic and swashbuckling story. It was all very exciting to us because we felt as though we knew you from Laylah's letters."

"What did Laylah have to say about it?" Fitz asked.

"Oh, of course she said that reporter had been bothering you for some time," Maluk answered. "You tried to be polite and helpful to him and then just because nobody could find you for a week while you were up negotiating oil leases, the reporter came out with that preposterous story."

Fitz was uncertain whether Laylah had even told her parents that she had gone to visit him in Dubai. However, Maluk cleared that mystery up for him in her next sentence. "Laylah said that the Arabian side of the Gulf was fascinating and that she really enjoyed her visit to Dubai. She wrote us about the drive across the desert. My, that sounded frightening. I wish she wouldn't take chances like that."

"I'm afraid that was my fault. I thought it would be a shortcut. I learned a lot more about the desert that day than I've ever known before. Actually we were never in any real danger."

The three were silent a moment as they all sipped their cocktails. Then Maluk, as though unable to hold back the question any longer, virtually blurted out, "What about Harcourt Thornwell? Apparently she's been seeing quite a bit of him. Hoving of course checked on him immediately. The Thornwells are an old Boston banking family. Courty apparently got away from the banking end and was interested for a long time in television and newspaper work."

The mention of Thornwell and the fact that Laylah had written her parents about him distressed Fitz.

"Thornwell is a rather interesting person," Fitz said in measured tones. "He seems to still have a big interest in the communications field. He asked me to help him meet some of the Arab leaders with an eye to obtaining financing from them for some sort of a communications network in this country. I couldn't give Courty as much help as he felt I should, so we drifted into a parting of the ways. But I understand he's still actively seeking Arab financial help."

"Very interesting," Hoving mused.

"Now tell me, Fitz," Maluk gushed, "do you think there's anything serious between them? I mean, she mentions him so frequently in her letters. She's certainly old enough to be ready for marriage now."

What he felt was akin to a knife stab in the stomach. So this was their impression from Laylah's letters. Fitz the old and trusted friend, the wise counselor. But of course no romantic involvement. He wanted to blurt out: I'm in love with your daughter. I thought she was in love with me. I thought we were going to get married. Thornwell is moving in on Laylah. He's trying to use her for his own purposes.

Fitz picked up his cocktail glass and drank a long gulp from it. He set the glass down deliberately, slowly. Then he turned to Maluk. "I don't know whether there's anything, as you put it, serious there or not. When I last saw Laylah she merely told me that she and Thornwell do enjoy each other's company. Also I think Laylah has been of some help to Thornwell in his quest for Arab and, for that matter, Iranian financing." That was about as much as Fitz could manage.

"Well, I say Laylah should take her time before she does anything like getting married," Hoving Smith declared. "I'm sure Courty Thornwell is a fine young man. But I don't want to see her rushed."

Hoving nodded to himself and picked up his martini. Maluk

had been studying Fitz and he thought that in a flash of comprehension she now understood how he felt about Laylah although
she said nothing. She turned to her husband. "Tell Fitz more
about what you've done," Maluk suggested.

"Right. Well, Fitz, the man you're going to meet on Saturday
night, his name is Cameron Davidson. As I said, he's the chairman of the State Republican Committee. Naturally his biggest
job is fund raising. And he is very close to the White House.
When it comes to patronage Cameron Davidson has a big say. As
you know, the U. S. Ambassador to the Court of St. James's is
from Pennsylvania. You and Cameron can have an opportunity to
discuss this tomorrow night. It would be a welcome change to
have the White House appoint an ambassador who was qualified
for the job. It doesn't happen very often." There was a discernible
edge of bitterness in Hoving's voice. Fitz remembered that Laylah
said he had not been recognized to the full extent of his capabilities at the State Department.

"It does help to have an ambassador who speaks the language
of the country to which he's been appointed," Smith continued.
"We would never have been surprised at Pearl Harbor if we
hadn't had such an incompetent nincompoop representing us in
Tokyo. The ambassador, you know, steadfastly refused to learn
Japanese and was completely dependent upon the Japanese-speak-
ing members of his embassy to tell him what was going on. To
send a man to an Arabian country who can't speak Arabic and
doesn't know the customs intimately would be to me the height
of folly."

Hoving Smith noticed that Fitz's glass was empty. "How about
the other wing? Then we'll go into dinner." He took Fitz's martini glass and his own and went over to the sideboard.

"I called Lorenz Cannon in New York. Cannon is the president
and, I believe, the founder of Hemisphere Petroleum Company.
They're one of the biggest of the so-called independent companies. I know that Lorenz has had quite a bit of experience in
Arabia. He's looking forward to meeting you as soon as you can
get to New York. I told him I thought you were going there next."

"That's right, Hoving. My plan is to fly to New York Sunday
evening."

"Good. Then give Lorenz a phone call on Monday morning. I'll write it all down for you. He's definitely looking forward to meeting you."

Fitz was still in a semi-comatose state. Of course, he told himself, maybe Laylah was using Thornwell as a stalking horse just to get her mother and father used to the fact that she might be wanting to get married. It was a comforting thought, though Fitz did not really believe it. In an effort to make conversation and divert attention from himself, Fitz said to Hoving Smith, "By the way, I had lunch yesterday with a State Department type who knew you. His name is Matt McConnell."

The name brought an immediate reaction. Hoving Smith's eyebrows jumped. "Matt McConnell! Sure. The spook. He's an old-line fellow over at State. As I suppose you know, basically he's with Central Intelligence."

"Yes, that's what I was told. I understand he has a lot to say about who gets posted to what countries, especially at the ambassadorial level."

"That's right. Matt's been able to stop a lot of patronage appointments to sensitive spots. He's lasted a long time. A full eight Eisenhower years, then Jack Kennedy and Lyndon Johnson, then back with Nixon. Fortunately for Matt, he and Nixon were good friends when Nixon was Vice-President. I remember then Matt saying Nixon was going to go a long way, might even be the next President, and Matt went to great efforts to give special briefings to the Vice-President, told him stuff that Ike never did. So once again old Matt McConnell is right firmly in the saddle. Nobody at State or the Agency disagrees too strenuously with him. For what you have in mind you couldn't have met a better man."

"Glad to hear that, Hoving. He said the same about you."

"Well, let's hope it all works out. Here's to it." He took a long pull on his martini and Fitz followed his example. Before dinner was over, Fitz told his hosts about his lunch date the following day with Bill at Valley Forge. As long as they were of the opinion that Fitz was just a friend of Laylah's and Courty Thornwell was the real contender, there was no reason for not telling them about his son.

CHAPTER 32

Lunch with his son, Bill, the next day had been by and large a pleasant experience for Fitz. The two, even though they had spent so little time together, had no trouble communicating. Bill had decided that he would like to try a military career and he was proud of his father's reported adventures on the Arabian Sea. Fitz had tried to minimize the newspaper stories but Bill had become a hero of sorts at the military school because of his father's exploits.

Fitz was particularly pleased at Bill's interest in geography and his son's desire to visit his father in the Middle East despite his mother's objections. Fitz promised to do his utmost to get Marie to allow her son to spend some time on the Arabian Gulf.

Returning Bill to his school after lunch, Fitz allowed himself to be exhibited briefly to some of Bill's selected friends who all wanted to hear about how he killed those "gooks." The boys had learned two previous generations of disdain for non-Caucasian natives fast, he thought ruefully. Once again he found himself regretful at being admired for all the wrong reasons as he drove back to the Smiths' home from Bill's school.

That evening after dinner Fitz and Cameron Davidson, the Republican state chairman, moved off to the side of the parlor away from the other dinner guests and discussed the question of campaign contributions and how Fitz could most advantageously give. The very fact that Fitz was willing and able to make an extremely substantial contribution to the Republican finance committee was confirmation enough, as far as Cameron Davidson was concerned, of the veracity of the news stories he had read about Fitz. However, money has a way of overcoming all aversions.

"The big push now is on the mid-term congressional elections,"

Cameron Davidson was telling Fitz. "The President is very concerned about losing any more Republican members of the Senate and House. Nineteen seventy will be an important year to the Republican committee. What did you have in mind as a total contribution?"

"I was thinking in terms of about a hundred thousand dollars."

"Those are very fine terms in which to think," the state chairman replied. "Very fine terms indeed. Naturally it is a feather in my cap to come up with a contribution of that amount made through the Pennsylvania State Republican Committee, particularly from someone who is not even resident in Pennsylvania."

"Hoving felt that perhaps you more than any other state chairman that he knows or has access to could help me achieve the goal I'm after."

"Well, certainly Pennsylvania has been given at least its fair share of patronage, if not more. If anybody can help you it would be us."

"I hate to think of my application as being a patronage case. But I suppose that's the only way you can look at it, like it or not. I feel I'm the most qualified individual for the job."

"Of your qualifications I am absolutely convinced. But that has very little to do with it. Something, of course, but not the final answer. What I might suggest is making a fifty-thousand-dollar contribution early in 1970. This would be used by the national committee along with the other funds they raise in an effort to put more Republicans into the Congress of the United States. Then somewhere along the end of 1971 or early 1972 you could make the other fifty-thousand-dollar contribution for the election of the President. Now at the time we receive the first fifty thousand I'll personally start putting on the pressure for you. By the way, if you don't mind me asking, why do you particularly want to be the ambassador to some country that hasn't even been formed yet and God knows what will come of it? For a hundred thousand dollars you could probably get Jamaica, Trinidad, most any of the Latin countries, Ceylon, and for another fifty thousand, say a hundred fifty thousand dollars, you might even get a European country or perhaps Mexico."

"In the first place I can't speak Spanish."

"That's no problem. There's always interpreters. Besides, you could take a quick Berlitz course if it happened you wanted to go to a Spanish-speaking country. I understand it's very good living for an ambassador there."

Fitz spent another twenty minutes trying to convince Cameron Davidson that he sincerely believed that he could do the best job for the United States in an Arab country. He was also convinced, he said, that he could do a better job in an Arab country than any other ambassador the State Department could produce. They then turned to the method by which the contribution would be made. The committee was always delighted to get cash. Checks could sometimes prove to be embarrassing. Only half joking, Fitz asked, "How about gold bullion? Two hundred pounds would be about equal to a hundred thousand dollars at prices today."

"Fitz," Davidson said firmly, "you had better not say gold bullion to anybody again. All it does is make them remember the stories in the newspapers."

"I stand chastened and corrected," Fitz replied good-naturedly.

On Sunday, Fitz said goodbye to Laylah's parents.

"We enjoyed your visit." Hoving wrung Fitz's hand warmly. "Give our love to Laylah when you see her."

"I hope that will be in not much more than a week's time," Fitz answered. "I'm flying directly to Tehran and then I'll go back to Dubai."

Maluk put one hand on each of Fitz's arms and looked searchingly into his face. "I hope you get what you want. Everything you want, Fitz. But just remember the old saying, beware of wanting something too much, you might get it."

Fitz realized that Maluk Smith was aware of the fact that he was in love with Laylah. He wondered if she had told Hoving her thoughts on this matter. Probably not, Fitz thought. The chances are he wouldn't have been quite so agreeable. After once again profusely thanking his hosts, Fitz got into his car and drove off for the turnpike which would eventually take him to the airport. One thing he wanted to avoid was driving a car into or even near New York City.

CHAPTER 33

The hotel in New York at which most of Fitz's military friends stayed when they went to the big city was the Warwick. Some of the officers told pretty juicy stories, he remembered, about staying at the Warwick. If you didn't know anybody in town and wanted a date, there were always beautiful women around the Warwick bar. That wasn't, of course, his reason for staying there. The Warwick was well located in midtown New York.

He checked in about seven o'clock in the evening and then went down to the bar for a drink. After a half hour, a very attractive woman came in and sat down at the bar just one stool away from him. She saw him looking at her and smiled back. She had long black hair and suddenly Fitz thought of Laylah. He toyed with the idea of making an approach to this girl and try to imagine he was with Laylah. He was on his second drink when he invited the girl to join him. She looked at the door to the bar expectantly and then back at Fitz. "I'm waiting to meet someone," she replied. Then, after a pause, "He's very unreliable, maybe we could have one together before he gets here."

The young woman moved over to the stool next to Fitz and introduced herself as Lily. They talked for an hour about the various conventions that were in New York starting that night and when Fitz admitted he was not a conventioneer but just in on some oil business, Lily became even more interested.

Bitterly Fitz wondered what Laylah would be doing about now. It was six in the morning in Tehran. Was she just waking up with Courty Thornwell as she used to with him? Fitz had never picked up a girl in a bar before. As he talked to this girl he felt a throbbing in his groin. It had been a long time since he had had a woman. Lily had a very intimate way of talking to him, her hands frequently touching his. The fact that the girl's name was Lily, so close to Laylah, further excited him. If he squinted his eyes a bit Lily indeed became Laylah. Finally Fitz said, "I'm getting really hungry. Would you join me for dinner? Perhaps you know a good restaurant."

Lily, her hands holding his, leaned close to him. "That would be nice. Just one thing, Fitz. I am a working girl if you know what I mean. I get a hundred fifty dollars for a night."

"The entire night?" Fitz asked.

"I'll see you to sleep anyway."

Fitz thought about the proposition a moment, then in the same low tone he replied, "Tell you what, Lily. Let's make it two hundred dollars and you stay for breakfast with me in the morning. How's that?"

Lily nodded and smiled. "If you mean it, certainly, Fitz."

Fitz reached into his suit-coat pocket, pulled out a wallet, and extracted a hundred-dollar bill. He did it so casually and with such aplomb that neither the bartender nor other people at the bar realized what he was doing as he pressed the crisp note into Lily's hand. "This is what we call the signature bonus. The rest of the payment will be made when we are alone. O.K.?"

"O.K., Fitz," Lily breathed, slipping the bill into her oversize handbag.

Fitz finished the rest of his drink, paid the bill, gave the bartender an overly generous tip, and with Lily on his arm they left the Warwick Hotel and walked a block east to the St. Regis Hotel on Fifth Avenue.

Fitz was feeling better than he had since the remark had been made Friday night by the Smiths that made him realize Laylah was not really in love with him. Lily helped him order the most expensive meal that the exclusive little downstairs restaurant at the St. Regis had to offer. The champagne of course was Dom Pérignon at fifty dollars a bottle. Lily said she had seldom been treated so lavishly by a client and they both greatly enjoyed dinner.

When it was almost midnight, Lily whispered in Fitz's ear with a chuckle, "Don't you think it's time we went back to the Warwick?" By now to Fitz's troubled and somewhat drink-muddled brain, Lily had become Laylah.

Lily looked at Fitz, smiled, and watched him pull out his wallet

and peel off two one-hundred-dollar bills from a not so incon-
siderable sheaf of crisp money to pay the check and tip. Then
they left the restaurant, walked up the stairs, and out onto Fifty-
fifth Street. It was a pleasant fall evening as they walked the block
from Fifth to Sixth Avenue and then entered the Warwick. They
went up to his room on the twenty-eighth floor. It was a beautiful
room with a large double bed. Fitz was glad that he was not going
to be alone in it tonight.

Lily closed and locked the door behind them as Fitz walked
over to the phone and asked for a bottle of champagne and two
glasses to be sent up to the room. Then he turned to Lily.
"Laylah, it will be just like Bandar Abbas all over again."

"I'll do my best, Fitz," Lily said. "Where's Bandar Abbas?"

"In Iran on the Persian Gulf at the Straits of Hormuz."

Fitz took her in his arms and kissed her. Lily's lips parted and
her tongue darted out to meet his. Fitz reached into his jacket
and pulled out his wallet. From the wallet he extracted another
hundred-dollar bill.

Lily kissed him again. "Now, Fitz, I've got to go to the bathroom for a few minutes. Will you be a good patient boy?"

"Of course, Laylah. I'll be right here waiting for you. And the
champagne should be here by the time you're through."

Lily picked up her large handbag and walked into the bathroom, closing it after her. When the door was closed Fitz took off
his coat and removed the wallet. Holding the wallet in one hand,
he started looking around the room. He pulled open some drawers
and closed them again. Finally he pulled back the bedspread on
the double bed. He lifted up the mattress and placed his wallet in
the very center of the area between the bedsprings and mattress
and pulled the mattress back on top of it. Moments later the
doorbell rang and he opened it. A waiter with a bottle of champagne and two glasses was outside. Fitz beckoned him in and
pointed to the bedside table. The waiter placed the tray on it and
handed Fitz the check. Fitz signed the check and added a large
tip. Then, smiling, he gave the check back to the waiter, who
thanked him profusely and bowed himself out of the room. Fitz
locked the door, pulled the chain across, and then began to un-
dress.

When he was wearing nothing but his underpants, he went to

the bottle of champagne and popped the cork. He spilled the bub-
bly liquid into the two champagne glasses and then took a long
sip of one of them. Lily emerged from the bathroom wearing only
the sheerest shortie nightgown.

Fitz clinked his glass with hers. "I thought this would be a
pleasant way to end the evening. We won't see each other again
for dinner until you come to Dubai."

As Lily and Fitz sipped the champagne he went on talking. "I'll
make a million dollars in two years and buy an ambassadorship
somewhere out here. Will you be my ambassadress?" He held out
his arms and Lily came into them, pressing her body to his.

"Of course I will." She put her fingers on the waistband of his
underpants and pulled them down so that he was standing
undressed before her. Lily pulled her frail negligee up and over
her shoulders and posed naked in front of him.

Fitz threw his arms around her and pulled her down on the
bed. Lily reached down and stroked Fitz's hardness. "Oh, Fitz,
what have we got here?" With that she moved around on him
and took his maleness in her lips. Fitz lay on the bed, his eyes
tightly closed, his hands in the long, flowing, heavy black hair.

Lily was Laylah. Laylah had improved in her technique, Fitz
thought. Her fingers caressing him, her mouth devouring him,
Fitz lay moaning, "Laylah, Laylah, Laylah, darling." He had
wanted to prolong the moment but he couldn't. He felt the heat
and strength surge from deep within him and erupt into her
mouth and throat. Lily-Laylah never ceased her manipulations as
Fitz felt himself expending everything within him. "Oh, Laylah, I
love you," he cried, and fell back into an almost coma-like sleep.

Later, he had no conception of time, the depth of his sleep was
disturbed. He came reluctantly awake, feeling himself being
shaken. When he completely woke up he was conscious of the
fact that the mattress upon which he was lying was being shaken.
Then he realized that the girl was reaching under the mattress.
Suddenly reconstructing the evening behind him, he saw it wasn't
Laylah's head at mattress level, her arm reaching underneath. It
was Lily, the whore he'd picked up. He'd enjoyed the little fan-
tasy. But that was over now. Lily had been Laylah, but now she
was Lily. He grinned at her. "What are you up to, Lily?"

"Oh hi, Fitz. You're awake. Good. I was just trying to wake you up and say good night. You don't really want me any longer, do you?"

Fitz thought about Laylah. He wanted Laylah very much. But Lily was no longer Laylah. "No, I guess not. I enjoyed what we had."

Lily slid her hand out from underneath the mattress. She stroked his shoulders with the hand. "Because if you do want me again now, Fitz, you're entitled."

Fitz felt a little sick about the whole thing, but Lily had served her purpose. She had helped him expel something troublesome from his system. He was still in love with Laylah but the hurt was less.

"Thanks, Lily. I guess not. I want you to know you really did something for me."

Lily was completely dressed, Fitz noticed. He realized it was a good thing he had shoved the wallet into the exact middle of the bed. But he didn't begrudge her trying. After all, a whore is a whore. And she had done well by him.

CHAPTER 34

When Fitz woke up in the morning he had more than a trace of a hangover. He lifted the mattress and retrieved his wallet. Then he ordered a hearty breakfast, which he knew he'd probably have to force down, and took a long shower, first hot and then cold. The aspirin seemed to help and by the time breakfast had arrived he was feeling well enough to take some nourishment.

By nine o'clock he had finished eating and felt capable of facing the world. At nine-thirty he called the offices of Hemisphere Petroleum Company and reached Lorenz Cannon's secretary. She told him to come over to the offices of Hemisphere at ten-thirty.

Next he called the First Commercial Bank of New York. He had the name of the foreign-trust officer there who would be handling his New York account. Tim McLaren had sent letters of introduction to the New York branch. He reached the banker on the phone and the man invited him to have lunch. He accepted, promising to be at the bank at noon.

Hemisphere Petroleum Company was in one of the large new office buildings on Park Avenue. He noticed that the company occupied three floors of offices. It was exactly ten-thirty when he announced himself to the receptionist. Moments later Lorenz Cannon's secretary appeared and led him down a maze of corridors into the huge corner office of the president.

Lorenz Cannon was a short man, perhaps five feet five, Fitz thought, who exuded vitality and vigor. He had been standing behind his desk when Fitz entered. Now he walked around his desk and across the room and took Fitz's hand in his own.

"It's a pleasure to meet you, Mr. Lodd. Hoving Smith told me what you have in mind."

Cannon gestured toward a large leather sofa with a long table in front of it. "Sit down, and let's go over the whole situation. I know something about this area that you are interested in. As a matter of fact, I have frequently suggested to our people that we try to secure a concession somewhere in the Persian Gulf area."

"Then I came to the right place," Fitz said. He placed the neat leather attaché case on the table in front of them.

"O.K., let me have the whole situation, Mr. Lodd," Cannon said, getting down to business.

Fitz explained how he and a group of businessmen had come across the seismic information which indicated there was a structure nine miles off the island of Abu Musa in the territorial waters of Kajmira which almost certainly indicated the presence of an oil field. For five years a Texas group held the concession but had done nothing with it. Fitz described how he had met Shaikh Hamed and negotiated with him.

Lorenz Cannon interrupted him for a moment. "It seems to me you've made remarkably rapid progress with this Shaikh Hamed. I'm well aware of the time-consuming process it is when you start negotiating with these shaikhs for a concession. Do you mind if I ask you how it was you moved ahead so fast?"

Fitz looked at Cannon speculatively. Deciding to take the most cautious route and knowing what an astute individual Cannon was and the fact that undoubtedly Fitz had been checked out thoroughly, he decided it was time to completely explain the unfortunate misrepresentation of his statements to the reporter Sam Gold more than a year ago in Tehran.

When he had finished his story Fitz paused and studied Lorenz Cannon's face. He hoped he was getting through. "This is all very interesting to me," Cannon said. "It's too bad the reporter distorted your statement and made you appear to be an anti-Semite. As you may have heard," Cannon continued, "I am of Jewish extraction. However, I worship at a church I believe in, the Unitarian Church. I guess the Unitarian Church could be called a neutral secular institution. Many of my Jewish friends consider me to be somewhat of a traitor. I've never given a dime to the UJA nor have I been involved with any Jewish causes. As a matter of fact, I guess most people don't even realize that I am, religious or not, a Jew. In any case, I was interested in your explanation."

"Thank you, Mr. Cannon," Fitz replied, and went on. "The story which resulted in my early retirement was widely circulated in the Arab countries. They all considered me to be somewhat of a hero. An American, an Army officer telling the people of his country that the Jews are hysterical."

Fitz shrugged his shoulders helplessly. "Such success as I've enjoyed in business along the Arabian Gulf is, I'm afraid, attributable to one gigantic misunderstanding. That, plus the fact I had some rather influential partners in the deal, was why the concession was signed in record time."

"Thank you for being so forthright, Mr. Lodd. And it's only fair to say that if I had been what some people might term a professional Jew I wouldn't be in this aspect of the oil business today. The success of Hemisphere Petroleum has been its ability to explore for oil on a worldwide basis and that of course includes Arab countries, where I have spent much time. As a matter of fact, I know Kajmira and I have sat in Shaikh Hamed's majlis. Now before we start looking at leases and pertinent documents, perhaps you'll tell me exactly what it is you would expect of Hemisphere Petroleum Company if we came into this deal with you."

"My partners and I put up the signature bonus of three quarters of a million dollars to be paid in three equal installments a year apart. However, if we are to start drilling before three years are up the entire amount of signature bonus, another half million dollars, is due and payable. If at the end of three years we have not started drilling operations, then the concession is terminated. I have the seismic report here, which I will give you. My partners and I could finance the construction of the rig, placing it over the structure, which is at a depth of two hundred feet. One of my partners, Fender Browne, runs an oil field supply service along the Trucial Coast and actually has much of the equipment in his warehouses. That is his contribution to the consortium."

"It looks to me, Mr. Lodd, as though you don't really need Hemisphere or anyone else. In fact, it looks to me as though you will end up with your own successful independent oil company."

"Yes, it might look that way to you. That's certainly the way it appeared to us. However, we are at best fledglings at this business. We don't have the great international influence that comes from many years in the oil business. We don't, in a word, have muscle."

"It certainly looks to me as though you had enough muscle to secure a promising concession more quickly and less expensively than any existing oil company, major or independent, could have done."

"Yes, that's probably true. Nevertheless, when I knew I was coming to the United States I persuaded my partners to allow me to investigate the possibilities of getting a well-established oil producer into business with us."

Lorenz Cannon's eyes strayed to the briefcase. "You have the lease there?"

"Yes, sir." Fitz opened his briefcase and took out a large envelope full of documents. He closed the briefcase and laid the envelope on the table. "Everything is in here, Mr. Cannon."

For twenty minutes Lorenz Cannon studied the agreement between Shaikh Hamed and Fitz's group. The terms of the lease neatly typed in English on the left-hand half of each page and Arabic on the right impressed Cannon. No major oil company, he pointed out, could have made as good a deal with the Shaikh.

When Cannon had finished reading the lease he nodded thoughtfully. "You fledglings could teach my experienced negotiators something."

From the envelope Fitz took two more pieces of paper. "Here's the chart clearly showing our concession given to us by the British Foreign Office Arabian Department."

Fitz waited until Lorenz Cannon was finished examining the chart. "As you are aware I'm sure, Mr. Cannon, whenever a Ruler signs an oil concession, the British Foreign Office becomes very much a part of the act. Shaikh Hamed's son, Shaikh Saqr, who was acting on his father's behalf, turned over a letter at the time of our signing to the Brits agreeing that we could not in any way transfer our concession without British approval. It was at this same time that Brian Falmey, the Brit Political Agent, gave us the chart before you. So therefore we have a guarantee from the British as well as from the Shaikh of Kajmira that our concession is valid."

"Oh, there's no doubt in my mind, Mr. Lodd, that this concession is thoroughly and legally and, if you will, morally tied up. As I said before, you've done a fine job. Naturally we at Hemisphere would be interested in coming in with you on this situation. What sort of a deal do you propose?"

"Our suggestion is that Hemisphere take over our concession on the following basis. You pay us the money we've put in to date. You assume responsibility for making all further payments to the Ruler of Kajmira. You pay us a signature bonus of half a million dollars. You finance all drilling operations from this day forward. And we receive twenty-five percent of your profits."

Fitz, Fender Browne, Majid, and other experienced oil people had discussed this deal at length. It was fair, equitable, and if anything somewhat more in Hemisphere's favor than their own. Hemisphere had what they knew would be a very valuable concession for less than they could have negotiated with Kajmira. They had been spared tremendous amounts of time, travel, and legal fees. Fitz knew he was making Lorenz Cannon an eminently equitable proposition, one that he really almost couldn't turn down.

Cannon looked searchingly at Fitz. "That's it? In broad strokes that's the deal you propose?"

Fitz nodded. "Yes, sir, that's it. Oh, by the way, I didn't give you our seismic information." He pulled out of the envelope the field report of the Marine seismic survey made by Fender Browne and himself in the survey ship. Lorenz Cannon glanced through it. "I've seen an old survey of those waters," he said. "This is a new one, is it?"

"Yes, it's one we made ourselves just a month ago. There's a big field down there. We feel the reserves may prove out to two maybe even three billion barrels and could go higher."

Lorenz Cannon nodded appreciatively. "I take it then that you feel disinclined to continue risking your money and in fact would like to get out with a quick profit right now plus a percentage."

"We don't think there is any risk. Of course, there is always some element of doubt when you drill but this is about as foolproof as you could get."

"I'm inclined to believe you, Mr. Lodd. I believe we should definitely follow through on this situation. From what you've shown me and told me I think we can make a deal. Are you authorized to sign on behalf of your consortium?"

"Yes, I am, sir. The powers of attorney are enclosed with the other data. I'll leave it for you to go over at leisure and give to your lawyers."

"If all this stands up, you've got yourself a deal, Mr. Lodd. A good one for you and a good one for us. We at Hemisphere pride ourselves on being able to operate fast, much faster than our competitors. That's one of the reasons we have been as successful as we have."

"When do you think we could actually close this, Mr. Cannon? I have some urgent business to take care of back in Dubai. Also, I need to go to Tehran as soon as possible."

"You've certainly kept yourself busy since your retirement."

"I had counted on at least ten more very active years in the military." A wry expression came to Fitz's face. "However, as it's turned out everything seems to be working out for the best. At least almost everything," he added.

If Lorenz Cannon detected a note of discouragement, he did not comment on it. "Hoving Smith has done me a real service in getting the two of us together. Had he not sent you to me, what would you have done?"

"My partners and I had made a list of the ten most likely people to go to see. Hemisphere was on the list but there were several other companies that we probably would have approached first."

Fitz had been having an internal wrestling match with his conscience. Should he reveal to Lorenz Cannon the information that Laylah had given him. Certainly Hemisphere as a company and Lorenz Cannon as a man had proved their integrity many times. Cannon's remark about a financial reward to Laylah's father, who was certainly not expecting anything more than a chance to help a friend of Laylah's, emphasized to Fitz how reputable business people operate.

Majid Jabir, Fender Browne, and Sepah had all left it to Fitz's discretion as to whether he would reveal the information on the possibility of the extension of the three-mile limit to twelve miles around Abu Musa. He decided he owed it not only to Lorenz Cannon and Hoving Smith but also to his own sense of integrity to completely reveal everything. Cannon was obviously delighted with the proposition, and as Fitz watched, the president of Hemisphere shuffled through the seismic report again.

"There is one more thing you should know, Mr. Cannon." Fitz had made the decision. "Our partnership has been granted an ironclad British guarantee of this concession. Isn't that the way you would read it?"

"Certainly I would read it that way. I've been involved in many of these deals where the Brits have for half a century or more given Arab leaders all the trappings of ruling themselves but the strings have always been pulled in London."

"Right, Mr. Cannon. I'm glad you see it that way. Now let me tell you what I heard in Tehran last week. As I mentioned to you, Hoving Smith's daughter Laylah and I have been friends, quite close friends, for two years. She is probably the most popular and knowledgeable young unmarried woman in Tehran. Because her mother is Iranian she speaks the language fluently. Her mother's relatives are all very highly placed in government and business. There is nothing going on that she either does not know or that she couldn't find out. Laylah knew all about my interest in the Kajmira oil concession. She also knew that the actual field we wanted to develop was nine miles off the island of Abu Musa."

Cannon's eyes held his unwaveringly. Was he blowing the deal? Fitz asked himself. "As you know, I suppose, the Shah of Iran has vigorously and vociferously claimed the island of Bahrain as rightfully Iranian territory. Saudi Arabia has in a more restrained way also claimed it. Bahrain, of course, is an oil-producing emirate and the British have political, military, and commercial interests there. They would not like to see Bahrain taken over by the Shah. Laylah discovered that the Brits offered to let the Shah claim half of Abu Musa and half of all its potential oil revenue for a quitclaim on Bahrain."

Fitz saw that Cannon was listening intently. This was his last chance to change his mind about revealing the vital information. But Fitz plunged on. "Now the hitch is that there is no oil within the three-mile limit of Abu Musa. Therefore, what the British have told the Shah is that they will support him if he and the Trucial state of Sharjah should declare that the three-mile limit around Abu Musa is unilaterally declared extended to a twelve-mile limit, which would clearly take in our structure."

Lorenz Cannon studied the chart silently for a few moments. He stirred through the other agreements and then looked up at Fitz. "They can't do that. It is absolutely illegal. The British have guaranteed this concession. I know the Shah of Iran personally. He is certainly a most acquisitive individual. However, I can't believe that he would defy international law and opinion by unilaterally taking away from the little Emirate of Kajmira the most valuable part of its oil concession. How was it that Laylah heard this?"

"She has a friend who is number-one assistant to the Chairman of NIOC in Tehran."

"It is possible that such a maneuver has been discussed but I cannot believe it could really occur. Is it this piece of information that caused you to come to us?"

"I suppose so," Fitz admitted. "Although we found we were getting in much deeper than we thought. We thought that with perhaps a million or so dollars we could finance this deal. Now we see it's really not enough money."

"No, under normal circumstances it certainly wouldn't be. However, I have great respect for your resourcefulness and I feel you probably would have made the thing work. This information of yours does not change my mind about going into this deal, incidentally. However, my respect for you has increased as a result of your honesty. Obviously you are much more disturbed than we would be by Miss Smith's secondhand report from Tehran."

"It is certainly true that we alone couldn't take on a combined British and Iranian power play," Fitz answered.

"Your information is interesting, Mr. Lodd. And as I said, what's most interesting is the fact that you gave it to me at all. I would appreciate it if you could give me until Thursday to try to put this whole deal together. In the meantime perhaps you would join my wife and me for dinner tonight. I may even have some more information for you by then as to how fast we can move."

"Thank you very much, Mr. Cannon. I'd like that."

Cannon took a personal card from his pocket. "Here is where you'll meet us. We live on Fifty-seventh Street just east of Fifth. We'll look for you about seven-thirty."

Several of the officers of the First Commercial Bank of New York took Fitz to lunch at the Four Seasons restaurant. He was made to feel very important as he shared cocktails with the three executives. They wanted to hear stories about the Persian Gulf and Fitz obliged them without denying his personal involvement in the gold smuggling that had been attributed to him. He had been handed a checkbook with his name embossed on the blue leather cover when he called at the bank. Opening it, he noticed a

balance of fifty thousand dollars which had been transferred from
the bank in Dubai. He was also handed a letter of credit for up to
a hundred thousand dollars if he needed it in the United States.

Before leaving for the luncheon he had asked to be given a
certified check for five thousand dollars made out to Marie Lodd.
Today she would be getting her divorce decree in Santo Domingo
and tomorrow she would be on her way back to Washington.

Over lunch Fitz and the bank officers discussed and agreed
upon the mechanics for setting up a trust fund for his son, Bill.
He would put in one hundred thousand dollars to start it and add
to the body of the trust with remittances from Dubai.

Dinner that evening with the Cannons had been interesting.
They stayed at home and a maid and butler waited on them. This
was unusual in the United States these days, Fitz realized.
Jeanette Cannon had been particularly interested in Fitz's marital
status since she said she was having a dinner party on Thursday.
Fitz thought for a minute after Jeanette asked the question and
realized that at this moment his divorce decree down in the
Dominican Republic was indeed final.

"No, Mrs. Cannon, I am not married. I have a fourteen-year-
old son but my wife and I are divorced." Then, remembering
Lorenz Cannon's appreciation of candor, he added, "as of today I
am no longer married. The divorce was supposed to have been
final at four this afternoon or thereabout."

Over a brandy after dinner Cannon told Fitz that his top executives were all enthusiastic about the project. He had discussed the
unilateral extension of the three-mile limit to twelve miles with
his legal staff and all of them agreed that there was no way this
could be done. Any international court would forbid it.

Fitz had little or no faith in international courts when it came
to raw power. However, he had done his duty, he had warned
Lorenz, as he had been asked by Hemisphere's president to call
him. It wasn't up to Fitz to point out that if the British Navy
combined with the Iranian Air Force decided not to let Hemisphere put up a rig offshore, the rig wouldn't go up and the
drill bit would not go down.

CHAPTER 35

Fitz returned from New York the next morning to the Twin
Bridge Marriott Hotel in time to lunch with Dick Healey and a
short, pudgy, bald man wearing thick spectacles and a rumpled,
nondescript suit. This was Sy Annis, one of the "Company's" top
electronics surveillance experts. After lunch in Fitz's hotel room
Annis gave him a thorough course in bugging and left an attaché
case full of equipment to take back to Dubai.

Late in the afternoon Marie called him. She had returned with
the divorce decree. Fitz invited her to have dinner with him, and
over cocktails, after she had handed him his copy of the divorce
decree, Fitz gave her a certified check for five thousand dollars.
First Marie was grateful; then chagrined that he had so convinc-
ingly pleaded poverty. However, when he told her he had set up
the trust fund for Bill and would be adding to it, Marie was totally appreciative. She even agreed that at an appropriate time in
the near future Bill could visit him in the Middle East.

The following day Fitz again lunched with Dick Healey and
they were joined by a State Department bureaucrat named Philip
Briscoe. Fitz, who tried to like everyone, felt an immediate an-
tipathy to the short, rumpled, officious man with an egg-shaped
bald head whose steel-rimmed glasses picked up all stray rays of
light and gleamed them back at whomever he was facing.

Nevertheless, Dick had warned Fitz that Briscoe was one of the
top officials on the Middle East desk and any ambassadorial appointments of a political or patronage nature would come to his
attention. Perhaps Briscoe had been sounded out on his behalf,
Fitz thought, and was already antagonistic toward him. Briscoe
had, however, done Fitz one large favor before meeting him.

At Dick's request Briscoe had sent a message from Fitz through to Laylah via diplomatic channels. His cable had read: "Arriving Tehran Saturday with subject documents of last conversation. Please clear time for discussion of same."

That evening when Fitz was having dinner with Dick and Jenna at their home, Dick reported that Briscoe, as a matter of course, fought all political appointments but hopefully would support Fitz when, as, and if his name came through for comment. No reply had yet been received to Fitz's cable but Dick was sure that the answer would come through the next day.

Fitz gave Dick the phone number of Lorenz Cannon's office. He would be there from eleven in the morning until sometime in the afternoon. He was planning to leave Thursday night for the long trip to Tehran via London and Beirut. Dick promised to get word to Fitz as soon as the State Department signal reached him.

At nine o'clock Thursday morning Fitz took the Air Shuttle back to New York and arrived at the Hemisphere Petroleum Company offices at ten forty-five. At eleven he was ushered into Lorenz Cannon's office, where Cannon introduced Fitz to the oil company's chief counsel, Irwin Shuster.

"Nobody can believe this deal you worked out, Fitz. The boys spend years putting a concession like this together." For the next forty-five minutes Cannon and his lawyer discussed all aspects of the concession and methods of drilling and oil storage. It was generally agreed that the best route to follow would be to try to get permission to set up a tank farm on Abu Musa, which had been Fitz's idea in the first place.

Finally Cannon brought up the point that Fitz's information indicated that Sharjah and Iran might attempt the unilateral extension of the three-mile limit around the island to twelve miles. Both Shuster and Cannon were not really worried about it. In the first place, it seemed to them that the information was at best third-hand. Also, as Cannon had said at their last meeting, the British would never attest an agreement with an Arab ruler and then go back on their word.

"There is one point, however, upon which Irwin is very strong," Cannon said. "It is possible that Sharjah or Iran, if indeed it really is given half of Abu Musa, might actually bring up the subject of extending their limit to twelve miles in order to take over the oil field. Therefore, we want to have the British attest to the agreement between Hemisphere and your present consortium."

"Yes, I agree," Fitz replied. "Probably the best way to do it would be to close in London."

A secretary walked into the room. She looked at Fitz. "Mr. Lodd, there's a telephone call for you from Washington. Do you want to take it in here?"

"You can go into another office if you want to, Fitz," Cannon offered.

"Not necessary. I know who's calling. I'll take it right here." He walked over to the telephone on Lorenz Cannon's desk and picked it up. "Lodd here," he announced.

"Fitz, it's Dick. We just got the answer for you from Tehran. I'll read it to you verbatim. 'New Embassy assignment taking me away from Tehran for ten days to two weeks. Stop Urgent you get word to Mr. James Fitzroy Lodd not to arrive Tehran with intention of discussions with me. Inform Lodd I will contact him in Dubai.'

"That's it, Fitz." There was a sympathetic tone to Dick's voice. "Sorry about that. I know you were looking forward to seeing her."

"Thank you, Dick. Much appreciate your efforts." Fitz had turned his back to the others while listening to Laylah's message. "Give my best to Jenna. I'll see you next time I get back to the States." Fitz hung up, composed himself for a moment, and turned around.

Cannon clearly saw that Fitz was deeply disturbed about whatever message he had just been given. "Well, Fitz," he said cheerfully, "what say you and Irwin and I go out and have a little lunch. We'll bring you up to date on some of the other things we've all talked about." In a state of semi-shock which he tried to conceal, Fitz followed Lorenz Cannon and Irwin Shuster out of the office.

They walked down Park Avenue to the Waldorf. "I suggest we try the Bull and Bear. The drinks are good and the food is hearty. One of my favorite spots for lunch." Fitz nodded silently and docilely walked beside Cannon into the Waldorf through the large crowded lobbies to the Lexington Avenue end of the hotel and then down a flight of stairs to the Bull and Bear restaurant. A headwaiter jumped to attention, greeted Cannon effusively, and escorted the three men to a table in the corner. They ordered martinis and then Cannon asked, "Did you get a piece of bad news?"

"I guess so. I'd been planning to see Hoving Smith's daughter Laylah in Tehran. I sent her a cable through the State Department and I just got her answer back. She's going to be away from Tehran on a special Embassy assignment for the next ten days."

"And that was the only reason you were planning to go to Tehran?" Cannon smiled sympathetically.

Fitz nodded. The drinks arrived. Cannon held his glass up; Fitz did likewise. "Well, here's to our mutual success in Kajmira." They drank to that. It was obvious Fitz was having a problem concentrating on the oil deal. They drank their martinis quietly. Finally Cannon got down to business again. "One of the points in this deal Fitz is that we want you to be our man on the Arabian Gulf. Naturally, aside from your profit sharing and the signature bonus, you would be on a retainer to Hemisphere. As I said, none of my boys could believe your deal. It wasn't even made in London, where all Gulf oil deals are made. Everybody agreed that your continued identification with this whole project was a necessity." The chief counsel nodded his head in emphasis. "Is this acceptable to you? Naturally we'll have to talk money. But in principle, do you agree?"

"Yes," Fitz replied. "I'd like very much to be identified with Hemisphere. I'll do everything I can to represent you with distinction."

"That's what we wanted to know."

Fitz finished his martini and Cannon immediately ordered three more. Fitz tried to expunge the hurt from his emotions and talk in a businesslike way to Cannon and the lawyer. "There is one possibility—at least I hope it's a possibility—which might someday prevent me from being your man on the Gulf."

A look of concern came across Cannon's features. "What's that?"

"Actually it's nothing that could do anything but help Hemisphere. I am planning to actively seek the position of U. S. Ambassador to the new Union of Arab Emirates or whatever the present Trucial States are called when they become a nation. That was one of the reasons I went to see Hoving, to get some advice from him. I've also been working on it in Washington."

"Well, that is certainly a noble ambition, Fitz. I have a number of very powerful Washington contacts in the Senate and elsewhere whom I would ask to help you. Naturally it would be quite an honor for Hemisphere to have its representative on the Gulf chosen by the United States to be ambassador. As a matter of fact, you could probably do us more good in that position than in any other way I can think of."

Fitz found that the pain of Laylah's rejection came in waves. First it went away and then suddenly came back and engulfed him again. Fortunately the second martini was put in front of him just as the feeling of loss swept over him. He took a long sip of the cocktail.

"Maybe it's for the better that she can't see you for a week, Fitz," Cannon said. "It was going to be my suggestion anyway that you leave tonight for London. I want you to see my very good friend and associate Abdul Hummard. Abdul knows the oil business as few people do. He's a Palestinian traveling on a Jordanian passport. Abdul is what you might call a lone wolf. He knows everybody. I believe Abdul can be very helpful in setting up a meeting with the British Foreign Office to attest the new deal we're going to make. Abdul's contacts are legend. I'll call him after lunch. Can you leave for London tonight?"

"I certainly can," Fitz replied. "It will be a good change for me to stop in London on my way back to Dubai."

"You'll find Abdul a most engaging fellow. I know among his many accomplishments he has a wide acquaintanceship with attractive women in London. I have a feeling Abdul Hummard is just the man to help you get your mind off the situation that is troubling you right now."

"Well, if I can advance our deal, that in itself will be a good mind occupier for me," Fitz replied.

Lorenz Cannon picked up the menu and Fitz took his and glanced at it halfheartedly. Even the martinis hadn't restored his appetite. At this point he didn't know whether he really wanted to be an ambassador any more or not. Half the reason for it was to make Laylah proud of him.

The first-class Pan American flight to London was always an enjoyable experience. The stewardesses were pleasant and helpful and the champagne flowed copiously. It would be Friday morning London time when they actually arrived at the airport. He was due at Abdul Hummard's office by eleven o'clock.

Twice Fitz had tried to put his head back and catch some sleep. But both times he found he could only think of Laylah and much as he hated it he couldn't avoid picturing her doing with Courty Thornwell what she had with him. He was surprised at the near physical aspect of the pain he felt as his errant mind kept visualizing the intimate details of Laylah experiencing the ecstasy of orgasm with Courty. Did Courty's tongue bestow the exquisitely intimate caresses she so loved? Did he cause those large tears to well from her eyes?

Fitz rang for the stewardess and asked her to exchange the champagne for a martini.

Somehow Fitz managed to get a couple of hours' sleep toward the end of the flight. The plane landed on time and by seven o'clock Fitz was leaving London's Heathrow Airport by cab for the Westbury Hotel.

Fitz checked in at eight-thirty, went up to his room, showered, shaved, changed clothes, and felt considerably better. He left the hotel at ten-thirty and was walking into No. 27 Red Lion Square just before eleven. In the typically venerable British office building Fitz walked up two flights of stairs and found the door to Abdul's office, labeled as Lorenz Cannon had described: Office of Arabian Gulf Oil Affairs. It looked like a branch of a government. He opened the door and walked into a dowdy reception room where a dowdy middle-aged woman looked up from her typewriter at him.

"Mr. Lodd?" Fitz nodded. "I'll take you into Mr. Hummard."

Abdul Hummard sat behind a huge table piled high with maps, correspondence, blueprints, books, magazines, and miscellaneous documents. He stood up as Fitz was ushered in and, smiling broadly, he walked around the table, behind which were two windows looking out over the Square. His large room resembled a lawyer's office, with reference books filling floor-to-ceiling shelves. Abdul was short and his thinning black hair revealed patches of brown scalp. He wore horn-rimmed glasses over brown eyes that twinkled with good humor. He greeted Fitz warmly.

"I was so delighted when Lorenz called about you," he began. "Being a Palestinian, I have wanted to meet you since I first read about your remarks on the Israeli conflict and I always hoped our paths might cross one day. I visit Dubai several times a year. My friend Majid Jabir is a partner of yours, I understand, in this Kajmira concession. I have long been aware of the structure off Abu Musa but you know how it is, one doesn't get around to doing everything. Have you got the documents with you?"

Fitz nodded and Abdul gestured at a chair pulled up to the table. The Palestinian was about Lorenz Cannon's height, Fitz decided. Maybe that's why Lorenz liked him. "Just put your case on the table, you can push one of those trash piles away."

Fitz did as he was bidden and opened the attaché case, taking out one complete set of photostated documents. "Here's everything," Fitz said.

"Good. Now I want to go through all these documents thoroughly in the next hour and then we'll have some lunch. You can sit in here if you like, perhaps read oil trade magazines or—"

He pushed through a mound of magazines and handed Fitz a loose-leaf scrapbook. "Here are pictures of some of the lovely girls I know in London, any of whom you'd enjoy meeting. Lorenz mentioned you may have reached an impasse in a love affair. I'm sure we can eliminate the pain from your soul."

Fitz smiled at the obliging Palestinian. "Very thoughtful," he remarked. "But I think I'll take a walk around the area here and return in an hour. It's been a long time since I've been in London."

"Fine, suit yourself, Fitz. See you in an hour."

The hour passed quickly and Fitz reappeared in front of Miss Mardy, as she had been introduced to him on the way out, at exactly noon. She told him to go into Hummard's office.

"Simply amazing," Hummard greeted him. "To think you did the entire thing without coming to London. I know Shaikh Hamed and his son Shaikh Saqr. In fact, I've taken care of Saqr here more than once. Old Hamed is a hard old desert Bedou. You must have really made him like you. But even so, this is a very good lease arrangement. I can see why Lorenz was excited about it. Now, my job is to get the Foreign Office to attest to a new agreement between you and Hemisphere wherein you give to

Hemisphere all rights granted you in this concession in return for which you get your invested capital back plus the half-million-dollar signature bonus. Usually only Arab rulers get signature bonuses."

"The first quarter of a million goes to reimburse us for what we've paid out and we've spent another hundred and fifty thousand in exploration costs," Fitz explained. "Do you think the Foreign Office will go along?"

"I see no reason why not as long as Hamed raises no objections. Perhaps you and I will visit Kajmira together and discuss with him this transfer of concession rights."

"That has bothered me," Fitz admitted. "You see, we told Hamed that this is just what we were not going to do."

"I can help you appease him on that score. You know, with all my contacts, my spies, my informants, my pretty girls who learn so much as they sleep around, I never heard a breath of the story of the three-mile limit around Abu Musa being extended. I always thought that the Shah, the old thief, would try to take all the islands in the Gulf, but it would be pretty audacious for him to also extend the three-mile limit by nine miles into another country's concession area. If this is really a plan being worked out between the British and the Shah, Shaikh Hamed should be happy to have the influence and prestige of a major oil company like Hemisphere behind him. Between the two of us we will convince him. Now are we ready for lunch?"

At the second-floor restaurant which Abdul had picked he ordered a bottle of champagne and a pitcher of orange juice. "I don't know whether you'll like this or not, Fitz. Half a champagne glass of orange juice and fill it up with champagne. A nice light drink."

Fitz had been drinking so much hard liquor for the last week that he was happy at an opportunity to have something as soft as orange juice and champagne. He found that he really didn't like the concoction much.

"Now, Fitz," Abdul said, "I'm going to really have to make an effort to get to my highest contacts at the Foreign Office. If it is true that at the very top level they are planning to back up an extension of the three-mile limit, then they're not apt to double their culpability by attesting to the deal a second time. I'll have to try to go around the edges on this. Perhaps we'll bring Shaikh Saqr to London with his father's official seal so that we avoid getting Brian Falmey involved. He seems to be the prime architect of the whole idea."

"That sounds good to me. When can I be on my way back to Dubai?"

"I think you'll have to stay with us a few more days. I promise you we'll see that it's not a dull time. I'll try to get to my Foreign Office friends this afternoon and see if something can be done over the weekend. Probably not, though. The British haven't changed one bit as far as long weekends in the country parts are concerned.

During lunch Abdul Hummard did most of the talking. Fitz didn't have to worry about holding up his share of the conversation, for which he was thankful. As they drank champagne and orange juice and ordered lunch, Fitz occasionally threw in a question just to keep Abdul going. "What sort of deals are you working on now?" Fitz asked.

"Most of what I do I have to keep confidential. For instance, tonight I'm giving a party for five young Saudi Arabian Arabs. These are boys who have been studying in the United States for several years. They have learned the technical end of oil production. They've also studied business administration at the Harvard Business School. These are typical of the new breed of young men who will be actually running the oil production in Saudi Arabia in another few years. They're all related to King Faisal one way or another and as they progress in the oil business in Saudi Arabia they will become increasingly important and influential." The Palestinian took another long sip from his orange juice and champagne and set it down. "Fitz, I know you know the Arabs and the Gulf. What do you think about the chances of another oil embargo in the near future? Like the one they pulled in 1967 after the Six Day War?"

"I don't know, Abdul. I suppose it's possible. Particularly when, and you notice I say when not if, the next Israeli-Arab war breaks out."

"That's just what I think. What I'm trying to do now in advance of the situation is to become a personal friend of the younger, technically trained Arabs who will be managing production and export of Saudi Arabian oil. Then when the next embargo comes and everybody is desperate for oil, I believe I'll be in a position to use my friends to see that oil is exported to those who need it."

"And make yourself a fortune doing it," Fitz added.

"That's the business I'm in, Fitz."

With luncheon served they ate in silence for a while before Abdul said, "Why don't you come to my party tonight for these young Arabs? It wouldn't do you any harm to get to know them and furthermore you'll have a very good time. I've invited some of the most interesting women in my scrapbook to come up to this party."

"Might be fun. I have nothing else to do until you let me go back to Dubai. I'm building a restaurant and bar there. It would be a shame if the place had to open without the owner present."

"You mean Shaikh Rashid allowed you to have a restaurant and bar that serves hard liquor?" Abdul reacted.

"That is correct, Abdul."

"I wish I'd met you sooner. Your bar should be a very useful means of collecting information," Abdul suggested.

"I hadn't really thought about it that way," Fitz replied, thinking of the suitcase full of bugging equipment at the hotel.

When they finished lunch Abdul suggested to Fitz that he go back to the hotel and have a good nap. It was going to be a long evening. Fitz admitted he was tired. The combination of jet lag and sitting up all night was getting to him. "And where is the party?" he asked.

"My place in Chelsea." Abdul Hummard handed Fitz a card with his home address on it. "We should get the proceedings started by about eight-thirty, I'd say."

Fitz took a cab back to the Westbury Hotel, went up to his room, took off his shoes, hung up his suit, and fell asleep. He was awakened by the persistent ringing of the phone beside his bed. It was Abdul. "I ran into a little luck, Fitz. I was able to reach my man. He has agreed to have a meeting tomorrow morning since he apparently is not going out of London for the weekend. This will mean perhaps you can get away sooner than we'd originally thought."

"That is good news," Fitz replied. "See you tonight." He was feeling refreshed from his sleep and beginning to resign himself to a life without Laylah as his wife. "I just hope you have enough girls to go around."

Abdul laughed on the other end of the phone. "Now you're sounding better. Don't worry about the girls. If we run low I can always call up for some more. See you later, Fitz."

CHAPTER 36

At eight-thirty Fitz arrived at the apartment address Abdul Hummard had given him. When Fitz knocked on the door of Abdul's apartment he was expecting some sort of orgiastic exercise in party giving. Instead he was let in by an Arab servant complete with *dish dasha* and *kuffiyah* and shown to a large living room overlooking the Thames River. These riverside apartments in Chelsea were, Fitz knew, some of the most expensive in London. Abdul undoubtedly did extremely well in his Gulf Oil Affairs office.

Sitting in chairs around the richly carpeted floor were five young Arabs—Fitz guessed they must be in their mid to late twenties—and their host, Abdul. They were all wearing Western garb. Shirts without ties, slacks and lightweight sports jackets. All were decorously sipping coffee and talking. Abdul introduced Fitz to the five Saudi Arabians and as he sat down Fitz was offered a cup of coffee, which he took.

"Ah, Fitz," Abdul said exuberantly. "We've been talking about the two subjects dearest to the Arab heart—oil and war." The Saudi Arabian young men seemed to prefer speaking in English rather than in their native language. And for half an hour Fitz chatted with them about first the oil situation along the Arabian Gulf and then the inevitable war with Israel. Although very definitely and outspokenly pro-American, these young men, typical of the new crop of Arabs trained in the United States, were aggressively nationalistic. In talking about the Arab-American oil company, they delighted in saying how they were looking forward within five years to taking the "am" out of Aramco, the Arabian-American Company. Fitz pointed out that there was already an oil company called Arco. The Arabs knew this and said that the company would be known as Saudico. Fitz flashed a hopeless look at Abdul. Then he asked the Arabs, "You feel you can get rid of all the Americans in Saudi Arabia and do it all yourself?"

"Certainly not," the Arabs chimed in. "We want the Americans there. We need them. We'll always need them. But the time has come for them to work for us, to serve Arab interests, not just their own. Americans working for Saudico and for that matter working for any area of Arab enterprise will be the best-paid Americans in the world today. But just as you Americans would be shocked if we Arabs owned your banks and automotive companies, so we feel that we should own our own oil-production companies within the borders of our country."

Abdul stood up and walked over to a sideboard and opened up the cabinet. "Would anyone like to shift from coffee to whiskey?" he asked. There was an immediate clatter of cups and saucers being placed on the nearest coffee table. The Arabs had learned more than technical expertise in the United States. They too stood up and walked over to the sideboard. Abdul's servant appeared with a large bucket of ice and glasses and the drinks were poured.

As the Saudi Arabians loosened up, Fitz said he, as an American, would have no objection to the Arabs nationalizing their own oil production but the least they could do if the American firms were willing to turn over their interests to Saudi Arabia would be to guarantee there'd be no more embargos, like the unsuccessful attempt after the Six Day War, against the United States or for that matter any industrialized nation.

One of the Arabs, Jamiel, was vociferous on the subject of embargos. "We will embargo the United States and any other country that helps Israel."

"The United States helps Saudi Arabia and the other Arab countries just as much if not more than it helps Israel," Fitz argued.

"Until Palestine is returned to the Palestinians, no Arab nation will be satisfied with affairs in the Middle East." With that statement Jamiel downed his scotch and walked over to the sideboard to fill up his glass again.

To the Arabs, Abdul Hummard said, "I am a Palestinian and the return of Palestinian lands to their rightful owners is a fundamental precept with me. However, oil embargos help no one, including the Palestinians. It is merely a manner of releasing emotion. If it would help I'd be all for it. But it doesn't. All it does is hurt international business."

Another of the young Arabs got up and went over to the sideboard and Abdul chose this moment to escalate the party into a more agreeable milieu. "My friends," he said, "are you finished with business and political talk? The girls will be here shortly." Inhibitions becoming dissolved in alcohol, the Arabs began to speak less guardedly with Fitz as they waited for the girls to arrive. The young technical men did agree that an embargo served nobody well. They discussed with Fitz and Abdul some of the ways in which an embargo could be enforced. All were agreed on one point. The Americans and British had been responsible for circumventing the embargo after the Six Day War. The Arabs had not been sufficiently technically advanced to stop the oil from being loaded aboard tankers which were going to countries specifically on the embargo list. Now, however, they knew precisely how to prevent this.

"Just one thing before the girls arrive, my friends," Abdul said. "Not only am I an Arab, I'm a Palestinian. It is the lands of my people that have been taken and someday I want Palestine returned to its rightful population. However, when the next Israeli war occurs and the next embargo is declared, I want you to remember Abdul Hummard. If I come to you and say such and such a tanker will be filled and its destination unquestioned, you must help me. Because I am working in my own way for the return of Palestine to our people just as you are in your way. So, now with your American education behind you, with your new duties in Saudi Arabia ahead of you, do not let raw emotion interfere with practical business. It is only through enlightened business practices that we will regain Palestine."

The young Arabs had listened attentively to Abdul Hummard. They nodded their assent. Jamiel, who seemed to be the oldest and the leader of the five, said, "We will trust your judgment in the event of a future embargo. Naturally the United States will be the target of our boycott." Having made the speech, Jamiel went over and filled up his drink again just as the doorbell rang.

Two blond girls were escorted into the room by Abdul and introduced to the young Arabs. One was a German named Heidi, the other was a Dutch girl named Christa, and the Arabs were immediately outdoing each other to offer the girls drinks. Shortly afterward another girl, a brunette, arrived. She had a camera case over one shoulder, Fitz noticed. Abdul took the camera case from her and left it in the reception room before bringing her in to meet the Arabs. The brunette girl was English and introduced as Lynn. She was beautiful and young, and even though Arabs prefer blondes, they were delighted with Lynn also. Lynn had long, thick black tresses and violet eyes. She wore a tight-fitting black sheath with a gap in the front of it which revealed much of both breasts. Fitz felt the old hurt as he looked at Lynn and realized that she was much the same physically as Laylah.

Over the next twenty minutes four other girls arrived and the Arabs were having the time of their lives, a last fling before going to the desolate, sandy wastes of their homeland where sex was forbidden to the unmarried young Arab man and woman. When the five Arabs were completely occupied with the girls, Fitz pulled Abdul aside in the reception room. "Are these girls prostitutes or what?"

"Not really. They're party girls. I have been able to do many favors for them. Get them on to weekends. They love to go on a jet party to Beirut or Cairo, the Caribbean, you name it. The French Riviera of course is a favorite. One of my shaikhs will take a girl to Cannes for a long weekend and she will come back several thousand dollars richer and beautifully decorated with jewelry. Tonight the boys will be well taken care of. Tomorrow I will see that the girls are rewarded one way or another. They know this."

"How about that brunette? She is something! And somehow she doesn't seem like the others." He stared at her.

"Lynn, yes, she is different. She is not the ordinary party girl. In fact, she isn't even a party girl really. She is a fine professional photographer who specializes in candid shots. You see, I want photographs of this party. You never know when they might come in handy in the future. These five young examples of the future of Saudi Arabia will probably prefer group sex to merely taking a girl to the bedroom. It seems to be an Arab tradition. They will probably all have all the girls before the evening is over. Now if a man were to take pictures it would kill the party. However, if a girl is

doing it—say, taking Polaroid shots which she then gives to them
—*that* they don't mind. In fact, they think it rather sporting. Just
so long as they take all the pictures with them."

"Then why bother to take pictures at all?" Fitz asked.

"Oh," Abdul responded. "Lynn has developed a unique technique. A miniature camera that looks like it is the sight of the big
Polaroid takes a picture simultaneously."

"Very unique indeed," Fitz agreed.

"Yes. Comes that next embargo and my friends forget the
promise they made me, I will be able to remind them of this party
most vividly. While they love to have an orgy, even your Ameri-
canized Arab is very prudish at heart publicly. A picture of them
drinking and playing with blond women would raise havoc with
their careers even though every one of them is related to King
Faisal himself. As a matter of fact, Jamiel is the son of Faisal's
brother, former King Saud."

"So Lynn is really an honest business girl, not a play-for-pay
girl?" Fitz felt a sense of relief, even happiness, to hear this. She
was the only girl at the party to whom he was attracted. He realized that his interest stemmed from her resemblance to Laylah.
But she was also a woman who completely on her own would
have quickened his pulse.

Fitz sidled up to her. "I guess we're both basically observers
here. When do you start shooting?"

"Abdul has told you of my mission?" The girl seemed surprised.
Fitz nodded and smiled. "Well," Lynn said, "I expect I shall get
a smashing set of photos from this little bash."

"I'm certainly looking forward to watching your technique. Fortunately most Arabs don't drink too well, so they probably won't
notice what's going on."

As the Arabs became more amorous and sexually aggressive, the
blondes girded themselves for the inevitable and made no attempt
to stave off advances.

When Jamiel reached under the dress his girl was wearing and
hooked his thumbs over her panties, pulling them down to the
floor, she neatly stepped out of them and put them around his
head.

"Yah!" she cried. The other four looked over at Jamiel and
burst into laughter. At that moment there was a flash and Lynn

had caught her first picture of the evening. While a very funny scene, in sober Arab quarters this would be interpreted as a serious breach of respect for the traditional Arab Headdress. For a moment the five young Arabs were startled and then they turned on Lynn.

"I thought you boys would like a memento of the occasion," she said. "You can have the picture." The Arabs saw the Polaroid camera and then they laughed and relaxed. They were well acquainted with Polaroid cameras and knew that the picture when it came out would be an original with no negative that could be reproduced. They also knew that they would not leave any picture taken of them behind.

Sixty seconds later Lynn took the color picture out of the back of the Polaroid camera and handed it to Jamiel. He was still wearing Christa's panties over his head and when he saw the picture he burst out laughing himself. Then he handed it around the room and everybody laughed.

Abdul said quietly into Fitz's ear, "At this point either get with the party or go into the next room. I don't want these boys to feel inhibited." Fitz nodded and walked out into the foyer, where the Arabs couldn't see the fully clothed American.

Following Jamiel's lead, the other Arabs de-pantied their dates and all wore the undergarments as *kuffiyahs*, Lynn snapping Polaroid pictures and handing them out to the Arabs, who laughed and then thoroughly destroyed them.

The party progressed as slacks and shirts were discarded and dresses pulled over heads. Champagne was consumed and the orgy got under way. However, despite the alcoholic lubrication of Arab passions, one of the five, as if by predetermination, was always watching Lynn. Each time the bulb flashed a young Arab was at her side to take the picture. Jamiel was photographed in a most interesting pose, entering his blond girl friend from the rear, her dress hanging from her head to the floor so that her face could not be seen. The others cheered as he thrust himself deep into her and her shrieks reverberated through the room.

All the girls had come to the party knowing some Arabs had a proclivity for anal sex, all of them having experienced it. Jamiel, while indulging himself in this sexual abnormality, never let go of the bottle of champagne, from the neck of which he was drinking

as he finished off with Christa. The incident was duly recorded on
the Polaroid camera as well as on Lynn's miniature. And the party
continued. The girls laughed and giggled as they were assaulted in
various manners by the lusty Arabs.

Drinks were filled and spilled and Lynn's flash pops continued
to go off, with an alert Arab grabbing the picture out of the camera, showing it around, everybody laughing, and then destroying
it.

Abdul in an open shirt and open pants left the blonde he was
playing with and walked out into the foyer, where Fitz was drinking and observing. "Quite a party, Abdul," Fitz laughed. "Your
place must be a mess after one of these."

Abdul laughed. "It makes no difference. This is just my party
flat. I never stay here. My own flat is above this one."

When Lynn came out into the foyer to reload her camera, her
dress half hanging off, Fitz whispered, "Don't you think you have
enough pictures now?"

"I guess so. I haven't missed one of those Arabs in a compromising position."

"Don't you get kind of turned on at scenes like this?"

"If they weren't Arabs I might. I'm Jewish myself."

Fitz thought about the statement. Then: "If you've taken
enough pictures, why don't we go someplace else together. I think
we could both use a drink in a nice cocktail lounge. Maybe my
place, the Westbury."

"That's a good idea, Fitz. Getting out of here, I mean. I don't
know so much about your hotel room."

"I meant the cocktail lounge, not my suite."

Lynn smiled and nodded. "O.K. Quite honestly I don't like the
orgy scene but I get paid very well for doing my photographic act.
Let's go then." She pulled her dress back into some semblance of
order.

Abdul was just taking his blonde through the foyer into the
bedroom when he noticed Fitz and Lynn leaving. "Going already?" he asked.

"Yes," Fitz replied. "I'll call you at the office tomorrow. What
time is our meeting?"

"Eleven-thirty tomorrow morning. Over at the Foreign Office.
Meet me in my office at eleven. Maybe you and Lynn will come

together." He chuckled and then pulled his blonde into the bedroom, closing the door behind him.

Fitz let Lynn and himself out the front door of the flat. He closed the door after him. Turning to Lynn, he asked, "Would you like me to carry your camera case?"

Lynn shook her head. "No, I'd be quite lost without it. I'd think that I was missing something." They walked down the stairs and out onto the quay.

"Fitz," Lynn said, taking his arm, "I can't go to a nice place like the Westbury. What I've got on was only suitable for the sort of party we just left. Do you mind if we stop by my place so I can change?"

"Of course not." He hailed a cab, helped Lynn inside, and Lynn gave the driver her address.

Lynn's flat was a large studio with a bedroom adjoining it. The studio was obviously that of a working photographer. A portrait camera faced a white screen in one corner of the studio. Fitz looked around approvingly. "You really are a hard-working girl, aren't you?"

"Yes, I certainly am. I love my work." There was a long pause. "Except for things like tonight. But that's how I make enough money to experiment with the sort of photography that means so much to me. I love to do landscapes, city street scenes. I enjoy preserving slices of life that I see and I also like the portrait assignments." She gestured toward the large wooden box camera on a tripod. "One of the scenes I did for Abdul paid for that camera."

"Does Abdul mind that you're Jewish?"

"No. Abdul is a very enlightened Palestinian. We talk about it sometimes. Even though I'm Jewish I've never been to Israel, so I don't suppose I have much right to talk about the situation. However, someday when I save enough money I'm going to take a trip to Israel. I'd love to photograph the old city of Jerusalem. And I'd like to go out into the countryside and photograph the kibbutzes and all the things I've heard about."

"I know you'll do it," Fitz said.

"How about a drink, Fitz?"

"I could do with one."

Lynn made two scotch and sodas. She handed one to Fitz. "You can sit down on the sofa while I put on something more sedate." She disappeared into the bedroom and before he'd finished his drink she reappeared. Now she was wearing a plain black dress with two diamond clips, one at each corner of the square bodice. Around her neck was a double strand of pearls. She looked both pretty and proper, Fitz thought, a vision of Laylah fleeting through his mind.

"I'm all ready, Fitz. May I make one suggestion?"

"Of course."

"You know, the lounge at the Westbury is really rather dull. Let me take you to a club I belong to in Curzon Street. I think you'll love the White Elephant."

"You're on. Let's go."

Fitz and Lynn did enjoy the evening at the White Elephant, although after two more drinks Fitz found it difficult to always say "Lynn." Twice his tongue slipped and starting with the L sound he ended up with "Laylah." The third time he did it, which was late in the evening, Lynn looked up at him quizzically. "Laylah is a beautiful name, Fitz. But it's not mine. Do you know a Laylah somewhere?"

"Laylah lives in Tehran. We were quite close for a while. And then I was away a lot and . . ." He shrugged. "The old story. Absence makes the heart grow fonder—of someone else."

There was a bitter edge to Lynn's laugh. "Yes, I know what you mean."

"Is there some special man in your life right now?" Fitz asked.

"No, not really. I meet people, I enjoy them, like you. It's my work that really matters to me."

It had been a long time since Fitz had danced but Lynn encouraged him to try. Fitz quickly remembered and held her closely to him. It could have been Laylah. Her hair was the same length. Then he realized he had to stop thinking of Laylah. Lynn danced perfectly with him. How she followed his clumsy steps he didn't know, but she made him feel as though he were an accomplished dancer. And he felt himself wanting her, wanting to make love to her and not just tonight. That was the story, that was the problem with him. He was always moving from one place to another. When they sat down he asked, "If I gave you a ticket to fly from London to Beirut to Dubai to Tehran to Israel and back to London, would you do it?"

Lynn looked at Fitz appraisingly. "You mean it?"

"Of course I mean it."

"How much longer are you going to be in London?"

"I don't know. I guess Abdul's going to need me around for a few days, maybe a week."

"Well, Fitz, if you really mean it why don't we plan to see each other a lot for the next few days. Then if you still want me, I'll come." A frown crossed her face. "Dubai is one of those Arab countries, isn't it? Will they let somebody Jewish in?"

"No problem if you're coming to see me. In fact, there's no problem anyway. How are they going to know whether you're Jewish or not?"

"Fitz, you haven't even asked me what my last name is?"

"What is it?"

"It's Goldstein. Lynn Goldstein."

"If you're coming to see me there'll be no problem. I'll be out at the airport to meet you and have Customs and Immigration expecting you. It is true, of course, that it's impossible to get into an Arab country if you have an Israeli stamp on your passport."

"It's an exciting thought, Fitz. Let's think about it." She looked around the room. "You know, Fitz, I think we've had it here. Let's go home and I'll fix you a nightcap."

In the early hours of the morning, after two nightcaps and extensive kissing, Lynn sighed. "All right, Fitz, you might as well stay over with me. It's what we both want of course." Fitz meekly followed Lynn into the bedroom, which was very intimately feminine in comparison to the photographic studio. Again it was hard for him not to think about Laylah's bedroom in Tehran.

The similarity of the situation struck him. He was naked in Lynn's bed waiting for her to come out of the bathroom. Just the way it had been the first time with Laylah except that he'd kept his shorts on until the last minute. He smiled at the shyness he had felt with her. Somehow he felt much more confident about his first time with Lynn.

She finally walked out of her bathroom standing straight and tall, her breasts firm and upturned, her hair falling loosely about her bare shoulders. My God, he thought to himself, is every girl I meet with long black hair going to be Laylah?

Lynn smiled at him. "You like?"

"I love." He threw back the covers and Lynn turned off the bedside light and got in bed beside him. Light drifted through the windows from the street lamps outside, and when his eyes became accustomed to the darkness, he could see Lynn quite clearly. They reached out for each other. Lynn was caressing him gently in the groin, giving him excruciatingly delightful pleasure, and although he was concerned about the number of drinks he'd had and the fact that he was tired, nevertheless he was responding admirably to the occasion.

Fitz positioned himself between her legs and felt her hand guiding him into her. As he filled her she gasped and cried out with pleasure. Her hunger, desire, and need matched his. No preliminaries had been necessary. Each was eminently ready for the other. He had wanted her so much all evening and now the all-encompassing sensation threatened to bring him to immediate climax. He desperately struggled to hold himself back but finally he could retain the passion and pressure within him no longer.

"Oh God, Laylah, I love you. I can't hold my love back any longer."

"Give it all to me, Bill. I love you too." Lynn shuddered and whimpered in climax as Fitz was still filling her with his strength. Then they both went limp and lay for some moments. Finally pulling apart, they lay beside each other on their backs. Sleepily Fitz asked, "Who's Bill?"

Lynn laughed throatily. "Who's Laylah?" After a pause: "You Fitz, me Lynn. O.K.?"

Fitz chuckled. "You Lynn. I guess I'm just very tired. I was on the airplane all last night."

"Get some sleep, Fitz. I'll wake you up in the morning."

Sleepily Fitz said, "All right. And then you'll come to Dubai with me?"

CHAPTER 37

It took Fitz some moments to remember where he was when he woke up. He was alone in a big double bed in a woman's apartment. Sunlight was streaming through the window. Then he remembered. Lynn. The beautiful photographer. He turned his head but she was not with him. Quickly he got up, went into the bathroom, washed, brushed his teeth with a new toothbrush she had left out for him, and then started to dress. In his shirt sleeves he walked out into the studio. Lynn was just walking out of what seemed to be a closet. She was holding several photographs in her hands. He realized she had been working in her dark room.

"Abdul's going to love these pictures." She handed them to Fitz, who took a look at them and whistled.

"My God. I'd almost forgotten it."

She looked up at a large round clock hanging on the wall. "Well, my darling, it's ten forty-five. You have time for some coffee before we have to leave for Abdul's office. She pointed at the small built-in kitchen. "Just light the gas. I have a couple of more pictures to do and then away we go." She disappeared back into the dark room.

They made the trip in record time to Red Lion Square and were in Abdul's office at eleven-fifteen. He was a little concerned since it was at least a fifteen- to twenty-minute cab trip to the Foreign Office. However, Abdul was delighted with the photographs. He sorted through them muttering happily. Then he looked up at Fitz. "Come on, we've got to go."

Fitz turned to Lynn. "Where will we meet?"

"Come back to my flat when you're finished and we'll have lunch together."

"I'll take you both to lunch," Abdul said magnanimously. "As a matter of fact, I've already booked for one o'clock."

"You're on, Abdul," Lynn replied. "And don't forget to bring your checkbook."

As Fitz and Abdul drove over to the Foreign Office in a cab, Abdul gave him a briefing on what was probably in store for them. They were going to meet Sir Hugh MacIntosh, formerly a political resident in Kuwait with a fine knowledge of Persian Gulf affairs. Prior to the Kuwait assignment he had been a Foreign Office representative in Palestine during the British occupation right after World War II. "Abdul, it looks like to me as though you have everything under control and you don't even need me."

"Not true. Sir Hugh MacIntosh specifically wanted to talk to the representative of the group presently controlling the concession. He's also going to want to talk to a representative of Shaikh Hamed."

They arrived at the Foreign Office on the Mall and Abdul expertly led Fitz upstairs and down corridors to the Arabian Department. The musty old building seemed deserted. Finally Abdul stopped, pushed open an ancient creaking oak door, and walked into a reception room which was empty. Looking around, Fitz saw an open door into a large office with windows looking out over the Mall. A white-haired, tall, ruddy-cheeked man was sitting behind an outsize mahogany desk. He stood up as Abdul and Fitz walked in.

"Good of you to meet with us today, Sir Hugh." Abdul walked to the desk, reached across, and shook hands. "Mr. Lodd is anxious to get back to the Arabian Gulf and his pressing business there. We are both grateful to you." To himself Fitz thought that the business in the Gulf didn't seem as pressing now as it had yesterday.

"As it turns out, I had to be in this morning for a while anyway," Sir Hugh MacIntosh said pleasantly. "Please sit down." Fitz and Abdul sat down on chairs across the desk from Sir Hugh. Eloquently Abdul explained the situation between Fitz's group and Hemisphere Petroleum Company.

Sir Hugh broke in. "I remember Hamed very well. He must be about the oldest of the rulers still around in the Trucial States. A great old fellow. He used to love to bend coins in his fingers as he talked. A disconcerting thing. In reviewing the papers you sent over to me yesterday I cannot help but be surprised, perhaps impressed would be a more apt word, at the terms of the concession which Mr. Lodd negotiated with Shaikh Hamed. However, it will be good for Hamed if you really do start producing oil. Now the question is, as I understand it, Mr. Lodd, you feel that it is necessary to enlarge your consortium and take in Hemisphere Petroleum with you people. Is that right?"

"That's precisely right, Sir Hugh."

"Do you have a draft of the new agreement between yourselves and Hemisphere?"

Abdul answered the question. "No, sir. I only started on this matter yesterday morning. However, by next Tuesday I can have on your desk an English draft copy of the agreement. You don't need the Arabic translation to give us your approval in principle?"

"No. Of course, I want to read the Arabic translation before we give you the political attestment to the arrangement. However, that can wait."

"Lawyers from Hemisphere are on their way over to London and will be meeting with me first thing Monday morning. Will you want Mr. Lodd present for another meeting?"

"It would be useful for him to tell me himself that he has read the new agreement and it meets with his approval. Then of course we'll have to get Hamed or his representative here to London for a final signing. As I understand it, the signature bonus has already been paid Hamed. Therefore, there shouldn't be another signature bonus paid to him. Correct?"

"That's certainly the way it should be, Sir Hugh," Abdul replied. "However, I believe that when Hamed discovers that Lodd's group is making an immediate profit after reimbursement for expenditures, he will object."

"That's something you people will have to work out. You show me the agreement between Lodd and yourselves and I'll tell you whether we can attest it."

Fitz leaned forward intently. "Sir Hugh, did you see the diagram given us by the Arabian Department of the Foreign Office at the time we signed in Kajmira?"

"Certainly. It's right here before me, as a matter of fact."

"Then it is all right as is? There'll be no change in the concession area?"

"I certainly see no reason why there should be. If it was

attested two months ago, why should anybody go back on the agreement today?"

"No reason, no reason at all, Sir Hugh. It's just that since we are changing the deal we originally made with Hamed, I want to make sure there is no change in the concession area."

"None at all that I can see, Mr. Lodd."

As they rode back in the taxi cab to Abdul's office Fitz was silent and contemplative. "I can read your mind, Fitz," Abdul said. "You now doubt that your information was correct. Maybe it was, maybe it wasn't. In any event, your group is much better off with Hemisphere. It would be a very hard go for you all financially."

"True, but we would have made it."

"Yes, you probably would have."

"Oh, we're going to go through with the deal all right, whether or not there is a real plan to change the three-mile limit to a twelve-mile limit around Abu Musa. Now that I've met Lorenz Cannon and you, I'm convinced we did the right thing anyway."

"Good fellow. Lorenz Cannon is expecting to hear from me between nine and ten his time. That gives us a nice luxurious two-hour luncheon with the beautiful girl photographer. It shouldn't be unpleasant for you to stay over in London until next Wednesday. Actually you could get out Tuesday night if you wanted to."

"Wednesday will be just fine. In fact, who knows, I might even stay until Thursday."

Abdul chuckled happily. "Lynn was exactly what the doctor ordered."

Except for meetings on Monday and Tuesday morning with the lawyers for Hemisphere and an afternoon meeting with Sir Hugh MacIntosh, Fitz and Lynn were never apart. He regarded it as a particularly good sign that he had yet to repeat his mistake of the first night they were together and call Lynn Laylah. He hardly thought about Laylah. Lynn made it easy.

On Wednesday he told Lynn that he would have to be back in London again in three to four weeks with a representative of Shaikh Hamed to sign the Hemisphere Petroleum agreement. "Then I'll take you back to Dubai with me. Stay as long as you can and I'll put you on a plane to Tehran, where you can change for Israel. It's an exciting period of time in Israel these days. Now that the Israelis have the entire city of Jerusalem and the west bank of the Jordan River, you can see the Holy City as it was impossible to see it up until the 1967 war."

"Oh, Fitz, I'm so excited. I really have always wanted to make this trip. I'm going to work hard and earn every penny I can so that I will really be able to enjoy Israel."

"Do me a favor. No more of those photographic orgy sessions. When you get to Dubai there'll be a commission waiting for you. Fifteen hundred dollars to take photographs of my restaurant, the Ten Tola Bar. How does that sound?"

"Super. I'm so happy, Fitz."

"So am I, Lynn. I'll give you plenty of advance warning when I'll be in London."

It was not until Friday morning that Fitz finally tore himself away from Lynn and took the Middle East Airlines flight to Beirut and Dubai. Fitz realized more than ever how fortunate he was to have Joe Ryan on the scene managing things, seeing to final stages of construction and decoration so that he could travel freely.

CHAPTER 38

Vigorously Fitz stroked and kicked several lengths of his new swimming pool and then pulled himself out of the cold fresh water and sat for a few moments on a plastic chaise longue in the late-afternoon sun. The large patio with the pool in its center was surrounded on three sides by a high whitewashed wall. The fourth side was the front of his new duplex apartment, which abutted the Ten Tola Bar. The club had been open a week now and from the moment it had opened its doors had been a resounding success.

When the sun had dried him Fitz stepped into his home. On the first floor was a bedroom and bath adjoining the spacious living room and dining room, which connected through a butler's pantry to the main kitchen of the restaurant. Upstairs another bedroom and living room were connected to Fitz's office, for which there was only one key, which he always kept on his person.

The office had two secrets. A one-way plate-glass window looked down on the entire restaurant. A large painting of a picturesque Arab dhow was hinged over the window and could be swung aside when Fitz wanted to check the action below. On a table directly in front of the one-way glass panel, what looked like a collection of miniature portable radios was arrayed. This was the second secret. Each transistor radio was tuned to a different high-frequency setting and was capable of picking up all the conversation at the table in which Fitz had installed the hidden transmitter emitting the corresponding wavelength.

Fitz padded up the stairs in his bare feet. He unlocked and opened the door to his office. Shutting it behind him, he swung the picture aside and looked down at his creation. He had to give a lot of credit to Joe Ryan, who had handled all the finishing touches while he was away. The Ten Tola Bar was a long, rectangular structure set back fifty feet from the main road between the airport and downtown Deira. The entrance was in the center of the long side of the high-ceilinged building. Directly across from the entrance on the far long side of the room was the long mahogany bar. Around the edges of the room were booths. Arabesque lattice screens between each booth provided additional privacy. The four circular booths at each corner of the room could accommodate as many as eight people and gave the illusion of being exceptionally private and intimate. Since the day the Ten Tola Bar opened, Joe Ryan received phone calls every afternoon reserving the corner booths for the night. Already Fitz had decided to install more of these circular banquette-type booths, walling them off for the privacy most of the patrons of the Ten Tola Bar seemed to require.

In the middle of the room, around a small dance floor, twenty tables were placed. They had been half occupied all week. And the Americans were only just beginning to start the occupation of Dubai. The petroleum families were scheduled to begin their influx within months as the drilling on the Fatah Field was completed and oil commenced to be produced.

So Fitz had, in two years from the day of his retirement, created the core of his little empire. It was very satisfying, though even as he surveyed his domain the ache of not having Laylah to share all this gnawed at him.

Joe Ryan had his own comfortable apartment walled in beside Fitz and beyond that was the six-bedroom motel-like guest house with its swimming pool for imported staff. Joe had brought in an attractive English girl singer from London via Beirut and four pretty blond waitresses who were particularly pleasing to the Arab taste. At least half the Ten Tola Bar business consisted of Arab men who, true to their customs, never took women out but were glad to see Western girls at the places they went. Only in this one place throughout the Arabian Gulf could such an establishment exist. Dubai was the supreme monument to free enterprise and it was the Ruler's excellent business judgment that made Dubai the most important Arab port on the Gulf. Dubai had achieved impressive wealth before oil had been found. Now there was no limit to the commercial heights this small emirate could achieve.

Fitz regarded with distaste the bugging devices on the table in front of him. He did not like the idea of eavesdropping and he had no intention of doing more than occasionally testing the equipment to make sure it was working in case Abe Ferutti, his CIA control, came down from Beirut to see how the Agency's asset in Dubai was doing. Now that Laylah had apparently fallen in love with Courty Thornwell, his desire to become an ambassador had ebbed. And with his growing disinterest in the diplomatic post he could see little reason to cooperate with his country's espionage activities.

Although the Ten Tola Bar right from the start was a late-night place, there was always a respectable dinner crowd. Joe Ryan had brought a fine chef in from Tehran and the food had, in just the short time the place had been opened, established a reputation for being the best place in the Emirates to eat.

At seven-thirty Fitz was in the restaurant watching his customers arrive. Although it was efficiently air-conditioned, three antique four-bladed fans hung from the high ceiling, turning lazily.

Naturally his investment in the Ten Tola Bar had far exceeded initial estimates but fortunately Sepah's second successful voyage had taken care of the overage. Also Tim McLaren was happy to increase the size of the short-term loan the bank had made. It was immediately apparent to everyone from the Shaikh on down that this was a highly profitable venture. Costs and expenses were high but in this boom-town atmosphere so were the prices Fitz could charge. Majid Jabir was a very happy silent partner with a twenty percent interest in the place. Fitz was happy too. This was a lot cheaper than the taxes he'd have to pay in any other country with a comparable lack of competition and dizzying economic growth.

Fitz walked around his place, greeting guests and spreading encouraging phrases among the employees. One of the girls, Ingrid, had caught his eye and he asked her if all was going well. "Oh, yes," she replied. "An Arab pulled a gorgeous yellow diamond out of his *dish dasha* last night and wanted to give it to me."

"You know what it means if you take it," Fitz answered. "Once you take up with a customer you and I are both in trouble—you more than I."

"Once in a while it would be fun to have a real date," she pouted. Ingrid was Norwegian, just the type the Arabs liked best, blue eyes, long blond hair. Fitz knew that there would have to be a fast turnover in girls but Joe Ryan seemed to feel the source was inexhaustible. Scandinavian girls were adventuresome and loved to get away from their long cold winters and find the hot sun.

"Well, take my advice and stick to Westerners. They're in and out of here. The Arabs are very possessive. You make it with an Arab and we might not see you again. And it's their country, not ours, so there's very little I could do to help you. Why don't you concentrate on making money. Your tips are good, aren't they?"

Fitz thought of asking her over to his house for a drink after work but remembered that the flight from London and Beirut would be arriving at its usual time, about two-thirty this morning, and Abdul Hummard would be aboard. The Palestinian oil man would have time for a short sleep and then they would have to start out for Kajmira. Shaikh Hamed and his son Shaikh Saqr were expecting them at nine. But perhaps tomorrow night he'd give Ingrid a night off and let Peter serve Abdul and Ingrid dinner at his house. He owed Abdul something for Lynn. Also the Hemisphere deal was a godsend as far as he was concerned. Financing the oil field was over his head when he looked at it realistically.

With the opening of the Ten Tola Bar, Fitz had become something of a celebrity in the Emirates and everybody who came here wanted to say hello to the owner. His acquaintanceship with Arabs and Westerners alike increased every night. It was tiring but necessary. The tempo quickened as the hours went on and by midnight even the tables in the center section were almost all taken.

At two in the morning Fitz drove to the airport, only a short distance from the bar, to wait for Abdul's plane. A phenomenon he had observed in the past three nights was occurring at the Ten Tola Bar. Businessmen and various government bureaucrats were flying into Dubai, going directly to the Ten Tola Bar for meetings, and then returning to the airport and flying out. Dubai boasted a heavy schedule of midnight to 6 A.M. flights landing and taking off.

The flight from London and Beirut was somewhat late but when it finally landed Abdul was the first passenger out of the first-class section. Majid Jabir had alerted Customs and Immigration and Abdul was whisked through and Fitz drove him back to his place.

"You might as well get settled in. Then if you want to see the

action in my bar I'll take you in. It's not much by London standards, I'm afraid," Fitz apologized. "But for out here it goes just
fine."

Fitz showed Abdul through his pantry into the kitchen and
then out into the bar. A group was just arriving from the airport
for conferences at the corner booths.

"Al-lah! This place is fantastic." Abdul looked around the
crowded restaurant. "At two-thirty in the morning!" His eyes lit
on Ingrid. "She'd be a number-one choice anywhere. And those
others. Who does your pimping, Fitz?"

"A half Persian, half American from Tehran and Beirut named
Joe Ryan," Fitz replied. He pointed at the manager. "I have a
feeling the two of you have a lot in common." Fitz looked over at
Ingrid. "You like her? Get the deal made with Shaikh Hamed this
morning and the two of you can have dinner alone on my patio.
Other than that you're on your own."

"Blondes," he sighed. "I don't know what it is with us Arabs
and blondes."

"Do you want to get a few hours of sleep before we leave?"

Abdul's eyes darted around the room and then, reluctantly, he
turned toward the kitchen. "Human flesh is frail. I think it would
be sensible for me to sleep a little. But I really don't anticipate
any problems with Hamed."

CHAPTER 39

Over the sands, along the beach, and back over the sands again to Shaikh Hamed's residence in Kajmira was about a two-hour drive. "I wish they'd get started on the paved road. It will go along the coast all the way from Abu Dhabi to Ras al Khaimah," Fitz remarked as he drove the Land Rover toward their destination.

Abdul Hummard nodded. The sand tires of the Land Rover dug through the desert, propelling the vehicle onward. It was just before nine o'clock in the morning when they arrived in the town of Kajmira, situated on the point of a long finger of sandy land which separated a silted back-bay from the Gulf. They drove along the outside of the finger of sand toward an ancient fortress tower which stood on the point guarding the entrance to the harbor. Shaikh Hamed had employed a British construction firm to remodel the fort into an attractive beach house for himself. Shaikh Hamed and his wife each had a beach house. He also maintained a formal majlis as an adjunct to his house on the beach. But when he felt affairs demanded special attention and should not be aired in an open majlis, he conducted the meetings within the security and safety of the old fort. It was in the fort that Fitz and his group had signed the concession with Hamed the first time.

The Arab guards, armed with old British Enfield rifles, came to attention. The Land Rover stopped and Fitz and Abdul Hummard descended to the sand. As they approached the heavy double doors to the fort one of the doors swung open and a robed and headdressed Arab greeted them and showed them in. He closed the door behind them against the heat outside. The air-conditioned interior was a welcome relief, as refreshing as a plunge into cool waters. From the reception room they were led into the small, more intimate majlis which Hamed preferred.

Hamed was sitting in a comfortable overstuffed chair. The table beside him was piled with documents. Beside the Ruler sat his son Shaikh Saqr; four of Shaikh Hamed's most trusted advisers sat two on each side of him sipping coffee. As Fitz and Abdul Hummard entered the room the four advisers moved away from Shaikh Hamed, leaving two seats next to the Shaikh for Fitz and Abdul Hummard. Abdul not only knew Hamed and Saqr well but also the advisers. He called each of them by name, shook hands, Fitz doing the same, and then they took their seats beside Hamed. The lavish phrases Shaikh Hamed used to greet Abdul Hummard indicated the Ruler's esteem for the Palestinian business arranger.

On the drive from Deira to Kajmira, Hummard had mentioned to Fitz that he had a special surprise for the Shaikh. Fitz should not be concerned, he said, if during the discussions Abdul turned the subject matter to another matter. As Abdul and Hamed professed their profound respect for each other and the honor which both of them felt at being in each other's presence, the coffee servant came around and poured everybody coffee.

Abdul Hummard began the conversation by explaining that he was personally associated with one of the world's most influential and successful oil companies, Hemisphere Petroleum Company of New York and London. Hamed said that of course he knew Hemisphere. At one time he had even talked to a Hemisphere Petroleum Company geologist who had been to Kajmira. However, Hamed pointed out, nothing had ever come of that meeting, and when the very prominent pro-Arab American, Lodd, had approached him, and Lodd's associates, who were so well known to Hamed, joined the American in making a proposal, Hamed felt that this would be the right group of people with whom to do business.

Abdul Hummard agreed with Hamed completely. The Ruler could not have made a better choice of men with integrity and knowledge of the business than the group with whom he signed the concession. However, he explained, Mr. Lodd had for the last two weeks been in the United States on personal business and while he was in New York he had mentioned to Mr. Lorenz Cannon, president of Hemisphere Petroleum, that he and his associates were preparing to drill in a concession granted by the Emirate of Kajmira. "Mr. Cannon," Abdul continued, "expressed extreme interest in the Kajmira concession."

A look of slight agitation passed over the Ruler's features as Hummard went on talking. However, he did not stop the Palestinian until he had completed his story. "Mr. Cannon," Hummard continued, "became so interested in the Kajmira concession and the officers of Hemisphere were so excited about the prospects of being part of Shaikh Hamed's success that they prevailed upon Lodd and his associates to take them into the operation." What Mr. Lodd, therefore, and he, Abdul Hummard, an associate and representative of Hemisphere, were here to ask of Shaikh Hamed was his blessings on a deal in which the Lodd group joined forces with Hemisphere to fully develop the oil possibilities offshore of Kajmira.

A long silence ensued. Shaikh Saqr looked anxiously at his father to see what the Ruler's reaction would be. Whatever the Ruler's reaction, that would also be the son's. Hamed turned to Fitz. "You told me on many occasions that you are not acting as an agent who would go and take the concession and in effect sell it elsewhere. You told me that this was going to be something that you and Sepah and your friend Fender Browne, who we all know is one of the most knowledgeable oil men on the Gulf, along with prominent Arab residents of the Trucial States, would do yourself. It was going to be your oil company. It would be owned and operated entirely by people whose home was here on the Gulf. Now it appears to me as though you are doing just what you said you would not do."

"We had every intention of operating this concession ourselves, Your Highness. And we are still prepared to do so. Had not Mr. Cannon and his very experienced group of oil men made such a strong case for their participation we never would have considered doing it in any other way but by ourselves. Also, Your Highness, certain other disturbing possibilities have surfaced here on the Gulf. These possibilities made it even more logical to consider bringing Hemisphere into our concession."

The Ruler lifted an eyebrow questioningly. "Disturbing possibilities?" he asked.

At this point Abdul Hummard once more entered the conversation. At length he explained to Shaikh Hamed about British

desires to leave the Arabian Gulf in good order so that
British businessmen could continue operating there. Hamed
had, of course, heard frequently that the Shah of Iran was laying
claim to the island of Bahrain. Hamed knew that British interests
were particularly strong in Bahrain. It would certainly be disastrous both to the British and to the Arab side of the Gulf for the
Iranians to take over Bahrain. They were trying to take over every
island in the Gulf as it was.

Hummard then related the information Fitz had received in
Iran. Fitz had actually talked to the *mua'atamad*, at the American Embassy. Fitz had learned through sources of his own about
certain trading going on between the British and the Shah. Hummard explained the Sharjah trade-off of Abu Musa to the Shah.

Hamed listened and the look of concern on his face deepened.
He was realizing at last that the situation went further than the
American and his associates trying to make a fast profit for them-
selves. There was a possibility that Kajmira could lose the oil in its
offshore concession to the Emirate of Sharjah allied with Iran.
This was a situation that had never occurred to him until now.

Fitz knew that in the Arab mind proof lay in logic. Although
there was no factual proof of what Fitz and Hummard were telling
the Ruler of Kajmira, the logic of it was all too clear. This would
be just what the British would do in order to ensure peace in the
Gulf when they left.

Abdul, Fitz knew, had as little faith in the possibility of Iran
and Sharjah getting away with extending the three-mile limit to
twelve miles as did Cannon and his chief counsel, Irwin Shuster.
It was difficult for Fitz not to smile at the deep concern the Palestinian expressed at this threat to the prosperity of Shaikh Hamed
and Kajmira.

Hummard went on to tell Hamed that he personally had conducted several meetings with the British Foreign Office Arabian
Department, and while they had not confirmed the possibilities
he had just outlined, they had not denied them either. What is
necessary to obtain, Hummard pressed, is a meeting in London
with the Foreign Office and His Highness, the Ruler's representative, who, Hummard assumed, would be Shaikh Saqr.

Shaikh Saqr was openly delighted at the possibility of a trip to
London. He was well aware of the extent of Hummard's hospitality to visiting Arabs.

At this meeting, Hummard continued, Saqr on behalf of the Ruler would confirm His Highness's approval of the new agreement between Hemisphere and the Lodd group. At the same time the Foreign Office would issue a new political letter approving the transaction. It would be impossible under any sort of international law for the British to then condone changing the three-mile limit to a twelve-mile limit around Abu Musa. If, however, such a move was made the entire power of Hemisphere Petroleum and the United States Government would be brought to bear against Britain's, Iran's, and the Emirate of Sharjah's efforts to make such a unilateral change in the limits.

"Would there be a new signature bonus?" Hamed asked hopefully. Hummard looked at Fitz, who answered the question.

"Yes, Your Highness. In the deal I made with Hemisphere they pay our group half a million dollars when we sign the agreement with them. This means we would get back from Hemisphere the money we have invested plus a certain profit."

"A profit of a quarter of a million dollars," Hamed said pointedly.

"They have spent already considerable amounts of money on exploration and developing new seismic information," Hummard said, leaping to the defense of Fitz. "Lodd and his group could have kept the deal to themselves and not brought in the powerful and influential Hemisphere Petroleum Company. They could have become very rich men by their standards. Though of course poor in comparison to what Your Highness will realize from this project," he hastily added.

"Nevertheless," Hummard continued, "Mr. Lodd chose to protect Your Highness by obtaining the enormous power and influence of Hemisphere Petroleum on your behalf. Should Sharjah and Iran have extended the limits with British power behind them, there was very little that Mr. Lodd's group could have done to protect Kajmira's interests. However, Hemisphere can virtually guarantee that such a unilateral extension could not successfully be declared."

Fitz could read Shaikh Hamed's Arab mind. All this business about Sharjah and Iran may or may not have a basis in absolute fact. It was a logical move, however. But what Hamed saw was Fitz and his group making a quarter of a million dollars' profit for themselves, getting all their money back, and still owning twenty-five percent of the company. It was too good a deal for him not to share in it, the Ruler was undoubtedly thinking.

During the break in the conversation as Hamed considered all the possibilities being presented to him, Abdul Hummard opened the attaché case he had carried with him and took from it a page of colorful postage stamps. He handed the page of stamps to Hamed.

"De La Mue gave me these just before I left London. They are having a little trouble clearing the stamp at the International Postal Union in Switzerland."

Shaikh Hamed let out a guffaw as he looked at the stamp and handed it to his son Shaikh Saqr. "As long as nobody in my country ever sees that stamp, everything will be all right," he laughed, lightening the charged atmosphere. Shaikh Saqr also laughed and handed the stamps back to Hummard, who passed them to Fitz. Fitz saw that the stamp displayed a virtually nude, very Western-looking girl, blond, long-legged, and heavy-busted. He chuckled at the stamp himself. "Do you mean to say that the International Postal Union will recognize these postage stamps as valid?"

"I brought with me several hundred envelopes, all addressed to stamp collectors of note throughout the world. De La Mue, who printed these stamps, actually paid for the building of the Kajmira post office. When we leave here we will go to the post office and I will stamp each envelope and put it in the mail. We fully expect that the International Postal Union will try to ban the stamp. They will probably say it is lewd and indecent and this will cause an enormous furor throughout the stamp-collecting world. Everybody will want one of these stamps for their collection. In a year or two years each one of these stamps should be worth thousands of dollars. Due to the controversial nature of the issue, the value may rise even sooner."

"I thought I knew all the rackets around here," Fitz said with a grin. "But this beats all of them."

"It isn't good for enormous fortune making but it certainly could be worth a few hundred thousand dollars to Shaikh Hamed and to the printers. I get my commission in stamps."

"The Arabs with all their professed prudery in public would, I think, repudiate this issue," Fitz observed.

"With the money involved they don't worry about prudery.

That little lady"—he leered at the sheet of stamps—"is going to make us all a lot of money. The last time I was here Shaikh Hamed and I discussed this at great length. At first, of course, he was horrified but when I explained about how controversy sells stamps, books, movies, anything, he quickly realized we had a good thing here and approved the design." He winked at Fitz. "As I said, old boy, a diversionary tactic, you know."

Once more Abdul Hummard reached into his briefcase and pulled out a copy of the agreement which had been drafted between the Lodd group and Hemisphere Petroleum Company. The left-hand side of the page was written in English and the right-hand side of the page in Arabic. He handed the documents to Shaikh Hamed. "This is the agreement Lodd is prepared to sign with Hemisphere with your approval. Verbally we have told you what's in it. Now you can study it yourself and let us hear what your reactions are. Needless to say, Your Highness, the sooner we do this, the better. When I left the British Foreign Office in London they were willing to give me a political letter attesting to this agreement. But the arrangements with the Shah could come anytime. So the sooner you could send a representative to London, the sooner we can close."

Fitz saw the dubious look on Hamed's face. Much as Fitz would have liked to have turned a quick profit on the signature bonus, he could see that what the old Shaikh really had in mind—girlie stamps notwithstanding—was the fact that Fitz and his group were going to make money in a hurry. If anybody was going to make money in a hurry it should be Shaikh Hamed and not the American, no matter how pro-Arab he was. Fitz had discussed this contingency with Fender Browne, Sepah, and Majid Jabir at length. Majid had also anticipated the old Ruler's reaction. The consensus had been that if it was necessary to give the signature bonus to Hamed, thus increasing his total signature bonus by another quarter of a million dollars, Fitz should do it. They were still getting twenty-five percent of a huge oil concession and this they really couldn't jeopardize for the two hundred fifty thousand dollars.

In English, Fitz said to Abdul, "There's no such thing as a diversionary tactic when an Arab is thinking about money." He then turned to the Ruler. "Your Highness, I and other members of our consortium want nothing but a totally successful conclusion to this matter. Since they left final decisions on these negotiations in my hands, I know that they will feel as I do that we do not want to make a profit from changing our deal with you. Therefore, I know that Majid Jabir, Fender Browne, and Sepah will approve my decision that we split fifty-fifty with you the total signature bonus. That means that we will get back the money we directly gave to you. We will not get back the money we spent on exploration but we feel this is our contribution to the success of the enterprise. Therefore, when this arrangement is signed by the British Foreign Office and by your duly appointed representative in London, two hundred and fifty thousand dollars will go to you and the other two hundred and fifty thousand dollars to reimburse us for the money we've already given you."

A benevolent smile spread across Hamed's bearded face. He nodded. Saqr nodded and smiled too, no doubt thinking about his week or so in London with Abdul Hummard catering to such sexual fantasies as he might develop.

"My son," Hamed said to Fitz, "we Arabs know that you are truly one of us. You understand us, you have chosen to become a part of us. I can understand why you would see fit to change the arrangements we made. However, since this is best for you we will sign the new agreement. Shaikh Saqr will take my seal to London."

Fitz smiled manfully. He had just tossed away a quarter-million-dollar immediate profit, but all their actual expenses would be reimbursed at the commencement of production before profits were divided. At least he had all of his capital back and no outlay in the future expected of him. Also, his fee for being Hemisphere's man on the Gulf had been agreed upon at fifty thousand dollars a year. Fitz had done all right for himself and for his group.

Fitz and Abdul arrived back at the Ten Tola Bar during the middle of luncheon. Most of the Western offices and all of the Arab offices closed at twelve-thirty for the day. Long lunches were the custom, and while people had been in the habit of going to their homes for lunch, now more and more they were going out. The Ten Tola Bar was the chief recipient of the luncheon expenditures by Arabs and Westerners alike. The four circular corner booths were taken by the time Fitz and Abdul walked in.

"This is quite a little gold mine you have, Fitz," Abdul commented. "And it is a badly needed amenity in this community. Quite a life you've made for yourself on the Arabian Gulf."

"I like it, I guess."

Abdul caught the wistful expression. "You still haven't gotten over her, have you, Fitz? With all the beautiful girls you've got right here and all your business interests, you should be able to forget this girl."

"Yes, I suppose so." Fitz started for the bar. "Come on, let's have a drink. I brought in orange juice and champagne just for you." Over their drinks Fitz said, "Am I going to have a chance to return some of the fine hospitality you showed me in London? Shall I give Ingrid the evening off?"

Abdul sighed sadly. "Not for me, Fitz. I'll take the four-o'clock flight back to Beirut. I can make a connection for London which will get me there in time for a few hours' sleep and be in the office at ten in the morning. There's a tremendous amount of work to do before we sign the agreement. And I want to keep after my Foreign Office contacts every day to make sure that nothing is going to happen that would prevent them from giving us the second political letter."

"You still aren't really very worried about the Abu Musa situation, are you?"

"I think it's highly unlikely that such a thing could happen, particularly if we get the political letter. And even if such an attempt was made we can forestall it. However, you on your own might have had trouble."

"Sorry to see you leave so soon."

"Don't worry, I'll be back. And by the way, save those stamps I gave you. They'll be valuable some day soon."

"They will be a treasured addition to my Arabian Gulf memorabilia." He stopped a passing waitress and took a menu from her which he handed to Abdul. "Take a look. At least I can give you a good luncheon before we send you off."

CHAPTER 40

Joe Ryan conducted Majid Jabir and Sepah to Fitz's table, the first one on the right after entering the Ten Tola Bar. It had quickly become known as the "majlis." Here was where Fitz conducted most of his business from luncheon time until two or later the following morning, taking time out for a swim and sunbathing in the afternoon.

Fitz stood up from his seat at the head of the coffin-shaped table and welcomed Majid Jabir and Sepah to his majlis. With the time for the London closing fast approaching, all the principals in the deal conferred almost daily, and Shaikh Saqr frequently drove down to the Ten Tola Bar from Kajmira. While ostensibly Saqr's visits were for the purpose of discussing matters with Fitz, actually he was enamored of all the blond waitresses and particularly, Fitz had noticed, Ingrid.

Majid Jabir sat on one side of Fitz and Sepah on the other. They had hardly ordered coffee when Fender Browne and Tim McLaren joined them. They talked among themselves for a while, laughing at Saqr, who seemed to be propositioning every girl in the place. Fitz always worried about the volatile situation between the Arabs and the girls who worked in the restaurant. So far none of the girls had found themselves in trouble but there was bound to be a first time. Frequently Fitz had thought of doing away with the girls altogether but it was they who gave the place so much atmosphere and brought in large numbers of customers.

"I see Jean Louis Serrat in his usual corner booth hatching out some kind of trouble," Tim McLaren observed.

Fender Browne grinned. "I'd love to hear what's being said at some of these tables. The biggest deals on the Gulf these days are made right here at the Ten Tola Bar."

Majid Jabir glanced unobtrusively at Serrat. "I'd like to know what he's plotting with that Iraqi banker from Ras al Khaimah. That other fellow looks like an Iraqi too and he's got a Chinaman at his table."

"I knew about Serrat when I was in Beirut," Fender Browne said. "He's arranging some sort of a sale of French guns, I can tell you that. He was in on that sale of the French jet fighters to the Israelis, you know."

"Fender, you hear all kinds of rumors. Even about me," Fitz admitted. "And I guess giving out inscribed ten-tola bars to the best customers doesn't help any." Fitz laughed. "As far as I'm concerned, Monsieur Serrat is the representative of the French interests in the Dubai Oil Drilling Operations and one or two other oil-producing companies on the Gulf."

For a moment Fitz considered going up to his office and tuning into Serrat's conversation. He was well aware of the fact that the main provocateurs in the Gulf area were Iraqis and of course in Oman the Chinese were involved in training and leading the People's Front for Liberation of the Occupied Arabian Gulf, PFLOAG, fighting to overthrow the Sultan and establish a Communist state. He had yet to actually use the devices he had installed to eavesdrop on a conversation. But to leave his guests would have been rude. The group was discussing the London closing scheduled ten days hence. There was still mixed opinion among them about not holding on to their concession. Only Majid Jabir strongly sided with Fitz. The logic of the Abu Musa situation was such that he believed it to be true.

"It must be getting late," Tim McLaren remarked. "Here comes the group from the Beirut flight."

Fitz looked at his watch. "The plane must have been on time for a change." Several men and one couple were ushered to seats by Joe Ryan, joining groups waiting for them. "I wish I had one percent of every deal that's made in this place," Fitz said laughingly.

"You'd be richer than Rashid, Zayed, and Faisal altogether if you could work such a thing," Tim McLaren agreed.

Joe Ryan slipped up behind Fitz. "There's a Mr. Tony DeMarco just arrived from Beirut who wants to see you, boss. He says a General Boless sent him."

Fitz nodded. "I wondered when he'd get here. Bring him over."

And to the others at the table Fitz explained quickly, "This guy's coming here to try to put twenty to twenty-five million dollars away in Dubai. It was dirty money when it left Vietnam but I suppose here it's just plain money like any other money."

"I'll be delighted to help him, Fitz," Tim McLaren declared. McLaren and Sepah moved down one seat and when DeMarco was brought to the table Fitz gestured to the open chair at his right. "Welcome to my majlis, Mr. DeMarco."

Tony DeMarco was a stocky, burly man. His thick gray hair jutted out in a shock above his brows. Even at night and indoors he was wearing dark glasses. If there really was such a thing as the Mafia, Fitz thought, he was looking at the prototype of a Mafioso.

Fitz introduced Tony DeMarco to the men at the table. "From what General Boless told me in Washington, Tony, you're sitting with just the right group. Majid Jabir here is the man who makes things happen in the Trucial States. Sepah is one of the leading proponents of risk-capital investment in this part of the Arabian Gulf. Tim McLaren is your friendly banker. He runs the Dubai branch of the First Commercial Bank of New York. And he also presides over the safest system of secret numbered bank accounts in the world today. And across from him is Fender Browne, one of the most knowledgeable men in oil drilling anywhere in Arabia. So, Tony, we are all at your service."

"I never thought I'd find a place like this out here." Tony DeMarco's head swiveled about the restaurant. "I was set for a siege in the real boonies."

"You'll find us every bit as civilized as Saigon," Fitz said dryly. "Unless the Pearl of the Orient has changed one helluva lot since I was last there."

"The International Club has improved since your day, Fitz," Tony said. "But it's sure nothing like this."

"You can talk freely in this group. I'll just have to go to them anyway when you tell me what's on your mind. General Boless and I talked at some length in Washington."

Fitz had motioned for Ingrid to come to the table. She arrived and asked Tony DeMarco what he wanted. The look on his face clearly said "you, baby." However, he ordered a scotch and soda.

"For openers," DeMarco began, "I have a bank draft for

twenty million dollars. It's written on the Commercial Trading Bank in Hong Kong. I have a list of individual names for whom I want to set up numbered accounts. The twenty million will be placed into these various accounts."

"That's easy enough," Tim McLaren said affably.

DeMarco looked at Sepah. "I have another bank draft for five million dollars. My syndicate wants to put this into a high profit potential situation. We know we're taking a risk and if we lose we lose. But we'd like to get into a little action here. It looks like some deal around here paid off big for ole Fitz." DeMarco waved around the room.

Fitz turned to Sepah. "Can you take care of five million dollars?"

"I *will* be able to. Right now we have problems but I expect to solve them within the next two months." Fitz thought of suggesting to DeMarco that he put the five million dollars into their oil deal and then he would cancel with Hemisphere Petroleum. However, he still had faith in the accuracy of Laylah's report on Abu Musa. He also knew the people behind DeMarco; gangsters and murderers even though they were soldiers or to all outward appearances legitimate civilian businessmen operating in the Orient. He had no desire to be personally responsible for losing their money. It was best that he merely let DeMarco and Sepah see what sort of business they could do together. He would stay out of it.

"Well, Tony, you hit the right place at the right time," Fitz said heartily. "In ten minutes you've made all the contacts you're going to need. Now I'll just leave it up to you and Tim to work out your banking deal together and you and Sepah can work out whatever else you have in mind."

"General Boless said that you would personally watch out for this money. There's a lot more where it came from just looking for a home. The U. S. Government has cracked the Swiss numbered accounts. Also the damn Swiss bankers now are putting a thirty percent tax on money coming in to numbered accounts."

"Here the Ruler doesn't allow anybody, not even the United States Senate, to look into numbered bank accounts. Why don't you come around to the bank tomorrow morning around eight-thirty or nine and we'll get things started for you. Fitz will bring you by."

"When you've finished with Tim, Fitz will bring you over to my house," Sepah added. "I'll explain to you, with Fitz's help, precisely how our business works. Despite the risks the odds are good."

"If you want to get into the oil business you can come see me, Tony," Fender Browne threw in, not wanting to be left out of an infusion of cash into the Dubai economy.

It was now getting close to three o'clock and slowly the Ten Tola Bar was clearing out. There still seemed to be several business conferences going on in the corner booths but the tables in the middle of the room were entirely empty now.

"I came directly here, Fitz," Tony said. "I didn't bother to try to get a hotel room first. Can you arrange something for me?"

"Sure, Tony. You can stay with me while you're here. Did you fly in directly from Hong Kong?"

"That's right. I've been in the air a long time. From Hong Kong to Beirut with a couple of stops in between and then the flight down here. I don't know when I last got in a bed."

"Maybe you'd like to put off the meetings a day. Get rested up and recover from the jet lag," Fitz suggested.

"No, this is something I've got to take care of fast. As I say, if it all works out I'll have some really large chunks of cash to drop off here. We've had a good thing going now for about two years but what with this goddam new administration in Washington trying to wind down the war, plus an investigation some senator is trying to pull off who wants to get re-elected next fall, I give us six months, a year at the most, before we have to find a new area of operations."

"I'll show you your room," Fitz offered. "It's a funny thing about Dubai, the minute people get here they try to figure out how fast they can get out. Well, we can move quickly. Where are your suitcases?"

"Your man at the door said he'd watch them for me."

Fitz clapped his hands and a Pakistani busboy appeared. "Take the suitcases that Mr. Joe"—that was how he referred to Joe Ryan when talking to the other employees—"is taking care of and carry

them through the kitchen to my quarters." The Pakistani nodded
and hurried over to the door.

"O.K., Tony. Anytime you're ready."

"Now," DeMarco said wearily.

Fitz stood up. "We'll see you all tomorrow."

CHAPTER 41

The following morning Fitz woke up a very tired Tony DeMarco and suggested a plunge in the pool before breakfast. DeMarco accepted the challenge, struggled out to the patio, and jumped into the cold water. After a few minutes of thrashing around he pulled his heavy-set naked frame out of the water and toweled himself dry.

Peter served them breakfast and Fitz and Tony DeMarco drove in the Land Rover across the bridge from Deira to Dubai and then down into the town.

The First Commercial Bank of New York, Dubai Branch, was just being completed. It was a beautiful building, with arabesque cement latticework covering the square, functional structure, giving it a modern Arabic look.

Inside the air-conditioned interior there were lines of Arabs, Indians, and other denizens of the Gulf lined up at all the tellers' cages. "This is the busiest bank in this part of the Gulf," Fitz said.

"Looks it," DeMarco agreed.

Fitz led Tony DeMarco to the fence separating the officers from the rest of the bank. He pushed a gate open and walked through, the officers and their secretaries nodding to him. He came in to see McLaren so frequently that he was considered a bank employee.

Tim was standing behind his desk as Fitz and DeMarco walked into his office. He shook hands with DeMarco and motioned him to be seated. Fitz remained standing.

"I'm going to leave you two fellows to your business. You can brief me later. I'm going to collect my mail and then I'll be back and wait for you."

Fitz left the office and walked back through the bank and outside to where he had parked his Land Rover. He jumped in and drove to the post office nearby. Inside, he opened his mail box and took out the letters. The familiar blue envelope with Laylah's name embossed in white on the upper left-hand corner made his heart flip over. He wanted to open it and read it right here in the post office but there were too many people milling about. He would have to wait until he was in the sanctuary of an empty bank office.

Fiercely he drove through the crowds and across the sandy roads back to the bank. Inside he stalked across the marble floor of the main banking area, through the gate, and back to an unused office, where he sat down at the desk and pulled the envelope open.

The letter began with what Laylah was doing at the Embassy these days and then he learned as he read on that Laylah was seeing Courty most of the time and doing her best to help him with the Shah. He had had one audience with the Shah already and the Persian Ruler had definitely expressed real interest in buying into a large communications setup in the United States. Courty was discouraged at how long it was taking because both *Life* magazine and the American Broadcasting Company, he felt, could be purchased with a large infusion of cash if he could just get these oil rulers to act.

In the next paragraph there was a frank reply to a letter Fitz had written her some weeks before right after he had arrived in London and before he'd met Lynn. He had expressed his desire to come to Tehran and spend a few days with her, talking things out. He had told her, of course, that he now had his final divorce decree with him. He wanted her to see it.

"Fitz," she wrote, "please try to understand and not feel I have in some way betrayed you. There would really be no point in your coming to Tehran. I'm very happy your divorce is final. That was something you had to do anyway. I'm sure it's the best thing for both your ex-wife and yourself. I am seeing Courty now and he has proposed to me."

The pain became sharper. "I have not given him an answer, since I don't really know whether or not I want to get married at this time. But, Fitz, as a very dear friend, I must tell you that I do love Courty. I never thought it would happen. I thought he was a selfish young man using a very sad political problem to his own advantage. I know Courty much better now. When he proposed he suggested that we get married after he has succeeded in putting his financing together. Then we will go back to the States, where he will be working on acquisitions. So even if I accepted, I guess it would be another year before we actually got married.

"Please try to understand things, Fitz. I'll always love you in a very special way. But I really think it would be best if for the time being at least you did not come to Tehran specifically to see me. If you're coming anyway I'll plan to have a drink with you while you're here, but, as I said, don't come just on my account. I hope all goes well in Dubai. I'm sorry I couldn't come to see your wonderful restaurant opened. I'm sure it will be the greatest success in all those Arab countries. With my deepest affection, Laylah."

Fitz sat staring at the letter for long moments. He was hardly aware of Tony DeMarco and Tim McLaren standing at the open door. Finally he looked up and saw them, folded the letter, put it in his pocket, and stood up. It wasn't that she had told him something he didn't already know. It was just seeing it spelled out in her own hand that was so devastating. Fortunately Tim McLaren and Tony DeMarco were talking so animatedly that they did not notice Fitz's dazed look before he composed himself.

"I'll be over and have lunch with you and Tony when we close up here," McLaren said to Fitz.

"Good. We need the business."

"Now you're taking Tony over to see Sepah, right?"

"Right," Fitz replied. He turned to Tony. "I just got a letter from Boless. I haven't even opened it yet. Probably telling me to expect your arrival."

"He probably told you something else that you and I will talk about after we see Sepah."

Outside the bank Fitz pointed directly across the Creek to where several dhows were tied up at a dock. "The quickest way to get from here to Sepah's office would be to take one of these little abras, have them row us right across. However, I don't want to leave my car here. So we'll make a thirty-minute drive. The way things are going in Dubai, with business booming and so much construction being planned, I shouldn't wonder if one of these British engineering firms that make so much money here will talk the Ruler into building a downtown tunnel from the Dubai side to the Deira side.

"From what McLaren tells me, that is not out of the realm of possibility. You know, I'm more convinced than ever that this is where we should come while we can still get in on something close to the ground floor."

It was almost eleven in the morning when they arrived at Sepah's office.

"I'm afraid you picked a bad day to come see me about investing in one of my gold syndicates," Sepah said, opening the conversation.

"An accident?" Fitz asked.

"Yes, I'm afraid so. The first one I've had since before you joined the syndicate. I suppose it could have been worse. At least the dhow and its crew got back alive."

"How did it happen?" Fitz asked.

"The Indians have something new. They somehow acquired three hovercraft from the British. These hovercraft are even faster than their patrol launches. They travel at sixty miles an hour over the water. You know the principle. They don't actually touch the surface of the water, they float on a cushion of air about a foot above the water. Fortunately I took your advice, Fitz. We removed all the guns from the dhow for this trip. When the hovercraft forced us into the path of the patrol launch and they boarded us, not only had we jettisoned the gold but there was nothing incriminating aboard. The Indians made their search, found nothing, and left the dhow to return empty."

"How far off the coast did this happen?" Fitz asked.

"Seventy-five to a hundred miles. The hovercraft have about a three-hundred-mile range. Issa said that the hovercraft was armed with guns bigger than even the twenty-millimeter cannons that we carried."

"The hovercraft would probably have two forty-millimeter cannons," Fitz remarked. "No way you can fight that with twenties."

Sepah smiled sadly at Tony DeMarco. "Until I'm able to neutralize the hovercrafts on the ground in India, I don't think we'll try another shipment."

To Fitz he said, "I'm sorry. This was the fourth trip and the last one in which you had an interest."

"How do you intend to neutralize the hovercraft?" DeMarco asked.

"My organization in India is infiltrating the base where the hovercraft are maintained," Sepah answered. "So far we have put two mechanics into the base. In another month, two at the most, we will have all of the mechanics working for us. At that time we will arrange with them to have all the hovercraft in the maintenance shop whenever a dhow of mine approaches the Indian coast."

"Very clever," Tony DeMarco said. "You must have quite an operation going for you in India."

"The most important part of this entire business, my friend, is the machinery within India. It took me two years to set it up."

"My group is ready to shoot craps with you for five million dollars," DeMarco said earnestly. "Can you take that much?"

Sepah looked puzzled. Fitz chuckled. "That's an American expression for 'take a big chance with you.' "

Sepah regarded DeMarco for some moments. "There are many ways of investing in a gold syndicate. I would take your five million dollars and spread it over four or even five shipments. Each shipment that gets through means your money has tripled. If we have one accident out of five you're very much ahead of the game, as you can see. Even if we have two accidents out of five you still make a profit."

"There must be a hell of a lot of gold down there under the ocean near Bombay."

"Yes, I'm afraid there is. Unfortunately the ocean bottom in that part of the coastal region is neither rock nor sand but very soft silty material, so that the gold is quickly buried underneath the silt."

Tony DeMarco turned to Fitz. "My people left it up to me to decide how to play the action. I'm turning over to Fitz the responsibility of how the five million is bet. O.K.?"

"I might mention, Mr. DeMarco," Sepah remarked, "that there are many far less risky ventures into which you could put this investment capital. Cigarette smuggling into Persia, for instance. And liquor into the countries where it's forbidden. Dubai is probably the most important port on the Arabian side of the Gulf with the possible exception of Kuwait. You could profitably buy and ship a lot of cargo with that money."

"That would be pretty slow return on the money, wouldn't it?"

"Slow, but sure."

"When I'm ready to come down here and get into business myself, I'll go into that, but for the time being we'll go with you on the gold."

"With Fitz as your representative we will be happy to accept you into our syndicate. He certainly knows the business."

"I'm sure you'll make a lot of money for us and yourselves." Tony DeMarco turned to Fitz. "Let's get back. I want to get out of here late this afternoon and be in Hong Kong tomorrow night. It was nice to have met you, Sepah. I'll look forward to being back here again."

Back in Fitz's house Tony DeMarco was talking persuasively to a reluctant Fitz. "Come on, Fitz," DeMarco exhorted. "You're one of us. You're a pirate too. That's why we want you to represent us." Fitz wondered why he still felt shock when he was compared with an element he considered to be criminal.

"Fitz," DeMarco went on unctuously, "you're the best in this business. We wouldn't put up this money if we didn't know you were watching out for it. And naturally we don't want you to do it for nothing. We'll give you five percent of everything you can make with our five million. I also mentioned to McLaren that maybe you should be protected on the twenty million I put on deposit with his bank. If it wasn't for you he wouldn't have that deposit. He said he was going to talk to you about it."

"I don't want any commission on steering the right people to each other," Fitz said. "But what if we put this five million dollars into four or five trips and he comes up with three accidents. You end up losing."

"What's the chance of having three out of five accidents?"

"With Sepah I'd say slender, but it's a possibility."

"Of course it's a possibility. That's why you make so much money if you win. If you even double our money, just think what five percent of five million dollars is. Quarter of a million, right?" Fitz nodded. "Oh, I know what you're thinking, Fitz. If by any chance the money is lost you figure we'll be over here looking for you. No way. I give you my word. We just want the best there is working for us and if it doesn't work out we take our loss. Just the interest on that deposit in the numbered accounts with your friend's bank will do very nicely by us. What I'm saying, Fitz, is that we can afford to lose the five million. We don't want to, but we can afford to. So you just do the best you can for us, will you? Just think of that half million bucks you make and you got nothing to lose."

Fitz finally agreed with trepidation to manage the five-million-dollar fund and put it into the gold-re-exporting business via Sepah. DeMarco patted him on the back. "You've just made a decision you'll never regret."

At one o'clock Tim McLaren joined them and the three had a cocktail before lunch. DeMarco gave instructions to McLaren for Fitz to draw five million dollars out of the account at Fitz's discretion. McLaren nodded.

At that moment Joe Ryan came up to Fitz and asked him if he could see him for a moment. Fitz excused himself.

"What's the matter, Joe?" he asked.

"It's Ingrid. She disappeared sometime last night."

"Disappeared?"

"I went up to wake her for the luncheon business and she wasn't in her room. Her bed hadn't been slept in," Joe said. "Occasionally the girls have a date after work but they never stay out all night and certainly they get back in the morning in time for lunch."

"Any ideas, Joe?"

"One. Saqr. He was sitting at one of her tables as usual last night. I noticed he was being pretty attentive to her. He might have gotten her out of the place on the pretext of going for a ride in his Mercedes-Benz or something like that," Joe speculated.

Fitz thought about the possibility and remembered his conversation with Ingrid about not taking diamonds from the Arab customers. "That dumb bitch. I tried to tell her to be careful. Well, maybe everything's all right, she's just having a roll with Saqr and she'll be back for dinner."

"I'll certainly speak harshly to her," Joe promised.

"You do that. And afterward tell her to come see me." With that he returned to the table.

"Problems?" DeMarco asked.

Fitz nodded. "Ingrid seems to have disappeared from the premises. We think she's run off with Shaikh Saqr, the son of Shaikh Hamed."

Tim McLaren looked up in interest. "Saqr? His father keeps him on a pretty tight leash. I'm sure if Hamed thought that Saqr was even in a place like the Ten Tola Bar he'd deal very severely with his son. Hamed's one of the old-school shaikhs. He has very little use for Western customs. In fact, I think Fitz is the only Western man that Hamed ever took to."

"What are you going to do, Fitz?" DeMarco asked.

"There's not a damn thing I can do except hope that Saqr brings her back here in time for the evening trade." He made a helpless gesture with his hands. "There's nothing I can do about it now. We might as well enjoy our lunch."

Tim McLaren and Fitz saw Tony DeMarco off on the Beirut flight from the Dubai International Airport and then returned to the Ten Tola Bar. He found Joe and asked whether Ingrid had come back. Joe shook his head glumly.

Tim and Fitz sat at the majlis. They each ordered a drink and then Tim put a hand on Fitz's shoulder. "DeMarco suggested, and I quite concur, that you did a big service to the bank in bringing DeMarco to me. I want to work out some form of recognition."

"For me it's enough to have helped the economy of Dubai. Not that I had that much to do with it."

"DeMarco and I had a very frank talk for a full hour," Tim continued. "I could only come to the conclusion that the Vietnam War must be costing us about one hundred percent over its list price when I hear of the systematic rape of the American economy. Not that it's my business really. My business is money. If DeMarco hadn't given me two checks, one for twenty million dollars and another for five million, certified bank drafts on the Commercial Trading Bank of Hong Kong, I might doubt the enormity of the situation as he described it. DeMarco pointed out to me probably one of the most valuable pieces of deductive information that I've come across as a banker. There is no doubt in my mind after hearing of the financing depredations in Vietnam that the American dollar will have to be devalued, probably, I would say, by the end of 1971, certainly in 1972. DeMarco feels the same way. I'm going to write a special communiqué to the executive committee of the bank in New York and tell them why we can expect a devaluation of the American dollar."

"What does that mean to someone like me?" Fitz asked.

"It means, Fitz, that you are a very lucky American because you're living here. You can buy gold, all you want, and store it in our vaults. The price of gold has got to go way up from 35 dollars an ounce. It will probably hit 100 dollars an ounce, maybe even a little more, within six months after the devaluation of the American dollar."

"In other words, in the long run those Indians who are buying the gold smuggled into their country are getting a pretty good deal."

"Right. Sepah tells me he's selling gold for anywhere from 110 to 120 dollars an ounce in India right now. He's making a 200 percent profit on each one of those gold shipments. It wouldn't surprise me if by 1973, perhaps 1974, the Indians will be shipping their gold right back here and making a big profit on it. Even at the 110 to 120 they're paying the smugglers now."

Fitz considered the implications of Tim McLaren's statement. Finally he said, "Perhaps you have repaid any service I might have done you and the bank. How much longer do you think we'll be buying gold at 35 dollars an ounce?"

"At the most one year."

"In that case, Sepah had better work his dhows overtime for the next year. And I'm giving you an official order right now to take twenty thousand dollars out of my account and transfer it into ten-tola bars."

"I'm certainly going to do the same. If I can get permission from New York I'm going to buy gold for the bank's account. My God, it's stupefying how the economy of the United States is being raped and bled off in Vietnam." McLaren finished his drink. "Well, I'm going back to my house and take a plunge in the Gulf. Don't you miss your house on the beach?"

"Yes, I do, but of course it's better for me to be next to the place here. And in any case Sepah was more than generous to let me spend a full year in his house when he could have rented it at a high price."

"You certainly repaid him twenty times for that favor, Fitz.

Well, if you get a chance, drop over. I think the time has come to bring Emmy to Dubai. The house is finished, the new bank is complete, and I see at last real longevity for me as the bank's man on the Gulf."

"Good idea, Tim." Fitz looked unusually sad for a moment. "Every man should have his wife with him if he's really going to stay here."

CHAPTER 42

As Fitz waited beside the trim little Piper Cherokee outside the Trucial States Flying School hangar, he looked across the runway of the Sharjah airport. The three big four-engine Shackletons stood there, symbolic of the British political and military presence still very much in evidence on the Gulf. These were the airplanes used for RAF long-range reconnaissance flights. They were one of the many British tools for keeping close surveillance on all activities in and around the Arabian Gulf and the Indian Ocean as well as the Gulf of Oman, which the British still considered part of Her Majesty's territories and protectorates. He wondered if Brian Falmey had ordered a Shackleton to search for Sepah's dhow. Of course, basically the British supported the gold-exporting trade since a segment of the profits eventually went back into paying British firms for construction and engineering jobs in the Trucial States.

When the pilot had pulled the propeller through a few times and then stepped up into his seat, Fitz climbed in, sitting on the right. The Pakistani pilot started the engine and took off. On a map Fitz had shown the pilot the approximate location of the oasis where he knew Shaikh Saqr maintained his desert stronghold. Fitz, binoculars hanging around his neck, watched the ground as the pilot pulled into the air and headed northeast up the coastline toward Kajmira. It was a short flight to the town of Kajmira and through the binoculars Fitz recognized the old fort which Shaikh Hamed used as a beach house and special majlis. From the fort the plane turned east out over the trackless desert. Twenty minutes later Fitz was looking down at the oasis. It was completely walled in, about twenty acres of it, and within the walls was another walled-in tract of about five acres, he estimated. Saqr's residence stood inside it.

Telling the pilot to keep circling, Fitz probed the windows, which were nothing more than gaping apertures in the mud-brick fortress-like structure. For five minutes Fitz peered into the desert hideaway. He had seen and been in enough Arab residences to be able to recognize the women's wing or harem. This area had wooden louvered windows which could be closed against the heat, sun, and flying sand. He thought he saw forms at the louvered windows and then suddenly an unmistakably white arm reached out between the louvers and frantically waved. Moments later the arm was abruptly, violently jerked back out of sight. At the same time a squad of white-robed Arabs appeared on the roof of the large desert keep and aimed their rifles at the plane. The pilot gunned away from Saqr's residence, fighting for altitude with all the horsepower the small Cherokee had at its command. Fitz saw puffs of smoke come from the barrels of the rifles. However, he did not hear the telltale whine of a bullet through the fuselage. Well, he had established what it was he had flown here to find out. Ingrid indeed was in Saqr's harem and, since she had tried to signal the plane, was probably being held there against her will.

As the pilot flew back to the Sharjah airport Fitz considered his various courses of action. He could go to Ken Buttres and ask the Trucial Oman Scouts to send a motorized company to Saqr's desert fortress. However, in the first place, he doubted that Buttres would actually interfere with the doings of a son of the Ruler of Kajmira. In the second place, Fitz would be calling attention to the fact that the Ten Tola Bar was causing disruptions in the Trucial States by having women working there. And thirdly, Saqr and Fitz would be sitting together at a table in London in a week signing a very important oil-concession agreement. Grimly he remembered the repeated warnings he had given not only to Ingrid but to all the girls. They were there to make as much money as they could on tips and on the salary paid them by the Ten Tola Bar. They were making much more money than they could make in any other way short of out-and-out prostitution. In fact, they were probably making more money as waitresses at the Ten Tola Bar than they could have earned as whores. But they were in a dangerous part of the world for unmarried women. Undoubtedly Ingrid got a little greedy or maybe she really liked Saqr. He would like to think that she was enjoying her stay in the harem, but the sight of that wildly gesticulating arm made him doubt it.

Fitz noticed that they were two thirds of the distance from the Arabian Gulf to Oman. On an impulse he asked the pilot to fly over to the mountains and down the mountain line. He was curious to see the rolling sand dunes that he and Laylah had driven over coming back from Al Ain. The pilot reached the edge of the mountains and flew along them, the mountains on the pilot's side of the ship, the desert to Fitz's right outside his window. He examined the edge of the mountains with his binoculars. He picked out the pass which permitted entry into the hills and mountains of Oman. Just beyond the pass to the southwest Fitz could see the formidable miles of devastating sand hills he had driven through from Al Ain to get to Dubai.

The route from the coast of the Gulf to the mountain pass paralleled these miles of treacherous high sand dunes for eight miles before it wound its way into the forbidding wadis and crevices of the mountain areas where a large force of Communist PFLOAG guerrillas was building up. Once strong enough, this rebel force would surely surge up and spill over into the Musandam Peninsula and command the Arabian side of the Straits of Hormuz. Thus the Communists would be able to interdict at will the oil lifeline of the Western industrialized world.

When Fitz got back to his house he immediately summoned Joe Ryan. When Joe arrived he told him what had occurred. Joe nodded. "Just what I thought. The only way she'll get out is when he gets tired of her."

"I want you to get all the girls together in the guest-house lounge. I want to talk to them."

Thirty minutes later Fitz told the girls precisely what had happened to Ingrid and how he had seen her arm—at least he presumed it was Ingrid's arm—waving for help when the plane had flown over. He explained to the girls why there was no way he could help Ingrid. If he caused an incident now, every one of them would be deported from the Emirate and undoubtedly the Ten Tola Bar would have to operate with totally male personnel from then on.

"Ingrid was not kidnapped," Fitz pointed out. "She went

willingly with Saqr. And she disobeyed the most fundamental rule we have here. A girl does not go out with a customer after hours."

That evening Fitz sat around the Ten Tola Bar with a heavy heart. He hated the thought of the misuse to which he knew Ingrid was being put. Over and over again he asked himself what he could do and the answer was always the same. Nothing.

Two days before Fitz and Saqr were to leave for London to sign the new concession agreement, a wan, hollow-cheeked, stricken-looking Ingrid walked through the front door of the bar. It was six o'clock in the evening when Joe Ryan saw her come in. Despite her harried expression and bearing, Joe noticed that on the fingers of each of her hands she was wearing beautiful emerald, diamond, and ruby rings. Around her neck was a strand of what to Joe's practiced eye were natural white pearls. She was wearing the finest-quality caftan made for Arab women and the veil which would have concealed her features on the trip from Saqr's desert place to the Ten Tola Bar was thrown back from her head now. Joe took Ingrid by one of her bejeweled hands. "Come with me," he said severely. "We're going right in to see Mr. Lodd." Then: "Well, whatever he did to you, with you, up you, or down you he surely paid well for it."

Meekly Ingrid submitted to Joe's forceful pull on her hand and followed him across the crowded restaurant into the kitchen and through the pantry into Fitz's house. Joe called out for Fitz and he came downstairs from his office. When he saw Ingrid, he breathed a sigh of relief. Haggard as she looked, at least she seemed to be all right. Fitz noticed the rings on her fingers. "Was it worth it?"

Ingrid shook her head. "No," she whispered.

"You could have put us all in one hell of a lot of trouble. I almost got shot that day I flew over Saqr's place."

"Thank God you did. Maybe he wouldn't have sent me back if he didn't know that you knew where I was."

"Don't you realize what a terrible position you put yourself and all of us in? If I'd made a complaint, every girl in this establishment would have been kicked out of Dubai."

"I'm sorry," Ingrid whimpered.

Unable to restrain his curiosity, Fitz asked, "Well, at least tell me what happened?"

"I just wanted to go out for a ride on the desert. He said he had four-wheel drive with sand tires and it was very beautiful at night on the desert. Once he got me in the car he didn't stop driving for four hours. The sun was up when we got to his castle. Then he took me up to the harem. The other girls were all nice to me but I couldn't speak to them. None of them could speak English and I couldn't speak whatever it is they talk. For three days—" She started to break down and sob. Then she recovered her composure somewhat. "Then for three days he used me so violently and in so many horrible ways I couldn't believe it. He told me he was in love with me, that I would become his wife and the next queen of Kajmira. I knew he had three other wives because I'd seen them. Plus there were other Arab girls in the harem. They weren't much help. They're all afraid of him. He owns them like he owns furniture and his cars. Oh, what he did to me was dreadful." Involuntarily both of her hands went to her buttocks as though to protect the area between them.

Fitz nodded sympathetically to her. "Ingrid, you know you'll have to leave. I'd like to have you out of Dubai the very minute you feel well enough to go. Do you think you need medical attention?"

Ingrid shook her head. "It's too late now. I'll be all right. I know I have to leave. Can I just stay tonight? I'll go back to Beirut on any flight you tell me to tomorrow. I have friends there."

"Yes, and of course you have money too now. Not only what you made so far here but—" He took both of her hands and looked at the rings. "The jewelers in Beirut should pay you quite handsomely for those."

Ingrid started to cry. Fitz put an arm on her shoulder. "Just consider yourself a very, very lucky girl. All over Arabia there are blondes, captives for life, in places like the one you just left." He turned to Joe. "See that Ingrid is comfortable and make a reservation for her tomorrow on the first available flight to Beirut."

CHAPTER 43

Fitz arrived at Dubai International Airport to find the Kajmira contingent checking in for their flight. They were wearing the traditional *dish dasha* and *kuffiyah* as they prepared to board the jet to London. Saqr and his group were in high spirits. Any opportunity to get to Beirut, Switzerland, Paris, and particularly London was eagerly grasped. Neither Saqr nor Fitz made the slightest reference either by look or by verbal allusion to the abducted blond waitress.

Fitz, carrying in his briefcase the powers of attorney to sign for Sepah, Fender Browne, and Majid Jabir, sat in a different part of the first-class section from Saqr and his retinue. He would leave it to Abdul Hummard to handle the niceties of Saqr's visit. In his pocket Fitz had a letter he'd received two days ago from Laylah. This was a letter which he perhaps would and perhaps would not show to Lorenz Cannon and Abdul Hummard.

Once the jet had become airborne heading north toward Beirut, Fitz opened Laylah's letter and read it again. She made little mention of Thornwell since this communication was to apprise Fitz of the latest developments that she had learned regarding the Abu Musa situation. With the end of British domination of the Arabian Gulf in sight, further negotiations were taking place with the Shah and NIOC. The Shah had completely relinquished all the vigorous claims he had previously made on the island of Bahrain. The British Political Resident in Bahrain along with Brian Falmey, Political Agent in the Trucial States, which within the year would become known as the United Arab Emirates, had assured NIOC that they would be able to persuade the British Foreign Office Arabian Department to back up Iranian claims on Abu Musa and the extension of the three-mile limit to twelve miles, thus capturing the oil field in the concession Fitz had purchased.

Although no date had been set for Iran's takeover of half of Abu Musa, the time was not far off. Fitz should be prepared for an early declaration of the double sovereignty of Abu Musa which would be followed in a matter of weeks by the announcement of the unilateral extension which the Shah had been assured would be backed up by the British Navy if necessary. The letter ended with "I hope this is all of interest and use to you, Fitz. I know you're doing the right thing making the deal with Hemisphere. If any company can fight this cozy little international conspiracy, Hemisphere can. I just hope you can get the deal signed with them before they learn how imminent this declaration is. Affectionately, Laylah."

When the plane was an hour away from Beirut, Saqr and his group one by one went into the men's room and returned wearing Western garb, their robes in the suitcase in which they'd been carrying their suits. By the time the plane landed in Beirut four very Westernized Arabs had just finished a bottle of champagne and were preparing for landing. The layover in Beirut was an hour and then they were herded back on the plane again, which took off for London.

Flying from east to west they made up several hours because of the time difference between Beirut and London, and it was just getting dark when they deplaned. Abdul Hummard was there to meet them. He and Saqr embraced and then Abdul shook hands with the other members of Saqr's delegation. Abdul also warmly welcomed Fitz to London and told him that his favorite photographer would be waiting for him at her flat. "I'll take Saqr to the suites we have arranged for him at the Grosvenor House. You take a cab over to Lynn's and I'll call you there later. I've arranged a party for tomorrow night. However, if Saqr is impatient for entertainment we can provide him with such tonight as well."

"I think Lynn ought to do her photo number again," said Fitz.

"Of course. Although she told me you didn't like her doing that."

"In this case it is apt to prove valuable."

Fitz put his suitcases in a taxi and gave the driver Lynn's address in Kensington. Less than an hour later he was walking up the stairs to Lynn's photographic studio. She opened the door for him and he dropped his suitcases and hugged her. Lynn held him tightly as they kissed passionately for long moments. "Are you still coming back with me, love?" he asked finally.

"Of course I am, my darling. I can hardly wait."

"Great."

"Are you hungry?"

"Yes." He grinned suggestively at her. "As for food, Middle East Airlines took exceptionally good care of me." With the door closed behind them Fitz again embraced Lynn and waltzed her slowly across the expanse of her photographic studio through the open door of the bedroom. He was pleased to see that the bedspread had been turned down and the bed itself opened and turned back.

"Fitz," she laughed. "What have you got in mind?"

"What I've had in mind each day I've been waiting to get back here," he replied.

He kissed her and she sat down on her bed, pulling him down beside her. The loose sweater and tweed skirt she wore looked as though they would come off easily. Lynn could see what he was thinking. She winked impishly. "Your mind isn't really very hard to read, Fitz. Why don't you take your shoes off and get comfortable."

Fitz kicked off his loafers and took his jacket off, swinging it onto the back of a chair. Then he undid his tie and threw that on top of his jacket. They stood up together and Fitz ran his hands underneath the sweater Lynn had on. His hands found her skin and ran up to the full unrestrained breasts.

Lynn reached above her head with both hands and in one simple movement Fitz pulled the sweater up over her head and threw it onto the chair. Then he buried his face between her breasts for a moment, his hands holding them, thumbs caressing her nipples. Lynn reached for his belt, unbuckled it, pulled open his pants, and started to push them down his legs. Fitz stepped out of first one leg and then the other and kicked the pants onto the chair. In moments they were both naked and tumbling into bed together.

It was as good as their first time all over again. Gently, her fingers stroking and caressing, she guided him into her and then cried out, "Oh God, Fitz, I've needed it so."

Frenziedly they moved together, crying out to each other, and in thirty seconds they had consummated a total mutual climax to their lovemaking. Afterward they lay entwined for far longer than the brief moments it had taken to achieve the state of euphoric satisfaction they now both knew. Time slipped away and then they were suddenly startled, their calm shattered, by the strident ringing of the telephone.

"Abdul," Lynn snorted in disgust. "Well, it could have been worse. He could have called us about twenty minutes ago." She picked up the phone. It was Abdul and he asked if he could speak to Fitz. Lethargically Lynn handed Fitz the receiver.

"Yes, Abdul," he said.

Fitz heard Abdul chuckling on the other end of the line. "I tried to give you two children as long as I could before calling but I have to talk to you now. Saqr is all for the party tomorrow but he also wants me to do something for him tonight. I think I've taken good enough care of him. Lorenz Cannon will be in tomorrow morning from New York. His chief counsel, Shuster, is here now and several of his executives. The signing is set for the day after tomorrow. It's really just a formality since everyone has approved the papers."

Fitz breathed a sigh of relief. "Then why can't we have the signing tomorrow and get it over with?" he asked.

"Because we have Saqr and his Arab legion here, all of them expecting one big party. Now I've set up an orgy, a hell of an orgy, the same girls we had at the last one, all blondes, you remember?"

"Yeah, I remember them of course. Does that mean you need Lynn?"

"She's the best I know for this sort of a job. By the way, Saqr definitely told me he wanted to keep tomorrow's party an all-Arab show, if you know what I mean. I think he feels your presence might be a bit inhibiting. Anything happen in Dubai between you and Saqr?"

"I'll tell you all about it. You remember Ingrid?"

"Do I remember Ingrid!"

"O.K. Saqr kidnapped her and held her out in the desert for a week. I guess every time he sees me he feels a little guilty."

Abdul Hummard chuckled. "So that's it? Well, there's nothing more for you to do tonight. Just be in the office tomorrow morning at ten. And tell Lynn she's got a job tomorrow night."

Lynn took the phone receiver from Fitz and hung it up. Then she turned to him. "How about a little nightcap and some cheese and crackers or something?" she asked. "Middle East Airlines did not take care of me."

Fitz was waiting impatiently for Lynn at her apartment. She was still doing her photographic scene on Saqr and his companions. Fitz had dined with Lorenz Cannon and his group. The Hemisphere Petroleum Company executives were all in high spirits at the prospect of soon spudding in offshore in the Arabian Gulf. They were producing oil in Libya but the alarming trend toward the nationalization of the oil production by the wild-eyed, fanatical revolutionary Colonel Qaddafi, the military dictator of the country, had reduced every oil-producing company in Libya to a nervous state.

Fitz decided that it would be in nobody's best interests to disclose that Laylah had written to him repeating her previous warnings. He chose to bask in the general atmosphere of optimism that prevailed. It was planned that just as soon as Fender Browne, working with McDermott out of Kuwait, had constructed the platform, it would be towed out to the site, set up over the structure, and drilling operations would begin.

Lynn finally returned from Hummard's party about midnight and described the orgy. "That Saqr is a wild blood." She shuddered. "He really likes to make the girls scream when he buggers them. The randy desert bastard didn't let a one of them escape his rather special attention."

Fitz winced. "I wish you hadn't seen it. And you never will again," he added positively.

"What is the panic with Saqr?"

"You never know when we'll need a little muscle with him," Fitz replied noncommittally. "And now that that bit of nastiness is done with, let's get on to happier pursuits."

"That suits me, darling. Mind if I have a nightcap first, or with, if you like?" She grinned and went to her efficiency kitchen.

The signing on the following afternoon had been planned as an impressive occasion. The Western parties to the agreement had provided a dozen souvenir pens, all of which would be used in signing. The Arabian Department of the Foreign Office had made

available a formal meeting room and a photographer had been
hired by Abdul, a male photographer, to record the occasion for
posterity.

Shaikh Saqr sat behind the desk, wearing his *dish dasha* and
kuffiyah. The Arab robes were a concession to the photographer, whose pictures of this occasion would be widely viewed
back on the Arabian Gulf. His retinue was standing behind him.
Lorenz Cannon stood to one side of Saqr and Fitz on the other.
Sir Hugh MacIntosh and two clerks from the Arabian Department stood at the end of the table, and then the documents, decorated with red seals and green ribbons, were placed on the table
before Shaikh Saqr.

Every word in the documents had been carefully checked over
during the previous day and initialed in pencil by lawyers for
Shaikh Hamed, Hemisphere, and the law firm Majid Jabir used in
London. Also, Sir Hugh had carefully perused the agreements and
had prepared a letter addressed to himself, as head of the Arabian
Department, Foreign and Commonwealth Office, which would be
signed by Shaikh Saqr. Its second paragraph read: "In application
of our rights under Article 19 of the Concession Agreement with
Hemisphere Petroleum Company and James F. Lodd et al., we
shall not give our approval to the transfer of the concession to any
person or company except on the recommendation of Her Majesty's Government."

Sir Hugh MacIntosh opened the proceedings with flowery formal phrases and then suggested that Mr. Cannon and Mr. Lodd
sign. A chair was provided for Lorenz Cannon first, and then Fitz,
to sit down and sign with all twelve pens the concession
agreement. At that point Lorenz Cannon placed a bank
draft for two hundred fifty thousand dollars before Shaikh Saqr,
who examined it a moment, with ill-concealed satisfaction. This
brought the total signature bonus to one million dollars. Then,
letter by letter, pen by pen, he signed his name and with his father's signet ring he stamped the official seal of Kajmira on the
document. All the signatories to the agreement signed four additional copies and then Saqr signed the political agreement with
the Arabian Department and in return received Sir Hugh's letter
attesting to British acceptance of the concession, and the formal

proceedings were over. Now must come the traditional party, not like the orgiastic scene Abdul had arranged the night before. This was to be a party in a suite at the Grosvenor House.

Congratulations were extended all around and Cannon handed Fitz the check for a quarter of a million dollars to reimburse his group for what they had already paid to the Ruler of Kajmira.

The party was rather stiff at first and Saqr still seemed to be avoiding Fitz as much as possible. After the first two rounds of drinks, however, Saqr seemed a little more at ease. Fitz decided that in the interests of future relations he had better make the move to show the Ruler's son that there was no animosity on his part as a result of Ingrid's kidnapping. Indeed, the solemnity of the occasion had been such that Fitz wondered if a man like himself, who entered into important negotiations and closings, should own a place like the Ten Tola Bar. But that was something he would face up to at a later date.

"I look forward to many prosperous years working with you, Shaikh Saqr, and of course with His Highness, your father."

Fitz put his hand out. Saqr shook it and obviously appreciated the sign of appeasement. His mouth contorted into a wide, toothy smile behind his black beard, the mustache melting into the heavy chin cover.

"I, too, and my father look forward to a long and profitable relationship, Mr. Lodd," he replied warmly if formally.

Sir Hugh MacIntosh joined them and talked convivially of old times on the Gulf and of his fond memories of Saqr's father. Fitz, with Laylah's last letter still on his person, could not fathom the British outlook. Surely Sir Hugh would have some inkling about the plotting between the Gulf Political Resident, his subordinate Brian Falmey, Political Agent in Dubai, and the Shah's Director of the NIOC. Had Sir Hugh just attested an agreement which Her Majesty's Government would later repudiate? If so, had he done so knowingly?

After two hours of drinks and canapés Fitz told Lorenz Cannon he would meet him the next morning and map final plans for the Kajmira operation, and then bidding Saqr and Abdul Hummard good evening—Sir Hugh had already taken his leave—Fitz left the waning party and made for Lynn's flat posthaste.

Majid Jabir was at the airport at two in the morning to meet
Fitz and Lynn and shepherd them through Customs and Immigration. Before he left Dubai, Fitz had confided in Majid that he
was bringing back a young woman of whom he was very fond to
spend a few days with him in Dubai. He also admitted to his
friend and partner that she was of Jewish origin but completely
nonpolitical. Her interest and her livelihood was photography. He
did not mention she would be making her pilgrimage to Jerusalem
after leaving Dubai.

Fitz briefly filled Majid in on what had happened in London.
He would take Lynn to his apartment, get her settled, and then
they would join him at the majlis, where, late though it was, the
group—Fender Browne, Tim McLaren, and Sepah—were waiting.

Lynn was enthusiastic at the idea of seeing his place immediately and she let Fitz merely pile her suitcases on the living-room
floor while she went to the bathroom and then walked with him
through the kitchen into the restaurant, surprisingly busy for almost three in the morning.

"My God! I don't believe what I'm seeing," she exclaimed,
glancing at her watch.

"It's boom town, Arabia," Fitz replied. His seat at the majlis
and a seat to his right were open and Fitz and Lynn sat down. He
introduced her around the table and then brought his partners up
to date. Everything had been signed. They all speculated on the
strange fact that the British would have attested the agreement
fully expecting, if Laylah Smith's information was correct, to vio-
late it.

From his pocket Fitz withdrew the check for two hundred fifty
thousand dollars and handed it to Tim McLaren. "O.K., we're
out of this deal with most of our money back and twenty-five percent of future profits. Personally I think we're going to do all
right."

"I feel we've done the wisest thing," Majid Jabir agreed. "Never
forget 'perfidious Albion.'"

After more guarded discussion—nobody was sure of Lynn yet—
the majlis adjourned, and Fitz, after saying hello to Joe Ryan, escorted Lynn back through the kitchen to his quarters.

"What would you think of a swim?" he suggested. "It's all very
private back here and it's a beautiful hot night."

"I'd love it, Fitz." And without more ado Lynn stripped off her clothes and plunged into the pool. Fitz was right behind her.

"What an exciting milieu you have created, Fitz." Lynn lay on her back in the water, her fluttering hands keeping her on the surface. "I love it already. I can hardly wait to start taking pictures. I think I'm really going to love the Middle East. What a tragedy that there has to be this terrible schism out here. Why is it that we can't all live together and enjoy each other's countries?"

"After you've been out here awhile you'll begin to understand. Of course, here in the Trucial States people are removed from the conflict and their only thought is business. Tomorrow you'll see the Creek in action."

Lynn turned over in the water and swam around the pool, ending up beside Fitz. They held each other tightly in waist-high water at the shallow end of the pool. "This is what a working girl in London dreams about," she sighed. "Nude under an Arabian night sky, in a swimming pool, being held by a virile lover. Have you done this much, Fitz?" she asked. "You have enough lovely girls working for you."

"As a matter of fact, this is the first time I have played in this pool naked with a girl. I was telling you the truth in London when I said you're the only girl I've been with since the first time we were together in your studio."

Lynn planted a watery kiss on his lips. "How beautiful to be doing something with you when it's the first time for both of us."

"You will also take the virginity of my house," he said seriously and then laughed at himself. "Lord, I sound like a stuffy one, even to myself. Anyway, shall we go in and start building memorable moments in the history of my home?"

"I think that's a lovely idea." Lynn walked up the steps and out of the pool. Fitz admired her form and the graceful way she walked across the patio, and then followed her.

The luncheon customers were arriving by the time Fitz and Lynn had arisen, taken a swim, eaten breakfast, and dressed. "In the interests of some photographic experimentation I'm going to show you something that nobody in Dubai but my manager, Joe Ryan, has seen," Fitz announced as they were standing in the upstairs lounge between the bedroom and the office. "This is really my one big secret."

"I feel honored that I'm receiving so many firsts. To be the first girl you've made love to in your new house and now—whatever is now."

Fitz unlocked the door to his office. "This is where I work, keep my records, make phone calls, and in general keep my business in order." He closed the door after them and walked over to the picture of the dhow, which he swung back, giving a panoramic view of the interior of the Ten Tola Bar.

Lynn caught her breath in surprise. She hadn't even thought about Fitz's house being directly adjacent to the wall of the restaurant. "What does it look like from the other side?" she asked.

"Just decorative glass paneling."

Lynn moved closer to the one-way window and watched the activity below. "You must feel like quite the lord and master up here surveying his domain."

"Could you take pictures through the window?" Fitz asked.

"Yes. There's enough light. If I'd brought a telephoto lens I could probably get close-ups of all your guests. Now if you could just hear what they're saying you'd know everything that's going on in this part of the world."

Fitz laughed uneasily. Nobody, not even Joe Ryan, knew about the bugs he himself had planted in the strategic tables. "Sometime you might try to snap a few shots for posterity." He pointed out one of the corner tables. "Over there sits Jean Louis Serrat, the mysterious Frenchman who is involved in oil, arms, and reputedly such raw materials of the dope trade as opium and hashish. I wouldn't mind having a picture of everyone who comes in here to have a conference with him."

"I'll do the best I can for you, Fitz," Lynn answered cheerfully. "Why didn't you tell me to bring a telephoto lens?"

"Never thought of it. Ready for lunch?" Lynn nodded. "Let's go. And don't stare up at the other side of this window when we're down below."

Fitz and Lynn enjoyed a leisurely week together during which he took her to Fender Browne's oil field supply storage facilities on the Deira side of the Creek above the bridge. Although he had not heard any more about the Abu Musa limits being extended, he was anxious to get on location and started drilling. He and Fender Browne discussed the progress being made on the rig. It was going slower than it should, Fitz thought, and he was frankly worried. He was the only representative of Hemisphere on the spot, he reminded Browne, and it was his responsibility to get the rig ready on time.

Their last night together before Lynn would leave for Tehran and Israel they did not visit the Ten Tola Bar. Peter served them dinner on the patio beside the pool.

"Fitz, it's been a beautiful vacation," Lynn said after they had finished eating and were sipping an after-dinner drink. "It just went so fast. I hate leaving you."

"Then don't," he replied ardently. "I wish you'd settle in with me here."

"I can't. My schedule is all very sensibly worked out and I'll have one week of sightseeing and photographing in Israel before going home just in time to get back to work before I lose all my clients."

"I hope you lose Abdul."

"I promise, darling, no more orgies except for those you and I have alone together."

"You'll send me the shots you took here when you get back?"

"Of course. You really should have a dark room so I could develop everything for you here."

"Come back and set it up for me. As a matter of fact, you could go around asking people if they want their pictures taken for ten rials. The photo girls make a lot of money in New York and London nightclubs."

"I'll keep that in mind. It would be better than handling Abdul's jobs."

Neither Fitz nor Lynn overly sentimentalized their relationship. They loved each other but were not in love. Sexually they were beautifully satisfying to each other and Lynn had thought up some exciting and innovative experiments. First in and around the pool and then one midnight her *pièce de résistance*. They had left the restaurant for a swim and afterward Fitz followed her upstairs, but instead of turning into the bedroom she stood there, drops of water spangling her body, and asked Fitz to open his office. He got the key, opened it, and went in after her, closing the door, as always, behind him.

Lynn went over to the painting which shielded the one-way glass window and pulled it back, standing there in the nude looking down at the capacity-business room. Then she lay on the table beside the secret pane of glass, her buttocks on the edge of the table, her feet on the floor. Fitz felt himself becoming fully, overwhelmingly aroused despite the hundred and fifty or more faces just below them, many looking directly at the glass separating Lynn's enticing body from their gaze.

Slowly Lynn raised her legs until they formed a V above her. The calves of her legs rested against his shoulders as this fantastic girl ripped away the last shreds of his inhibitions, about which she liked to tease him. He leaned over her, his arms sliding under her back and shoulders, and held her tightly as the full force of his vigor plunged to her. She turned her head to look down at the customers a moment and he followed her glance.

"None of you people ever got it like this," she shouted, and then devoted all attention and energies to meeting Fitz's passionate thrusts.

Fitz thought about that moment as they sipped their apéritifs. Lynn was leaving him with many memorable moments on which to reflect when he was alone in his home. "I hope you come back for another visit, Lynn," he said sincerely.

"I want to, Fitz. Let's write often and when you're ready for me to come back, let me know. I'll see if I can get away. I'm planning to take an advanced course in cinematography when I get back. I'm just sorry we didn't get up to Kajmira this trip."

"Supposing we ran into Saqr. He must be back from London by now. Although he's probably out in the desert resting up after his exertions closing the deal." They both snickered.

At the airport Fitz saw Lynn off for Tehran the next morning. "I think I love you more than casually, Fitz," she said, as though admitting to breaching an agreement between them. "Just as well I'm going."

"I'm not sure I'm staying so casual myself," Fitz replied. "Come back whenever you want to."

"I don't want to go."

They walked out as far as Fitz was allowed to accompany her.

"I wish we could kiss again," he said, "but the Arabs consider it poor taste in public."

"I know. I'll think about the kiss we had at the pool this morning. *Au revoir*, Fitz."

She turned from him and presented her passport and ticket to the guard at the gate and after being cleared walked through. Fitz waited at the airport until Lynn's flight took off for Tehran. He couldn't help think about the time he put Laylah on this flight. For a moment he felt the old void in his psyche he had known when he first realized Laylah was no longer in love with him, if indeed she ever had been.

CHAPTER 44

Through the one-way window in his office Fitz watched the girls wait on the Western businessmen and Arabs having lunch at the Ten Tola Bar. It was three months since Lynn's visit. Sometimes, as the girls came and went, he was tempted to take one for himself, but he had vowed he would never let himself become intimate with any of the girls that worked at the Ten Tola Bar and so far he had kept the promise.

It was important to preserve strict discipline at all times—he did not want a repeat of the Saqr incident. The desert lecher had taken to coming to the Ten Tola Bar and ogling the blondes, but now when a girl joined the staff, she was told by Joe Ryan in no uncertain terms not to date the customers. Then the terrible case history of Ingrid was cited. It became more grisly each time it was told. All the girls knew about Ingrid, the beautiful blonde who had been kidnapped by Shaikh Saqr and taken out to his desert palace. The sexual abuse that the girls could expect from certain Arabs was made clear to them. Saqr never again persuaded a girl to take a late-night drive with him.

Fitz of late had been listening to conversations that might be interesting to his CIA contact in Beirut. Abe Ferutti had made several visits to Dubai and had complimented Fitz highly on the manner in which he had bugged the tables in his restaurant. The spy spent hours looking down through the one-way window, tuning in on one conversation after another. So far it had become obvious that small shipments of guns and ammunition were coming through the various creeks, ports, and beaches along this part of the Arabian Gulf. They assumed that most of the arms were being sold to the Communist-led rebels in the mountains of Oman.

When Fitz obtained any positive information about a definite

OIL   389

landing point for arms or the time and route of a truckload of
guns going across the desert to the Oman hills, he passed it on to
Ken Buttres. The commander of the Trucial Oman Scouts was always grateful for this information. However, he had yet to interdict the first arms truck on its way into Oman.

When Fitz asked him why he hadn't taken a squadron out and
stopped and searched a truck, the answer was always the same. It
was the job of the Trucial Oman Scouts to keep peace between
the various rulers and ensure that the objectives of the Political
Agents and the Political Resident on behalf of Her Majesty's
Government were carried out. Interdicting contraband was the
job of the police, not the Trucial Oman Scouts.

Frequently, and without revealing his source, Ken Buttres had
informed the local police commandants about possible loads of
contraband coming through their area of responsibility. Even the
police were reluctant to stop and search trucks that might be on a
mission backed by one of the local rulers to whom they were con-
tracted. As Ken Buttres said to Fitz, "We don't hesitate to carry
out the important missions. Anything of direct interest to Her
Majesty's Government receives immediate and thorough attention."

As usual, Fitz noted with satisfaction, the luncheon crowd was
heavy. There were even people waiting at the bar for a table.
Somehow Joe Ryan managed to make everybody feel important,
and even when he had to seat people at the bar and ask them to
wait, he did it in a way that made them feel he had a personal interest in them.

There was a knock at his office door. Fitz swung the picture
over the window and went to the door. He looked through the
peephole and saw Peter, his servant. Peter handed him a familiar-
looking blue envelope. It had been almost two months since he
last heard from Laylah. He wrote frequent letters to her, telling
her about the Ten Tola Bar and passing on any information of an
intelligence nature which might be interesting to the U. S. Embassy in Tehran. Sometimes she replied and sometimes she did
not, but those few letters he received expressed her appreciation
for the scraps of intelligence he was able to send her.

He tore open the letter from her and devoured it. Every week or
ten days, she reported, she had dinner with the deputy to the Di-

rector of the NIOC, who by now was hopelessly enamored of her. It made Courty angry, she said, but her friend thoroughly unburdened himself each time they were together and gave her information about oil policy which had been highly useful to the American Ambassador. She had just returned home from dinner and was immediately writing to him. Apparently the Trucial state of Sharjah, which claimed sovereignty over the island of Abu Musa, although recognizing Iran's right to use it for a military base to protect the Gulf and also recognizing Iran's right to split oil revenues, had just completed a deal with an oil company which would operate the oil field nine miles off the Abu Musa coast. Iran was now ready to back Sharjah in its declaration of a twelve-mile limit.

"Fitz, I don't know what you can do about this," she wrote. "You had better inform Mr. Cannon right away. I don't know whether you are actually drilling yet or not. I do know that the British Government is firmly behind this move and the Shah has dropped his claim on Bahrain. So obviously a deal was made and it is about to be consummated."

Laylah went on to mention that Thornwell had definitely decided that there was no point in pursuing the financing for his communications network at this time. Not that he was giving up. He would go back to the United States and wait for the Arabs to start and lose another war and then be right back again. Fitz detected a wistful note in the letter. Apparently Thornwell had not asked her to accompany him back to the States. He wondered whether he should take another trip to Tehran. Probably it would be best to wait until Thornwell was well out of Iran.

Fitz swung the painting of the dhow back away from the one-way window and looked down to see whether Fender Browne had come into the Ten Tola Bar for lunch as he almost always did. He didn't see him but decided to go down and wait.

By the time Fitz had walked into the Ten Tola Bar, Fender Browne had arrived. They sat at the majlis together. Fitz told Browne about the letter he had just received. Browne nodded. "I've heard that Sharjah is about to grant a concession to an oil company. The interesting thing is that no seismic exploration has been conducted of the Sharjah territorial waters. So obviously they expect to take over our oil field."

"When can we start to place the well jacket and put up the platform?"

"As a matter of fact, I heard from McDermott this morning. The barges are being marshaled now just below Kuwait. They're already loading the platform and rig. They should be ready to come down in a few days. I've already chartered the survey ship *Marlin*. It's on its way now from Bahrain and should be tied up on the Creek tomorrow."

"I'm going to try and call Cannon now and tell him what the situation is," Fitz said. "As soon as the *Marlin* gets into the Creek, you and I had better go out and set the marker buoy. Everything we can do to hurry the operation is important. If we have the marker buoy set by the time the barges get to the site, they can start right in placing the well jacket." Fitz looked at his watch. "If I get through before you leave I'll come back and join you."

"I'll wait here for you, Fitz. We could actually go out in the *Marlin* tomorrow and start setting the buoy."

It took Fitz over an hour to get through to Cannon in New York. The president of Hemisphere Petroleum Company barked back instructions. "You get the survey ship out on the site the minute it comes into Dubai. Tell them to get that marker buoy down as fast as they can. I want you to stay right where you are so that I can reach you if I have to. I'm sending Irwin Shuster to London on the next plane and from there he'll go on to Dubai. Jack Tepper is already in London. I'll call him now and tell him to get down to you as soon as possible. Get the well jacket placed and start putting down the platform the instant the barges arrive on site."

"Right," Fitz replied. "Any and all muscle Hemisphere has in London they'd better get busy using."

"I told you before, Fitz, that Political Agent down there in Dubai can't get away with breaking international law. I'll have Irwin go to the Foreign Minister, Douglas-Home, personally, as soon as he gets to London. Let's get busy now."

The following morning Fitz went down to the survey craft, where Fender Browne was waiting for him. The survey ship was a sturdy one-hundred-foot vessel on which the equipment had been

loaded to locate the underwater structure and place the marker
buoy. The pinger locator would give the exact spot where it had
been decided to place the well jacket. Then into the two hundred
feet of water the anchor would be dropped and the marker buoy
would float above it. The captain of the *Marlin* was British and
the ship was British-registered. The Union Jack floated in the
wind that blew down the Creek.

"We'll stay in touch by the radiotelephone," Fitz said to
Fender Browne. "After you've set the marker buoy remain out
there until the barges come in and then get them started placing
the jacket. In the meantime I'll try to keep track of political developments here and let you know as things progress. Obviously time
is of the essence. If we can just start drilling before Brian Falmey
decides to do something to stop us I think we'll be all right. I
don't see how they can stop us once we've spudded in no matter
what kind of phony declarations Sharjah makes unilaterally."

Within the hour the *Marlin* pulled away from its berth beside
the Creek and started out toward the Gulf beyond.

Before dark Fitz contacted Fender Browne on his radio. Fitz
had installed a radio tower above his house and put in an expensive but highly useful radiotelephone system. He could talk to
ships, and on shortwave he could contact the worldwide network
of ham radio operators. He expected that Hemisphere would soon
have its own helicopter and airplane, both of which he would be
able to talk to on his radio. Fitz got through to the *Marlin* and
Fender Browne was soon on with him. "How's it going out there?"
Fitz asked.

"We've been followed ever since we left the Creek. That goddam Shackleton from Sharjah has been flying around us for the
last four hours. We'll start pinging first thing in the morning and
we ought to have the marker buoy set before the end of the day."

"That's good," Fitz replied. "I'll try to put a call through now
to Cannon and tell him what's happening."

Brian Falmey stared out the window of his office in the Ruler's
headquarters building. It was noontime. The *Marlin*'s departure
from the Creek had not escaped his notice. He had seen the
Marlin enter the Creek and stay several hours at the oil field supply dock. Then she'd gone back out into the Gulf. Falmey imme-

diately called the RAF station in Sharjah and assigned a four-
engine Shackleton to keep the *Marlin* under surveillance from the
air. Now twenty-four hours later the reports were coming in.

The survey ship had spent six hours following a grid pattern
and had apparently located the structure, since as of now a marker
buoy was floating on the surface of the Gulf nine miles off Abu
Musa Island indicating the spudding-in point for the offshore rig
when it arrived. The Shackleton had also sighted a barge convoy
carrying the platform and rig coming down the Gulf from Kuwait.
The Shackleton report indicated that within twenty-four hours
the barges should be on the site of the marker buoy.

Falmey had his orders from his superior, the Political Resident
in Bahrain. Now it was up to him to act. Impatiently he stood up
and walked into the reception room where an English girl was
typing furiously. He watched as she finished her task and pulled
the last piece of paper from the typewriter and handed him the
document.

He read: "Supplementary decree concerning the territorial sea
of the Emirate of Sharjah and its dependencies." His eye went on
down the page and he smiled grimly as he read Article 1. "The
territorial sea of the Emirate of Sharjah and its dependencies extends into the open sea to a distance of twelve nautical miles from
the base lines on the coast or the mainland and of the islands of
the Emirate." He read the next page and a half and, satisfied that
it was in order, he placed the document and several copies in his
attaché case.

"Now, Miss Frober, I don't expect to be back in the office again
today. If the PR calls from Bahrain, I can be reached at Shaikh
Khalid's office in Sharjah and after that I'll be going up to Kajmira to see Shaikh Hamed." With that Falmey left his office and
walked out into the automobile enclosure. His driver was waiting
for him.

Shaikh Khalid received the *mua'atamad* with much deference,
and, smiling broadly in satisfaction, he signed the declaration unilaterally claiming a twelve-mile limit around the island of Abu
Musa. Falmey left the original with Shaikh Khalid and took two
signed copies with him.

Falmey's next stop was the RAF headquarters at the Sharjah air
base. He walked into the flight operations center and asked for a

helicopter. Ten minutes later he was airborne heading up the coast for Kajmira.

One thing about the helicopter, Falmey thought. You don't have to send a signal that you're coming. The helicopter settled down on an empty patch of sand not far from the fort Hamed used for his private meetings. Falmey waited until the sandstorm created by the helicopter's rotors had subsided and then he stepped out and walked across to the fort. The two guards came to attention, the door opened, and Falmey walked in.

Shaikh Hamed and his son Shaikh Saqr were sitting in the small meeting room. Falmey walked in holding his attaché case and went through the usual greetings. After a second cup of coffee he finally got down to business. "As Your Highness is aware, Shaikh Khalid of Sharjah has for a number of years claimed that Sharjah territorial limits run twelve miles into the sea, not three miles as has been customary. It is the Ruler of Sharjah's contention, Your Highness, that the concession you granted to Hemisphere Petroleum unlawfully extends to within three miles of Abu Musa. It has further come to our attention that the Hemisphere Petroleum Company is moving barges down from Kuwait and has already placed a marker nine miles from Abu Musa where obviously it intends to drill."

Falmey opened his attaché case with a sharp snap and removed a copy of the signed document, which he handed to Shaikh Hamed. "Here is the document which proclaims the twelve-mile limit. I believe that eventually we will be able to mediate this dispute. However, in the meantime I would recommend to you that you tell your concessionaire, Hemisphere, not to start drilling operations until the dispute is settled. I'm sure that it will not be much more than three or four months before we settle this situation. I know you'll understand, Your Highness."

Hamed listened and was silent for some moments. He was not taken by surprise since Fitz had called him the day before to warn him that he might receive this call from the *mud'atamad*. Hamed weighed his words carefully. He was very well aware of the consequences of defying the British and yet this representative of Her Majesty's Government was preparing to take away from Shaikh Hamed and his small state their big opportunity for wealth and progress. Hamed knew that there would never be a settlement of the dispute in his favor.

"I signed the agreement with Hemisphere Petroleum granting them a concession which ran to within three miles of the Abu Musa shores. It was you yourself who gave Mr. Lodd the chart of the concession so that there would be no misunderstanding of where he could and where he could not take his drilling rig. This same chart was attested to in London when we signed the agreement a second time taking Hemisphere Petroleum into the consortium. The head of the Arabian Department of the British Foreign Office was at the signing and attested to it. Therefore I do not see how you can do anything but guarantee the concession which I gave to Hemisphere."

"Your Highness probably doesn't realize it but a new factor has emerged which we consider to have serious implications. This is in regards to the attitude of Iran. The Iranian Government has made it clear to us that if Hemisphere goes ahead with exploration in the disputed area, it would take action to stop the company's operations. You know what that means? It means that the Iranian Navy would if necessary destroy the barges and rigs."

"Her Majesty's Government could easily stop the Iranian Navy from carrying out such a threat." Hamed followed the riposte with a long silence. Then: "The future well-being of my country and all my subjects depends upon the successful operations of Hemisphere Petroleum. We have always looked to England to guarantee our interests. When we signed the political agreement it meant to me, as it does to the other rulers, British backing. Now you tell me that after giving your guarantee you want to go back on it. You want me to go to my concessionaires. You want me to tell them, after they've already paid the signature bonus and have spent millions of dollars of their money on putting together the equipment necessary to carry out this drilling program —you want me to tell them they must stop."

Hamed could not conceal the agitation he felt. His aged hands shook as he talked. His voice quivered. "No, I do not see how I can ask them to stop. I will discuss this situation with them. Perhaps voluntarily they will stop for a while to see what transpires. But I have no faith in a fair settlement unless the British Government backs up its guarantee."

"HMG didn't guarantee anything," Falmey shot back. "We merely acknowledged the fact that we are aware of the agreement that you signed with Hemisphere." There was a silence as the impasse hung forebodingly between the *mua'atamad* and the Ruler.

Finally Falmey stood up. "Before I leave Your Highness, let me once more strongly recommend that you stop Hemisphere Petroleum from going ahead with its plans to drill on the concession presently granted, if that drilling is to take place within the twelve-mile limit around Abu Musa. Her Majesty's Government will take steps to ensure that the settlement is completed in the shortest possible time. As regards the attitude of Iran, Her Majesty's Government will use their best efforts to try and clear up the present unsatisfactory situation." And concluding, Falmey unctuously went through the ritual. "Please accept my highest regards and respects, Your Highness." With that he turned and left the majlis.

Hardly had the helicopter started to charge up its rotors to take the Political Agent back to Sharjah when Shaikh Hamed had his son Shaikh Saqr on the phone to summon Fitz to Kajmira to discuss the situation. Fitz had been in conversation with Fender Browne over the *Marlin*'s radiotelephone off and on all morning when the call came through from Saqr.

"The Shackletons have been circling us ever since we left Dubai yesterday," Fender Browne's words were crackling over the radio as Saqr's telephone call came through. "An hour ago a helicopter was hovering over us."

"Stand by," Fitz called over the radio. "A call from Kajmira is coming through." Fitz talked with Saqr a few minutes, promised to leave immediately for Kajmira, and then went back to the radio.

"When the barges arrive, Fender, immediately start placing the well jacket. The Brits are making their move now."

"I'll do the best I can, Fitz," Fender Browne called back. "It looks like they've got permanent surveillance on us. That damned Shackleton just keeps flying around and around us like a buzzard waiting for something to die."

"We aren't going to die for them," Fitz shot back with more assurance than he felt. "I'm leaving for Kajmira now. I'll radio you when I get back. Out."

"*Marlin* out."

CHAPTER 45

At Shaikh Hamed's remodeled fort Fitz listened sympathetically to the old Ruler's report of the meeting with Brian Falmey earlier that day. Fitz tried to persuade Hamed to defy the British Political Agent unequivocally. "We'll start drilling in a matter of days. The well jacket should be in place by the day after tomorrow. Tell that bloody Brit to get out of your emirate and stay out," Fitz counseled.

Sadly Hamed shook his head. "You don't know how the British react to that sort of defiance, Mr. Lodd. We rulers know exactly what the procedure is. When they depose a ruler he is escorted forthwith from his residence. Then there is the ride in the Trucial Oman Scouts' Land Rover from the palace to the RAF aircraft which is waiting. Next the trip on the RAF aircraft to Bahrain. In Bahrain there is the spacious hotel suite waiting. Then there may be another aircraft trip to London and exile. The British call us rulers but we only rule according to the recommendations of the British. Nevertheless, I will do everything in my power to resist the British on this matter." He sighed heavily.

"As the Ruler of Kajmira, I must do the best I can for my people. To give up my state's oil wealth easily would not be ruling my state in its best interests. This is something I have tried to do for the forty years I have been Ruler of Kajmira. I'm an old man but I shall rule as my father ruled and his father before him."

Fitz felt tremendous sympathy for the old Shaikh, and the thought of Saqr ruling was a grim one.

"The barges are on their way," Fitz repeated. "We expect they'll arrive tomorrow night or early the following morning. We start operations immediately. The only thing that can stop us is a direct written order from you to cease operations. We're certainly not going to let the British tell us what we can do. You are the

Ruler, you granted us the concession, it was yours to grant. Just don't let the British pressure you into signing a letter ordering us out of that part of the concession claimed by Sharjah before we have actually commenced drilling operations. Then it will be too late for them to stop us. I think we could expect help from the United States Government in the form of some show of naval force in the Gulf should Sharjah or Iran try to stop us when we actually had the platform set."

"I will try, Mr. Lodd. I will do everything I can to resist. But if I am indeed carried away and my son becomes Ruler, they will surely force him to stop your operations."

"Just play for time. The general counsel for Hemisphere Petroleum will arrive at two-thirty in the morning. I'll be back tomorrow morning and we'll form a plan."

Fitz made the long drive through the sand back to the Dubai Creek and the Ten Tola Bar. For an hour, until it got completely dark, he swam in his swimming pool. Then he went back to his office and contacted the *Marlin* by radio. The ship was anchored in twenty feet of water just off the island of Abu Musa. Fender Browne was in frequent radio communications with the slowly moving McDermott spread as the barges moved down the Gulf toward the island. That evening Colonel Buttres arrived at the Ten Tola Bar about ten o'clock. He joined Fitz at the majlis and handed him a note. Fitz looked at it. "Shall I open it now?"

"It doesn't matter," Buttres replied. "It's a request that you and the solicitor for Hemisphere Petroleum meet at ten-thirty tomorrow morning at TOS Headquarters in Sharjah. Brian Falmey will be there and we think the Political Resident in Bahrain will be flying in for the meeting."

"Make it eleven-thirty and we'll be there," Fitz replied.

Buttres assented to the time change and sat with Fitz for an hour. Finally he left and Fitz walked around the restaurant greeting people and occasionally buying drinks. He drove out to the airport to meet Irwin Shuster and Jack Tepper.

"I know it's late," Fitz addressed them as they approached the hotel. "However, a lot of things are happening and I think we ought to have an early meeting in the morning and decide what we are going to do."

At eight o'clock in the morning Fitz was back at the Carlton Hotel having coffee with Shuster and Tepper in their suite.

That Brian Falmey was keeping a watchful eye on every aspect of Hemisphere Petroleum Company's operations was evident when at eight-thirty a uniformed British officer of the colonial police knocked on the door of Irwin Shuster's suite.

Fitz opened the door and accepted the proffered envelope. "I'll take the letter. I'm Hemisphere's representative here." The colonial police officer handed it to Fitz, turned smartly on his heel, and walked down the corridor.

Fitz gave the communication to the lawyer. "Here's a letter from the Commandant of Police, Sharjah."

In abrupt and formal language the communiqué, addressed to Hemisphere Petroleum Company, 420 Park Avenue, New York, New York, U.S.A., stated that His Highness, the Ruler of Sharjah, has been advised that Hemisphere's drilling platform has arrived within twenty miles of Sharjah's island of Abu Musa. His Highness was gravely concerned that Hemisphere intended to move the platform into the twelve-mile territorial sea belt of Abu Musa.

"He forbids such an intrusion," the communiqué continued. "And he will regard it as a trespass if it occurs." The communiqué went on to say that His Highness would submit the controversy to mediation but in the meantime the Government of Sharjah will hold Hemisphere and its affiliates responsible for all consequences of any intrusion into the territorial waters of Sharjah, including Abu Musa's twelve-mile belt.

"They aren't wasting any time putting us on notice," Shuster said glumly.

"I've already heard from Falmey myself. He wants us to meet at the office of the Trucial Oman Scouts commander, Ken Buttres. I want to see Shaikh Hamed first. I'll meet you in Colonel Buttres's office."

Fitz made the arduous drive along the coastline through other emirates to Kajmira, arriving there about ten o'clock. He walked into the fort, where Shaikh Hamed and Shaikh Saqr were waiting for him. Fitz was offered the usual cup of coffee and then handed the official British letter—Arabic on one side of the page, English on the other. Fitz read the three-page epistle. It was merely putting into official language what Falmey had already told Hamed verbally. Falmey, as Her Britannic Majesty's Political Agent, was formally recommending (demanding) that Shaikh Hamed immediately and formally tell Hemisphere Petroleum that they cannot operate within the twelve-mile limit of Abu Musa. Fitz handed the letter back to the Ruler.

"What are you going to do, Your Highness?" Fitz asked. He didn't know what to counter-recommend and he was in full sympathy with Hamed's predicament.

"I've discussed this with my son and we have both decided not to impose operating limits on Hemisphere Petroleum at this time." He shrugged his shoulders expressively, his eyes rolling upward. "We all know the futility and foolishness of trying to oppose the British. With their Trucial Oman Scouts, their airplanes, their officials running the police of all of the states here, with their Army unit stationed in Sharjah, what can we ultimately do?"

"Hold out as long as you can, Your Highness," Fitz replied.

More than ever Fitz was convinced that his strongest recommendation to Hemisphere would be to purchase a helicopter as he drove once more through the sands back to Sharjah. He arrived at the headquarters of the Trucial Oman Scouts and was escorted by his friend Major Tom Rudd, the oldest British officer in point of service in the Trucial States, into the office of Colonel Buttres. Already Brian Falmey was there with his deputy and both Shuster and Jack Tepper had arrived.

"I take it you've just come down from Kajmira," Falmey said, a triumphant sneer on his lips.

"That's correct," Fitz said tightly.

"Then you've read the letter?"

Fitz turned to Shuster and Tepper. "I just read a three-page document from Her Britannic Majesty's Political Agent to the Ruler of Kajmira. In this letter Falmey recommends"—Fitz smiled wryly at Shuster and Tepper—"you know what 'recommends' means out here if it's by the *mua'atamad*. He recommends that Shaikh Hamed direct us formally to cease all operations within the twelve-mile territorial limit of Abu Musa. And incidentally, Shaikh Hamed has not done so yet. I was just with him."

"Shaikh Hamed, the Ruler of Kajmira, will very soon impose

operating restrictions on Hemisphere." Falmey's voice was positive, not to be denied. The significance of the location of this meeting was not lost on Fitz or for that matter on Shuster and Tepper. The Trucial Oman Scouts represented the constant threat of force in carrying out the objectives of Her Majesty's Government. Colonel Buttres, looking somewhat sympathetically at Fitz from behind his desk, was the individual who would apply such force as and when necessary to support political decisions. A fruitless, rambling discussion went on for forty-five minutes in which Falmey over and over reiterated the reasons why Hemisphere could not proceed with operations within the twelve-mile limit of Abu Musa until the situation had been mediated. That would probably take three months, perhaps a little more. Her Majesty's Government was prepared to ensure that these negotiations moved ahead promptly.

Shuster, the New York corporation counsel, was completely at a loss to know how to deal with the situation. The British Government had clearly double-crossed Hemisphere. Yet there was no law here but British force. Over and over again Shuster reiterated that according to their agreements attested to by the British Foreign Office they were within their rights to drill. Finally when it was obvious that no amount of discussion was going to resolve the situation, Fitz suggested that they adjourn the meeting.

"Now, Mr. Shuster, just precisely what are your intentions at the moment?" Falmey asked.

"My company, Hemisphere Petroleum, reserves the right to act in accordance with its agreements and in its own best interests under those agreements. We reserve the right to exercise any appropriate option consistent with the agreement signed by ourselves, Shaikh Hamed, and the British Foreign Office."

With that Shuster stood up, followed by Tepper and Fitz. Fitz waved goodbye to Colonel Buttres and they left the headquarters building. Outside Fitz suggested they meet back at the Ten Tola Bar and decide what to do. Majid Jabir would join them.

As usual, the Ten Tola Bar was filled when they arrived. They sat down at Fitz's table and compared notes. They had just ordered drinks when Majid Jabir showed up. He was completely briefed. After some thought it was Majid's advice both as a government official and as a partner in the enterprise to go ahead with operations. In the meanwhile he suggested drafting a letter to Her Majesty's Government from Hamed laying out all the reasons why the Ruler of Kajmira is not planning to stop his concessionaires from developing the area inside the twelve-mile limit.

"You know, I hate to say this," Shuster began. "I couldn't prove it but I think Brian Falmey is in league with that obscure oil company that just made the deal with Sharjah. They're the ones that are going to profit in this whole situation."

"It would seem that way, I suppose, to an American," Majid replied thoughtfully. "But as an Arab who has dealt with the British, as an Arab who deeply resents the British tentacles that make it impossible for Arab rulers to make their own decisions, as an Arab who has personally seen three rulers deposed by the British in short order when the rulers became contentious, still I do not agree with you, Mr. Shuster. I have yet to personally encounter corruption among the British political agents or political residents. Stupidity, yes. Pettiness, certainly. They are frequently vain and of course all hunger for first the OBE, which Brian Falmey has, and then of course the ultimate, the KBE, knighthood. Brian Falmey is the type of man who is far more interested in someday being known as Sir Brian Falmey than he is of picking up his baksheesh from an oil company. However, if I was at the root of this whole situation you can be very certain that some form of quid pro quo would be forthcoming."

"As so often it has," Fitz agreed in benediction. "I'll have Sepah take me out to the *Marlin* in his high-speed dhow so that I'll be there when the McDermott spread arrives," Fitz went on decisively. "We should just be able to make it before dark. In the meantime, Irwin"—he looked at Shuster—"you had better draft up that letter for Hamed to sign and then be sure it is delivered to Falmey's office on the Creek. We'll try to rush operations and get the well jacket placed by tomorrow night."

"It looks like that's the only way," Shuster agreed. "This is a pretty tough place to practice law," he commented.

CHAPTER 46

Fitz had alerted Sepah to the possibility that he might need to use the high-speed dhow, which at the moment was back from one trip and waiting to go on another. Issa was aboard and waiting. The ropes were slipped and the dhow moved out into the Creek, heading for open water.

Issa pushed the throttles up to flank speed and with no cargo aboard the dhow fairly leapt ahead as it passed out of the Creek and into the Gulf. They were less than two hours out of Dubai when they spotted the impressive spread of barges which had come down from Kuwait carrying the platform, well jacket, and drilling rig. It looked like an invasion flotilla and as Fitz scanned the line of barges the sheer financial outlay of this operation impressed itself on him. Indeed they had done the correct thing in having Hemisphere take over the entire project. He was looking at millions of dollars moving into position to start producing oil. The dhow came alongside the *Marlin* and Fitz jumped into the survey ship. Fortunately there was little tide and no swells. The dhow stood by in case Fitz needed to make a fast trip back to Dubai.

Fender Browne was elated as he watched barge after barge move into position around the bobbing red marker buoy. Captain Clayton, master of the *Marlin*, a long-time British seafaring man, welcomed Fitz aboard his ship. Fender Browne was directing operations over the radio, talking to the various barge captains and marshaling the equipment into position. Almost as an afterthought Fender Browne pointed a finger straight up in the air. Fitz followed the pointed finger and noticed a four-engine aircraft flying high above them. It seemed to be circling and was obviously keeping the barges and the survey ship under observation. Fitz nodded as Fender Browne continued to talk to the crane barge, which was carrying the 365-ton well jacket. It was starting to get dark and Fender Browne decided that with daylight they would commence operations to swing the well jacket from the deck of the barge and lower it to the ocean floor. The *Marlin* dropped its anchor and the crew prepared to spend the night on location.

It was a long night for Fitz and Fender Browne. Captain Clayton was blissfully unaware of the crisis approaching. Fitz and Fender Browne, standing alone on the bow of the ship late that night, speculated on what Clayton would do if Falmey should get to him and appeal to him as a British subject to take the survey ship away. The McDermott spread was manned entirely by Americans.

With the first pink light appearing in the eastern sky the men on the barge which was floating the well jacket began to make preparations to lower it onto the structure two hundred feet below the surface. Machinery was whirring and the divers who would set the jacket in the correct position were getting ready to suit up. The rest of the flotilla was standing by. By the time the sun had risen into the sky, lighting up the Gulf, the supervisor on the crane barge was talking to Fender Browne over the radio.

A sudden throaty roar of engines came from overhead and one of the Shackletons flew low over the barge and the *Marlin*. It circled and came back again. "Limey bastards!" Fender Browne muttered. "Sons of bitches think they own the world."

"It looks like they still own this part of the world," Fitz commented. "I used to think the Russians were the enemy."

Captain Clayton of the *Marlin* came up to where Fitz and Fender Browne were standing. He looked up concerned at the airplane. "What do you think they're up to?" he asked.

"That's your Shackleton. That's how they keep track of everything that's going on in the Gulf. You must have seen them before."

"Sure I've seen them before but never down this low. It looks almost as though they're trying to tell us something."

"They're telling us that Big Brother is watching," Fitz commented dryly. Then to Fender Browne: "I'll be glad when that jacket starts sinking in the water and the divers are setting it."

"Now what the bloody hell are they up to!" Captain Clayton was looking out over the starboard bow as a British minesweeper approached at flank speed. It cut through the sea toward them, two great white geysers of spray shooting up from either side of the bow. A quarter of a mile away the minesweeper began to make a turn and in moments was circling the crane barge and the *Marlin*.

The minesweeper made a full circle around the two ships and then cut its engines back to dead-slow speed as it drifted up close to the *Marlin*. As Fitz watched, the minesweeper, which he could now make out was HMS *Bulware*, put a dinghy over the side into the water. Two British officers and a sailor climbed down a rope ladder into the dinghy. The two officers stood at the forward end of the dinghy while the sailor started the engine and headed in the direction of the crane barge, which was on the verge of lifting the well jacket off the deck.

Obviously they wanted to prevent the barge from actually starting to place the jacket. Suddenly the unmistakable chuffing of a helicopter from directly above the *Marlin* caught Fitz's attention. He looked up and saw the RAF helicopter. At the same time a second plane, this one a fighter, zoomed across the barges and the *Marlin* while a second minesweeper appeared on the other side of the crane barge. Fitz and Fender Browne were awed at this abrupt display of force. As they watched, the two British officers boarded the crane barge and confronted the master of the barge. Fitz and Fender stood by the radio waiting for a report from the barge master. Finally the radio crackled.

"Mr. Browne," the voice came over the radio. "We've just been given the following written orders. Do you want me to read the statement?"

Fitz and Fender Browne looked at each other. Fitz nodded. "Read away," Fender Browne ordered.

"Here's what it says. In caps it says WARNING and then: 'Yesterday Her Majesty's Government recommended to the Ruler of Kajmira in accordance with their political agreement with him that he should not, for a period of three months, permit operations of any kind by his oil concessionaires in the area claimed by the Ruler of Sharjah. The Ruler of Kajmira has instructed Hemisphere Petroleum Company accordingly.'"

There was a pause and then the voice of the master of the barge came over again. "There's one more paragraph here. I'm instructed to tell you that the movement around the area in question belonging to Hemisphere Petroleum Company or under its control, or the control of its agents, would be regarded as a contravention of the operating limits which have now been imposed! This little document, sir, is signed by one G. S. Jones, Lieutenant Royal Navy in Command, who is standing looking down my throat right now. What do I do?"

Fitz and Fender Browne looked at each other. "The Ruler hadn't signed anything when I left yesterday and I'm sure he hasn't yet," Fitz said.

The second minesweeper came up close to the survey ship. Fitz heard the bellowing over the bullhorn. "Ahoy, Captain," the strident voice boomed out. Clayton walked over to the other side of his ship and looked up at the 150-foot-long minesweeper. Fitz and Fender Browne stood with Clayton. They were staring into a considerable amount of armament. One three-inch cannon was mounted on the front deck; a 40-mm. single-mount cannon was placed behind it. Four 20-mm. cannons were placed strategically to the rear of the bridge and a .30-caliber machine gun was mounted on each wing of the bridge. Gun crews were standing by all of the weapons.

As Fitz looked up at the bridge a civilian walked out of the wheelhouse and stood beside the commander of the ship. Fitz immediately recognized Brian Falmey. Falmey looked down and across the water at the smaller survey ship and saw Fitz standing at the rail.

Through the bullhorn the commander of the ship was addressing the captain of the *Marlin*. "You will turn around and leave the territorial waters of the island of Abu Musa. You will be escorted to the twelve-mile belt. You will not come back inside these waters."

Captain Clayton looked up at the minesweeper and the gun crews standing alertly awaiting orders. "Let's get the hell out of here!" Clayton cried.

"Let me use your bullhorn," Fitz said.

"It's in the deckhouse. Get it yourself. They mean business."

Fitz ran across the deck to the wheelhouse and found the bullhorn hanging above the wheel. He took it off the hook and walked back outside again. Putting it to his mouth, he called over the horn, "If you want us to leave show me the order signed by the Ruler of Kajmira. We are lawfully in his territorial waters at this moment."

From the minesweeper blasted back, "We'll send a dinghy for you."

Fitz watched the second minesweeper drop a dinghy and crewman. It disengaged itself from the davits and started over to the *Marlin*. When the dinghy came alongside, Fitz slid over the rail and dropped into the dinghy. Five minutes later he was climbing the ladder onto the minesweeper. Falmey was waiting for him on the deck.

Half amused, half annoyed, Falmey said, "Well, Lodd. If you aren't the number-one troublemaker in all these Trucial States. You know, you're lucky I haven't recommended to the Ruler of Dubai that he suspend your visa and deport you."

"Maybe you can push poor old Hamed around but I don't think you want to tangle with Shaikh Rashid. Now let me see the order signed by Shaikh Hamed restricting our operations."

"Actually he's in the process of signing it now."

"Well, until you get that signed document and bring it out to me we're going to go ahead here. You have no legal right telling us we cannot continue with our operations."

Falmey gave Fitz a quizzical look and turned to the commander of the ship. "Order the barge with the derrick to move out immediately!"

"Yes, sir," the Lieutenant replied. He gave orders to the gun crew, and a formidable display of artillery was trained on the barge.

"Keep one twenty-millimeter on the dhow over there," Falmey ordered, staring at Sepah's dhow, which was drifting beside the *Marlin*. Then the Political Agent turned to Fitz. "You still keep your private gunboat with you, I see."

"You've gone power-mad, Falmey. You wouldn't dare fire on that barge."

"It has nothing to do with daring or not daring, Lodd. What's at stake here is Her Majesty's Government's best interests. And those best interests are for this spread to move out of here right now."

It was obvious that the master of the barge was in no frame of mind to test how far the British Navy was prepared to go in furthering Britain's best interests. The tugboat pulling the barge headed out into the Gulf, bending full power to the objective of getting out of the twelve-mile limit and out from under the guns of the British minesweepers.

Victoriously Falmey fixed Fitz with a steady stare. "Now, Lodd, if you have nothing further on your mind the dinghy will take you back to the *Marlin* and the *Marlin* will take you beyond the twelve-mile limit. By the time you get back to the mainland Shaikh Hamed will present you with a signed order limiting your concession."

Defeated, Fitz turned from Falmey, walked to the rail, flung himself over and down the rope ladder, dropping into the dinghy, which took him back to the *Marlin*. The survey ship had already weighed anchor and was only waiting for Fitz to board before moving out to an area safely beyond the twelve-mile limit. The other barges of the McDermott spread were also moving out, following the crane barge. The helicopters, the Shackleton, and the fighter plane were still circling overhead as the minesweepers escorted the ships out of the area and well beyond the twelve-mile limit.

Once they had reached undisputed waters, Fitz watched the minesweeper with Falmey on it speeding off toward the mainland. The other minesweeper was staying in the area to make sure there was no return by the barges or the survey ship. They needn't have worried about the survey ship. Captain Clayton was in no mood to challenge his own nation's navy.

Fitz turned to Fender Browne, "I'm going back on the dhow. You might as well come with me."

"Right." Fender turned to Captain Clayton. "Bring the *Marlin* back into the Creek and up to the supply warehouse docking facility. We'll see if we can find some answer to this whole mess back on land."

"Very good idea, Mr. Browne."

Issa brought the dhow up alongside the survey ship and Fitz and Fender Browne jumped aboard Sepah's high-speed boat and they were off for the Creek. Fitz and Fender Browne arrived at Sepah's dock on the Creek about one o'clock in the afternoon. They walked up the embankment along the Creek until they reached the Carlton Hotel. Inside they were told that Mr. Shuster and Mr. Tepper were in Mr. Shuster's suite.

As Irwin Shuster opened the door and saw Fitz and Fender Browne, a stricken look came over his face. "I thought you were placing the well jacket today, right now."

Fitz explained the morning's events to the Hemisphere corporate lawyer.

"As far as we know, Hamed has signed nothing yet," Shuster said. "Drive up now to Kajmira and see the Ruler."

"I'm sure that at this point the deputy Political Agent is with him trying to force him to sign the letter ordering us to respect the twelve-mile limit. As a matter of fact, between the minesweeper and helicopters I'm sure our friend Brian Falmey is up there in the fort right now."

"Then hurry on up there, Fitz. You should be able to dissuade the Political Agent from forcing the Ruler to sign the document, with the following arguments." The corporate counsel began a futile recitation of legal points. "Tell Falmey that: One, Hemisphere will make no further attempt to move equipment into the area until an agreement has been reached with the British Foreign Office. Two, we should be given time to file a suit against Her Majesty's Government in the high court in London. This would bring out all the facts in the case and help some settlement to be reached. Three, point out that there's nothing to be gained by further embarrassing Shaikh Hamed and causing him to renege on the agreement we originally signed. Perhaps if you present these arguments the Political Agent will not force the Ruler to actually sign the paper limiting our territorial concessions."

"After all that's happened, you think that Falmey is going to listen to those arguments?" Fitz shook his head. "At this point we need an army, not a lawyer. If you'd seen them training their guns on our barges and the survey ship you would realize that they are beyond logic. But . . ." he sighed, "I will present your arguments and let you know what happens."

"That's all you can do, Fitz. We'll be standing by here at the phone to hear from you."

Once again Fitz started out on a torturous trip from Dubai Creek to Kajmira. As he drove over the sand Fitz made up his mind that if Shaikh Rashid ever again asked him what he could do to make his life easier he would suggest getting the road built between Dubai and Kajmira.

Before Fitz reached the Kajmira border he observed the helicopters hovering above him, a fighter plane circling in the air, and then, as he came closer, he saw the armored vehicles flying the unmistakable red-and-white flag of the Trucial Oman Scouts. As he entered Kajmira two squads of British-officered Trucial Oman Scouts straddled the road, mounted thirty-caliber machine guns on their Land Rovers. They made no move to prevent Fitz from driving through but he knew that Brian Falmey had reached the final stage of enforcing British recommendations. Next step would be the Land Rover trip to Sharjah airport and a flight to Bahrain in the transport plane kept by the RAF for just such purposes.

As Fitz approached the remodeled fort he saw another squadron of Trucial Oman Scouts in their desert Land Rovers, obviously waiting for orders from the Political Agent. No move was made to prevent Fitz from striding up to the fort and the doors were opened for him by a guard.

He walked into the private majlis. Hamed was sitting in his customary seat, his son beside him, and both Brian Falmey and his deputy were seated next to Shaikh Hamed. Shaikh Saqr saw Fitz come in. He got up and walked over to him and shook his hand. Fitz regarded Falmey bitterly, and the Political Agent nodded back, a cold smile flitting across his features. He was winning. In low tones Shaikh Saqr explained to Fitz that his father, the Ruler, had not yet signed the letter limiting the concession.

Fitz nodded and turned to Falmey. As eloquently as possible he repeated the arguments that the Hemisphere Petroleum Company corporate counsel had asked him to deliver to the Political Agent. Falmey listened impassively. He made no comment. Clearly it was Falmey's resolve to walk out of the fort with the necessary papers signed by the Ruler. Fitz accepted a cup of coffee from the coffee server but Brian Falmey did not. There was almost total silence in the small majlis as Falmey waited, the papers on the table beside Shaikh Hamed for him to sign. Finally Falmey glanced at his watch, stood up, and turned to his deputy. "Tell Major Farquharson to bring the Land Rover up to the fort and provide an escort of three squadrons from here to Sharjah airport. Also tell him to have the plane in Sharjah ready to take off and a flight plan filed for Bahrain."

Shaikh Hamed turned to Fitz and motioned for him to come close. Fitz got up from his chair and moved closer to the Ruler. "My son Saqr will succeed me. He will sign the limitation on your concession as his first official act as Ruler of Kajmira. I leave it to you. In all my years as Ruler, over forty years, never have I failed to keep my word or repudiated an agreement I had already signed. I will not renege on our agreement now either unless you, Mr. Lodd, with whom I first signed it, tell me that I have no choice but to make the *mua'atamad*'s recommendation a decree by the Ruler."

Fitz looked into the sad but resolute eyes of the Ruler. This was a man of true nobility, he knew. He had always served his subjects to the best of his abilities and means. Fitz had already seen the results of the signature bonus in small but much appreciated improvements in the town of Kajmira and particularly at the docks. He could have transformed the life of all of his subjects with oil. Fitz glanced at Shaikh Saqr, indecisive, frightened, yet strangely lusting for the power of being the Ruler. Fitz knew that Brian Falmey was not bluffing. He heard the squealing of a Land Rover being halted just outside the double doors into the fort.

"I think Your Highness that the wisest course at this moment would be for you to sign the document that Her Majesty's Government has presented to you. I would also appreciate it if you would write a letter to me stating that you signed the concession limitation under extreme duress by Her Majesty's Government."

An annoyed look came over Falmey's face but he could hardly deny that he was applying pressure of the most extreme type. Hamed seemed relieved that the untenable situation had been at least temporarily alleviated. He nodded to one of his advisers, who brought him a pen. In quick strokes Hamed signed his name to the original and two copies of the document, stamping them with his signet ring. The deed was done and Hamed stood up. Brian Falmey handed Fitz a signed copy. "This resolves the impasse, Lodd. Shall I read it to you?"

"I can read, Falmey." Fitz read the short document.

"Letter to the local representative of Hemisphere Petroleum Company from H.H. the Ruler of Kajmira.

"On this date the Government of the United Kingdom recommended to me, in accordance with their agreement with me, that permission should not be given to your company to commence operations of any kind for a period of three months in the area claimed by the Ruler of Sharjah. I at once informed you, as local representative of the company, of these operating limits. To remove any misunderstanding, I hereby confirm these operating limits and request your company to observe them. More precise details of the limits will be notified to you as soon as possible."

Well, that was it, Fitz said to himself. Laylah had been right all along. Hemisphere would lose its investment, Kajmira would never enjoy its oil revenues, and Britain and the Shah had divided up the Gulf in a satisfactory manner before the final pull-out of British force east of Suez.

Fitz shook Hamed's hand. "Your Highness did what had to be done." As he was leaving he could hear the obsequious words pouring from Brian Falmey's mouth now that His Highness had bowed to British power and objectives.

Part IV
INSURGENCY
1971

CHAPTER 47

The CIA man was impressed. Abe Ferruti had not expected such a complete compilation of the potential points of intrigue on the Trucial Coast as Fitz had prepared for him. Below their vantage point in Fitz's office, the Ten Tola Bar was blasting along at full capacity. Everyone interested in business, politics, and intelligence information felt it behooved him to spend some time here every day catching up on the latest news. Most people chose the 10 P.M. to 1 A.M. shift. These were the customers Fitz and Abe were staring down at now.

On the table in front of the window were the various transistor receivers for the bugged tables about the restaurant. There was also a stack of photographs and a file of tape cassettes. Abe studied the photographs as he listened to the conversations being transmitted from the most private booths.

"You have beautiful quality in these telephoto shots," he remarked.

Fitz gestured at the scene beyond the window. "You can compliment Lynn Goldstein down there for them. After four months in London she decided to come back here. I once showed her this place. Except for you and Joe Ryan she's the only one who knows about it. She returned to me with just the right camera equipment to make those pictures."

"She is a very tawny girl," Abe opined. This, Fitz understood, was a high compliment coming from the impassive agent. "I'm looking forward to meeting her."

Fitz watched Lynn engage in vivacious conversation with the other patrons of the majlis, a woman sitting in un-Arabic style at the head of the table. Fender Browne, Tim McLaren, and several visiting American and British businessmen were basking in her femininity.

Suddenly Fitz let out an oath. "That son of a bitch Saqr!"

"What's up, Fitz?" Abe asked.

"See that Arab coming in the door?"

Abe nodded.

"That's Shaikh Saqr, son of the Ruler of Kajmira. Now that the oil deal is blown, he's trouble."

As they watched, Saqr and three other Arabs Fitz knew from Hamed's majlis were shown to a table by Joe Ryan. Saqr looked around the Ten Tola Bar and motioned toward a tall, stately blond girl. The other Arabs followed his gesture with their eyes.

"Tune in on that table, Abe," Fitz demanded. He pointed to the correct transistor. Immediately Saqr's harsh voice lashed through the office.

"That is the one I want."

"The bastard," Fitz muttered. "He's caused me enough trouble. The girl he's talking about is Gillian Rhodes."

"She's a beauty," Abe conceded. "You can't fault his taste."

Saqr went on talking to his retinue. "Two times the English woman has refused to sit with me or accompany me for a drive on the desert. It will be your mission to bring her to me, using whatever means necessary. Don't worry about the American. He is powerless in our land."

Fitz turned to Abe. "Did you hear that? He's going to try and kidnap Gillian."

"This is a rough part of the world," Abe agreed. "Anything you can do?"

Fitz nodded and walked across the office to his filing cabinet, which he unlocked. From inside he pulled out a folder and handed it to Abe as he closed and relocked the cabinet. Abe opened up the folder and a loud guffaw exploded from him.

"Where in hell did you get these pictures?"

Fitz gestured through the one-way window in the direction of his table, where Lynn was sitting.

"I'll be damned. Do you think she'd like to go to work for us? We'd pay top dollar for that kind of photographic talent."

"I would strongly advise her against it," Fitz replied. He took a sheet of paper from his desk and sat down, picking up a felt-tip pen and writing in flowing Arabic.

"My dear Shaikh Saqr," he began.

"I regret as much as you the bitter circumstances which have befallen our oil concession. To lessen the pain we all feel at losing the concession, I thought that the enclosed photographs might remind you of enjoyable moments in London at the time of the signature ceremonies. If you or your father would like more of these pictures to present to friends in Kajmira, the supply is unlimited. Needless to say, under existing circumstances these pictures would only be available to you. Let us in the future treat each other's remaining holdings with respect."

Abe read the letter, which Fitz did not sign, and gave a last look at the pictures. "I never saw anything like that before," he murmured. "Wouldn't the old Shaikh love to see his son in action!"

"I just hope Saqr doesn't recognize Lynn. But I'm sure he wouldn't. Not out here."

Over the transistor, as Fitz had been penning his message, various plans for effecting the abduction of Gillian had been discussed by Saqr's cohorts. None of them could have been effective as long as Gillian stayed within the Ten Tola Bar compound, but all the girls had to get out once in a while, even if just to see the sights and visit the souk. They were all fascinated with the marketplace.

Fitz slipped the note he had written into a large envelope, along with the most compromising pictures of Saqr and the blond party girls, in one case drinking from a bottle and engaging in deviate sex simultaneously.

"See you in a few minutes." Fitz left his office. Moments later he emerged on the restaurant floor and, holding the envelope in one hand, he moved toward Saqr's table, greeting his customers on the way. Reaching Saqr, he smiled and they shook hands.

"I came across some pictures taken in London I thought you might want to add to your collection. Take them home and look at them at leisure," Fitz said in Arabic.

Saqr nodded, took the envelope, and placed it on the table beside him.

"Can I send you a drink with my compliments?" Fitz asked.

"A Coca-Cola," Saqr requested piously.

Fitz left Saqr's table, giving the order to a waiter. He brushed by Gillian and whispered, "Keep away from Saqr."

"You don't have to tell me, boss," she replied coolly. "Anyway, Ken will soon be here."

Fitz walked over to his own table and sidled up beside Lynn. "I'm just finishing up a little business in the office and then I'll be with you."

The others at the table assured Fitz he could take his time, they would look out for Lynn. Fitz returned to his office.

"Has Saqr opened the envelope yet?" Fitz asked Abe.

Abe shook his head. "He's still plotting with his goons how to snatch Gillian."

Fitz sighed. "Sometimes I wonder if it's all worth it. We Westerners are encroaching on a separate culture and then we get disturbed when the Arabs won't change their ways to conform with ours."

"Don't get rid of this place, Fitz. It's too valuable."

"Maybe I'll just drop the girls." He looked down through the window.

Then he turned to Abe. "Anything interesting going on at Serrat's table?"

Abe shook his head. "They seem to be waiting for someone. The man with Serrat, whom your young lady has photographed on three different occasions here, is an agent for a French munitions cartel. He is well known in Beirut and of course he is active in narcotics. Arms and dope seem to go together."

"At your leisure you can study the tapes of conversations Serrat has conducted in here over the last ten days," Fitz said.

They watched as the front door to the Ten Tola Bar opened from outside and three men came in. "Now maybe we'll pick up something of interest," Fitz said. "That's Colonel Buttres of the Trucial Oman Scouts. With him is John Brush, acting Political Agent with Brian Falmey on leave, and Major Colin Richards, deputy commander of the Scouts. That English morsel Saqr is after, Gillian, has, with my encouragement, been seeing the Colonel. As a result, he spends a lot of time here in a corner table which transmits to this receiver."

Fitz picked out a small receiver from the neat row of transistors and turned it on. "What you'll hear mostly is the sad story of the decline and fall of Her Majesty's empire. You'll also get some insight into at least one reason why insurgency is on the rise in the hills behind us."

Gillian spent longer than necessary getting Buttres and his party seated and it was apparent that she and the Colonel were confirming a date for later. Meantime, Saqr's eyes never left Gillian. Fitz wondered if he would open the envelope before leaving the Ten Tola Bar.

With Gillian's withdrawal Buttres watched her, and his wistful voice came over the transistor. "You know, I shall be sorry when we pull out completely and I have to go. I'm just beginning to enjoy this posting."

"I'm afraid, Ken, your time is shorter than you think," the young acting Political Agent said. "We're getting things tidied up nicely. The rulers will still look to Britain for their needs even after our tooth-ons are all evacuated and our recommendations are no longer enforceable orders."

Hearing that come over the transistor, Fitz grimaced. "Tooth-ons is what the Brits call their first-line combat forces. They sure did us in on our oil deal."

Colonel Buttres was still talking at the table below. "I'm going to try to get back here to the new Union Defense Force when the United Arab Emirates is born," Buttres stated. "I guess Rashid and Zayed would give me a contract. Of course, Hamed probably would oppose any former officer of the TOS after the way Falmey used us to pressure the old boy."

"That's what we're here for, you know," Richards, the deputy, said realistically. Then more animatedly: "You should have been with us over in Oman when we gave that old bastard Sultan Sa'id bin Taimur the Land Rover ride to the airport. The people down in Salalah are still cheering."

Fitz slapped the table triumphantly, almost knocking over the receiver. "I knew it. Buttres tried to tell me that Sa'id's son, Qabus, engineered and carried out the whole overthrow and the Brits had nothing to do with it. That was patently impossible. Poor Qabus was imprisoned by his father for four years, right up to the moment he was suddenly proclaimed Sultan."

Abe smiled. "As that young acting PA, Brush, said, the final stage of tidying up is well along."

At the Colonel's table the drinks arrived. "Cheers. To the new order out here, whatever that will be," Brush proposed.

The others drank and then in dour tones Buttres muttered, "The latest new orders I have are: Do nothing. No more operations. You know Fitz? The chap that owns this place?" the Colonel asked Richards. The deputy shook his head. "That's right, when he was at headquarters you were standing by down in Oman." Buttres swallowed more of his drink.

"What about him?" Richards asked.

"He picks up a lot of useful information. Probably the girls overhear things—but Gillian is all right," he added hastily. "Don't worry about her. In any case, he has twice told me about arms shipments and there wasn't a thing I could do. The orders are: No unnecessary operations. Pull out, in effect." Glumly he regarded his glass.

Abe gave Fitz a sharp look. "You gave him stuff you picked up here?"

"Sure. One colonel to another. There's no way he could know how I got it. You heard what he said about the girls. Actually, there's not much point in telling him anything more, since he can't do anything."

At the table down below, the acting Political Agent considered what the Colonel had said. Then he gave his comment. "Just as well to let the odd arms shipments get through to the rebels in Oman. As long as they're a threat Qabus is going to need us to run his army and government. If he didn't have an internal security problem, and a serious one, Qabus might get to thinking that Oman should be run for Arabs by Arabs—Sandhurst-educated or not."

"There's no way that what Oman calls an army could stop a serious thrust by the Communists," Richards observed.

"Right," Brush concurred. "We might as well keep him spending his oil money with us for defense."

"I can tell you, Brush"—Buttres gestured for another round of drinks—"and try to keep this securely in your political mind, that whoever comes in here after us to keep this part of the world straight is going to have sizable problems. You know who the best troops in the Scouts are?"

"The Dhofars?" Brush asked.

"Right. They learned all about modern weapons and tactics from us. In a year they could be back in the Dhofar province fighting for the Communists in Salalah and they'll be damned hard to stop."

"A good Marxist insurrectionary force down there on the border of Saudi Arabia will help worry King Faisal," Brush returned. "He'll think twice before he applies another oil embargo against us and the Americans and loses our military aid."

Fitz laughed as this last speech by Brian Falmey's youthful number two came across. "You see the way they're brought up to think in the BFO? Always scheming for Her Britannic Majesty."

"Which is why Britain will always survive," Abe replied. "We could do with an infusion of hard-line British thinking in Washington."

"Here comes a man I've seen with Serrat before." Fitz pointed through the window. Abe tuned out the frustrated Brits and turned up the volume on Serrat's corner table.

Fitz looked down at his majlis directly opposite the window. Lynn was enjoying herself, though probably wondering how much longer he would be in the office with the Lebanese businessman who had unexpectedly arrived in Dubai from Beirut. Fitz had not introduced them pending instructions by Abe concerning his cover.

"Now I think we'll get some action." Abe was listening intently to the conversation in French, which as the newcomer arrived changed over to Arabic. "It's the man they've been waiting for. He's got an Arab with him."

"We've got pictures of him with Serrat," Fitz said. "He operates the Kajmira branch of the Bank of Iraq. He's become very close to the poorer herders and farmers. There's green grass and crops growing there, you know, and then there are the Shihu tribesmen in the hills that spill over into Oman's Musandam Peninsula. For the past two years the Bank of Iraq has been making low-interest loans and even forgiving them in certain hardship cases. As a result, the Iraqis through their bank are trusted by the potentially socialist-leaning people."

Having consumed two cups of coffee each, the Iraqi and Arab left the table. Their conversation had not been long but it was interesting.

A substantial number of expert guerrilla fighters had been smuggled into the Trucial States with the hundreds of Indian, Baluchi, and Pakistani immigrants needed for the labor force. They had created a camp in the mountains of the northern boundary of Oman, just south of the western territory on the Gulf of Oman owned by the Trucial States of Fujaira and Sharjah. These states cut a swath through Oman, separating the Sultanate from its patch of territory to the north, the Musandam Peninsula.

More trained guerrillas were coming in with the illegal immigrants every week and finding their way up to the camp. A large force of dissident Bedouins and Shihu mountain tribesmen had gathered around this hard-core cadre.

What was needed now was a large supply of arms, enough to last them a year, carried up to the mountains. Once fully armed and equipped, the force would divide in two, half fighting a guerrilla war against Oman Government police and troops in the area of the capital, Muscat, and its adjacent seaport, Matrah; the other half crossing the Trucial States through hills and wadis and starting the occupation of the Musandam Peninsula.

The Iraqi Government had financed the purchase of a huge shipment of French arms which were now ready to be shipped from Iraq's Gulf port of Basra down to a point on the Trucial coast where it could be safely landed and transported up to the mountains.

"Our weapons are many times, a hundred times better than the Chinese weapons the insurgents have been getting," Serrat had assured the Iraqi banker. The Arab, whose name was never spoken, was apparently a leader of some Arab socialist movement whose aim was to depose all the traditional rulers and substitute Marxist governments that would take the wealth of the shaikhs and divide it among the people.

"Just remember, when you revise the Oman Government and take over the oil fields, that it was French arms you used and that French oil companies should be substituted for the Dutch," Serrat remarked patronizingly.

"French arms, paid for in full by us," the Iraqi banker reminded Serrat dryly.

"When can the arms be transported across the desert?" the Arab asked impatiently.

"I will need a week or ten days to make arrangements for the trucks to carry them from the coast to the foot of the hills. From there they will have to go on camels through the wadis. There is no way the trucks can make it beyond the edge of the desert."

"I can provide the camels," the Arab said. "The trucks will bring the munitions along the hard-packed sand track that runs from Dubai out to the empty quarter. Then instead of turning across the sand dunes toward Al Ain the trucks will proceed directly to the hills. There will be time before daylight to load up the camels from the trucks and herd them into the wadis and mountains of Oman, where they will be impossible to find."

"Shall we set a date now?" Serrat asked. "It will require additional financing for trucks, drivers, and guards," he added. From the window Fitz and Abe could see the sharp look the Frenchman gave the Iraqi banker.

"The funds will be at your disposal," the Iraqi replied. "And the ship can leave our port within a week, I am told."

"Then let's settle on ten days, or rather nights, from today," the Arab decided. "The ship will approach the coast at the point we have been using to bring in the immigrants. Should there be any changes we shall notify each other through the Bank of Iraq in the usual way." And the conversation was abruptly terminated, although the Arab and Iraqi stayed at the table until they had finished their coffee, the Frenchmen sipping their Campari and soda.

Abe stared at the transistor. "Things are getting serious around here. I picked an instructive evening to come."

"Every night some unbelievable deal is hatched out," Fitz replied.

"Their plan must not be realized, Fitz. We're going to have to stop it."

"Don't say 'we.'" Fitz shook his head. "I promised to get you information. But I don't want to get into operations."

"I don't expect the Scouts will do anything about it, from what we heard out of the commander's own mouth. Fitz," Abe said seriously, "we have a big stake in this Gulf area. Someday we'll be operating here. The stronger the Communists get in the hills, the worse our job will be. If that load gets through it will keep them for a year. We can't let them get into a position to be able to use the Musandam Peninsula as a strong base of operations. All they'd have to do is drop a few mines from dhows into Hormuz to plug up the oil lanes. It would require a major military campaign to displace a well-entrenched insurgency force."

"Hold it!" Fitz exclaimed, interrupting Abe. "I think Saqr is going to have a look." He flipped on the transistor tuned in to Saqr's table.

Almost unconsciously, it seemed, Saqr's hands were opening the envelope as his eyes wandered about the Ten Tola Bar in search of Gillian, who had momentarily left the floor. From the one-way window Fitz could actually see the slick surface of the first photograph before Saqr, apparently giving up for the moment trying to locate Gillian, looked down at what he expected was another picture of the ceremonial signing or the subsequent party at the Grosvenor House.

A sudden convulsive tremor shook the Arab's body as he realized what he was seeing. He stared at the picture in disbelief, his head twitching spastically. Hands a-quiver, he jammed the photograph back into the envelope, looking around to see if anybody else had noticed the offensive picture. Then he stared for several moments in a near comatose state at the envelope in front of him before throwing wild glances about the restaurant.

"What is wrong, Shaikh?" one of his companions asked.

A strangled grunt could be heard over the transistor. Then Saqr rose unsteadily to his feet and, clutching the envelope, he blindly made for the door as other patrons watched him curiously.

"Well, we've given him a black face for sure," Fitz chuckled. "I doubt if he'll ever come back here again as long as I'm around." He turned from the one-way window as Saqr plunged out of the Ten Tola Bar.

"I understand the problem, my friend," Fitz said, returning to the subject of the insurgents. "I just don't want to be involved."

"I'll return to Beirut tomorrow and see what the Middle East station chief thinks."

"You have to leave? That's good news," Fitz answered ungraciously. "Are you ready to meet Lynn and eat?"

When Fitz and Lynn finally escaped the Ten Tola Bar and fell into the pool for their nightcap swim, Lynn asked, "Who's your

Lebanese friend? I mean really." She laughed. "After what I've seen, don't tell me he's just some businessman."

"The only thing I'm going to tell you is that all the time he was talking business to me I was looking down at you and wondering when we'd be in bed. O.K.?"

Parentheses formed at the edges of her lips and her eyes twinkled. "O.K."

He splashed water over her. "Enjoying your second trip to the Creek?"

"Yes." She climbed out of the pool. "Bed anyone?"

CHAPTER 48

Fitz was beginning to have the disquieting feeling that he was getting lazy, not progressing in his quest for success on the Arabian Gulf, as he sat watching Lynn sunning herself on a rubber raft floating in the pool. They had made love out in the sun and now were somnolently contemplating what they would do with the rest of their day.

Although he was still the representative of Hemisphere Petroleum on the Gulf, at a much reduced figure from what had been discussed when Lorenz Cannon had been anticipating high oil production, there was little for him to do beyond filing a series of complaints against the British Political Agent, the Political Resident in Bahrain, where he went every two weeks, and keeping track of what the other oil company with the Sharjah concession was doing and planning. The latter was easy enough since the head of the company discussed corporate policy and operations nightly in the Ten Tola Bar. Fitz had been bitterly disappointed at finding himself on the outside of Gulf oil production, the most important activity in this area of the world he had chosen for his home. Not to be in oil was not to be at the wellspring of political and financial power here.

He thought about the arms shipment and Abe's ominous statement of the night before. "We're going to have to stop it." Fitz's thirst for the power and the prerogatives of being U. S. Ambassador to the United Arab Emirates when the Union was finally brought into existence was considerably slaked. Without Laylah— He cut off this train of thought and concentrated on the voluptuous Lynn gaining an even tan over her entire body. She had been with him almost three weeks now and showed no signs of wanting to return to London. Besides the professional job she did taking pictures from the window overlooking the restaurant, she made him feel happy and contented. He still had not revealed, even to her, the secret of the bugs. That was something he was ashamed of and no amount of rationalization could change his feelings of self-disgust. Yet he did tune in whenever he thought there was something Abe and the "Company" should know about being discussed at one of the private booths.

Fitz just didn't know where he was going now. The Protestant work ethic with which he had been brought up and by which he had lived all his life, this fundamental precept within him was affronted. He had over two hundred and fifty thousand dollars in the bank and the Ten Tola Bar made an unconscionable profit for him every month, even after Majid Jabir came to collect His Highness's share. So what was the matter?

"Fitz," Lynn called softly. "Why don't you come in the pool with me? You'll get too hot just sitting there in the sun."

Obediently Fitz stood up, walked to the edge of the pool, and slid into the cool water. He paddled over to the deep end where Lynn was floating and held on to the raft.

"Something wrong, Fitz?" she asked. "You've been positively morose these past days."

"I suppose it's the Hemisphere fiasco. But damn it, I warned them."

"Nothing else?" There was an anxious look in her dark eyes. "Are you getting tired of me squatting on your turf?"

"Of course not. If you think I'm a bit on the sullen side now, you should have seen me before you came this time."

"You want me to stay, Fitz? I mean, sort of indefinitely?"

Fitz, way down deep, was not so sure. Lynn was a definite addition to his life here and he enjoyed her company and their intimacy tremendously. But indefinitely could be a long time. Nevertheless, he pulled the raft around so his face was beside hers and kissed her on the lips. "I want you to stay as long as you are happy here, Lynn. I mean it."

"You're sure?"

"Yes." He saw that the sun had passed its zenith. "Time for a gin and tonic." He grinned cheerfully.

At 1 P.M. the Ten Tola Bar was filled with the lunch crowd. Fitz and Lynn were sitting at the majlis, friends and associates dropping by to say hello, when to his surprise Fitz saw the tall, white-haired, distinguished-looking opportunist John Stakes walk into the restaurant. Joe Ryan led him to Fitz's table.

"Hello, John. I thought you were still hustling the Arab rulers for Courty Thornwell," Fitz greeted the Englishman. "Meet a fellow countrywoman of yours, an itinerant photographer, Lynn Goldstein. Join us. How's the project?" Fitz asked.

"Now that you ask," Stakes replied with a rueful smile, "I'm afraid I have to admit you were right. You just can't get Arabs to move together. Each ruler was as enthusiastic as Zayed but somehow Courty and I were unable to get them to agree with each other on methods, although they all agreed on the objective. In any case, there'll soon be another Arab-Israeli war. The Arabs will be whipped and looking for a way to convince their people and the world that they in fact won. Perhaps at that time out of necessity some sort of Arab solidarity program will develop. That's when Courty and I will pick up again where we left off. Meanwhile he's gone back to the U.S. to see what newspapers and radio and television stations can be purchased. He still hopes to buy an entire broadcast network."

"That's what I gathered from the occasional letter I received." He paused. Then with studied unconcern he asked, "Is Laylah going back with him?"

Fitz felt electric tension emanate from Lynn when he mentioned the name.

"No," Stakes answered, "I don't believe he suggested it, as a matter of fact. I must say, Fitz, young Thornwell seems just a bit of a cad, you know. He and I found Laylah extraordinarily helpful and I know he gave her to believe that marriage was in the offing and then he just said goodbye and took off for London and New York to wait for the next war out here."

Fitz noticed Lynn stiffening as Stakes went on. "Oh! That reminds me. She gave me a letter for you."

"You can give it to me later, John."

"Don't be silly, darling." There was an unmistakably hard edge to Lynn's tone. "Of course you want it now. There might be something important in it."

"I say, I'm not interrupting anything?" Stakes sensed the tension.

"Of course not." Lynn's voice was soothing. "When we don't want to be interrupted we don't sit out here."

Stakes reached inside the pocket of his lightweight suit and pulled out the familiar blue envelope with Laylah's initials in embossed white in the upper left-hand corner. Gingerly Fitz took the letter. He was wearing a sports shirt, so he had no pocket in which to put it. He placed it on the table beside him. "How about a drink, John?"

The drinks came and they sipped in silence. Finally Stakes asked, "What new opportunities are there here these days, Fitz? I heard about your bad luck on the oil deal. Very sorry. I wish I'd been here, might have been able to do something with that bugger of a Political Agent. Something I learned early on, never trust a Political Agent. In fact, never trust the Foreign Office."

"I'm afraid there's nothing anyone could have done." Fitz welcomed the opportunity to plug the awkward silence. "We were caught in British tidying up of the Gulf. Hemisphere is suing everyone they can find. It's a very fortunate thing for me that I didn't put everything I had into the operation or I'd be back where I started, only much worse." He thought about the loss of over half his pension to Marie.

"Laylah certainly saved you," Stakes commented. "Fender Browne, Sepah, and Majid owe her a lot."

"They know it." Fitz wanted to get off the subject of Laylah and he tried to edge the letter out of sight under a napkin, but Lynn's bright dark eyes instantly caught the move.

"Oh, go on and read it, Fitz. You won't be able to relax until you do." She stood up. "I'm going to the house for a few minutes. Be back soon." And she was gone, heading through the kitchen door.

"Sorry if I caused a problem, old boy," Stakes apologized.

"Not your fault," Fitz said absently, already opening Laylah's letter. He read:

Dear Fitz,

As John will tell you, he and Courty have temporarily given up on the big project. Courty has gone home and I am working harder than ever at the Embassy now that I'm not spending half my time trying to help establish a communications empire. Should business take you through Tehran, let me know and maybe we can share some vodka and caviar again.

As always, Laylah

Fitz looked up at Stakes. "Is she pretty upset about Courty not taking her back to the U.S. and marrying her?"

"I think she feels he's been pretty cavalier with her," Stakes answered. "I got to know Thornwell quite well, you know. I don't think he intends to tie himself up with marriage at this point in his life. Laylah was useful and a beautiful companion. That was about it."

"I think I'd better go over to Tehran and see her." Fitz fingered the letter. "She sounds as though she's depressed."

"If you can spare the time and"—Stakes inclined his head toward the seat Lynn had just vacated—"it isn't going to interfere with something else that's important in your life. I have the distinct feeling that Laylah needs you just now. Not that she was all that considerate of your feelings, but she's a young woman and perhaps this experience with Courty has given her a slightly more mature outlook."

"Thanks, John. I appreciate your frankness. I'll cable her this afternoon and go over tomorrow."

"Is there anything I can get into here you can think of?"

"I don't know. When the Kajmira deal blew that ended it for me, temporarily at any rate. All I've got going is what you can see around you."

"It's enough. I hear this place is better than an oil well."

"I'm fortunate but this isn't my idea of a life's work." He looked about. "I'd better go find Lynn. This is the first time I've seen her get temperamental."

"I didn't realize she was anything other than a—what did you call her?—an itinerant photographer or I wouldn't have talked about Laylah in front of her. I can see she is very attached to you. By the way, Fitz, it is odd, you having a Jewish guest in Arabia."

"I've never been a conventional type." Fitz stood. "Have whatever you want, John. I'll be back." Fitz walked across the crowded restaurant and through the kitchen, into his pantry, and then into the house. Lynn was sitting in the living room moodily staring out the window at the patio.

"When are you leaving?" she asked as he walked in.

"Leaving?"

"To see her. She lost her boy friend and now she wants you back, right?"

"That's not exactly it, Lynn. I am a friend now, that's all. And it seems like she needs a friend."

"So you are going back to her."

"I think I should see if there's anything I can do to make her feel better," Fitz replied weakly. "I'll only be gone a couple of days. It's the least I can do after what she did for me."

"Well, don't expect me to be here when you come back from offering yourself to her after she walked all over you for that society stud and got herself properly jilted."

"Oh God, Lynn! I'm not offering myself to her, just my friendship. If I can do anything to make her happier I owe it to her. If it hadn't been for Laylah I would be broke now. I would have had everything in that oil project. If you knew how much money it would have taken. I would have had the Ten Tola Bar and every cent stripped from me and still be in debt if I hadn't made the deal with Hemisphere. Do I just ignore all that because she's young and fell in love with a young man of her own class?"

"I understand, better than you. You're still in love with her. You can't help yourself. I thought I'd helped you get over it." Lynn started to weep and Fitz went to her and took her in his arms, but she shook her head and pulled away from him. "I never should have come back to Dubai."

"Of course you should have come back, Lynn. I want you here."

Her voice broke. "Go now. Please."

Fitz stared at Lynn helplessly for a moment, felt defeated, turned, and went back through the kitchen again. Instead of returning to his table he went to the small office Joe Ryan used, situated at the juncture of the kitchen with the restaurant floor. He sat down at Joe's desk and composed a cable to Laylah. Then he picked up the telephone and called Cable and Wireless.

With the cable on its way he went back to his table and rejoined John Stakes. Now that he had decided upon a definite course of action things were no longer confused.

Fitz had no idea whether or not Laylah would be waiting for him when he gave the address of her apartment to the cab driver at Tehran's International Airport. As the cab entered her district his heart pounded. Whatever happened he would always know he had tried to see her, comfort her, and let her know that he was still her friend. He knew he had lost Lynn. She had put up a good front but her plane had left for Beirut and London just ten minutes before he took off for Tehran. For the first time since he and Lynn had met they had slept in separate rooms when they could have been together. That was how crushed she was at his "impetuous, emotional, and irrational response" to Laylah's note.

As the cab wound its way up Laylah's street toward her apartment and the mountains beyond, Fitz felt an uncertainty that unnerved him. Finally he stepped out of the taxi in front of her apartment house. He pressed the button of her apartment.

The answering buzz startled him. He opened the inner door and started up the stairs. Her front door was open and Laylah was standing in it. Except for a darkness beneath her eyes which made her look slightly older and tired, she was the Laylah he had always known. Thick, black tresses hanging almost to her shoulders, the knowing look projected by violet eyes and quizzical lips, the cashmere sweater he had brought her on one of his trips last winter, the tweed skirt, reminiscent of Main Line Philadelphia. It was Laylah, and all the efforts he had made to forget her were in the instant dissipated.

"Hello, Fitz." Her voice was deep and warm. "I've got the vodka on ice and the caviar ready. You know where the facilities are if you want to get freshened up." He walked across her threshold and put down his suitcase. Laylah stood looking levelly at him. She was a tall girl, he remembered. With both hands free he placed them on her shoulders and drew her to him, giving her a tentative kiss. She kissed him back the same way and then drew apart from him.

"You're looking great, Laylah," Fitz managed. "No different from when I last saw you."

"No different?" she asked, surprised. "I'm older."

He shook his head as she gestured toward the bathroom and they sat down together on the sofa. The vodka was in a silver ice bucket, the caviar in the blue tin with the picture of the sturgeon on it, melba toast wrapped in a napkin on a silver tray, chopped egg yolk and onion in silver dishes. It was as though nothing had ever happened, everything the same down to the last detail.

"Tell me about yourself, Fitz," Laylah said. "I hope you were protected financially on that Abu Musa thing."

"Thanks to you, I was."

"My father was very disappointed. But he said that Lorenz Cannon admired you all the more for the way you tried to handle the situation and particularly because you completely disclosed the problem to him before getting him into the deal. My father was grateful for that too. He and Lorenz are old friends."

"Well, the Ten Tola Bar is doing well, better than well. Your friend Joe Ryan should be able to sock away a considerable amount of money over the next few years."

"Yes, I've heard about it even over here." They touched glasses. "Cheers, Fitz." They sipped and then Laylah asked, "What happened to your ambitions to become an ambassador?"

"They've waned considerably." He looked at her significantly. "I somehow lost the motivation since coming back from my trip to the United States."

Laylah looked down at her drink. "You are more qualified than ever after your last experience with the British Foreign Office. The United States needs a man who can build and maintain a strong position on the Arabian Gulf. Nobody would be better than you."

Fitz shrugged. "It just didn't have the same appeal. The American Ambassador should at least have a wife who understands the language and customs." There, he thought, he'd said it.

"My father thinks you can have it if you want it." She looked back at him and smiled. "Anyway, that's not something you have to think about now, is it?"

"No, although I guess I am again. Do you want to tell me about yourself and"—he paused—"everything that's happened here?"

"You mean about Courty?"

"Whatever you want to tell me."

"There isn't much to tell. He was here for over six months while he visited the Arab rulers with John Stakes. I was able to help them make contacts through my friends at the palace. And I guess I was able to use the Embassy on their behalf. The Ambassador knew Courty's family in Boston, of course. He's always impressed with old-line family money like the Thornwells'. I've always heard their fortune originated with the slave trade when Boston was the center for that kind of thing." She laughed. "Once when I got very cross with Courty—it happened more and more toward the end—I said he was nothing but an old blackbirder himself. He didn't think it was funny."

"What finally happened?"

"He went home and, as you can see, I'm here." She shrugged her shoulders. "Just as well."

"Supposing he came back. Wouldn't you two get together again?"

Laylah thought about the question and shrugged again. "I don't know, Fitz. Certainly not the way it was." She heaped two more pieces of melba toast with caviar and poured them each another pony of vodka.

Finally Laylah observed, "You certainly found business in Tehran fast after John Stakes gave you my letter. I appreciate it, Fitz. I really wanted to see you, as I guess you gathered. I felt so guilty about you getting the divorce for me and then I couldn't follow through."

"As you said at the time, it was something that had to be done eventually anyway," Fitz replied gently. After a long pause: "Where do we go from here?"

"I'd like to go dancing someplace." Laylah slid from the real purpose of the question.

"I made a reservation at the Darband Hotel. We could go there," Fitz suggested.

After dinner and dancing at the Darband the old warmth was returning. However, Fitz knew that it would not be salubrious to their reawakening intimacy if he pressed, or even suggested that he stay with her that night.

At the end of the evening Fitz took Laylah back to her apartment. By now they had made a date for the next day. He would come down to the Embassy, call on General Fielding, and the Ambassador if he was free, and then Laylah and he would go to La Résidence for lunch. They would also see each other again the following evening. That was as far as they made plans.

CHAPTER 49

Fitz returned to Dubai from Tehran with new resolve. He and
Laylah had sensed that eventually they could be even closer than
they were before. But Fitz didn't want Laylah on the rebound
from Courty. He knew she would have accepted a proposal from
him, but he was afraid that they might get married and when she
was completely over her affair with Courty she would regret marrying old-shoe friend Fitz Lodd.

Nevertheless, Fitz's heart sang once more and his face reflected
his happiness in the knowledge there was every likelihood that
Laylah and he would be together again. On this visit, although he
had badly wanted to make love to her, he resisted the driving
desire and stayed at the hotel.

When Fitz left Tehran he knew that the next time he came to
her or she to him their old intimacy, once shattered and now on
the mend, would blossom into a total relationship stronger and
even more exciting, if possible, than it had ever been.

It was late in the day when Fitz arrived at his home beside the
Ten Tola Bar. He had no sooner put down his suitcase than Peter
handed him a note and told him that the man from Beirut was in
the bar. Fitz read the message. Abe Ferutti had come in just a few
hours earlier. He had urgent communications for Fitz from
friends in Washington, D.C.

Gillian, the pretty English girl, had seated Abe Ferutti at the
majlis, knowing he was a business associate of Fitz's. The agent
looked up and, seeing Fitz coming across the room, vacated the
seat he had taken at the head of the table, leaving it open for its
rightful occupant.

"You seem to be happy as hell about something," Abe observed
as Fitz sat down.

"Things may work out all right after all," Fitz acknowledged.

"You have the look of a man loaded for bear, or maybe a camel caravan."

"I've had a couple of long teletype conversations with Washington. And I have a cable for you from our friend Colonel Dick Healey. I think we'd better talk up in your office."

Once ensconced in the office with the picture pulled back so Fitz could see who was coming into the restaurant, he and Abe started talking business. "The head of operations at the Agency would like to see that huge arms shipment destroyed," Abe began.

"I'll try to get Colonel Buttres off his Brit ass. It's a job for the Scouts."

"You and I both know that he can't do anything now."

"What did you have in mind then, Abe?"

"You're a resourceful old guerrilla fighter. How do we do it?"

"Seriously, Abe, I can't get personally into an operation."

"What about your caper on the Arabian Sea?"

"That was different."

"Because you were starting your fortune? This place?" He waved at the window. "By shooting up a few Indian patrol launches?"

"It's one thing to get into an armed conflict with pirates on the high seas and quite another to attack a desert convoy within the territorial limits of one of these emirates. For all I know, the shipment may have the blessing of one of the shaikhs. As far as I can gather, they're planning to land on the coast off Kajmira. That means that Hamed or Saqr or both are getting a cut out of the deal. Christ, I'd lose everything I've built up here, the chance of maybe even becoming a U.S. diplomatic representative, if I got caught pulling off a raid on a line of trucks. They'd say I was a hijacker."

"I'm not asking you to get caught." A sardonic smile came over Abe's face. He reached into his thin plastic briefcase and pulled out a decoded teletype message and handed it to Fitz.

"Fitz," the message which was sent to him under Dick Healey's name read, "the covert operations group really want this one pulled off. Abe will explain if necessary the importance of this. Do it for us. Remember our operation inside Cambodia when we shouldn't have been there back in '63? We set the Commies' timetable back a year on that one. This is the same thing. Your friends in Washington are working to get you what you want. So do this one for all of us."

Abe watched Fitz as he read the message and then turned to the CIA agent. "If I do this, and I say 'if' because I don't know whether or not I can, it is only because a certain young lady currently in Tehran remotivated me to want that ambassador job here in the Emirates."

"Good for her," Abe replied. "I'll see that she gets a promotion."

"If I pull this off I'm going to do everything to promote her from second assistant intelligence officer to wife of the Ambassador."

"How do we handle it, Fitz?" The CIA man radiated excitement.

"First I find Sepah. Are you going active on this operation?"

Abe shook his head. "I can't. If it misfires and I'm captured they'll establish direct U.S. complicity."

"But if you're only killed they can't interrogate you." Fitz well knew the language he was using. "You can carry a thermite grenade attached to your belt. If you're wounded you or I pull the cord and your body will be burned beyond recognition. That's the way Dick and I handled the Cambodian interdiction. If either of us had been hit and couldn't get out, the other would have burned him."

Abe's tough veneer deserted him momentarily. "Fitz, I'm under orders not to personally become involved in black operations. I'll send for a black operator if you want one, or even two. Non U.S. citizens."

"I'm a U.S. citizen," Fitz reminded Abe, taking some delight in the agent's discomfiture. "You don't think they'll say I was working for the Agency if I'm caught or killed?" he asked argumentatively.

"But since you are definitely not, since you retired from the Army somewhat under a cloud, it will be easy to make a denial of any alleged connection you might have with us stick."

Fitz raised a hand as though to ward off a blow. "O.K., O.K., Abe. I'll do it. And I don't want any goddamned black operator down here. If I do it, I do it my own way with my own people, if I can find them. I probably could use two good desert drivers."

The intelligence agent smiled to himself. He was well aware of Lieutenant Colonel Lodd's ability when it came to special combat operations. The arms shipment would be effectively interdicted.

That night Fitz and Abe monitored all the conversations at the bugged tables of the Ten Tola Bar. It was surprising how dull and inconsequential most of the talk was, but they hoped that someone might drop a hint about the arms shipment that would give them a better fix on the operation. Eventually, they hoped, Serrat would be in, if not tonight, then tomorrow night.

Fitz noticed that Majid Jabir was sitting in one of the corner booths with Ed Bass, the local head of the new Sharjah Petroleum Development Company, and two other American executives of the company. As local head of Hemisphere, these were the enemy and he wondered what Majid was doing with them, so he tuned in.

It was pretty much a foregone conclusion that the Sharjah-Kajmira dispute was going to be worked out in Sharjah's favor, especially with Iran's claim to half the island and half the oil revenues. Everybody played the game of appeasing the Shah at all costs. But in the conversation now taking place below Fitz learned something new.

"I have succeeded," Majid was telling the president of SPDC, "in securing the announcement that the arbitration has been decided in favor of Sharjah." Majid noticed, as did Fitz even from the distance of the one-way window, that the president seemed unimpressed by the statement.

"A foregone conclusion, you say," Majid continued. "Perhaps. But what does it mean to you to be able to start drilling next week instead of next year as would surely have happened? We are trying to form a Federation and all the states must agree to it. Therefore Kajmira must feel that full measure has been given to its claim. The arbitration could go on indefinitely.

"Perhaps," Majid continued persuasively, "you don't understand the subtleties of what is now called the Trucial States and will soon be known as the United Arab Emirates."

He sure as hell doesn't, Fitz thought as Majid tried to explain. "I have talked to the Ruler of Dubai and the Ruler of Abu Dhabi. Shaikh Zayed is supporting Sharjah's claim. I am negotiating on Rashid's part for strong Maktoum family representation in the leadership of the new Federation. If Rashid goes along with Zayed on the Sharjah claim it will be immediately decided and you can start drilling."

If Ed Bass couldn't fathom that, he ought to be back in Louisiana working a rig, Fitz thought. But Ed and his two top men seemed finally to comprehend. "You can make this happen, Majid?" Bass asked.

"But of course. That's why we're sitting here. I can have you drilling in a week. And there was another point holding up drilling, you know. The Shah of Iran insisted that Iran's half of the oil revenue come off the top. In other words, the Shah asked for fifty percent of the total money realized and the other expenses and bits and pieces paid out in percentages come strictly out of Sharjah's share. Now I am in a position to get Sharjah to agree to this."

Fitz shook his head. Majid was a slick operator. Fitz didn't feel it was disloyal of Majid to be working with Sharjah Petroleum. There was nothing more he could do to help Hemisphere.

"Well, that's just wonderful, Majid," Ed Bass said. "We didn't really think we'd be able to start drilling for a long time. The company much appreciates what you've done."

"It hasn't been done yet." Majid bestowed his most inscrutable smile on the Americans. "But it is ready to be done."

"Well, you go right ahead and do it, Majid. You can be sure the company will recognize your efforts."

"Yes, I will be sure. The company can pay me half when I start to put the final building blocks together and the other half when you begin drilling. Is that fair?"

"Of course, Majid." Then, cautiously: "What did you have in mind as a fee?"

"Four million dollars," Majid replied without hesitation.

"Four million?" Bass sputtered. "My God, Majid. There's no way the company could go for that."

"You would have had nothing if it hadn't been for British meddling, and even now, with Mr. Lodd pressing Hemisphere's claim so vigorously, there is always the possibility that some kind of compromise could be effected." Majid pointed all this out reasonably and logically. "However, if you feel my fee is too high," he went on after a dramatic pause, "why don't we just—cut it in half?"

"Good old Shaikh Cut-It-in-Half," Fitz commented to Abe.

"I'll pass the word along to my company." Ed Bass could be seen glancing at his watch. "I'll put a call through to Los Angeles now. It would be just coming up noon there." He stood up. "I'll get back to you, Majid, but you start moving those building blocks around. We want to see some production as soon as possible."

Majid nodded. "Of course, it costs a great deal of money to just be sitting and waiting."

"The way he's going he'll be richer than the Ruler in a few years," Fitz chuckled. "I'd better tell Fender Browne to get onto Sharjah Petroleum Development Company and sell them the equipment they'll need."

"Be careful how you dispense information, Fitz," the CIA man cautioned. "If you give out too much good stuff people will start wondering where you're getting it and some smart Brit Special Branch agent might just suspect that you've got an electronic surveillance system going in your pub."

"Abe, old friend," Fitz said, "when this black, covert, whatever you want to call it, operation is over, I'm ripping that damned system out of my gin mill once and for all. I don't like eavesdropping."

"But look at how valuable it can be." A note of alarm crept into Abe's tone. "I wish I had something like this in Beirut. You can't just shut down the most valuable listening post on the Gulf."

"When I've interdicted that arms shipment I've done more than enough for the Company to deserve its help in being recommended for the ambassadorial post. I'm an intelligence officer, or rather was, yes. But a spy? No."

Abe decided not to argue with Fitz. At the right time certain pressures could be brought to bear which would change his resolve.

Then the activity they had been awaiting occurred. Through the doors came Jean Louis Serrat and his French associate. Gillian took them to Serrat's usual table. Immediately Abe tuned in to their conversation.

For half an hour Abe listened to talk about girls in Beirut and speculation about the girls in the Ten Tola Band who they were sleeping with. Then the Iraqi banker from his area came in with his Arab associate and sat down at Serrat table. They sipped one cup of coffee and then quickly stated the progress which had been made.

It had been arranged that the shipment would be on the Kajmira coastline above the town in a small cove where Shaikh Saqr had a beach house. Saqr had been paid to allow landing craft to come into his cove on Thursday night, the night most Arabs celebrated since the next day was their holiday. Sat had arranged for a convoy of Bedford trucks to be waiting and it was planned to load the crates from the landing craft into the truck between ten-thirty and midnight. A Pakistani and Indian labor gang would be standing by.

"There's still the matter of the final payment," Serrat brought up.

"We have paid two million rials already," the banker declared. "The final one million will be paid in Oman. Your manufacturers in France should be very happy."

"When you are ready to buy some Mystère jets we'll talk real business," Serrat replied airily. "This is more in the way of being an accommodation job."

Fitz looked at Abe. "Some accommodation. Half a million dollars down, another quarter million in Oman."

"That's a quarter mil they'll never see," Abe grunted in satisfaction.

The Arab was speaking. "A squad of Dhofar fighting men from the Trucial Oman Scouts will desert their British officers and meet us, fully armed, at the landing point. They will provide protection for the trucks and then for the camel caravan which will carry the arms the last leg of their journey into the mountains. Then these trained men will become part of the cadre which will organize attacks on Oman Government installations while the others infiltrate and create bases in the Musandam Peninsula."

This intelligence was of real concern to Fitz. "Hell, Abe. Now we're in for a goddamned fire fight. Those Dhofars are the best fighters the Scouts have."

"You'll be able to handle them, Fitz," Abe said confidently.

"I wish I kr what kind of weapons they'll have."

"Why dor ou pump your friend Buttres on that matter? One colonel to a her?" Abe suggested. "Go ahead. I'll stay with the bugs in cas y more information develops at Serrat's table."

CHAPTER 50

The headquarters of the Trucial Oman Scouts did not have especially happy memories for Fitz. All he could think of was the frustrating meeting with Brian Falmey as he walked into the very British old-school atmosphere somehow re-created out on the Arabian Gulf by the English officers who founded the Trucial Oman Scouts. The general factotum of the Scouts, the officer who had served longest in time with the Scouts, Major Tom Rudd, led Fitz through the hallways adorned with pictures of previous commanders, flags, and military memorabilia to the rear of the building. Colonel Buttres's door was open and Fitz followed Tom Rudd in. The Colonel stood up and held out his hand, which Fitz took for a moment, and then they both sat down. The commander was wearing the faded blue uniform of the Scouts with red-trimmed epaulettes. His red and white checked *kuffiyah* hung over the post of a chair.

"Thank you for coming over, Fitz. From what little you said last night your information should be most interesting. Go ahead and tell us what you heard."

"As you may have surmised, we pick up snatches of information around the Ten Tola Bar and as an old intelligence officer I sometimes put the bits and pieces of information together in jigsaw-puzzle fashion and, as you know, I sometimes arrive at a conclusion."

"And you have recently arrived at a conclusion?" Buttres asked.

"Correct, Ken. And it is as follows. This is Tuesday morning. In two nights, Thursday, the night before the Arab weekend, a ship will put in on a cove north of the town of Kajmira. This ship is loaded with armaments to be transported by Bedford trucks from the cove where Saqr has his beach house. You know it?"

Buttres nodded. "Certainly. Go on."

"These arms will be transported across the desert to the point where the road from Dubai to the Buraimi Oasis turns south paralleling the mountains of Oman. The trucks will penetrate the mountains for a short distance and then the arms will be packed onto camels which will carry the crates of guns and ammunition through the wadis and hills up to the Communist cadre forming up there."

Buttres nodded his head thoughtfully, his lower lip twitching. "You have mentioned arms shipments before. Do you mean that people come into the Ten Tola Bar and within the hearing of the waitresses talk about smuggling guns?"

"Not exactly, Ken. As I said, one puts the pieces together."

"You seem to get a remarkably large basket of pieces." The commander of the Scouts glanced suspiciously at Fitz.

"Well, there is more. Are you expecting a desertion by any of your national groups in the Scouts?"

An alarmed flash flew between the Colonel and Tom Rudd, who abruptly stopped puffing on his pipe. "What else, Fitz?" Buttres asked. "Pity you aren't working for us."

"How much longer are you going to be here?" Fitz asked.

"Not much longer, that's the point. Now what about desertion?"

"I seem to come up with the fact that your Dhofars, or some of them anyway, plan to desert on Thursday, with their weapons, and join this arms shipment, which is supposed to carry a year's supply of guns and ammunition to the Communist insurgents in the hills of Oman. Their objective then will be to establish operating bases in the Musandam Peninsula. As you know, it is the Communist idea to control the Straits of Hormuz by subverting Oman."

"This is all very interesting, Fitz. From your sources, how good is this information?"

"Number one. It is possible that the plans may change but as of now this is what is scheduled."

"Is that Frenchman I see at the Ten Tola Bar, Serrat, mixed up in this?"

"Of course. That's his business, isn't it?"

Buttres sat in silence for some moments. "I appreciate your passing this on to me, Fitz. I don't just know what, if anything, I can do about it. I'll have to discuss the situation with Brian Falmey."

"Then you can be sure nothing will happen. Why don't you just take a squadron or two of the Scouts—non-Dhofars, I'd suggest—and blow up the trucks? You don't want to see a year's supply of arms get through no matter how much pressure that will put on Qabus to stick with Britain." Fitz regretted the statement as it came out of his mouth. Buttres leaned forward and shot a sharp look at Fitz. It was obvious that he recalled the statement of John Brush, Brian Falmey's number two, a week earlier at the Ten Tola Bar.

Finally Buttres sat back thoughtfully in his seat. "Fortunately Brian Falmey was due back yesterday from leave. I'll discuss the matter with him. Anything else, Fitz?"

"Isn't that enough?"

"Yes, of course. And really, we do appreciate these tips you pass on from time to time. Believe me, Fitz, if for one reason or another we don't appear to act on them it isn't my fault. I'm a very political soldier, you know. More so than ever now that we are pulling out of here."

"Yes, I'm well aware of the tidying up process that's going on. Well, maybe we'll have a drink tonight at the Ten Tola Bar, on me." Fitz stood up.

"I'll probably be around. Remind me to keep my mouth shut." He looked up at Fitz from under his brows, his head rising and falling slightly.

Everything seems to begin and end in Kajmira, Fitz thought as his Land Rover's balloon tires floated the vehicle over the sand. Today, however, he was not on his way to see Hamed or Saqr. Arriving in the town, Fitz drove up to the large warehouse which belonged to Sepah. He jumped down from the Land Rover and walked up to the small door inside the large sliding door of the corrugated-iron building and pulled it open.

Inside, due to a clever ventilating system, the big storage building was pleasantly cool. Crates, cartons, tools, and vehicles were stored all over the dimly lit interior. In the far corner Fitz recognized Mohammed, Juma, and Khalil, who were waiting for him.

They wore the costume of the laborer on the Gulf, loose-fitting slacks, a smock, and a ragged turban.

"*Keef Haalkum*," Fitz greeted them.

"*Al Hamdu lillah Zein*," they called back.

Sepah had done well, Fitz thought, to assemble on such short notice the three men he had taught how to be gunners. This was the total extent of his army. He explained at length to his three former pupils the extent of the mission two nights hence.

Fitz found the three Land Rovers Sepah had told him he could use and with the help of his stalwarts he began fastening the gun mounts to the back of the vehicles. The job took all day and they stopped only when it became too dark to see what they were doing.

That night Fitz wrote a letter to Laylah and, exhausted from the unaccustomed physical labor in the heat, he went to bed early. The following day was again spent with Mohammed, Khalil, and Juma, and by evening they had the guns mounted on three of the Land Rovers. Thursday was devoted to mounting the second 20-mm. cannon on the rear of Fitz's Land Rover. The job was completed by midday and then Fitz and his three-man strike force went to the Hemisphere Petroleum Company beach house to rest and review the strategy for that night.

Colonel Buttres had not appeared at the Ten Tola Bar since Fitz's meeting with him and Fitz knew for sure, although he had hoped otherwise to the last minute, that the TOS would not be interdicting the arms convoy. He prayed that at least Buttres had prevented the defection of the Dhofars.

Naturally Jean Louis Serrat had planned carefully. It was a moonless night that had been picked for the ship to land and the trucks to drive across the desert to Oman.

The bluff overlooking the sea and standing half a mile south of Shaikh Saqr's cove had once been the site of a Portuguese trading post. Potsherds showed white on the sand. They were scattered all over the dunes and by day frequently attracted picnickers who amused themselves by digging for ancient coins and artifacts.

Through the special light-intensifying binoculars he had been given in Washington, Fitz scanned the activity in the cove. A World War II-vintage landing craft was just sliding up on the beach and letting down its forward bulkhead, making a ramp onto the sand. A foreman drove the work party onto the ramp and into the landing craft and the laborers began moving crates off the boat and onto the beach. Other laborers hefted the crates onto the large Bedford trucks which had been backed down the incline of the beach as close to the landing craft as they could get without being mired in the soft, wet sand.

Fitz lowered his binoculars and walked back to his Land Rover parked below the brow of the hill. He flipped on the switch of the radio transceiver he had installed, placed earphones over his head, and blew into the microphone.

"Read you, Roy," Fitz heard Abe Ferutti's voice from the office in the Ten Tola Bar come over the radio. "What's happening?"

Roy was Fitz's radio code signal. "LCV on the beach. Unloading now in process. Looks like a much bigger operation than was originally planned. I can count ten Bedford trucks and two personnel carriers down there. Also, it looks as though they have about fifty laborers."

"What security do they have?"

"Looks like our friends at the TOS couldn't prevent the defection of about thirty-five men, presumably Dhofars. They're still in uniform. At least they didn't desert with their arms."

"Keep the operation under surveillance and let me know what's going on. I'll be right here. Base out."

"Roy out." Fitz walked from the Land Rover up to the hill and continued to scan the situation below. He quickly discovered that it made no difference whether or not the Dhofar fighting men had left their barracks unarmed. As he watched, crates were opened and the warriors from Oman's southernmost province of Dhofar were arming themselves directly from the shipment.

They were obviously a well-trained unit and they apportioned among themselves a balanced group of weapons. Fitz counted half a dozen grenade launchers, automatic rifles, submachine guns, high-powered sniper rifles, and hand guns being distributed. A formidable display of firepower against which there was only Fitz and his three Arab gunners to interdict the convoy. However, Fitz felt his plan would prevail.

The loading of the crates took the fifty laborers two hours to perform and at about midnight the caravan was ready to start. To

Fitz's horror the laborers were loaded into the trucks to sit on top of the munitions crates. These same workers, Fitz realized, would be employed to reload the crates on the backs of the camels, which, unlike even a Land Rover, much less a heavy truck, could straggle through the passes, wadis, and the hills of Oman.

The Dhofar unit split into two detachments—one rode in the personnel carrier at the head of the line of trucks, the other bringing up the rear. Grimly Fitz watched the year's supply of munitions for the PFLOAG insurgents in the Oman hills start out across the desert. Way off to the north he thought he detected a movement out on the dark desert. He scanned the area with the binoculars and picked up two Land Rovers, one of which had an open rear platform on which was mounted a naked .30-caliber machine gun. Was this the convoy's extra flank security? he wondered.

Once again Fitz flipped the radio switch and pulled the earphones over his head and blew into the microphone. The answering signal shot back.

"Base standing by. What's going on?"

Fitz reported all developments, expressing his concern for the laborers and even the Dhofars when he opened up on them with 20-mm. cannons. "There must be more than a hundred people involved in this convoy," he reiterated. "The Dhofars are well armed but we can stand off out of their range and annihilate them. It's the flank security they have out to the north at the moment that worries me. Probably it's Serrat, the other Frenchman, and the Arab in one vehicle, with a gun crew riding shotgun in the armed Land Rover escorting them."

"Rake them once with your twenty and a lot of problems will be solved for us in the Gulf. Maybe they'll have that Iraqi banker with them and you can get him too."

"We'll just have to play it as it comes, Base. I'm going to rendezvous with my three elements and we'll proceed to operation point."

It was about a twenty-minute drive back to the town of Kajmira and Fitz pulled up in front of Sepah's warehouse. The 20-mm. cannon mounted in the back of his Land Rover was covered with a canvas hood. Fitz leapt from the Land Rover and knocked at the door. Immediately the large sliding door eased open and three

Land Rovers with rear canopies concealing the mounted weapons drove out of the warehouse. The massive door slid closed behind them.

In each Land Rover an Arab gunner sat beside a driver who had been recruited by Abe from among his "black," or covert, agents. Fitz had not wanted a driver, preferring to handle his armed Land Rover completely by himself.

The three Land Rovers followed Fitz as he set out across the desert. The Land Rovers paralleling the route of the arms caravan ten miles to the south were able to travel considerably faster than the truck convoy. As he drove over the desert sands Fitz evolved an entirely new strategy for the interdiction of the convoy. The situation was drastically different from what he and Abe had envisioned when they developed their plan for dealing with the huge load of French arms.

It had taken them exactly two and a half hours to reach the point Fitz had decided upon for the ambush. He had twice flown over the area and photo-mapped it in detail. By now they were driving over the hard-packed gravel and sand that characterized the pass into the Oman hills from the Dubai road. They were following the same route the trucks would soon be churning across. To the south on their right lay the forbidding steep, high sand hills which Fitz had driven across with Laylah beside him. Was it really a year ago? Now he could afford to smile at the memory. Straight ahead of them awaited the safety of the rugged mountain passes through which no wheeled vehicle could ever proceed. To the left, on the north flank, lay only flat, open desert. Fortunately the darkness favored the ambushers in their relatively small, low vehicles over the large, noisy, cumbersome, heavily loaded trucks.

Fitz led his tiny mechanized strike force into the desert north of the hard-packed track and they stopped fifteen hundred yards out from where the convoy would have to pass. He jumped out of his vehicle and walked over to the other 20-mm. cannon. Juma was already pulling the canopy off the rear of the Land Rover, exposing his weapon. He grinned and patted it affectionately.

"We make a quick change, Juma," Fitz said. "Take off the silencer and flash suppressor."

"But they will then see me," Juma protested.

"That's what we want. They have no weapons that can reach us out here. I want to frighten them. We don't want to kill all those innocent workingmen."

Juma could see no reason for not killing every living thing associated with the convoy but he obeyed orders. With Fitz's help the silencer was removed and the Land Rover backed into position, the big gun commanding a wide sector of the track the trucks would soon be following.

It took Fitz about twenty minutes to place Juma, Khalil, and Mohammed. The two 20-mm. cannons were placed at the extremities of the ambush, about two hundred yards apart, and evenly spaced between them were the two .30-caliber machine guns, whose mission it was to protect the twenties as much as possible in case of counterattack. When the ambush was completely set up, Fitz once again radioed base.

"Roy here. We're all set up. But I've changed operating procedure." Fitz went on to explain. "I don't want to be responsible for killing those people. I've given orders to fire at the bottom of the trucks, blow off the wheels if possible but no firing into the canopies of the trucks. There must be five or six laborers in the back of each truck. And then there are two men up front in each truck, a driver and armed Dhofar as well as the Dhofars in the lead and tail personnel carriers."

"You're crazy, Roy!" Abe's voice carried his agitation clearly over the radio. "You could lie out of range and destroy every truck, blow up the ammo, kill the Communists, without ever taking a return round. Now they'll see you."

"I don't want to kill the Dhofars. They think they're fighting to keep their province independent."

"God damn it, Roy!" the anguished voice crackled. "What the hell's gone wrong with you?"

"Nothing. I'm doing what I promised. Not one of those crates of guns and ammo will get any further than this point. Tomorrow morning the Dubai and Sharjah police can come out and pick up the entire load, with a little help from the TOS if the Political Agent lets them. Isn't that the point of this mission? And anyway we shouldn't be talking so long in the clear. It's conceivable someone might pick up this frequency."

"Base to Roy. You're crazy! Good luck! Out!"

Fitz had stationed Khalil close enough to him so he could shout orders to him if necessary. He told both of the .30-caliber gunners to be on the watch for two Land Rovers, one of them armed with a machine gun, cruising along on the north flank of the convoy. Fitz now alternately scanned the desert behind him and the track in front of him. Through the light-intensifying binoculars he could see, almost as clearly as in daylight, anything upon which he trained them.

Then in the distance he heard the chuffing and rumbling of the heavy diesel trucks approaching. Finally the lead personnel carrier came into sight way off to the east on his right. Once again he flipped on the radio.

"Base. Lead truck in sight. Coming along steadily about twenty-five miles an hour. Estimate operation commence in about ten minutes." Again he swept the northern desert behind him but detected no signs of the Land Rovers. He took the AR-15 .223-caliber submachine gun from the rack on the dashboard of the Land Rover and placed it conveniently on the driver's seat along with four magazines of twenty rounds each and then he climbed onto the rear of the vehicle and swung the 20-mm. cannon in an arc covering the track ahead.

Minutes later he watched the convoy roll into the ambush. By now the first three trucks would have passed by Juma's position. One after another the Bedfords entered the destruction zone and then the personnel carrier was directly opposite Fitz's position. He let it go by, still well within his arc of fire. A second truck came abreast of him. Checking through the binoculars, he saw the last truck in the convoy was directly in Juma's range. He let the binoculars drop, hanging from the strap around his neck, and took careful aim on the front wheels and engine block of the personnel carrier. A driver and nine men were in it, he noticed.

Fitz stroked the trigger and the silent desert nighttime was rent with the throaty roar and bright flashes of the heavy rounds. Direct hit. The engine block fired and the wheels disintegrated, throwing the Dhofars suddenly, shockingly, through the air. They landed stunned and terrified on the sand as Fitz was blasting at the front wheels and engine block of the first Bedford. Bits and pieces of the truck and wheel base flew into the air as it knelt into the desert sand.

Fitz could hear Juma's twenty dealing destruction down the

line and the two .30-calibers added to the tumult, although the rounds, if they reached the convoy at all, would have been too spent to do damage. But the firing had the desired effect. All the trucks which hadn't been hit turned off to the right, spinning wheels churning into the desert and the sand dunes.

Fitz hoped that Juma was obeying orders. Shoot up only one truck and then deliberately aim above them to drive them into the sand dunes without taking a chance of inflicting casualties.

Fitz stopped firing long enough to survey the truck line through the binoculars. They were all, except for the first and last truck in line, which had been disabled, plunging through the cloying sand hills, powering up one dune, nearly toppling down the other side. Fitz laughed aloud. The heavily loaded trucks would never come out of those dunes. The drivers and laborers would easily enough be able to abandon them and struggle out of the sand, but the trucks and their cargo would never see the hundred or so camels waiting to receive the arms.

Now to notify Base. "Mission accomplished. Two trucks destroyed without inflicting casualties. All the other trucks hopelessly mired in the sand dunes. Drivers and workers abandoning them. Tell the cops they can come out and help themselves to a generous supply of weaponry for the Union Defense Force when it gets started."

"Good show, Roy. Now get out of there fast."

"Roy out." He reached under the dashboard for the flare gun and fired a green flare into the air, the signal for the drivers to pull out of the ambush fast and head back to Kajmira. He was just wondering what had happened to the flanking Land Rovers he had observed back at the coast when from the direction of the ambush, but much closer, a concentration of small-arms fire broke out.

The goddamned Dhofars! Fitz thought to himself. They were moving in on him fast, he realized, as he heard the sting of bullets probing the Land Rover.

Holding his head low and slinging the AR-15 over his shoulder, he started up the Land Rover and jackrabbited out of position, heading away from the firing. Just as he thought he was safe a splattering explosion shook the Land Rover and he felt a sudden sharp pain in his right thigh and the stickiness of blood running down his leg. The Land Rover had been jolted sideways by what he knew was a grenade from a launcher. There would be more. He struggled, despite the pain, to get the Land Rover headed away but the engine gasped and expired.

This had to be it, he thought. He checked his weapon, still slung over his shoulder, grabbed the magazines, and heaved himself out of his vehicle, now the target of Dhofar small-arms fire. Agonizingly he crawled away from the Land Rover toward the north. His binoculars had been lost in the explosion. Several more grenades exploded around the Land Rover as Fitz slithered, crawled, and rolled away from it. Flames began to lap about the vehicle's engine and in their glow he saw silhouetted the forms of three of the Dhofars who, following their training, had attacked directly into the ambush. The fighting men were looking into the vehicle for some sign of its former occupant and suddenly realized that he had escaped. They turned and started to fan out, heading toward Fitz. Before they could get out of the illuminating flames now fast consuming the Land Rover, Fitz leveled his AR-15 and with the weapon turned to single fire he took careful aim at one of the Dhofars and squeezed off a shot. The target seemed to blow apart as the deadly, long, thin, tumbling bullet tore into him. Before the other two could dive out of the circle of light Fitz fired twice more and hit them both. Even a grazing hit with the AR-15 sends a shock wave through the body sufficient to permanently disable. Three Dhofars would never fight again.

Knowing that their companions must be close behind, Fitz continued to struggle away from the flaming Land Rover, dragging his wounded leg behind him. He must have been hit by a piece of metal torn from his Land Rover, Fitz thought. His thigh felt as though the wound was a jagged one. He hoped that perhaps Khalil or Mohammed in the two Land Rovers with the .30-caliber machine guns might see his vehicle in flames and try to rescue him. However, Fitz had given specific orders that when they saw the green flare they would speed away from the ambush and get lost in the desert and then head back for Kajmira. Perhaps, if the Dhofars didn't find him, he could hide out in the desert until morning when the police came out. They would have little sympathy for the American but at least they would get him to a hospital.

And then he heard sporadic random fire from the location of his fast-burning Land Rover. More Dhofars had come upon the scene and found the bodies of their three companions, Fitz surmised. They would pursue him relentlessly all night. He was already feeling weak from shock and loss of blood. From his pocket he drew a handkerchief and tied it tightly around his pants leg over the wound. The pain from the pressure on the wound was excruciating but if he could stanch the bleeding he might still have a chance. Strangely enough, he found he had no regrets about the way he had handled the operation. It was ironic; in his desire to avoid inflicting casualties he had become one.

The shots kept up behind him but the Dhofars now were careful not to silhouette themselves. From the muzzle flashes Fitz determined that at least six or eight men were looking for him, hoping to hit him with a lucky shot.

Suddenly from the north, coming directly toward him, he heard the sound of a vehicle. Could it be one of his gunners? He doubted it. More likely the Frenchmen coming in to find out what had happened to the arms cargo, or perhaps the Iraqi. There was little he could do now. They would treat him no less harshly than the Dhofars.

As the vehicle approached he could clearly see it was not one of his. It was a Land Rover with a .30-caliber machine gun mounted on the rear and a man crouched behind the weapon. A second Land Rover was behind the first. Fitz placed his AR-15 to his shoulder, flipping the key to full automatic fire, trying to ignore the pain in his leg as he leveled the sights on the gunner.

He was about to fire when he heard a voice booming out over the desert in English. "Cease fire, cease fire. Trucial Oman Scouts!"

Fitz was horrified at how close he had come to opening fire on the Scouts. However, the Dhofars seemed to have no hesitation at firing on their former comrades in arms.

At least the Scouts wouldn't kill him, Fitz thought. "I'm here!" he shouted. "Lodd."

"What the hell are you doing out here, you old bugger?" Never was he happier to hear Ken Buttres's voice.

"Here!" Fitz shouted. "I'm hit." The intensity of the fire from the Dhofars increased as they ran toward the TOS vehicle, firing as they came.

An explosion rocked the TOS vehicle. "You'd better get out!" Fitz shouted. "They've got grenade launchers!" His voice sounded pathetically weak even to him. The unarmed Land Rover turned toward him.

"Where are you, Fitz?" Buttres called through the bullhorn.

Fitz raised his rifle and let off a burst into the air. He guided not only the TOS Land Rover to him but also the Dhofars.

The Land Rover reached him first, and while the escorting vehicle spat fire at the advancing Dhofars, from its .30-caliber machine gun, Buttres leaped out of the driver's seat, grabbed Fitz under the arms, and hauled him back into the front seat. Almost unconscious from pain, shock, and loss of blood, Fitz vaguely noticed that there was another man in the seat behind him. Buttres ran around behind the Land Rover and jumped in behind the wheel and gunned the engine. A grenade exploded just behind them, drawing angry bursts from the TOS escort gunner beside them.

Fitz heard the man behind him say, "This is the most extraordinary thing I could have imagined. Lodd out here trying to do the job of the Scouts."

It was Brian Falmey himself, Fitz realized. Feebly Fitz managed to say, "Thanks, Falmey, Ken. You damn near got yourselves killed. They had me."

"Now look here, you bloody, interfering Yank," Falmey sputtered angrily. "There's only one person who is going to kill you and that's me. I just want to do it when you're healthy."

A slight smile crept to Fitz's lips before he completely blacked out.

CHAPTER 51

Intermittently Fitz had conscious moments over the next three painful hours. He was vaguely aware of being carried out of the Land Rover and being worked on by a doctor in the Trucial Oman Scouts dispensary. How long a time had elapsed between his rescue and the moment he regained complete consciousness, Fitz did not know.

The British doctor was standing above the cot looking down at him. "You're with us again at last I see."

"What day is it?" Fitz asked.

"It's Saturday morning," the doctor replied. "You've been out of things for a day and a half, I'm afraid. Anyway, you're going to be all right. I had to take some nasty pieces of shrapnel out of your leg. It's a miracle that an artery wasn't severed."

"I'll be able to walk all right again?"

"Yes, of course. But not right away."

Fitz looked down at his leg. A sheet had been drawn over him up to his chest. His leg seemed to be all there. Then he became aware of the heat. Apparently the Trucial Oman Scouts dispensary was not equipped with air conditioning. He looked back up at the doctor. "When can I go home?"

"The problem is not whether you're here or at your home. The problem is moving you from here to your home. The wound is all nicely cleaned and sewed up and dressed. I'd hate to take a chance on having something come apart in the process of transporting you. I'm afraid you're going to have to stay with us for at least a week. Then I think we could take a chance on moving you. Of course, I'd rather keep you here longer."

"At least I have air conditioning," Fitz remarked.

"Sorry about that." The doctor smiled apologetically. "It does seem that the Foreign Office could have found it in its budget to provide air conditioning here. However, you are the first Western patient we've had here in some time."

"I suppose Colonel Buttres would like to talk to me."

"Oh yes, indeed he would. And so would several other people. I've had a hard time keeping them away from you. They wanted to wake you up. No regard for a wounded man whatsoever."

"The sooner I get it over with, the better."

Ten minutes later Colonel Ken Buttres was at Fitz's bedside. He gave Fitz a comradely grin. "You're not looking too bad."

"Thanks to you I'm not feeling too bad. How did you happen to be out there?"

"Well, needless to say, I was pretty upset that Falmey wouldn't give me permission to take a couple of squadrons out and do what you did single-handed apparently."

"I had some help."

"Well, whoever was helping you got away cleanly. It did seem a rather formidable job for one man to have done all by himself. In any case, Falmey did feel that we should at least keep an eye on the operation and learn as much as we could about what was going on. We thought perhaps Saqr had a hand in it somewhere, although it certainly was not to his advantage to help the insurgents over in Oman grow strong. When the shaikhs have to run their own defense force they'll learn about insurgency. Falmey and I watched the operation right from the moment the landing ship came in and started unloading. We followed the truck convoy from as distant a course as possible. As you know, old boy, you were quite right about the Dhofars defecting. Except for the three that were dead we rounded them all up in the desert first thing in the morning and brought them back here. They're in detention now."

"What about the arms?"

"Between the colonial police and ourselves we've collected enough armament to equip the entire Union Defense Force when it's formed. Unfortunately, however, the arms are all of French manufacture. We could never allow our Arab friends to have to go to the French for replacement parts and ammunition. We haven't quite decided what to do with all those munitions."

"Maybe you can sell them back to the French."

Buttres laughed. "They don't buy, they just sell. In any case, the main problem seems to be you. Old Falmey is in a real quandary about that question. He'll be here soon. I wouldn't want Falmey to know I told this to you, but we both feel you rendered all of us quite a service. Just six months ago the Scouts would have ripped that convoy apart. But now that our Foreign Minister has announced that we are leaving these parts forever, the impotence of this so-called military unit is staggering."

They both heard the squeaking sound of the screen door opening. Buttres turned. "Here's Brian now."

Falmey walked over to the bed and stood looking down at Fitz. It was undoubtedly an effort on his part but he somehow managed a rather benevolent, even a kindly look. "Ah, Lodd, glad to see you're feeling better. How did it happen that you decided to take on this mission of interdiction all on your own? I mean, obviously there was no profit motive here. And I can't for the life of me see why a man with your new-found wealth would risk his life to stop a large supply of arms from falling into the Communist insurgent movement in Oman."

"Those years I spent in Vietnam trying to defeat the Communists—it does become habit-forming."

Falmey shook his head. "It's hard for me to believe that was the sum total of your motivation in this matter. There's only one possible explanation. Either formally or informally you are part of the CIA. Damn it, but you boys have a ball for yourselves running around the world, mounting covert operations as you see fit. And then you say the British Foreign Office is meddlesome. My belief is reinforced by having met your—what do we call him?—business associate? Mr. Abe Ferutti from Beirut. We came across him when he was making discreet inquiries of Jack Harcross as to your whereabouts."

"Good old Abe." Fitz forced a laugh. "He was down here to see whether I'd be interested in opening an agency to sell American cars. All you can buy here are Toyotas, Datsuns, Mercedes', and British cars. I'd forgotten I had a meeting with him on Friday morning."

"Lodd, don't be inane. I won't press you on that ridiculous cover story. I am, however, surprised. Until now I thought you were nothing but another American freebooter. This I could understand. I didn't like it, but I could understand it. Now a new element comes in. I thought we had a very strict understanding with the Americans that they would not engage in covert operations in this part of Arabia until we had actually pulled out."

Fitz made no reply. Actually he was completely at the mercy of Brian Falmey now. If Falmey exposed this last caper pulled off by the notorious American rogue and cashiered colonel, James Fitzroy Lodd, that would blow all his chances of becoming part of the official American presence on the Arabian Gulf. The little ifs began to plague him. If he had followed Abe's instructions to blast out the column of trucks from afar and run, he wouldn't be in this position. If he had told the CIA agent in the first place that he absolutely would have nothing to do with covert operations, he wouldn't be in this position. If— He made himself stop thinking of his misjudgments.

"All right, Lodd." Falmey interrupted his thoughts. "I didn't expect you to admit the reason for your complicity in this matter. The fact is that other than your wounds, the mission was a resounding success. The only other person who knows you were involved is Jack Harcross. When the Dubai police drove out there, Harcross, of course, spotted your burned-out Land Rover. All identifying marks including the license plate were destroyed by the fire. However, there was the twenty-millimeter cannon. That particular weapon seems to be a trademark of one ex-colonel of the American Army named Lodd."

As he talked, the Political Agent paced about the foot of the bed, sometimes fixing Fitz with piercing stares, at other moments apparently talking aloud to himself.

"Jack Harcross was impressed with the operation, I might add, and the fact that he was notified, albeit from an anonymous caller, of what had happened. He and his men were the first on the scene. Now, while I did have to notify the British Foreign Office of what happened, they left disposition of any loose ends in the matter completely up to me. Nobody but Buttres, Harcross, and myself are aware of the true facts in the case. It would seem that it is to everybody's advantage that we take the position that some desert raiders attacked the convoy. As for ex-Colonel Lodd, he met with a motorcar accident from which he is making a rapid recovery. How does that suit you?"

"I'm very appreciative, Falmey. What more can I say?"

"What you can say, and do, is that you will inform your co-horts to keep hands off out here. At least until the British presence is no longer a force. Can't you chaps wait just another few months?"

"I'm planning a trip back to the States as soon as I am able to travel. If I see any friends who have a connection with our Central Intelligence Agency, I'll pass on what you have said."

"That would be most kind of you, Lodd. And now, if you'll excuse me, I'll leave you. I hope you are recovered soon." Falmey nodded and started to leave.

"Falmey," Fitz called after him. Falmey turned. "Thanks," Fitz said. "Someday I may be in a position to be of help. And on the oil deal, I understand perfectly. You were doing your job. I'm glad to see that your problems with the Iranian Government over Bahrain have come to a satisfactory conclusion."

A bleak smile crossed Falmey's lips. He nodded and then turned and left the dispensary.

CHAPTER 52

"There's got to be some way, Fitz darling." Laylah's voice dropped to its lowest register as she stood over the bed wearing a brief bikini. Fitz lay in the ground-floor bedroom of his house, his right leg, bandaged almost to his groin, rested on pillows. "I'm sure we'll discover it."

From the TOS dispensary Fitz had written to Laylah and told her, in guarded terms, what had happened. And now, just the day after he had been taken home, she was here, answering his letter in person.

In a matter of hours from the moment she arrived at his home they had re-established the old intimacy. Perhaps because of the handicap of his wounded leg rather than despite it, Laylah had decided that they should make love forthwith and try to wipe out the madness, as she called it, that had possessed her for a while.

"My leg doesn't hurt any more, it's just that the damn thing is immobile," Fitz explained.

"I have so much to make up to you, darling," Laylah said sadly. Gently she sat down beside him. "I'm going to work hard to make you forgive me." Fitz lay naked on the bed, a sheet drawn over him from toes to waist. "There's one thing I can do right now," she said.

She pulled back the sheet, and then deftly untying her bikini bra and letting it fall from her, she leaned over him, allowing his erect maleness to protrude between her breasts. "Just lie quietly, darling. I wouldn't want the doctor to say I can't come see you any more. Let me do everything."

She bent lower and took him between her lips and then deeply into her mouth, bobbing her head up and down as he groaned ecstatically. All he could see was the heavy black tresses swirling as Laylah, almost desperately it seemed, gave him the most exquisite pleasure. It was only for moments that he could contain himself before he felt himself let go from deep within.

Totally spent, Fitz lay back on the bed, his eyes closed. Laylah lay down beside him, pleased that she had been able to give Fitz such happiness. She realized more than ever that he had been the one constant factor, the one person beyond her immediate family who cared deeply, totally, and unselfishly about her.

After many minutes Fitz said quietly, "Laylah, I love you. Thank you for being here. It means more to me than anything."

"I know it, darling. I'm sorry I can only stay until Friday night but I am working very hard at the Embassy now. In a month I get my first leave."

"We'll be in the United States at the same time. I'll have this leg working in another two to three weeks at the most."

"I hope when I get back home I can help you get what you want," Laylah said. "You know I'll do everything I can."

Laylah seemed almost too desperate to help him, Fitz thought. It seemed as though she was almost in a frenzy to prove that she was finished with Thornwell.

By the time Laylah had to leave for Tehran the following evening, they had discovered how, with Laylah performing most of the activity, to make love in several different ways.

A week after Laylah's departure he was walking again, leaning heavily on a cane. The doctor had suggested that he try to walk and also that he swim. So each day he hobbled out to the pool, slid into its cool water, and swam on his back to and fro across the pool. Motivating his efforts to a speedy recovery was the thought that Laylah could arrive in the United States before him and probably, even if only for old times' sake, would be in touch with Thornwell. He never wanted to repeat the mistake of being absent from Laylah's side too long again.

Sepah brought Fitz particularly good news. He had now completely infiltrated the Indian hovercraft base with his own mechanics. At will he could order all three craft grounded. Two gold shipments financed by Tony DeMarco's money had made it through to India and returned 250 percent profit on invested capital. Fitz's 10 percent share of the profits had been deposited into his account with the First Commercial Bank.

Even though he was incapacitated, Fitz was getting richer every day. He sent Marie a check for ten thousand dollars and told her he would be back in a few weeks and would hope to be able to finalize plans for Bill to come visit him in Dubai. He hinted in his letter to his ex-wife that before long he would be in a high official capacity and it would be particularly educational for Bill at that time to be with him.

Everybody professed to believe Fitz's motor-vehicle-accident story and nobody ever questioned him about the incident. The Ruler had sent a particularly solicitous inquiry after the state of his health upon hearing of the accident. Fitz knew perfectly well that the Ruler had been told by Jack Harcross precisely what happened. Apparently the Shaikh approved wholeheartedly of Fitz's interdiction mission. The Ruler of Dubai, far more than any of the other rulers, was sensitive to the implications of a strong Communist insurgency movement on the Dubai border in Oman. The commerce of Dubai could be severely hampered if such a movement got out of hand, the Ruler knew. Hazards to commerce were the hazards to which the Ruler gave the most thought.

As Fitz felt his leg growing stronger and found that he leaned less and less heavily on the cane, he began making plans for his trip back to the United States. During the course of this planning he received a discouraging letter from Dick Healey. In carefully couched terms Healey reported satisfaction at the Agency with the job Fitz had accomplished. Matt McConnell was working on his behalf now. The State Department was considering a more formal diplomatic post with the new Arab Federation about to be created. A U.S. consulate in Abu Dhabi reporting to the United States Ambassador to Kuwait was presently the sole representation in the Emirates.

McConnell's proposal of Fitz for the job of ambassador had not been enthusiastically received at first. However, Matt was still hammering away and the head of the Middle East Department had the recommendation on his desk. Healey sent on to Fitz a verbatim report he had received from Matt McConnell on the subject of Fitz's quest for the ambassadorship to the Emirates.

For the third time Fitz carefully read McConnell's report:

The appointment of James Fitzroy Lodd has become controversial. There is the feeling that some members of

Congress with large Jewish constituencies might oppose
the appointment on the basis of the newspaper articles
that appeared a few years ago regarding Fitz Lodd's
statements when he was attached to the embassy in
Tehran. This problem can probably be circumvented.
The wild story about Lodd's shooting up units of the Indian Navy can also probably be discounted. But there is
a problem which has been mentioned. How can the
United States appoint the American owner of the biggest saloon on the Arabian Gulf to the post of ambassador to that region? Until Lodd divests himself of all interests in the enterprise known as the Ten Tola Bar, it
would be pointless to continue the advocacy of his appointment to an American ambassadorship there.

Divest himself of all interests in the Ten Tola Bar? It had become his life, his power base, and for that matter it had been responsible for his being able to help the United States Government to such an extent. That would also mean selling his home,
the place which had come to mean so much to him, the first real
home he had ever had in a lifetime of nomadic wandering. Yet
when he thought about McConnell's communiqué he realized
that it was valid. How indeed could an ambassador own a bar
and restaurant in the country to which he was being sent as
America's top representative?

Obviously the Ten Tola Bar would have to go. But to whom
could he sell it? The most knowledgeable man in business on this
part of the Arabian Gulf was Majid Jabir. Without more ado he
wrote a note, which he sent by his servant to Majid Jabir's office
in His Highness's office building, requesting Majid to pay a call
on him at his earliest convenience.

At six o'clock that evening Majid Jabir appeared at Fitz's house.
Fitz gestured to a chair and then heavily sat down, putting his leg
up on the table in front of his sofa. Fitz was careful to seat Majid
Jabir to his left, knowing the Arab's predilection for tapping arms
and, when sitting, nudging and tapping knees.

For the first time Fitz was discussing with an associate his
desire to become ambassador. He omitted all reference to the interdiction of the arms convoy and merely said that friends of his

in the United States in high positions were proposing him for the ambassadorship to the Emirates. Naturally, Fitz went on diplomatically, his friends Shaikh Zayed of Abu Dhabi and Shaikh Rashid of Dubai would have to approve this appointment. However, he hoped he had proved to them his loyalty to the Arab cause and the well-being of the future federation of Emirates.

Majid discussed the possible appointment, occasionally nudging Fitz's left leg as he made a point. Majid was convinced that the chief rulers of the Emirates would happily accept Fitz as the American Ambassador. In fact, Majid said, he could be counted upon to see that the rulers went so far as to request Fitz specifically. This was something Fitz hadn't thought of but he knew it would help the cause.

Finally Fitz came to the point, bringing up the Ten Tola Bar. Majid replied that he too had instantly thought about Fitz's ownership of the Ten Tola Bar as being a detriment to the appointment but hadn't wanted to bring it up himself. Fitz could see the well-oiled wheels and cogs turning in Majid Jabir's brain. How could he, Majid, profit by this unfortunate necessity facing his friend, Fitz Lodd?

Majid asked the all-important question. "What do you want for it?"

Fitz had been giving this question a considerable amount of thought. Invested in the Ten Tola Bar at the present was somewhere just under $150,000. "I'm giving it away for $200,000," he said. "If I went by the standard business rule that a business is worth five times its earnings, then based on projected earnings for the first year I would have to ask $500,000. However, I want to sell it before I go back to the United States on this trip. Have you any ideas? As a matter of fact, it would be a good investment for you, Majid. There are certain side benefits to ownership of this place which I have told nobody about."

Majid gave him a questioning look but did not directly ask about these benefits. "I too am thinking in terms of an ambassadorship. Therefore, while I would very much like to be at least one of the owners of the Ten Tola Bar, it would present me with the same problem it does you. I could own a shipping firm, I could own a prestige hotel, I could own shares in an oil company, but I could not own any share in a place with the primary purpose

466   DUBAI

of serving liquor if I hoped to achieve the post I'm presently negotiating for. However, let us say I can produce a buyer who will pay
you $250,000 for the Ten Tola Bar. Perhaps I could even find a
buyer who would pay $300,000 for it. Could I expect to keep as a
fee for handling this transaction whatever over $200,000 I can get
for you?"

Fitz remembered the conversation he'd heard Majid carrying on
with the Sharjah oil company executives. "Why don't we cut it in
half?" Fitz suggested. "If you get $100,000 over my price, then
we'll each take fifty. If on the other hand you get only $25,000
over the price, you keep it all. Have you a specific buyer in mind?"

"I will put together a group who will buy the Ten Tola Bar
from you, Fitz. You can count on having the money and the
transaction completed in one week."

"I suppose I should be happy at the speed with which you can
work. However, as you know, it is very painful for me. Your
buyers will be very happy clients."

"And you, my friend, will be a very happy ambassador to our
country. Your government could not make a wiser choice of a
man to represent it here than Fitz Lodd. It is always good to have
a man in high position that one can work with."

They talked for a while longer about the Ten Tola Bar and
then Majid got up to leave.

"*Fii Aman Illah,*" Fitz said in farewell.

"*Fii Aman Illah,*" Majid returned, and then left Fitz alone with
his sadness at having to give up his treasured creation.

CHAPTER 53

Fitz had arrived early at the Metropolitan Club. He was tired of killing time, something he had been doing considerably on this trip to the United States. He had been home, if that's what America was, for just over three weeks and had known about five effective days of accomplishment in that period. Still depending to some extent on his cane, he walked across the spacious foyer to the cocktail lounge where he was to meet Matt McConnell and Dick Healey at five-thirty. It was now ten after five.

Fitz was seated in the cocktail lounge to wait for Matt. He put his leg out straight in front of him; he would have liked to put it on a chair but the staid nature of the club overwhelmed him. Once again he was reminded that he possessed a near-unconquerable inferiority complex.

Matt McConnell would be delivering the response to his well-presented request in just a few minutes. Whatever the answer, Fitz had done his preparation as well as possible. At Hoving Smith's house three weeks ago he had presented Cameron Davidson a beautiful black leather attaché case with one hundred thousand dollars cash in hundred-dollar bills. This had been prepared for him by the First Commercial Bank of New York. The Republican state chairman had been thrilled. The President's campaign financial chairman was, to use Davidson's phrase, sucking up cash money around the nation like a vacuum cleaner. Davidson had promised fast action. The new Federation of Arab Emirates would be an independent nation within the month.

Laylah had just arrived a few days before, but Fitz had stayed in Washington, waiting for this meeting, talking to her on the phone every day. It was his intention to visit her and her parents as soon as he could announce that his name was being sent to the Senate for confirmation.

As Fitz waited, trying to suppress his anxiety, he went over again the forces he had marshaled. Even Lorenz Cannon had contacted several powerful senators with whom he did business to recommend Lodd for the diplomatic post to the State Department.

The only step he regretted taking to attempt to ensure his appointment was selling the Ten Tola Bar. Majid had put together a syndicate in which the Arab arranger was a very silent partner and paid Fitz two hundred and fifty thousand dollars. Majid pocketed another fifty thousand from the three-hundred-thousand-dollar selling price he had obtained.

Fitz chuckled as he sat in the Metropolitan Club lounge thinking of the amazement and then delight Majid Jabir had revealed when he was shown first the window and then the bugs. It was Fitz's last act before leaving his home and restaurant for the airport. Majid had said that if he had known about the bugged tables and the secret window he could have gotten an extra hundred thousand out of the syndicate just for the information they could pick up.

The headwaiter in the lounge brought Dick Healey over to the table. "Matt not here yet?" Dick sat down and glanced at his watch. "He's got five minutes before he's late." Dick's somewhat brusque manner concerned Fitz. Did he know that the news would be bad?

Dick ordered a martini and urged Fitz to have a drink. Fitz also ordered a martini. Dick talked about the coming peace in Vietnam, which merely meant clearing the way for a total Communist takeover. "And when that's happened let the rest of the world watch out. They'll be on the move everywhere, especially in the Arab oil countries." Once again Dick complimented Fitz on the success of the operation he had carried out so successfully.

"I did my part, in every way." Fitz glanced down at his leg, which still hurt him at times. "Now let's see what Matt McConnell has done." Just as Fitz and Dick Healey took the first sips from their martinis Matt McConnell and another man who looked familiar to Fitz arrived at the table and sat down.

"Good evening, Fitz," Matt said genially. "You remember Phil Briscoe from your last visit, just a year ago. He holds down the Middle East desk at State."

"Yes, of course I remember Mr. Briscoe," Fitz replied, shaking the State Department man's limply extended hand. Surely this had to be a good sign, Fitz thought. The Middle East chief would be instrumental in choosing American envoys to Arab lands.

For a few minutes they talked about Arabian Gulf affairs and Briscoe brought up the Hemisphere Petroleum business. "It's too bad we couldn't help Lorenz Cannon. God knows, we spent enough time with him trying to sort that situation out. But we just weren't prepared to buck the British in their Gulf maneuverings at the time. Now with our cousins across the sea about moved out, we may have a little more clout."

"I have some ideas on establishing just that," Fitz ventured.

"We want to hear all good ideas," Briscoe replied—evasively, Fitz thought.

"I insisted that Phil come over and meet with you because I wanted you to hear from State's top man in your area of expertise," Matt said in a businesslike way when the drinks he and the State Department man ordered had arrived. Fitz began to feel a presentiment of disaster.

Matt turned to Briscoe, his steel-rimmed spectacles gleaming, his already humorless look souring by the moment. Obviously this bureaucrat was the type who resented being pressured and equally apparent was the fact he had not wanted to attend this meeting but was ordered by superiors to do so.

"Now, Phil," Matt was saying seriously, "as you know, there is quite a group of us both on the political and career side who are interested in seeing Fitz Lodd appointed ambassador to that new Gulf country. Also, as you know, two of the local rulers have expressly requested Fitz for the job. You've seen both letters."

"You seem to have made a good impression on Rashid and Zayed," Briscoe conceded.

"Equally important, Central Intelligence has the highest regard for Mr. Lodd's capabilities and I personally discussed this with the Secretary, who assured me that every consideration would be given to the possibilities of his appointment."

"The Secretary talked to me about it," Briscoe answered noncommittally.

"When we were first discussing the matter, Phil, you brought up the point that it might not be seemly for an ambassador to own a restaurant in the country to which he was appointed. Mr.

Lodd, as I informed you, has completely divested himself of this enterprise. And I might add that as a direct result of the fact that he owned the Ten Tola Bar he was able to be of inestimable value to us in achieving certain urgent objectives on the Gulf."

"Yes, I heard something about that." Briscoe sounded as though he didn't like what he had heard.

"And of course there is one more thing. Mr. Lodd's support of the President's coming campaign has been more than generous. You may have heard from Mr. Stans on that score."

Briscoe nodded, the corners of his thin lips turning down, but made no comment.

"Therefore, on all counts, it would seem that Fitz Lodd is the ideal man for the job. Now, supposing we let you bring us up to date on your thinking, Phil."

Fitz knew with a certainty that Matt McConnell had been brought up to date and was well aware of what Briscoe was going to say. It was becoming exceedingly difficult for Fitz to disguise the dismay that was spreading through him.

"In the first place, Mr. Lodd, we fully expect at least one and more likely two Arab-Israeli wars in the next three or four years. We fear that before the end of 1975 we will be caught up in the culmination of the confrontation and may find ourselves on the brink of another world war."

"That may be true, Mr. Briscoe, but the Gulf states are not interested in a war with Israel. They are interested purely and simply in commerce and they have kept as aloof as possible from the confrontation states, beyond the expediency of sending money to the Palestinian cause."

"One has to consider the Arab states as a whole, Mr. Lodd." Briscoe's tone was severe, as though dealing with a wayward underling. "In any case, the National Security Council has made certain decisions regarding the Middle East. We anticipate extensive turmoil and we don't know how we will deal with it. Therefore we are not sending ambassadors at this time to the new Arab Federation, nor to Oman. We will continue with our present consulate in Abu Dhabi and we are considering opening a consulate in Oman. Of one thing I am certain, Mr. Lodd, we will not be making a political appointment to any of the Arab states."

"You can't consider me a political appointment," Fitz objected sharply. "I have been attached to the American Embassy in three different countries, Vietnam, Jordan, and Iran."

"We certainly can't consider you a career State Department hand," Briscoe snapped back. "If ever there was a time in Middle East affairs when the State Department required disciplined"—he pounced on the word—"career men, it is now."

"Imagination and a great deal of Arab experience are what you need. That's what I can offer."

"I'm sorry, Mr. Lodd." Briscoe sounded triumphant. "But what I have told you is the decision made jointly between the National Security Council and the Middle East experts."

"Don't you think in the light of Mr. Lodd's experience and recent services to us," McConnell, a pained look on his face, interjected, "that there might be a reconsideration of his case? You certainly have no more experienced man anywhere in the Department as far as Gulf affairs are concerned."

Briscoe, lips compressed, stared through his shining glasses. "I would like to be able to give Mr. Lodd some hope for the future but I think it would be doing him a disservice."

"Considering that you've already pushed me into shearing myself of my livelihood, I cannot see that there is any further disservice left you to do me," Fitz shot back.

Briscoe shrugged and gave Fitz a bland look. "I don't see how you can blame us if you divested yourself of the Ten Tola Bar."

The disappointment was too fierce for Fitz to bother answering. Matt smiled sadly. "We all did our best, Fitz. As a matter of fact, I called Hoving Smith this morning and told him what I expected the results would be of this meeting." Dick Healey sat glumly staring at his drink. Only Briscoe seemed, in his own dour way, to be cheerful about the proceedings.

"Now, Fitz," Matt went on, "I know that something can be worked out, directly with the Secretary," he said pointedly, glaring at Briscoe, "to show our appreciation for all you've done to help us. I asked Hoving to call Cameron Davidson to exert some further pressure."

"Matt, if you don't need me any longer, I have a late meeting back at State," Briscoe appealed.

"Sure, Phil. Go along."

The State Department man stood up. "Nice to meet you, Mr.

Lodd. Sorry we couldn't be of more help to you." Neither man offered his hand and Briscoe walked away.

"Christ," Fitz muttered, "if that's what we've got in the Middle East Department, the Arabs were one hundred percent better off with the British power structure. Do the Arabs actually have to see that guy?"

"I'm afraid so," McConnell sighed. "I'm sorry things worked out this way, Fitz. And I'm surprised that the political side double-crossed you, took your contribution, and let you down."

"If I was truly a political appointee, I could understand," Fitz said. He drained his glass. "Well, I'd better get busy pulling my life together." Stiffly Fitz stood up, supporting himself on the arm of the chair as he reached for his cane. "Thanks for the drink, Matt. I know you did your best."

"As I said, Fitz, let's talk again about what else State might be able to do for you."

"The problem is that there isn't anything else I could do for State."

"Are you coming over for dinner tonight, Fitz?" Dick asked. "Jenna said she would fix something special."

Fitz shook his head. "Not tonight. I've got a lot of figuring to do. Maybe try to call me tomorrow. You might let Abe Ferutti know what happened. He came down to see me a couple of times while I was laid up at home. He was interested to know how I made out."

"Sure, Fitz," Dick said.

Fitz walked heavily from the lounge, his cane thumping on the marble floor as he limped across the foyer and out into the Washington, D.C., fall evening. He hailed a cab and asked to be taken to the Twin Bridge Marriott Hotel.

No way he was going to propose to Laylah now. What could he offer her? Nothing except a disabled, very disappointed, middle-aged man with dubious prospects for the future.

At the hotel he didn't bother to check for messages, he had just been given the message. He went up to his room, let himself in, and sat down on the chair, putting his bad leg up on the bed. He didn't even want a drink. He tried to think about what he would do. Between the campaign contribution and the hundred and fifty thousand dollars he had added to the trust fund for his son, Bill, he was down to very modest means.

There was a knock on the door. Fitz looked at it, surprised. He wasn't expecting anybody. Maybe Dick Healey was feeling sorry for him and probably a little guilty. He didn't want sympathy, he wanted to be left alone. Wearily he pushed himself upright and, leaning on his cane, he went to the door. He would just have to explain to Dick that maybe tomorrow they'd get together. Tonight he wasn't prepared to talk to anyone.

Opening the door, Fitz started to say, "Look, pal, I'm sorry about tonight . . ."

Abruptly he stopped. It wasn't Dick Healey.

"Laylah!" He stared at her, wondering if despair, fatigue, and the dull ache in his leg had deranged him, causing him to hallucinate.

"Don't you check your messages, darling? I left word for you that Miss Smith was waiting in the cocktail lounge."

It really was Laylah. He opened the door wider and stepped back, forgetting his leg. She walked past him into the hotel room and he closed the door after her as she looked about.

"Well, we've had better accommodations. Remember Bandar Abbas?"

"I don't let myself remember too often." They were standing close and suddenly Laylah threw her arms around him.

"Oh, Fitz, I should have come to you the minute I got to Radnor but I hadn't seen Mother and Dad for so long. Besides, I kept thinking you'd be coming any day."

"I didn't get it," he said hollowly.

"Good, darling."

"I mean, I am not going to be any kind of an ambassador."

"I know. So is that the end of the world? It should be the beginning for us."

"I don't know what I'm going to do, Laylah." He stepped back from her and looked into her eyes earnestly. "After the campaign contribution and the trust fund for Bill, I don't have much money left. I don't have the Ten Tola Bar and I don't know what I'll do in the future."

"Good," Laylah said happily. "Then nobody can say I married you for prestige or money. And at this point it sure isn't on the rebound from Courty. It's just because I love you, Fitz. I want to be part of your life. And you know you can do anything you set your mind to. The two of us working together we can do it all."

Fitz stared at her, slightly bewildered. "You still want me?"

"I love you, Fitz. Can't you understand? I've grown up, and it's just as well I got that over with before we married."

"I can't believe it," he murmured in wonderment. But he was believing it. She loved him, really. Maybe that nagging sense of inferiority would go away. Laylah loved him.

"Why don't you tell me something nice and then kiss me, Fitz."

Suddenly despair and disappointment dissipated in a brilliant incandescence of joy. "Laylah, I love you. I've loved you since the time I met you in my office in Tehran when you first joined the Embassy. I may have asked this question before but, when will you marry me?"

"Mother is already planning it. She's just waiting for me to call. When we heard this afternoon what you were going to be told I ran for Broad Street Station to get the train to Washington."

Fitz took her in his arms, dropping his cane, unconscious of his leg, which had miraculously stopped hurting, and they kissed deeply for long moments.

Finally: "Fitz darling, let me call Mother. She'll break the news to Dad. Would four weeks from now be too long a time? They'll crash out the invitations. But I'm the only child. I can't deprive them of putting on a big bash and then you and I will go back to the Gulf and make our lives and fortune. I know that's where your heart is."

"It would be anywhere with you, Laylah, but, yes, I guess the Creek is for me, for us."

"Then to the Creek we'll go. And don't worry in the meantime. We aren't letting ancient conventions steal our nights together from us."

Laylah sat down on the bed. "Let me put through the call to Mother. Then we'll begin the rest of our lives together."